MARY QUEEN
A LEGACY
OF
FREEDOM

CYNTHIA MARLOWE

Φ

To the descendants of Queen,
an incredible woman of strength and courage.
You are her legacy.

To my mother, Sondra Jarvis, and my sister,
Catherine Alfaro,
who stayed excited about Queen with me,
and always encouraged me to keep going.

To my dear friend Frieda Gutkowski,
a front-liner in my editing team
who is always ready for the next book.

Author's Note

This book offers an opportunity to expand the scope of awareness to our history and culture. Not as a tale of slavery, but as a culture built from diverse ideas and religions that struggled to accept the humanity of being different. It offers a truth to the development of the many tendrils of racism, sexism, and religious intolerance. It is not intended to pass judgement or to condemn either the individuals or organizations who are mentioned. It can, however, demonstrate how victimization affects others and has shaped our culture into the image of today.

Hidden just below hatred and fear is the part of ourselves that is devoid of understanding those who are different from us. While it is human nature to cling to others who are like us, we cannot ignore the fact that we are each only one very tiny piece of what makes a culture thrive: diversity of knowledge, experience, and a foundation of truth. It is how those pieces fit together historically that shape who we are as a culture.

Finally, we are on the verge of truly understanding the pieces of our history that have created who we have become as a people. They have been hidden, locked in a place where the vision of a cohesive society cast out those who were different and was documented by people who embraced that vision, whitewashing the details to glorify the acts of those who shared the same perspectives and aspirations.

Over time, our memories have become like dust. We sweep away the particles that are uncomfortable and ugly, polishing them into something that is shiny and to be admired. But like dust, they always return and settle, dotting our lives with actions and reactions we don't understand, so we swipe them away again and again, hoping it remains invisible.

Much of American history occurred when the purpose of society was to eradicate the connections of family and community, dissolving individuals into either fibers that fit within the social norms of the masses or as beasts of burden. However, what we didn't realize was that within each of us live visions that are reflections from the past, before the time of our memories, which are locked in the cells of who we are.

I believe that we have a responsibility to look at them honestly. We must grasp the angst that we inexplicitly feel when confronted with someone different than ourselves as well as explore the elusive flicker of excitement when prodded by a new experience or idea. They are the insights to our past and the lessons that we carry from those who have gone before us. They are the true legacy of our ancestors.

Those of us who research early American history during the time period of slavery understand how difficult it is to find information about specific enslaved individuals. Like detectives, we must dig through old documents with magnifying lenses and a talent for unscrambling the quill scribbled script of the time. There is very little luck when documentation is found. It is won through tenacious dedication, minute scrutiny, and creative deduction.

When I began this book, it was with the intention to pick up from one of the characters of my previous book, *SOLD!* and to continue with the journey of the women who were taken from the harem of the palace of Koch Behar, India. What I did not realize was that I would learn so much. The primary lesson I learned was how much of our history of which I was ignorant.

I never knew that Catholics were so oppressed and criminalized, unallowed to hold public office with severe fines if they even attempted it, were declared incompetent witnesses in a court of law, or that repeating the Holy Trinity was outlawed, punishable by banishment or even death.

I didn't understand that there were so many mixed-race families who passed as white but developed racial intolerance. Secretly living as whites, if they were discovered they could be killed. Because entire families depended upon their income for support, they did not share with their mulatto or quadroon children the truth of their heritage. Their situation was so precarious that they were forced to shun everyone and everything that connected them to their culture. Their children were raised in isolation, ignorant and rejecting their roots, and a reverse discrimination developed.

I never knew of the Jesuits or their missions, the plight of privateers when peace reigned between warring countries, or that the early cannonballs didn't explode. I believed the decadent presentation of the English monarchy as shown in movies and embellished in novels. I learned how good people can do bad things and vice versa, and that either can be a catalyst to allow the threads of who we are, within the deepest fibers of our hearts, to move forward and grow.

By definition this novel is a work of fiction. The people are real, their locations and experiences are real and documented, however, no documentation exists that would disclose their actual conversations, thoughts, insights into their environment, or sexual proclivities. For those, I take full accountability.

Queen's story has become very personal for me. At first, she was a name introduced by the circumstance of her presence upon the *Merchant's Adventure* in my first novel, *SOLD!*. However, it was through the unlikely speculation of my mother that I realized we had a stronger link to her, and her story became far more personal.

My mother's maiden name is Sondra Brantley. She is the child of Thelma Barnhill Brantley who is the child of Lucinda Belle Queen Barnhill, the daughter of William Queen. And so it goes, back through time and the fibers of my family, to discover a link to Maryland and the Jesuit missions there. That knowledge has given me a special awe and a feeling of pride in not only the person who was Queen, but also who she became as she grew through the years in the hearts of my family and myself.

Preface

I was once known as Wajeeha Narayan. I was a member of the royal family of Koch Behar, India. I lived protected and pampered within the harem of the Maharaja until the palace was overthrown in a great battle to usurp the throne. To shame my family, the women were carried off to be sold as slaves.

Since then, I have been called by many names, Maria Queen, then Mary Queen or Queen Mary, even the Pawpaw Queen, but mostly just Queen. Some would call me a whore. I say I am an intelligent advantagest, if that is even a word.

Life taught me very quickly that the one and only constant is that nothing ever really sticks. Not people, places or circumstances. We give to each what we can then choose what to carry forward, taking only that which serves us well, and leave the rest behind. I chose with whom I would share of what was mine to give, my thoughts, my intellect, my skills, and my affection. I took and I gave in equal conquest with those I felt deserving or where I could be most benefited. I feel no shame.

It is also true that nothing is more certain but that sooner or later we all must part. When we do it is better never to go back. That we separate only once spares us the pain of yet another parting. So, while I have endeavored to love, it has always been with the reservation born from the constant knowledge of parting. Because of that, I have only managed to achieve a small affection with a couple of my partners, and there have been many. Never did I have love for a man, that emotion being reserved for children, mine and others, who are yet innocent.

In the end, only my children were of value to me. In the end, they were all that mattered. In the end it should be said that though I suffered, I grew wiser, and I lived wholly.

Though I was born in 1667, it was not until the year 1682 that I began to live. That is where my story begins.

Chapter One

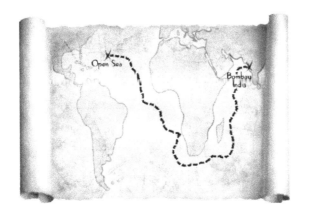

November 1682, Open Sea

My journey is finally over, breathed Wajeeha.

Past the shoulder pumping above her, the seagulls circled. Tighter and tighter they flew until their wings brushed against one another, screaming in protest to the atrocity happening below. Wajeeha closed her eyes briefly to acknowledge their tribute. She had tried to fight the sailors but was no match for so many. Shame engulfed her.

Her gaze slid towards the women of her family who were being cruelly led across the ship's deck by fists ensnared in their long hair. Painfully subdued by the threat of violence being demonstrated before them, they passed where she lay as another sailor mounted her. They tried not to look towards her shame, but the shock was too great and so their eyes reached for her. In them was horror, and worse, pity. She closed her eyes to their beloved faces. She had failed them all. Failed to prevent this cruel fate, failed to protect them, and could not save them from an even worse destiny.

The only thing she had left to do was to save herself by making a final escape. The world slipped away as she sank into a welcome void. Like washing black over dark shades of blue, it dimmed and faded.

Shrouded in a merciful trance of emptiness, Wajeeha did not feel the brutal thrusts of the sailor as he plunged into her, grasping her back by her hair only to deliver another punishing blow. She was unaware of the other sailors who replaced him. One after another they each pumped their lust into her unresisting body which yielded, broken to their demands. She did not hear the whistle of the whip as it uncoiled and snapped, licking the back of the sailor who rode her.

"Enough!" bellowed Captain Francis Townley.

Silence dropped over the raucous group as all eyes pinned to their fearless leader, except Jake's, who fell to the deck with an angry howl. Yanking up his britches from where they were bunched under his buttocks, he leapt to his feet and in a flash produced a knife.

Captain Townley groaned inwardly. Jake was going to have to die. It wasn't that he particularly cared one way or another about the man, but an experienced well-seasoned sailor was an asset, and these were hard times.

Frequently employed by the British crown to attack French and Spanish ships, Captain Townley was a legitimate privateer, attacking and looting their enemies. But as the differences between the countries were slowly being resolved, official appointments were more competitive and decent maritime employment was hard to find. He and his crew had found that the life of privateering suited them. So, as appointments dried up and times became desperate, desperate measures were also needed.

The excitement of a challenge and conquest had become a part of them, flowing wild and uninhibited through their veins. So what if they enjoyed an occasional raid that was not sanctioned or if it was sometimes against a British ship, though they preferred to leave their own countrymen unmolested. Besides, not having to share the bounty with the crown was far more lucrative.

Commanding a ship and crew of sailors was never an easy task, but the daring adventurous sort who risked crewing a vessel such as his was fraught with danger. As captain, he had to be feared as merciless. Infractions must always be punished swiftly and severely enough to serve as an absolute lesson and warning to any other who might dare to challenge him. One hint of weakness by him and he knew the men would spin out of control like an upset hive of bees, killing him to take over his ship and replace him with someone strong enough to do the job.

"We was funnin' wit the wench, Captain," Jake challenged sharply, sneering his superior's title. His cold, hard eyes were fixed upon the captain as he slowly raised the knife, "but ya buggered me back."

Captain Townley did not waver. Returning the man's icy glare, his hand hung to his side still grasping the handle of the whip. Its coil laid on the deck like a dead snake as he addressed the group.

"Men, by this time tomorrow Jake will be nearly fully consumed and floating in little pieces as he is shit out by the fish, once again into the sea."

Enraged at the insult, Jake lunged his bulk forward with a roar. Instantly the whip leapt back to life, snapping as it bit his knuckles, opening them in a neat line. His knife fell to the ground with a clatter. Another flick of the captain's wrist sent the whip springing to sweep it away. Jake froze. A loud whistle and a crack exploded above the sailors' heads. They heeded the warning and jumped back, out of harm's way.

The whip dipped down again and again, opening Jake's clothing and flesh in long ribbons of blood. In a desperate and foolish move, he dove for his knife but failed to reach it. The whip reached it first and pushed it away from him before gyrating back to land across his back with a vicious snap. Jake buckled in pain then turned and fled.

There was nowhere to go and nowhere to hide. The captain did not chase him but followed at a steady pace, the whip dancing through the air at his command. When Jake had run the full length of the ship, he pressed against the rail and the whip found him once more. He was pinned. With nowhere else to go, he threw himself up and over the rail, leaping wildly to his only route of escape. His howls were punctuated by a splash.

Captain Townley turned to his crew and slid an icy glare across them in an open challenge for anyone else who might want to dance with his whip. Keeping their eyes down, they nervously shifted. Satisfied that none would dare to defy him any further, he looked out to sea then shifted his gaze to the hapless creature laying on his deck. Naked and sprawled with her arm twisted awkwardly behind her, he could not see her face through the long dark strands of hair tossed over it.

"Is she still alive?" he asked to no one in particular.

One of the sailors stepped towards her, covered her face with a grimy hand, and paused.

"Still breathin', sir."

"Then take her to my cabin where she'll be safe and let's get back to the island."

Chapter Two

November 1682, British Caribbean

Captain Townley sat in his cabin nursing a bottle of some of the finest rum he had ever tasted. He didn't bother with a glass. It was the only good thing that had come out of his day's efforts. He and his crew had been looking for a challenge when the *Merchant's Adventure* was spotted. It sat high on the water and moved quickly, so he knew its holds weren't loaded.

Simply put, the added swiftness and maneuverability of an empty ship had promised some fun, just toying with it in a quick game of cat and mouse. It was disappointing when his adversary so easily abandoned ship, nearly handing it over to him.

Once his men boarded the ship, they discovered why it had been given up so easily. A few barrels of spice, a couple good cannons, and seven quality women slaves simply weren't worth risking your life for. The crew, though fine for a merchant ship, was of no real use to a privateering ship. With only a few good trainable men amongst them, the rest would be either sold or turned out at the next port. No point in wasting good provisions on dead weight. Even though they had mostly agreed to sail under his command, he knew they would sneak away to seek employment with another trade ship at the first opportunity.

Of course, a few resistors did have to be dealt with. One, a garrulously dressed man who flamboyantly threw his hands around in dramatic sweeping gestures while crying out names of English nobility he claimed would come to his aid, including King Charles. Captain Townley chuckled as he remembered the ridiculousness of the man. With no patience for such people, he had quickly dispatched him on to his maker with a musket ball to the head.

He had hoped that he would be able to acquire the ship, bringing it into his fleet with only a few alterations to avoid it being recognized. But a close inspection revealed a lot of hastily made repairs, so it was sent to the bottom of the sea.

In the end the rum was the only reward. No sporting excitement, no bounty, no crew worth having, no ship, and his bed was occupied.

He swirled the bottle in the air and watched the liquid churn. Little bubbles formed in a whirl then scattered as they raced to the top, clustering like foam on a stormy sea. He tilted the bottle to his mouth and took a swig, swashing it around before swallowing with a loud gulp. Fumes rose and pleasantly took his breath. The amber liquid burned down his throat to his belly and left behind a warmth that spread and flushed through his body. Reveling in the comfort of it, he glimpsed the woman sprawled across his bed laying just as she fell when flopped there by one of his crew.

He pushed himself up from his chair.

"Damn fine rum," he muttered, pausing to steady himself, "damn fine."

His feet steady, he walked to the bed to look at her more closely. She seemed pretty enough, but it was hard to tell in the low light with her hair still covering her face. Though he suspected she was awake, he decided to allow her the ruse of sleeping a while longer so he could enjoy the effect of good rum and ponder the situation.

He had learned from the crew of the *Merchant's Adventure* that they had sailed from India. Leaving hastily, their specific and sole agenda was to sell the women into slavery. It was very peculiar given the shape that the ship had been in. Especially since the East India Trading Company, who owned the *Merchant's Adventure* as well as hundreds of other ships, could have easily had quality repairs done and the holds filled before pushing it out to sea. Whatever had gone on, Captain Townley knew these were no ordinary women and he wanted no part of them.

Having sailed the world, he had learned a little about different cultures. He knew the women of the Orient, Persia, and India were very highly valued by their families, almost like goddesses. Accordingly, they were protected with a fierceness unparalleled. Families from those cultures generally ran wide and deep and they would never stop pursuit to gain the return of any of their women.

He had heard stories of men being chased the world over after having foolishly snuck away from one of those locales with a woman. When they were finally found, as they would be, if the woman were complicit in the arrangement and refused to go with her family, she was ordered to kill herself or be killed. Either way she was going to die and the family was getting their retribution for losing her. If they had to kill her, according to their beliefs, she went straight to hell. If she killed herself at least she went to heaven. He didn't want to know anything more about it, especially first-hand, so he wanted the women off his ship as quickly as possible.

He took another long deep draw from the bottle and recorked it. Closing his eyes, he slid into a warm alcohol induced haze which lulled him to sleep. When his breathing evened out and the bottle fell to the floor with a low thud against the thick rug, Wajeeha opened her eyes.

Taking inventory of her body, she focused upon each part, flexing the muscles and moving them ever so slightly. Her legs throbbed and her head was sore where small chunks of hair had been pulled from her scalp. Particularly sore from such violent misuse were her woman parts. She wanted to cry out in pain, fear, frustration and shame, but did not dare. Her fear of disturbing the man who sat guard over her was far greater than the sum of those urges.

She slowly turned her head to check out her surroundings. The cabin was large and well-appointed and was paneled in rich dark wood from the ceiling to the floors. The thickly padded bed where she lay took up an entire wall and was tucked into an enclave which could be concealed by heavy deep blue brocade curtains that were pushed to one side. On the wall to her right was a neat line of shining glass windows that framed a watery landscape and stretched down the entire length of the wall. Under the windows were a couple of large and obviously well-traveled trunks, as well as several small crates and wooden boxes. The next wall, opposite to the bed, supported a set of shelves that held stacks of folded clothing. Under the shelves were a row of cabinets. The door was on the remaining wall. It was tucked between shiny brass hooks that dangled some articles of clothing, a sword, a few whips, some chain, and several lengths of rope. A large ornately carved circular table stood in the center of the room and was strewn with maps, charts, a pistol, and a partially burned candle, its wax ribboned in layers. Four upholstered chairs surrounded the table and were partially tucked under it. In the corner where the windows and cabinets met, a small desk faced the room. Layered across the floor were thick rugs in a variety of colors that had been dimmed by use and time. A chair in the far corner was occupied by Captain Townley.

As Wajeeha's gaze slid over him, she saw he was staring at her, watching her through slitted eyes. Her breath hitched in fear as his icy gaze brought it all back. She had thought she was going to die and was disappointed to find herself amongst the living. What further torment would this man visit upon her? What could she do about it? Where could she go? There was nothing. She resisted the impulse to cower from him and proudly thrust up her chin to look at him, directly meeting his gaze.

Captain Townley saw her initial fear and was glad. He was a gentleman at heart, so he did not approve of what had been done to her, but she had every reason to be afraid while aboard his ship. After all, it was full of rowdy, hard-driven and mostly lawless sailors, so some healthy fear made things easier on them all. When she boldly jutted her delicate little chin up and met his gaze in an open challenge, his amusement bubbled up and he chuckled.

Wajeeha heard Captain Townley's chuckle and it infuriated her. When he saw outrage wash over her face, it caused him to burst into open laughter. She was not amused. How dare he! She had just suffered through months of the most extreme misery and was dismayed to have survived the ordeal. To be laughed at by such a despicable man was too much. She could endure no more.

"Do not laugh at me, you stinking goat!" she yelled, springing from the bed to her feet, "just kill me!"

Captain Townley couldn't understand what she said, but her anger was palatable. Such rage from someone so little and who was in such a vulnerable position amused him, so he laughed. His laughter turned into full belly howling when she lunged towards him with her fists flailing. Not alarmed with the onslaught and unconcerned for his own safety, he raised his arms to ward her off but continued in his hysteria.

Surprised with the strength of the chit, his amusement quickly turned to aggravation. Grasping her around the waist, he easily scooped her up and carried her back to the bed where he tossed her onto it as if she were no more than a discarded shirt.

"I will be amused this one time," he growled at her before he spun on his heels and stormed out the door, slamming it closed with a bang.

17

Wajeeha sprawled on the bed in stunned fury. Why hadn't he killed her? She had assaulted him and he had simply laughed. Unshed tears stung the back of her eyes as she slid off the bed and marched to the window. Far off in the distance she saw a dot that slowly grew. Land. As it got nearer a plan formulated.

She turned from the windows and went to the shelves with the clothing. Rifling through the neat stacks, she located some well-worn britches and slid into them. They were much too large for her. The legs were intended to gather just below the knees but on her they extended down to her ankles. The waist, more than twice her size, had loops for a belt. She grabbed the shortest length of rope that was hanging near the door and thread it through the loops, wrapping it twice around herself, then tied the ends into a knot over her belly. Returning to the shelf, she pulled out several shirts at a time, quickly looking them over and tossing them aside until she finally selected a white linen blouse, soft and billowy, and threw it over her head. The long tails reached below her knees. She stuffed them into the pants and rolled up the sleeves.

Once dressed, she returned to the window to watch the dot materialize into a bustling town. Water licked the shore on one side and a thick green forest towered behind. It looked as if the forest had been rolled back from the water just enough to squeeze in the strange row of structures. Threaded between the structures were roads that were filled with clouds of dust, horses, and people.

Captain Townley hesitated outside his cabin door, unsure of what to expect when he entered. Finally, he took a deep breath and opened the door. The last thing he expected to find was what he did. The girl had plundered his once neat stacks of clothing and strewn them across the floor in rumpled heaps. She stood by the window looking out to the wharf and was dressed, or draped, in a pair of his britches and a blouse. When he entered, she jolted and whipped around to face him.

Once again defiance instantly replaced a quick glimmer of fear. This time Captain Townley did not laugh. He froze. Her little frame draped in oversized clothing while standing so proudly determined made her at first appear as a stubborn child. Her long, dark, thick locks of hair, though matted in places, framed large chocolate-colored eyes with long butterfly lashes, a narrow nose that was pertly rounded at the tip, full rosy lips, though marred by a nasty bruise, and bright rosy cheeks over copper colored skin.

She was definitely no child. She was a bewitching seductress who had been abused by his crew and was rightfully angry, and she was sizing him up as if a combatant before battle. Enchanted, he could not move or speak. A clatter at the door behind him broke the spell.

"Here you go, Captain, just what ya need to keep ya hale and hearty!"

A short round man entered carrying a tray of jangling and clanking dishes which he set upon the table. He pulled a large flask from his oversized pockets. From it, he poured clear liquid into two shining silver goblets, then laid two places where he put plates loaded with a variety tantalizing smelling food at each. Once his task was complete, he stood back as if to admire his work.

That was when he first saw Wajeeha standing before the windows, still staring at the captain in open defiance. She didn't seem to have even noticed that he had entered. Frederick gulped.

"I… uh… brought… do… what…" he sputtered.

"Thank you, Frederick. I'm sure you have once again surpassed yourself," Captain Townley dismissed him.

"Yesss, ssssir," Frederick stammered nervously, unable to resist staring, "I brought ssssome for the lassie… of my own accord… I hope…"

"That is fine. Thank you again," interrupted Captain Townley.

Frederick hurried to the door, anxious to escape.

"Tell the men that there will be no shore leave today," the captain called after him, "Not for anyone. Not yet, and not in this port. Big Ron and his crew can see to the cargo. When they return, we pull anchor immediately."

Frederick paused in the open doorway and turned back.

"But sir, the men'll be needing a wee bit of fun…"

A cold look from his captain sent Frederick backing out of the room. With a nod he closed the door softly behind himself.

Wajeeha watched as Captain Townley went to the table and sat before one of the place settings. She knew his gesture towards her was an invitation to sit, but feigned ignorance. When she didn't move, he shrugged indifferently. Licking his lips, he picked up his knife to eat and Wajeeha turned back to the window to watch the activity outside.

The ship bobbed beside a long dock that extended from shore like an arm. Boards laid between the dock and the ship were used as a ramp. The rocking of the ship caused the boards to slide, so it didn't look very safe, but the sailors navigated them with ease as they hauled barrels back and forth across them. Wajeeha saw a few barrels that she recognized from the hold of the *Merchant's Adventure* when someone knocked, or rather pounded, on the door.

"Enter," growled Captain Townley, grasping his goblet to drink.

A large burly man with a wide bushy beard threw the door open. Oversized, he seemed to fill the whole room, thus his name, Big Ron. He had just collected the other women from the *Merchant's Adventure* and was ready to take them to the market.

"Sir, I'm ready to take the prisoners to market."

"Okay?" Captain Townley shoveled food into his mouth.

"Well, I was wonderin' 'bout that one." Big Ron gestured towards Wajeeha.

Captain Townley looked at Wajeeha, still draped in his oversized clothing, standing proudly as she stared out the window. Just as he swung his knife towards her in a gesture indicating for Big Ron to go ahead and take her, he paused. In a moment of rare sentiment, he realized that he didn't want her to go. Shocked with himself, the knife remained suspended as he began to laugh once more.

Big Ron didn't see what was so funny. The captain's laughter seemed misplaced and odd, even weird under the circumstances. Furthermore, the quiet resignation of the women made him uncomfortable. When he placed the chains on them to take them to market, he had been prepared for pleading, yelling, crying, even fighting, but the regal dignity they displayed almost made him feel bad for them... like he was doing something wrong. Not one to explore his conscience, he was anxious to be rid of them.

Ready to take the girl and go, Big Ron strode over to collect her. When he grasped her arm, she instantly spun around and yanked it away then kicked his shin with her bare foot. Surprised but ready for the sport, Big Ron lunged forward and easily scooped her up then tossed her over his shoulder.

"Stop," Captain Townley's voice boomed into the room.

Big Ron froze, gawking at him.

"Captain?" he asked, confused as he struggled to keep ahold of the girl while avoiding being kicked in his privates.

"I said to stop," Captain Townley yelled even louder and threw his napkin onto his plate.

He couldn't believe what he was about to say. He knew no good would ever come of it and that the girl would prove herself a headache and a problem.

"The girl won't be worth much all buggered up with bruises and... well.... I've decided to wait and sell her later, after she's healed and prettied back up."

"Captain! Have ya been drinking or are ya just touched?" Big Ron exclaimed in shock, "This ain't exactly a passenger ship and she ain't especially agreeable! We can find ya a good wench who'll sport with ya with a smile, then leave ya intact for the offering, right there in town!"

"Put her down and go," ordered Captain Townley irritably.

Big Ron simply opened his arms. Still thrashing, Wajeeha fell to the floor with a dull thud and scurried away from him. With a worried shrug, Big Ron took a deep breath.

"Ain't none of my business, but..."

"No, it isn't," Captain Townley interrupted sharply, "so I'll kindly ask you not to proceed. However, once you have returned from town, send to me one of the crew members from the *Merchant's Adventure* who can speak her language. Surely there's at least one in that high and mighty group that can."

"Yessir," mumbled Big Ron as he left.

Captain Townley looked to where Wajeeha sat staring at him in defiance.

"You sure are a bother," he mumbled as he went to his desk and plopped in the chair.

Chapter Three

Later that day, Open Sea

Shortly after they were back out to sea, Captain Townley was on deck when he was approached by a soft looking man who absolutely did not look anything like a sailor. Studious was a more apt description.

"Captain, Big Ron said you wanted to speak with me."

"Why in God's name would I want to speak with *you?*" asked Captain Townley sourly, wondering why they hadn't just thrown him overboard.

"I speak Hindi, sir," the man shifted nervously.

Captain Townley remembered and nodded.

"Go to my cabin and talk with the girl. Tell her she isn't in danger. Tell her I'm the captain of this ship and that no one will harm her again as long as she's under my protection."

"Yes, sir."

"Tell her I'm..." Captain Townley hesitated to see if anyone was around, then continued awkwardly, "...sorry... about what happened. Then teach her to speak English."

"Yes sir."

"What's your name sailor?"

"Percival sir."

"Percival! What kind of a name is that?"

"The kind my parents gave me sir."

Captain Townley groaned inwardly and looked out to sea.

He's no sailor.

"Yeah... well... Percival... you do a good job, get her speaking English, and I'll put you off at the first port afterwards. You'll be free to go."

"Yes sir!" Percival grinned broadly.

"But if you tell even *one* of these sailors what I said, about being sorry and all, I'll throw you overboard myself for the lie."

"Yes sir."

*****

Percival hurried to the captain's cabin. He was excited. Not being a sailor, he had simply volunteered because the only other option was to be thrown overboard. He had been a bookkeeper for the East India Trading Company and had only been aboard the *Merchant's Adventure* as a courtesy ride to take him to America. After living in India for five long years, he had worked and saved just long enough to get the money to buy himself a decent piece of land to set himself up properly in America.

Thankfully he had not traveled with all of his savings so his future was still secure. That is, until he had been taken and pressed into service. Fully aware that he wasn't cut out for the hard life of a sailor, much less a privateer, he had believed that all was lost for himself until he spoke with the captain. The assignment, he knew, was his saving grace and his opportunity for survival.

He entered the cabin and was instantly impressed with the fine paneling and craftmanship of it, particularly the elaborate carving around the bed closet. The girl, his pupil, sat in a chair by the window. She did not turn towards him when he entered.

"Hello. My name is Percival," he kept his voice soft, nonthreatening, and spoke to her in Hindi.

When Wajeeha heard her own language, she spun around to face him.

"Why are you here?" she asked suspiciously.

"This is the captain's cabin. The man who saved you was the captain, himself. He asked me to come to you and tell you that you are safe. No one will molest you further because you are now under his protection."

"What about my family? The Maharani? Are they safe?"

Percival instantly froze as his mind raced. He had not realized that one of the women they held, and sold, was the Maharani.

As a bookkeeper, he knew the East India Trading Company had financed and all but fought an insurrection in north-eastern India. It was a region sitting at the foothills of the Eastern Himalayan mountains that was along a valuable trade route. The Maharaja who controlled it was Basudev Narayan. He was willing to provide aid to foreigners traveling through but would not guarantee their safety. He particularly disliked the East India Trading Company, who was not fair in negotiating, greedily refusing to pay even fair market prices for goods or services, or respect his position as the Maharaja, reserving all such honor exclusively for their own exalted British king.

Frustrated, the company did not understand enough about the culture to resolve the issues. When approached by Jagat Narayan, a cousin to

Basudev who claimed to be the rightful Maharaja, they felt as if God had handed them the solution in an answer to their prayers.

Jagat and his brothers had been fighting to take back the throne for decades. They had a large faction who supported them and a small army of good fighting men. They had successfully stormed the palace on numerous occasions but were unable to hold it because they did not possess quality weapons or enough money for supplies and to properly feed their troops.

They struck up a bargain. The East India Trading Company would support the insurrection by providing enough funds and weapons to place Jagat upon the throne. In exchange, he would guarantee not only safe passage through the mountains, but also the exclusive first right to purchase spices, textiles, and other commodities from them.

Before Percival left India, he had heard that the palace had been taken in what would have been a successful campaign. However, before the palace was fully secured, soldiers from neighboring kingdoms showed up and defeated Jagat and his troops once more. When it was then discovered that all but one five-year-old male member of the royal family had been murdered, outrage erupted. The additional ghastly discovery that the royal female family members had been taken, caused such an outcry that even the earth seemed to shake in rage. It was so offensive to the people of India that none dared to even think of it much less form the words to speak of it.

When Percival boarded the *Merchant's Adventure* in India, he had seen the women standing in a huddle on deck. Their bright colorful silks, the finest he had ever seen, fluttered and danced in the sea breeze around them. It was so compellingly beautiful that he had not resisted the urge to move closer to stare at them in awe. They all wore a variety of bangles and jewels over their ankles, around their necks and waists, and up their arms. Several of them had golden chains laid over the top of their heads that supported bird-egg sized jewels that dangled over their brows. A couple of them even wore tiny gold bells which tinkled when they moved. They had been an enchanting spectacle of rich vibrant colors, gracefully dancing silks, and sparkling flashes of light as the sun reflected off of the glistening gold and silver. The clothes and jewels were in sharp contrast to the women, who stood trembling and reeking with the stench of fear and dirty unwashed bodies.

He was sure they were the missing women from the insurrection. He felt sorry for them, but mostly they frightened him. Their very presence on the ship put them all in extreme danger and he wanted no part of any of it. He had even tried to remove himself from the situation but in the time it took for him to retrieve his bags, the *Merchant's Adventure* had already weighed anchor and was on its way out to sea. He had run to the rail and contemplated jumping, but wasn't a strong swimmer and the distance was too great.

To now learn that one of the women was the actual Maharani was shocking. Normally, she would have killed herself, or been killed, rather than be taken. Terror slid through his veins with the awareness that the situation did not bode well. Overwhelmed with the revelation, he felt as if he couldn't breathe. The family would never rest until she was restored to them. Relief that she was no longer aboard the ship gushed through him.

To be tasked with a woman, royalty, whom he must teach to speak English before his own freedom could be secured was unsettling. That there was surely a league of vessels out looking for her, ready to kill everyone aboard in defense of her honor, was unnerving. He thought back to when he stood at the rail, watching India quickly fade in the distance, and wished he would have just taken his chances with swimming and jumped.

Unprepared to answer her questions, he turned to the table, still set with a lavish amount of food that looked untouched.

"Have you not eaten?" he asked, his tongue sliding over his lips hungrily.

"I will not eat that strange food. I prefer to die," Wajeeha shrugged indifferently.

"Then I don't suppose you would mind if I enjoyed some?" Percival asked hopefully.

With a quick flick of her wrist, she consented. She didn't care what he did or what happened to the food. He could indulge himself to his heart's desire.

"What is going to happen to me?"

"That, I don't exactly know," Percival garbled through an overstuffed mouth.

"Then why are you here?"

He washed down his food with long noisy gulps of water.

"Because the captain wants me to teach you to speak their language."

"No."

"No? What do you mean, 'no'?"

"Are you daft? I mean no. I will not learn it. I refuse."

Wajeeha stubbornly lifted her chin. Percival was aghast.

"But you must! You have no choice! I don't think you understand! These aren't exactly the most patient or kind men. You do what they say!"

"Or what...they *kill* me? I've been trying to induce that, but the stubborn man has not yet cooperated!" Wajeeha cried.

Percival wasn't surprised with her response. In fact, he had fully expected it. But he needed her participation to save his own self. Desperate, he tried another tactic.

"What is your name?" he asked as he pushed away from the table, stifling a belch.

Hours later, he explained the situation to the captain.

"Sir, she has lived her life ensconced within a harem of a very rich and very well-respected royal family. She has never even been looked at by any male other than her family. She was taken from the palace along with seven other family members. Those women included the mother of the Maharaja, their king, who is the very highly respected Valide. More importantly, one of them was the Maharani, the wife of the Maharaja, and thereby their Queen. To make matters worse, the Valide died upon the *Merchant's Adventure* and lay rotting for days in front of her family before the sailors finally noticed and removed her. Then, to stir everything up into horrible, she was deeply shamed when your men used her so poorly in front of her queen. In the face of that kind of shame, her culture calls for her death and she is trying to induce you to accommodate her."

Captain Townley remained silent to let what he heard sink in. He wasn't sure what he felt other than frustration and even that fact made it much more annoying. He was the fearless Captain Townley. A privateer commissioned by the king of England, Charles II, who bravely tormented Spanish and French fleets across the seas. That a chit of a woman bothered his conscience was embarrassing and unacceptable. But there he was. Simply ridding himself of her wasn't an option. He knew she would trouble him in his sleep, haunting his nights until he worked out what it was that so drew him to her.

"Follow me," he demanded as he stormed towards his cabin in long angry strides.

*****

Captain Townley burst through the door with Percival racing behind him and marched directly over to Wajeeha, who sat on the bed. Lifting her up as if she were a doll, he set her back down on her feet.

"Tell her I am *not* going to kill her," the captain demanded of Percival, never taking his angry glare from Wajeeha, "but if she persists in her antics, I very well may throttle her, just to make her suffer! A far graver fate than death!"

Percival was uncomfortable with the situation. He was sure that the tactic would not work and wanted to object, but knew that if he did it was to his own peril, so he relayed the message. Suddenly, Wajeeha surprised them both by bursting into tears. Stunned, the two men stood in confusion as she buried her face into her hands and sobbed.

Fear had dominated poor Wajeeha's life for months. From a pampered existence tucked away in a royal harem where she had been the Maharaja's Ikbal, or Fortunate One, she had been suddenly thrust into a world that she hadn't even known existed and was totally unprepared for.

The only males she had ever encountered, other than the Maharaja, were the eunuchs who served and protected them, but who had been rendered incapable of lust or masculine maturity. Lacking any male hormones, their voices remained soft and high, giving them a feminine tone and quality. Rarely did they speak harshly to the women of the harem or correct them in any way. That was the job of the Valide.

Wajeeha had been a very young girl, before she could even remember, when her father had gifted her to his cousin, the Maharaja, to serve as one of his royal concubines. She was placed in the royal harem where she was raised by the women there and educated in all matters of importance, governance, medicine, astronomy, literature, sex, childbirth, and even warfare.

Nothing had prepared her for the uncertainty and fear that she was experiencing. Never had she known that men were capable of such random violence and raw coarseness as that which had been inflicted upon her. Never could she have imagined the depth of shame she could feel until she realized that not only her family saw her being violated, but also her young Maharani.

She had pushed for death, welcoming it, yet these men had come to tell her that she was going to live and that she was going to have to endure whatever else they inflicted upon her. She turned from them and flung herself across the bed, crying through the night.

Chapter Four

Spring 1683, West Indies

Percival raked his hands through his hair. It had been nearly six months and it seemed Wajeeha was totally incapable of learning to speak English. Of course, they'd made progress in other areas. She had stopped crying, was no longer trying to get anyone to kill her, had not attacked anyone in months, and seemed generally content. But she still could not comprehend or speak English, and that was his only ticket to freedom. He was running out of patience with her but didn't know what to do about it.

"Wajeeha, why are you not trying?"

"I am trying! The language is just so crude and difficult! I cannot make those sounds no matter how hard I try!"

He had tried to force the issue, speaking to her only in English, but she sat for over a month in dazed confusion. Finally, he had no choice but to start over and begin anew. He had tried everything within his arsenal and had no more ideas.

Through it all, at some point he had begun to enjoy her company. But that would not gain him his freedom. They took daily walks on deck, talking as they strolled, so he had learned that she was actually quite brilliant. She was highly educated and well versed in most every subject he engaged her with, so he did not believe that she simply could not learn to speak English. The only conclusion he could come to was that she was simply being stubborn, refusing to cooperate in the only way she could.

"Let's go for a walk on deck, maybe the fresh air will do us some good," he suggested, more out of frustration than anything else.

"Maybe we can go ashore with the captain today?" Wajeeha asked hopefully.

Percival sighed. Once again, they were at a port. He wasn't exactly sure where. He only saw the ports from the distance of the captain's window and so they all seemed to blend together, just like the other details of life on board ship. A battle or a raid upon a ship or a village always brought new faces aboard. After a quick stop at port most of them disappeared. Then it happened all over again. There was an ebb and flow, but he made no effort to keep track of the details. The faces changed nearly as often as the weather.

No matter how many ports they visited they were never allowed to disembark. He was a prisoner until his task was complete, and Wajeeha would remain. Wajeeha knew that, so when she persisted in asking to go ashore with every stop, it irritated him. Without responding, he led her out onto the deck and into the warm tropical sunshine.

It was a clear sunny day with not a single cloud in the sky. A gentle tropical breeze wafted over the water carrying the distinct scents of green foliage, exotic spices and people. The ship rocked gently over mild rippling waves, making their walk easy. Not entirely comfortable on deck while Captain Townley was not aboard, instead of walking the entire perimeter, Percival led Wajeeha around to near the stern, where they stopped to watch the bustling little port town and the sailors unload the cargo.

"Well, ain't this a picture!"

A large and burly sailor with a leathery face that had been creased by age and the elements approached. Percival sensed trouble and stepped protectively in front of Wajeeha.

"Do not bother the lady sir, this is not a fight you wish to have," he warned the sailor sharply.

The sailor guffawed and snickered, then dramatically looked about as if seeking someone.

"Lady! I ain't seen no lady hereabouts!"

Wajeeha stiffened as Percival stepped towards the sailor. The sailor called to a friend that stood nearby.

"Suds! Ya seen any ladies around?" he laughed.

The sailor who stood nearby faded out of sight, back and around a stack of barrels where he could watch from a distance and escape any possible accusations of involvement. Seeing his friend abandon him did not daunt the sailor.

"How'd a bookish fop manage ta get ta share the captain's whore?" he sneered as he used the back of his hand to scrub the snot that dripped from his nose.

Before Percival could manage a response, Wajeeha grabbed a board that was left leaning against the base of the main mast. It had two long nails protruding through it, so she had just procured a nasty looking weapon which she promptly wielded with precision by whacking the sailor in the head.

A loud *thunk!* sounded as wood and metal met tissue and bone, embedding the nail in the sailor's left temple. The sailor howled in angry pain as his hands flew protectively to his face. Not willing to leave herself unarmed, Wajeeha kept ahold of the board by yanking it up to dislodge it. When it jerked free, she spun back and struck the sailor again on his right shoulder. Another spin and the board landed across his back then his groin. Unmanned, the sailor fell to his knees as blood spurt from his temple. Percival stood in frozen shock as the sailor folded himself into a protective ball, clutching his groin, and Wajeeha jammed her foot into his neck.

"I am no man's whore," she ground out in slow but perfect English.

Stepping over him, she marched, still gripping the board, towards the captain's cabin, until she remembered Percival and stopped.

"Are you coming or are you just going to stand there and gawk?" she asked, once again reverting to her native tongue.

Dumbfounded and angry, Percival quickly skittered around the groaning sailor and trailed after her.

*****

Following Wajeeha into the cabin, Percival slammed the door angrily. Wajeeha tossed the board to the corner and spun around to face him.

"Is that what they all think? That I am a toy being shared between you and the captain?"

Percival felt betrayed. Everything about the incident infuriated him.

"You understood everything that sailor said," he accused in barely restrained fury, "and then you spoke to him in perfect English!"

Still huffing in an indignant rage, Wajeeha was aware of her mistake so did not attempt to defend herself.

Percival realized that she was not going to back down. She didn't even seem to care that she had betrayed him for months, holding him hostage right along with her.

"You are a devil and a vixen! For months I have tried to teach you, patiently doing everything I could to help you, while you sat making a fool of me."

A dawning realization stole Percival's anger, replacing it with something more tenuous and intangible as it slowly formed.

"I've made excuses to Captain Townley for you, protected you, explained to him how you needed to work through your grief.... All the while you knew everything I said. You know I'm being held hostage, risking my life amongst sailors who will never accept me and would leap at the chance to catch me alone so they can throw me overboard. You also know that the captain said I can go once you can speak English. You used me, let me feel sorry for you, and then *selfishly* risked my life every day by keeping me here."

Wajeeha had not considered Percival's situation. Seeds of regret were planted. She could feel their little roots take hold and it was an uncomfortable feeling. She turned away from him to look out the windows. Sailors were pulling the gangway boards back to the ship, so they would soon be going back out to sea. She did not see Percival swipe at the tear that rolled down his cheek.

"You know what makes it even worse?" he asked her with a mournful sigh, "The fact is that you, a woman, are better prepared to defend yourself than me, a man."

It was a difficult fact to face but there was no denying it. Wajeeha, a mere slip of a woman, was more able to protect herself than even he was, a fully grown man. Somehow, she had been trained to fight and to do it well. She had quickly identified the board as a weapon and then applied it with precision. He could not get the image of her out of his mind. She had easily brought down a man more than twice her size then confidently placed her little foot across his neck to punctuate his defeat. There was no doubt about it. She was a trained warrior.

"I am sorry," whispered Wajeeha softly.

"No," cried Percival, "no more games! You will speak to me only in English!"

Wajeeha nodded hesitantly.

"How? How did you come to be trained as a warrior?"

Wajeeha did not understand and looked at him questioningly.

"Warrior? I do not understand this word."

Percival explained in simpler terms and Wajeeha gave him her answer in passably good English. When she struggled for a word, he supplied it for her then had her repeat it, using it in a sentence.

"Several of the women within the harem are trained to be the last defense to the Maharani. If the harem walls are broached and the eunuchs are defeated, then the women of the harem, including the Maharani, would be defenseless. That cannot happen.

"Whenever a palace is attacked, the women are all taken to a great room to hide and wait. There, the doors are sealed and armed eunuchs are placed both within and outside of them. In the back of the room there is a chamber which holds a great pyre with a large chimney. It is always prepared and stands ready for use. In the event of a breech, the pyre is to be lit.

"The job of the women warriors is to keep the Maharani safe long enough for her to get to that chamber. There, she must throw herself into the fire, along with other key family members, to avoid being taken. That way, they go with honor rather than to cause shame to either themselves or their family. The smoke from the pyre warns the people outside of the palace that it has fallen."

Percival gaped at Wajeeha. He had heard rumors to the effect of what she said but had never fully believed them. He knew that in India they cremated their dead, but the idea of willingly throwing oneself into a fire was alarming.

"But then, why are you here? How did that not happen?"

Wajeeha let out a long sorrowful sigh.

"Because of me. I was one of those warriors. What happened is my shame and it is very painful to me," she started wearily, "but the palace had been attacked many times by Mahi, an uncle, and his sons, who tried to take the throne of the Maharaja. Every time they were defeated. Every time we went to the safe room and waited. Every time we were later told to return to our rooms. Our soldiers were strong and well prepared, so we had no doubt of their victory.

"We won every time but the final time. That time, we ate and gossiped as if it were a party while we waited. The Maharani, still young, even played a game with the children. Then the doors burst open and the eunuchs fell. There was no time to get to the Maharani and move her to the chamber. The pyre was never even lit."

Percival watched Wajeeha struggle to maintain her composure. He knew just enough about the Indian people to understand a bit of how she thought. Though it didn't make sense to him, it wasn't his place to judge her, and her explanation gave him an even greater understanding of the full weight of her struggle. In the end, it had been her responsibility to prevent the women, particularly their queen, from being taken, and she had failed. However, he also realized that this new information and understanding about her changed nothing for either of them.

"What will you do now?" Wajeeha asked, "What will become of me?"

"I do not know," Percival sighed.

And so it was that Percival agreed to give Wajeeha some time before telling Captain Townley that she had learned English.

Chapter Five

Summer, 1683, British Caribbean

Wajeeha smiled at Percival as he admired the handiwork he had done with her hair. The winds were high that afternoon. When they took their daily walk on deck, Wajeeha had struggled to manage her hair. Constantly swiping it away from her face and out of her mouth, she finally tried to restrain it with her hands, but could not manage it at all.

They returned to the cabin where Percival located a ribbon. Remembering some of the simpler fashions worn by his mother, he twisted Wajeeha's hair into a long braid that nearly scraped the top of her hips, then coiling it to the back of her neck, he secured it with the ribbon.

"Perfect!" he exclaimed happily, proud of himself.

Wajeeha's hands fluttered to explore what he had done.

"Let's go back out and see if you have created a success," she smiled.

As they walked, they noticed a change in the air. It was warm, heavy and moist, and they knew they were once again approaching the Caribbean.

"Wajeeha, do you dislike the captain?"

She was uncomfortable with the question.

"I do not know how to answer that," she sighed as a flush stained her cheeks.

"When we are all together, he seems to be very kind to you. He inquires after you, joins you for meals, tries to engage you in conversation that he doesn't know you can understand. I know he sleeps beside you," Percival felt awkward, but he had to ask, "He does not mistreat you when I am gone, does he?"

Wajeeha searched Percival's face. She understood what he was asking and why they were having that particular conversation. He planned to leave her, and soon. She turned away from him and looked out to sea.

"He is nice enough," she sighed, "but I think we both know that it is you whom he would prefer to lay next to."

The revelation was no surprise to Percival. He had felt Captain Townley watching him. He knew the captain's eyes lingered upon him for too long when he thought no one was looking. It had become awkward and uncomfortable for Percival, but he continued to ignore the captain's subtle gestures, feigning ignorance to bland remarks which could be interpreted in other ways. He had heard of such men and knew that they were scorned by society with a vicious contempt. Captain Townley was widely feared as a hard and sometimes merciless, coarse man, but he was also respected as a loyal subject and valiant privateer, commissioned and held in high esteem by the King of England.

Percival understood that commanding the sort of sailors who were capable of the tasks of a privateer required just the sort of qualities found in the captain. It was especially frustrating because over the past months he and the captain had engaged in several long and thoughtful conversations about a variety of subjects, and Percival had found that he actually liked the captain.

Not being ignorant, Percival knew that the time was coming where the situation was going to have to change. Captain Townley was emboldened by Percival's silence which he misinterpreted as complaisance instead of self-preservation. After all, Percival never forgot that he was pressed into the captain's service under the authority of the King of England. Although technically he was not exactly a prisoner, he certainly wasn't free to go either. He knew he needed the captain's protection, not being of the same ilk as most of the sailors on board. If the situation progressed and the captain made an open gesture towards him, he would be forced to outright reject Captain Townley. In that event, Percival feared his life would be in danger. Eventually it was going to happen that everything would be brought out between them. Because they lived in such close quarters, he was concerned that when the time came there would be no hiding his outrage and distress, even to save his own life. If the sailors found out, both he and the captain would be immediately killed.

Unwilling to either confirm or deny Wajeeha's words, Percival also turned towards the sea to watch the porpoises play in the wake of the ship.

"Soon we will be back at port in the Caribbean."

"Will he let you go?" Wajeeha's stomach clenched.

"He said he would, and I do believe he's a man of his word."

Both nodded thoughtfully as Percival turned to Wajeeha. He grasped her face in his hands and gently encouraged her to look into his eyes.

"You must find a way to step into this life. There is no choice now, Wajeeha. It is time. You must tell him that you have become fluent in English. I would prefer that you do it, but if you do not, I will."

*****

Lying next to Captain Townley, Wajeeha listened to the steady rhythm of his breathing.

Very soon Percival would be leaving her, and she struggled to reconcile herself to that fact.

How can I ever accept this she thought, *when he is my only friend and ally?*

Percival had been the only one she had spoken with since she had arrived upon the ship. Of course, there had been multiple conversations with Captain Townley, but each of those had been interpreted by Percival, even when it had become unnecessary.

She drifted off into a restless sleep where the past revisited her, reminding her of the answer she held deep within her heart.

Sitting on the floor of the hold in the belly of the Merchant's Adventure, she heard Maharani crying during Valide's daily lesson. It angered Valide and she slapped Maharani! It was a shocking and horrifying scene! For anyone to challenge the Valide was unheard of, but for their Maharani to be struck in anger was appalling! The Valide gathered them together at her feet as she sat weakly upon a barrel.

"This you will always remember," she said, "Though we are upon this ship, we are not of this ship. We wear crude clothes and silks the same. None of those things shape who we are because this has already been determined. We are all women of quality. Wives and children of the most proud and highly honored maharajas of Koch Behar. Descendants of the royal Koch dynasty and the first maharaja, Chandran. That is who we are.

41

"Our bodies are but the chattel to pleasure and sow the seeds of a man, who can use any woman's body to do that. A woman's strength is in her mind and heart. A strong woman who gives her man good release with her body as well as safe relief for his spirit, is a wise woman who will rule her man.

"Be wise. Choose the seeds that will take root. Show not fear, for that breeds dominance and abuse. Be strong with yourself and your children, keeping your worries to yourself, and let others plague him with their frivolous concerns.

"Your eyes keep you blind. What you see with your mind's eye is a bigger picture of the universe as one. Remember that all of this is a part of life. It will help you to make noble decisions and stand up to challenges with courage, welcoming good thoughts. All these things are who you truly are and cannot be taken from you without your permission. They are what keep you free."

Wajeeha saw the Valide crumple and ran towards her but could not reach her.

"Valide! What am I to do, Valide?" Wajeeha pleaded for answers.

Suddenly the Valide opened her eyes and looked directly into Wajeeha's.

"You must not be afraid. Be brave. Rule. It matters not that he prefers another. Close your eyes and see. Be wise enough to rule through him. It will keep you free. Do not forget who you are, Wajeeha, and choose. Claim your destiny."

Frightened and confused, Wajeeha startled awake, disturbing Captain Townley who sat up to check on her. He wished that he could be more of a comfort to her but didn't know what to do for her. He placed his arm around her.

"Shhh, You're safe," he whispered.

"I am not afraid. I am angry," replied Wajeeha bitterly.

Captain Townley stilled. Wajeeha had spoken in perfect English. He had known that she understood far more English than she had wanted him to believe. He had known it for quite some time. Instead of confronting her or Percival about it, he watched them, wondering what they conspired and when it would manifest itself. He was tired and unprepared for a midnight confession, yet he didn't want her to think that she had fooled him.

"So, finally you speak," he chuckled and simply fell back onto the bed, pulled her close, and went back to sleep.

*****

September 1683, Open Sea

Captain Townley made a point to take extra time getting to know Wajeeha better after Percival's departure. He understood that her days felt longer without a companion, so he made it a habit to walk with her on deck as often as time allowed. Every evening they talked while they ate their dinner together.

"Once again you have outdone yourself," Captain Townley complimented Frederick as he finished laying out their dinner.

When all was complete and Frederick had departed, Captain Townley encouraged Wajeeha to hurry and join him. Everything smelled especially delicious, and he was hungry. After a lazy dinner filled with idle conversation, Captain Townley suddenly looked closely at Queen, studying her as if seeing her for the first time.

"Do you still miss Percival?" he asked, genuinely concerned.

"Not as much as before. You are great company and more than make up for his loss," sighed Wajeeha, forcing a smile.

"Then what troubles you, my dear?"

"Why do you not want me?" asked Wajeeha shyly.

Captain Townley's brows drew up as his eyes widened with surprise.

"Of course I want you! Why on earth do you think that you are here?"

Wajeeha fumbled with her fork and idly pushed the food around her plate.

"You want me as a companion to talk to and a pet to keep you warm at night."

Captain Townley laughed.

"A pet!" he exclaimed, "Never! I want you as my queen! To be cherished and spoiled! You have ruled my heart since I first laid eyes upon you, though why I do not quite understand."

"Your queen," Wajeeha objected doubtfully, "I could never be your queen! I believe I am much too plain to be a queen."

"My dear, queen is a title, a role you play. It isn't who you are on the inside," Captain Townley laughed and exclaimed in mock anger, then added, "and you are nothing even close to being plain."

Wajeeha smiled and laughed with him. She enjoyed the captain when his spirits were high and his mood was playful.

"Besides, I do not want to be as idle as a queen," she stated softly, then looked at him hopefully.

"Then, my queen," he smiled warmly at her as he grasped her hands and tilted her chin up to him, "you shall be as industrious as you choose."

Chapter Six

March 1685 Gulf de San Miguel, Panama

Surrounded by French and English ships, Captain Townley was excited.

"Queen!" he called across deck, searching, "Goddamnit, Queen, where the hell are you?"

In the crow's nest, perched at the top of the mainmast in the center of the ship, Queen heard him yelling for her. With a quick wink to the sailor posted there, she tucked her long knife between her teeth and grasped the rope secured by the mast and the shroud. Sliding down, she dropped neatly in front of the captain.

"Why," she asked, exasperated and out of breath, "must you shriek? The ship is only so big. You can be assured that I do hear you but am busy."

"I have been looking for you," exclaimed Captain Townley as he kicked aside a goat who wandered across his path, "because we've immediate decisions to make."

She nodded and followed him to their quarters. Once in private, she kissed him boldly upon his temple then went and sat behind his desk to wait for him to speak. Obviously, she had noticed the additional ships that had joined them. Though she was curious about them, she refused to admit it or to ask him about them. When he was not forthcoming with information, she glanced up, seemingly bored, and dropped her chin into her hands to wait until he could stand it no more.

"Well," he began as he always did, "we will be joining with additional forces. French forces."

"Hmmm."

"Is that all? Just, 'hmmm'?"

Captain Townley was incredulous. Surrounding them were an additional eight ships holding nearly one thousand men, all with canoes zipping back and forth between them. He knew without doubt that she had seen them. For that matter, even a blind person would know they were there. The noxious fumes wafting from them could not be ignored. How could she not be even the tiniest bit curious about them?

It wasn't entirely unusual for them to join forces with other ships, oftentimes to take another ship just for the sport of it. However, with peace being obtained between the English and the French, official assignments were scant. The Spanish were the only real targets left and the crown had withdrawn most of the commissions against them. It was a miserable situation for many sailors.

The privateer ships were not suitable as merchant ships, nor could their crews be trusted. Peace simply meant that there were many unemployed sailors, all seeking other options. A joint force of this size for the specific purpose of unsanctioned plundering meant they were crossing over into becoming official buccaneers, or pirates. For Captain Townley, it was a significant transition of identity and he wanted Queen to understand that.

"What else would you have me say? I don't have your loyalty difficulties regarding the French, Spanish, *or* the English."

Captain Townley laughed. Since becoming a part of his crew, Queen had developed into a very valuable asset. She could navigate as well as he could and wield a knife better than most any man. She had surpassed him in her technique with the whip, could mend the sails faster and with more precision than any of the sailors, and provide medical treatment whenever it was required. Additionally, although she was outweighed by every man aboard, if left unrestrained she could outfight any of them in hand-to-hand combat. Though at first some of the sailors had been unhappy with her presence, they had mostly come to accept and respect her.

"I have invited the leader of the French fleet aboard to dine with us this evening. Interesting fellow by the name of Francois Grogniet. I would like you to present yourself respectably," Captain Townley knew he was about to anger Queen and coughed subtly into his sleeve, "as a *proper* lady, in a dress."

Queen sucked in her breath and narrowed her eyes. He was goading her and she knew it. Smiling prettily, she slowly pressed her hands, dirty from working in the crow's nest repairing a small tear in the sail, onto her chest and drew them down to her belly, leaving long dark smudges against the soft white linen. Though she intended to shock the captain, her actions only served to humor him further.

*****

Captain Townley and Francois Grogniet were completing discussions regarding the joining of their forces when Frederick arrived heavily burdened with an oversized tray. Too large to fit through the doorway while he gripped it, he shifted his hands underneath the tray and then passed it through to the captain before he entered to set their places.

The Captain took the tray, inquiring about Queen as he did.

"Frederick, will you please let Queen know that she is keeping our guest waiting?"

Captain Townley was usually amused by Queen's antics. This time he was not because he very much wanted to make a good impression upon his guest.

Captain Grogniet was the youngest son of a good family and had worked as a privateer under the French crown for years. He had a fine ship, a good crew that was mostly orderly and often sober, and a beautiful woman by his side. Because Captain Townley was yet uncomfortable with the transition from privateer to pirate, he wanted to compare favorably to Captain Grogniet and to appear just as respectable as he did. It didn't matter that Captain Grogniet was in the same position.

The food smelled delicious and was meant to be served hot. To have it sit before his guest, untouched, was appalling. Captain Townley pushed up from his chair and went to the door in long angry strides. Harshly throwing it open to go find Queen himself, he nearly collided with her. Relieved, he quickly pulled her into the room.

"Ah, well, she has finally arrived! Captain Grogniet, allow me to introduce you to my dear friend and companion, Queen."

Gesturing to her, he turned and was about to complete the introductions when he realized what she was wearing. Not only had she defied him by not wearing the dress he had ordered her to, but she remained in the same clothing she had worn earlier in the day. Handprint stains were joined with additional grime, several small holes at the shoulder and back, and a partially torn cuff.

Aware that her appearance had rendered Captain Townley speechless, Queen took over. She smiled graciously and extended her hand towards Captain Grogniet in greeting. Then, after a quick glance at her soiled hand, she withdrew it, and spit into it. After rubbing her hands together, she wiped them down her thighs and across her pants, transferring the grime to them, then once again thrust her hand back out to their guest.

Captain Grogniet, also stunned speechless, looked at the hand she proffered, unsure of what to do and unwilling to grasp it. Finally, breeding overcoming caution, he grasped her wrist. Turning her hand palm down, he dipped his head and brushed a kiss to the back of it.

"So very pleased to make your acquaintance, Miss Queen," he stated in heavily accented English with an amused chuckle.

"Just Queen," she replied, well-pleased with her affect upon the two gentlemen.

She moved to the table and took her seat, absolving the men of their indecision regarding whether or not to assist her. Unable to recover so quickly from the shock of her, neither man was able to speak even after they had all been seated. The silence was deafening. Queen rescued them from the awkwardness of the situation and directed the conversation. Topics ranging from navigation to tactics were discussed and debated between them with the wisdom of experience.

Captain Grogniet was an intelligent man who could see through Queen's antics. He saw the rare beauty she concealed behind the layers of dirt and understood that she needed to be seen as a competent sailor in her own right, not just as an ornament. By the night's end, not only had she impressed him, but she had also thoroughly enchanted him.

Chapter Seven

May 28, 1685, Near the Island of Pacheca, Pearl Islands

The morning sky was washed the color of ripe plums. Long brushstrokes of yellow swept out from a watery orange sun that rose just above the water. Enjoying the balmy morning air, Queen navigated around the many sailors on deck who were still sleeping huddled under blankets and large pieces of sail, their only protection against the night's rain.

Choosing the solace of the crow's nest, she easily climbed the nettings to gain access, scaring off several gulls that had perched there for the night. She swiped at a stray tendril of hair that had escaped its braid and was tickling her neck, and looked out to sea. It stretched dark and endless but sparkled as the sun tore through the morning mist. It was going to be a beautiful day.

She stretched her leg down the length of the ropes and leaned against the mast to watch the sun rise. First, as was her habit, she glanced to check the other five boats in their fleet. Satisfied to see them bobbing over the waves, she was just settling in when she saw movement just beyond their fleet. Springing to full attention, she pulled the scope from her side to look closer. In the horizon, rapidly bearing down upon them, were several Spanish ships.

"Ho ahead!" she yelled to alert the crew.

The deck became a hive of activity. Instantly alert, the sails were tossed and the sailors were on their feet, springing to man their battle positions. It was a perilous situation in that they had no cannons. The only firepower aboard, due to malfunctions and other losses, were small firearms. Sliding down the lines to the deck, she ran to inform Captain Townley.

*****

"We can lower canoes with the men, drop back, and let them do their job with machetes and handguns. Once they've breached the hull, we'll move in."

Captain Townley was excited at the prospect of taking such a fine Spanish ship. Though his had been a fine vessel when he acquired it, it was beginning to show the signs of wear and tear. Plus, it was heavy and outdated. He was anxious to replace it.

"Those ships are well armed and moving towards us swiftly! We don't have time and we can't out-gun them. Our only option is to run! Save this fight for another day!"

Captain Townley checked his maps and charts.

"There's nowhere to go, Queen. We are against a narrow passage, maybe forty feet in width, and it's shallow."

Queen looked at the map.

"I can do it," she announced confidently, "I can get us through. The Spanish ships are too heavy, so they'll never be able to follow us in."

Panama was held by the Spanish and had been raided and ransacked by pirates for far too long. The Spanish, tired of being assaulted, outfitted a fleet of ships designed specifically to clear their waters of them. Heavily armed and designed for easy maneuverability, they sported multiple large sails to ensure speed. They were nearly impossible to beat, thus they were referred to as man-o-war vessels. However, because of the weight of weapons and ammunition, their hulls rode deep, so they could not enter shallow waters.

It was a daring and dangerous plan. If they failed, they were doomed. If they went down, they would all be scooped out of the water and escorted directly to a firing squad. Captain Townley had been on the seas most of his life. He knew that no responsible captain would do what Queen, with only a handful of years in experience, was suggesting and yet...

Queen locked gazes with Captain Townley. She didn't know how or why she so confidently believed in her plan, but she did.

"It's a gamble, but right now, in a crippled vessel," Queen threw her hand towards the Spanish ships, "confronting them isn't a gamble, it's death. At least this way, if we go out, we go out fighting. Let them live to die another day."

Captain Townley narrowed his eyes to slits and stubbornly jutted out his chin, a habit he had adapted from her.

Sensing he was nearly ready to fold, she pushed.

"Please." It was as close to a begging plea that he would ever receive from her.

"God damnit!" his decision made, Captain Townley raked his hand through his hair and sprang into action, "You take the lead then, Queen, and if this fails, it's been one helluva ride. Thank you for your loyalty and service."

"It will not fail," Queen promised with a silent prayer.

Captain Townley turned his ship towards the narrow channel and fled. One of the Spanish ships followed swiftly behind them. Cannonballs plopped into the sea all around Captain Townley's ship in great splashing waves, tossing it wildly about. As it approached the shallower waters, Queen deftly navigated into the channel, forcing the Spanish ship to stop pursuit. The rest of their fleet, with their weapons still functional, continued to engage the other ships in a short battle before also turning to flee. Outgunned, the pirates were defeated.

Rejoining later, a rift ensued amongst the captains. The French, under Captain Grogniet, blamed Captain Townley for fleeing. Captain Townley, boisterous and arrogant, blamed Captain Grogniet, who was positioned closer to the Spanish fleets, for not engaging in battle soon enough. Grave insults and baseless accusations were tossed back and forth until indignant outrage and self-righteous fury peaked. The result was an angry separation of their forces.

Captain Townley's fleet turned towards Nicaragua where they raided multiple towns and villages with only minimal gain, then proceeded on to the Mexican coast. There, they briefly reunited with the French to establish a blockade in an effort to force the Mexicans into a payoff in exchange for being left unmolested. Used to the tactics of privateers, and then pirates, the Mexicans refused to pay the ransom. After months of fruitless effort, they finally gave up and moved on.

*****

March 22, 1686, The Gulf of Nicoya, Costa Rica

Queen anxiously searched the coastline as she sat in the crow's nest over the main mast. Captain Townley had been gone for too long and she was worried. They had been preparing for an expedition to Granada and their supplies were low, so the captain had gone ashore to secure them.

Taking several crews in canoes, Captain Townley had left the previous morning to secure food, water, and wood. It wasn't too unusual that he hadn't returned by evening. Sometimes additional convincing was needed to induce the farmers to relinquish their stock and food supplies. The crew would never have tried to return to the ship in the dark, it was simply too dangerous. That they had not yet appeared by mid-day the following day was highly unusual.

If they were attacked, then all of the sailors wouldn't have been lost, she thought, *some of them would have returned. Yet I've seen no one.*

Most concerning was that the previous night a tornado had swept through. The swells that washed over the deck had been so large that the men had been forced to secure themselves to the masts with ropes to prevent being washed out to sea. The ship was tossed and turned until it was nearly spinning. Not ones to suffer from the constant movement of being aboard a ship, most of the crew, including Queen, had been surprised to find themselves doubled over a barrel, heaving in protest of the storm.

Worry and fear for her crew dominated Queen's focus so completely that she did not notice the approach of a familiar French ship until it was very nearly upon them. With an inward groan, she grasped the rope and slid down to the deck to greet their visitors.

When Captain Grogniet climbed aboard he was shocked to find that the ship was almost completely unmanned. Amused to have found it so exposed and vulnerable, he strode arrogantly across the deck with his arms fully stretched out in a great sweeping question. When he spotted Queen swooping down to meet him, his laughter froze in his throat, nearly choking him.

My God, she is an angel swooping down to me, he breathed, *I would follow her to heaven, or hell, wherever she would lead.*

Queen, in her customary pants and blouse, appeared as a vision. Her skin, tanned a rich and healthy copper, glowed with the sun behind her. Her hair, like a raven's wing, flew out behind her in shining glory. When she landed upon the deck, it danced and settled around her shoulders, then down her back, and framed her face in a vision of loveliness. Though she had to be wary of his presence due to the circumstances of their last parting, she appeared confident, neither welcoming nor inhospitable.

"Captain Grogniet, what brings you aboard our ship?"

He smiled as the smooth timbre of her voice caressed him. When she spoke, it afforded him a view of her white perfectly even teeth. In the sunshine they sparkled and nearly glowed in bright contrast to her sunbaked skin. Only slightly winded from her flight, her chest rose and fell enticingly. Though she was agitated, Captain Grogniet knew he would spend a lifetime trying to appease her if only he could see her every day. He bowed a deep and courtly bow.

"Lady Queen, I've come to pay my regards to you and your captain."

Queen narrowed her eyes. They were pirates. They did not pay regards or owe respects such as these. She knew he was up to something and didn't like it.

"Well, as you can see, Captain Townley is off securing provisions," she scoffed, "but I'll be sure to tell him you... dropped by...."

Captain Grogniet did not think as he grabbed Queen by the waist and drew her to his body. Pressing his lips against hers, he planted a solid kiss. It happened on such a strong impulse that he hadn't even been aware he was going to do it until the deed had been done. Just as quickly, he released her.

"That... was quite rude of me," he sputtered in embarrassment, not noticing that her hand had gone up and around to his back, "please... accept my... *most* humble... apology."

Living amongst lusty sailors, Queen was prepared for such things and had also reacted on impulse, withdrawing the knife she carried at her waist from its pouch.

"Because you are quick to correct your mistake, I will allow it just once," she whispered as she pressed the tip of the blade she held formidably against his back, "I am not a forgiving woman, Captain Grogniet. You would do well to remember that."

Captain Grogniet felt the threat of the blade and was once again enchanted. His brows raised and his eyes danced with excitement.

"My God, Queen," he exclaimed laughing heartily, "you are spectacular! Bravo!"

Remaining on board to wait for the return of Captain Townley and the rest of the crew, Captain Grogniet made plans to teach Captain Townley a lesson, as revenge for his insults that followed the Pearl Island incident.

Later that day, when Captain Townley and his men returned they found the ship under siege. Immediately taken into custody upon boarding, they were told they had become prisoners. For five hours the ruse continued. When finally the ship and possessions were restored back to Captain Townley, the men enjoyed a good laugh and some excellent rum before they sailed together towards Granada.

Chapter Eight

May 19, 1686, Open Sea

Queen was frightened and uncomfortable with the feeling, for rarely did she experience it. Though at first Captain Townley had been hesitant to engage in piracy, he had since embraced it so wholly that his former self was no longer recognizable. His actions of the past months were intolerable, and she feared the effect of them. Obviously, raiding and sacking carried the probability that there would be deaths. To kill or be killed was honorable in the course of war, however, Granada had been different.

Granada, in New Spain, was one of the most beautiful countries Queen had ever seen. It possessed a lush countryside splattered with vast neatly laid sugar plantations. It was so covered with color and life it reminded her of the vibrant silks of the women of the harem.

Then there were the churches. Magnificent churches built of stone that reached way up into the clouds. They had huge windows of colored glass that twinkled in the sunlight and splashed dancing color over the great open halls below. All built to honor their god. Though she did not particularly care about their god or their beliefs, she could not help but feel a certain reverence when she entered those churches. It repelled her that the sailors, bent on destruction, desecrated them. Though she had encouraged them to simply seek their plunder and go, she was ignored. Once they had collected what they needed, to what purpose did it serve to destroy a place of faith? It did not sit well within her heart.

That they had taken a priest prisoner was beyond unacceptable to her. He was a man of faith over a small and isolated community and had no wealth or political significance. Taking him could serve no purpose. He was not even worth the Spaniards ransoming and was physically incapable of contributing onboard the ship. He was useless as a prisoner.

Days earlier, in the city of Ria Lexia, they had arrived in need of food and supplies but had been unable to find any. The people there, tired of having their cattle and other livestock plundered, had moved them to safety, inland, far away from the coast. Obviously, it was inconvenient and a disappointment to the sailors, but who could blame the people?

In retaliation, Captain Townley not only ordered that all of their fine churches be relieved of anything valuable and then be destroyed, but he also took over one hundred of its inhabitants' prisoner. When the sailors who delivered the messages to the Spanish leaders did not reappear, he beheaded several of the prisoners and sent their heads with the threat that more would follow unless his men were returned along with the requested provisions. The Spaniards quickly complied, and Captain Townley and his crew departed, cheering exuberantly over their victory.

Queen enjoyed combat at sea and generally suffered no conscience from taking prisoners. If they were taken on land, citizens were normally released. Those that were taken at sea were sold. Sailors were either employed or killed. After all, if you were riding the seas then you were in the game. Everyone knew the risks, so all was fair.

She also had no problem sweeping onto shore and taking a cow or a pig, some grain, or raiding for valuables to support themselves and the crew. It was a necessary evil. It wasn't as if they took *every* cow a farmer had, or the *only* one. Although sometimes people got hurt, they did their very best to avoid it.

To be so violent against citizens, including women and children, even beheading them, was appalling. To do so when they were not working within the auspices of a commission, possessing no Letter of Marque, meant that they were acting as criminals and so had no protection under the law.

True, they had become pirates, but Captain Townley was becoming reckless. When set upon a mission, he pursued it with a single-minded determination that completely lacked any objectivity. He had become arrogant, egotistical, and vicious to any who dared to stand in his way. It made him dangerous to everyone, including his crew and himself. Queen had tried to talk to him about it but he would not listen. The captain was self-imploding and would take everyone who assisted him towards that goal with him. Something must be done.

She met with Captain Grogniet earlier in the day. He, too, was uneasy with the apparent unraveling of Captain Townley and was preparing to separate himself from it. Encouraging her to depart with him, he gave her only a few hours to decide. She knew what she must do. *Be wise.* It didn't make it any easier.

Over the years she had developed a fond affection for Captain Townley. He had saved her from the horrible fate of becoming a slave when he took her in, and then showed her a life of adventure and excitement that she would never have known existed. Although she cared for him, she owed him nothing. She took what he offered, but then she gave back to him in an even greater return. Though she knew he would miss her, she was equally sure she could be replaced, just as anyone could. She had no doubt that he was bound towards destruction and she had no wish to be with him when the day arrived. Gathering her few simple possessions, she waited for him in their cabin.

*****

Captain Townley entered tired and weary, slamming the door behind himself.

"Damn Grogniet must think me a fool," he exclaimed, "I rescued him from that damned island, and this is the way he repays me. He wants to divide the spoils, as if we are equals, then part ways once again. As if he won't come crawling back, yet again, when his coffers are empty and his equally empty head has no ideas about how to refill them! Absolutely *not!*"

Unsure if he wanted a response or was simply releasing his frustration, Queen watched him rip his shirt open, shrug out of it, then discard it with a toss. It floated in a billowing cloud and settled in a lazy heap on the floor before she spoke.

"You did not rescue him from that island," she stated, aware that she was challenging him about details he did not want to be reminded of, but nonetheless remained true, "If you recall, his ship was crippled by the storm of the night before and you simply helped to repair it. He took your vessel fair and square when he arrived and you were ashore, then repaid your earlier kindness by giving it back. Honor did not demand that he return it to you, yet he did."

Captain Townley was outraged.

"Only because it is mine!"

Queen smiled, mildly amused.

"At that moment it was not yours, it was his," she replied sharply, "that he chose to return it to you speaks of his character."

"Bah!" Captain Townley grabbed a bottle of rum and pulled the cork with his teeth. He shot it away with a huff of breath and it flew like a cannon ball to the floor where it bounced and rolled to rest between two barrels. He raised the bottle to his mouth. Before he could take a drink, Queen firmly placed her hand over it and lowered it from his mouth, poised to indulge.

"I need to speak to you and want you to be completely sober so we both know that there is no misunderstanding between us," she stated firmly, allowing him no reasonable objection.

Captain Townley was irritated, yet he knew Queen's temper. Rarely did she offer advice unless it pertained to the ship, the men, or missions. Then, she never prefaced it with an announcement that they needed to talk or of his need to be sober. This was obviously going to be personal, and he most assuredly didn't want to hear it. When things became personal with Queen, she developed an obstinate resolve that couldn't be broken. He placed his unoccupied hand against her cheek and smiled at her charmingly.

"What, my beautiful Queen, could trouble you so?" he asked, his voice was warm but dripped with indulgent sarcasm.

Queen brushed his hand away.

"I told you in Granada that I do not approve of the uninhibited way the men sacked the churches or treated the people there. Then, in Ria Lexia, you allowed it to happen again. Only instead of simply taking a useless priest, you took over a hundred innocent people and beheaded several of them! That is wrong and you well know it!"

Captain Townley was sick of hearing it.

"Innocent?" he cried in outrage, "there *are* no innocent people!"

Queen looked at him sadly. Saying nothing, she studied him. Uncomfortable under her scrutiny, Captain Townley dramatically threw himself into a chair. Nearly missing it, he stumbled, spilling the uncorked rum across his chest and over his lap in the process. When he looked to see if she noticed his stumble, she saw a strange gleam in his eyes that had not been there before. It was accompanied with the wide-eyed arrogance and denial borne of one who would not, could not, be found lacking.

He has become quite mad, thought Queen, turning her thoughts back to the words of Valide while they had been aboard the *Merchant's Adventure.*

> *"Be wise. Do not forget... your eyes keep you blind... you see with your mind's eye a bigger picture of the universe as one.... All is a part of the activities of life... make noble decisions, stand up to challenges with courage...these things are who you truly are and cannot be taken from you without your permission. They are what keep you free.*

Talking to him was of no use. There was no way to soften the blow.

"Captain, in life there are always consequences for our actions and for the actions of those whom we surround ourselves with. Quite frankly, I can no longer accept the inevitability of the consequences of your actions. No good will come of it."

Captain Townley leaned slowly toward her. Narrowing his eyes to a mere slit, he pushed the bottle of rum he still held up to his mouth. Drawing long and deep from it, he closed his eyes and swallowed in a loud gulp before leveling his gaze back to her.

"And what, exactly, do you intend to do about it?" he challenged menacingly.

Undaunted, Queen stepped towards him. Standing before him, she mirrored his glare. Words were not necessary. She was not afraid of him and would not be intimidated. Leaning down, she placed an icy kiss upon his brow then turned to the bed where her pack lay ready.

"Nothing," she stated, calmly gathering her belongings, "I do not intend to do a damn thing about you, but I assure you that I can do something about myself."

As she rowed away, she heard him calling after her in crazed drunkenness.

"Don't ever come back, Queen! I made you, damnit, and I will break you! How dare you leave me! Queen, I need you! Queen!"

And so it was that in June 1686, just two months later, Captain Townley sacked the city of Lavelia, Panama, taking three hundred prisoners. When the President of Panama refused to pay the demanded ransom, Captain Townley sent a canoe containing twenty disembodied heads as a warning to him, along with the dire threat of doing the same to all of the remaining prisoners. Although his demands were finally met, it was not without consequences. Captain Townley died from wounds he sustained in the battle, crying out for his Queen with his final breath.

Chapter Nine

Evening May 19, 1686, Open Sea

Queen easily navigated the ladder and dropped onto the deck of Captain Francois Grogniet's ship. It was very much like Captain Townley's ship, with various animals such as goats, ducks, a few pigs, several monkeys, a pack of dogs, multitudes of cats and rabbits, all scurrying around. Though the smell was noxious, she was accustomed to it, so she did not mind. Overhead, more than a dozen scavenger birds flew, swooping in if they saw an opportunity to snatch one of the smaller animals for a quick and easy meal. Circling the ship were the customary sharks who traveled along with it, waiting for the scrapings of the deck to fall. Men, about one hundred and sixty by her estimate, scrambled around in varied states of drunkenness, but still able to complete their tasks with efficiency. The familiar scene did not help to make her feel more comfortable.

Captain Grogniet stood not ten paces away, smiling in adoring welcome. He knew Queen was an asset to any ship and was happy to welcome her aboard. More than that, he had been enchanted with her since their first meeting. She was beautiful, had a quick wit, was an unparalleled warrior, and was one of the finest sailors he had ever met. Never had he been able to understand what her attraction to Captain Townley was, but neither did he have any real expectations of being able to lure her away from him. However, against all odds, fate had her standing before him as a member of his crew and a companion to warm his bed.

"Queen," the smile stretched slowly across his face, first touching his eyes then spreading across his cheeks and mouth, where he displayed a fine row of mostly white teeth, "Bienvenu, welcome."

Drawing upon her courage, Queen sucked in a deep breath. Holding it, she stepped toward him.

"Captain, thank you for welcoming me aboard," she stated confidently, sliding her eyes across the deck to note the sailor's varied reactions to her.

Of course they knew her. They had worked several times together in the joint fleets. They had seen her in action many times, but that did not guarantee a warm welcome and she was under no delusions about it.

*****

Queen climbed up to the crow's nest where she was most comfortable, and sat, dropping her legs over the edge where they dangled, swinging back and forth. She looked out to sea and couldn't help but search in the fading horizon for Captain Townley's vessel. It was long gone. A pang gripped her gut as she remembered him yelling after her. Knitting her brows together in silent pain, she coaxed herself to relax with the knowledge that she had done what was best.

Distracting herself, the knot in her belly eased as she watched the men move about on the deck below, preparing for the days end. Some sought a place to sleep, hoisting their bedrolls into canoes or other less congested places. Several played cards, or some other game that involved an equal amount of excitement, complete with both cheers and grumbling. A few fought. Their comrades quieted the disagreements before blood was drawn, or worse, they drew the attention of the captain. Others, it seemed, like the livestock, simply wandered.

Unsure of where she was to sleep, never before having been faced with that complication, she easily slid into the decision to secure herself where she was, in the crow's nest, perched high above it all. She knew Captain Grogniet wanted her. Although he had always been respectful of her presumed relationship with Captain Townley, he'd also certainly not hidden from her his desire for her, though subtly. His eyes lingered on her overly long when speaking with her and always seemed to be scanning the ship, seeking her, when he wasn't. She knew she could simply go to him, offering herself, and take up residence in his cabin, but she didn't want to make it that easy. He had to come for her. He had to ask. He had to want her enough to set his pride aside. Until then, she would remain elusive…making no obvious assumptions.

Although she had proven herself with Captain Townley's crew, she wasn't ignorant to the fact that she would have to also prove herself with this crew. Running straight to the captain's cabin without an official invitation would only complicate things with them. She was aware of the inevitability of the situation. It didn't frighten her. Being realistic, she knew it was going to be difficult. After all, there were some practical concerns that, being the sole female member of the crew, affected her differently.

"Queen! Bon Dieu! Merde, Queen, where are you?"

Queen watched Captain Grogniet as he moved about below, weaving amongst the groups and sleeping forms of the sailors. He covered the entire span of the deck grasping every sailor he passed. Squinting at them through the darkness, he quickly searched their faces before moving on. His actions intrigued her, so she continued to watch without bothering to respond. Finally, she saw one of the sailors point up towards her. The captain spread his arms out in question as he looked up at her, sitting as a shadow under the light of the moon. She pretended not to see him. He had to come to her.

Climbing the lines to the crow's nest, once he got to her, he looped his arm through the shrouds just a few feet away from where she sat. There he hung, slightly swaying with the rock of the ship, silently grinning. Then, as if they were children playing a game of hide and seek and he was proud of himself to have found her, a broad expectant smile stretched across his face.

"Why do you hide from me, mon Cheri?"

"Hide from you? I wasn't aware you were looking for me."

"Ah! So, we play this game," laughed Captain Grogniet, "but mon dieu, I am not so good with games."

*****

Queen found that Captain Grogniet's cabin compared equally to Captain Townley's. However, Captain Grogniet wasn't the same man. There could be no comparison. He was a man, fully, with desires and longings such as a woman would expect from a man. Though she had been relieved that Captain Townley was not, she felt drawn to Captain Grogniet in a primal and very womanly way. Turning to him, she was overcome with desire.

In a single step he closed the gap between them.

"I seem to recall you telling me that you would allow me the mischief of grabbing you just once, mon Cheri," he whispered gruffly. Placing his hand over her temple, he just nearly touched it and drew it down over her cheek to her jaw, where it hovered, "and that I must remember that you are an unforgiving woman, should I commit such a faux pas once more."

Queen could feel the heat of his hand as if he actually touched her. Leaning into it, she placed her hand over his and slowly guided it, pulling it down her body.

*****

February 1687, Nicoya, New Spain

Nighttime was crawling in after another long and difficult day. The mood was heavy amongst the sailors. They had just returned from a raid where they hoped to at least re-supply their food and medicine provisions as well as collect some silver from the church as compensation for their efforts. There was barely a goat or a pig to be found and the few chickens that were there refused to cooperate, so the sailors left almost empty handed. It was a huge disappointment, especially since their luck had been down lately.

"Captain, it ain't worth it," cried one of the men who was joined by another and then more until it became an angry chant.

Captain Grogniet drew out his pistol and shot into the air. It blasted through the chants and rang into the night, reverberating over the water, repeating and fading until the sea breeze carried it away. The men mostly quieted. A few stubborn protestors were quickly silenced with a warning glare.

"Men, I know it's been difficult lately," Captain Grogniet tried to appease them, "but these waters and lands have been overly abused by us for far too long."

"Ain't never see'd that afore! It's the wench! Wenches is bad luck on a ship!" cried one angry sailor to a chorus of rumbled agreement.

Captain Grogniet knew that being aboard his ship, any ship, could be dangerous for Queen. He had to get them to accept her presence amongst them and quickly, but he was desperate about how to accomplish it. She was a better sailor than most of them and more loyal by far than any of them. Hell, she could teach them a few things if they'd let her, but for as long as he could remember sailors had always believed that bad luck came if the fairer sex stepped upon a deck while at sea.

To make the situation even more tense, when they raided Lavelia, it produced nothing more than a headache. Then at Caldera Bay, three of his men were taken prisoner by the Spanish. After that, desperate at the Bay of Ampalla, they marched many leagues inland to a gold mine. There, they found very little gold because it had just recently been carted away, but the mine was fully staffed. To prevent the worker's from sounding an alarm, the sailors had no choice but to take them prisoner until they could return safely to their ship. In the end they got just enough food to provide for their prisoners. The entire venture turned out to be a fiasco.

Each time they went ashore, when Queen unfurled her whip, it was as if Durga, the goddess of war and strength, had arrived. The very air crackled and snapped, alive with the flick of her wrist and a toss of the whip. She appeared as the embodiment of a fearless warrior upon a righteous path. And though she was amazing and enchanting, superstitious demons are powerful.

"Either with or without Queen the circumstances would have been the same," Captain Grogniet reasoned with his crew, "the Spanish have moved their people, animals, and valuables inland. They are over-raided."

"Captain, it's the wench," the sailors argued, "and the luck she brings!"

"Must I remind you that she sailed successfully with Captain Townley for years?" he reasoned, "Hell, she was their saving grace, their good-luck charm."

"So we starve?" yelled several of the men, encouraged by the others.

"No," replied Captain Grogniet, "we sail for new waters where they aren't being quite so careful, or stingy, with their livestock and property."

And so it was that they joined with several other ships to create a fleet that would make the long journey to the city of Guayaquil.

Chapter Ten

April 20, 1687, Guayaquil, Audiencia de Quito, Peru

From the captain's cabin, Queen looked out the window and across the water through the bay to the town of Guayaquil, eerily transformed. The once quiet coastal village seemed a surreal display of hell rising. Flames licked the sky, dancing like devils as they ate the landscape and everything in its path. Structures built from the lumber of the trees which grew where they stood, groaned their resistance then crumbled with a mighty roar. Others gave in more gracefully, first the rooves fell with a crash, then the walls, as if they refused to fight, simply folded in quick supplication for a speedy end. Throughout it all, dark shadows clashed together, then apart, as the cities inhabitants fought against their invaders. In the water, dozens of canoes approached the ship carrying bone weary sailors, many of whom were wounded.

While at first everything seemed to have gone perfectly, it was unbelievable how quickly the situation had turned so very wrong. Their contingent had taken the city with relative ease, securing a vast number of jewels, merchandise, silver, and prisoners. Even the Governor and his family were caught under their net! A prize to be sure.

Negotiations for the release of the city had gone well, lasting only a few days, and ended in a treaty on April 20, 1687. Under the treaty, the parties agreed that the pirates would return the city, fort, shipping, and all prisoners including the governor, in exchange for over a million pieces of gold and four hundred packages of flour. To hasten the exchange, the Vicar General of the Roman Catholic Church, held by the pirates, was released to personally go and get the money from Quito, their capital. The pirates agreed to leave the people, including the city and churches, unmolested and undisturbed until his return. That is where things turned very bad.

Somehow, the very next day a fire erupted. Even as they battled the fire, the citizens of Guayaquil blamed the pirates for igniting their city and violating the treaty, which they would never have done so great was the prize they expected. The pirates retaliated by blaming the citizens of Guayaquil for burning their city to avoid paying the ransom, something they would also never have done. Either way, both parties were angry and violence erupted.

Captain Grogniet, with Queen by his side, rushed from skirmish to skirmish and tried to dispel the violence. They desperately implored the parties to work together to extinguish the fire instead of fighting one another. It was useless.

In the end, Captain Grogniet was shot. Before he was fully down, Queen fell across him, shielding him with her body even as her whip danced above them.

"Queen," gasped the captain, "spare yourself! All is lost here. Get to the ship!"

"Francois," heaved Queen, pulling at him, "I cannot carry you and will not leave you. If you do not help me, we will both die."

"It is no use," he argued, resisting her pull, "save yourself, mon amour!"

"Listen to me," she ordered sharply, lacing her arm under his, "you will lean on me and help me to help you, or I will die trying to save you."

"No," he resisted.

Queen knew that he cared for her and would fight to protect her. When she saw that he had given up, she used his feelings for her to encourage him.

"Save me, Francois," she demanded in a desperate plea, "by helping me."

He nodded weakly, but a spark ignited in his eyes.

She pulled on him to help him to his feet. He stumbled but then stood. When his eyes glazed, she struck him. Barking orders at him, she commanded that he focus only upon helping her to get to safety. Slowly, they wove their way through the city. Only half conscious, he leaned heavily upon her, hearing only the sound of her voice demanding that he save her by helping her get to the ship.

Queen appeared as a vision of a warrior goddess as she moved through the rapidly burning city. Supporting a man twice her size, she did not buckle under his weight even as she fought. With one arm circled around his waist grasping his belt to help support him, her other stayed in constant movement. She directed her whip with precision in an elaborate dance to protect Captain Grogniet and herself. Cracking and whirling, snapping and hissing, it danced overhead, seeking anyone who might harm them, striking any who dared to approach.

They emerged as shadows through a blanket of smoke, surrounded by flames which strained to reach them. Covered in soot and singed from the heat, the pair was barely recognizable to the sailors who guarded the canoes.

Once they helped to situate the captain in the bottom of the canoe, the sailors began a debate over who was to transport them to the ship. Without a word, Queen wasted no time as she grabbed the oars and pushed off. By the time the sailors turned back to her, she had already faded into the smoke and haze and was rapidly skimming across the water.

Rowing across the bay with musket balls whistling past them, Queen pressed on.

"Francois, just so you know," she huffed as several quick thuds followed by splintering wood jolted the canoe, "you definitely owe me for this, and you can't collect from a dead man, so you'd better not die."

She pressed on without pausing until only the plopping sound of the balls falling into the water assured her of their safety. She quickly checked on the captain, splattered some water across her face and neck, then rowed on.

"*Hey ho ahead,*" she called as she approached the ship, "man down. It's the captain and I need help!"

When she reached the ship, several sailors were waiting to help. Balancing the captain across their shoulders, they clambered single file up the narrow rope ladder then easily lifted him up and over the side and onto the ship. Taking him straight to his cabin, they helped Queen remove his clothing and wash him, assisting her in any way they could before leaving her to tend him.

Queen removed the musket balls from his leg and chest, then gave him a draught of rum mixed with opium to help ease his pain and allow him to sleep. Once she had done all she could, she went to the windows and sadly watched the flames consume the city of Guayaquil.

"Queen," Captain Grogniet weakly called for her.

Before she could respond, he called for her again.

"Do you love me, Queen?" he asked in a voice just above a whisper.

She went to him and sat gingerly on the side of the bed, careful not to disturb him. Smiling, she took his hand into hers and rested it upon his chest.

"What is love but a fanciful fog of emotion?" she answered his question with a question.

Captain Grogniet grimaced in pain.

"Ma chérie, can't you just say it to me, even once?" he asked, searching her face through drug glazed eyes, "s'il te plaît?"

Queen didn't know how to respond. She had always accepted each moment they had together without ever considering her feelings for him. As she struggled for a response, someone knocked on the door. With a gentle smile and a quick squeeze to Captain Grogniet's hands, she left his side to answer it. When one of the sailors told her that she was needed most urgently on deck, she looked back to the captain, already drifting off to sleep, and stepped out of the cabin, softly closing the door behind her so as not to disturb him.

*****

Queen stepped onto the deck and was immediately surrounded. As the crew, rowdy and drunk, hurled insults and accusations at her, a jolt of the ship told her that they had pulled anchor and were heading down the river, back out towards sea. Recognizing she was in trouble, she reached for the whip she kept hanging from her belt. It wasn't there. She had left it, forgotten over the concern for the captain, in the canoe.

When she tried to return to her cabin, the angry sailors barred her way. To escape them, she leaped to the ropes hanging overhead, but was pulled back. The sailors had stirred themselves into a frenzied mob, shaking their fists in anger and frustration as they heaped upon her all of the blame for the past failed expeditions. Suddenly, in the peak of their rage, they scooped Queen off her feet and carried her, struggling over their heads, across deck. With a great and mighty *heave ho*, they tossed her into the sea.

Queen never knew that about a week later, on May 2, 1687, Captain Francois Grogniet died. Some said it was from his wounds, others swore it was grief over the loss of his Queen.

For many years afterwards, sailors all over the world sang a merry shanty about her.

The Queen of the High Seas.

Spin me a tale, a mighty tale, of a queen upon the high seas.
With raven's hair and skin so fair, she enchants every sailor she sees.
Show me a queen who'll bring ya down in luck and from victory.
She swims now, we don't know how, 'cept she's the queen of the high seas.

unknown

Chapter Eleven

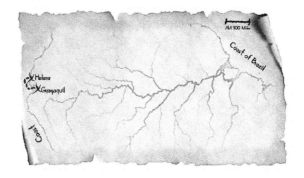

April 23, 1687, Village of Helene, Audiencia de Quito, Peru

In the year 1540, Pope Paul III, over the Catholic Church headquartered in Rome, approved a request by Ignatius de Loyola to establish a society consecrated under the patronage of the Blessed Virgin Mary. Named the Society of Jesus, its mission was to develop the evangelical missionary branch of the Catholic faith, reaching out to nations all over the world. Their aim was to stop the spread of Protestantism, an anti-Catholicism movement developed in response to perceived abuses and excesses within the Catholic Church.

The education required to be ordained was rigorous, taking many years, and included not only training in their faith, but also classical literature, languages, philosophy, science, the arts and rhetoric, as well as a host of other subjects. An extreme vow of poverty, chastity, and obedience, particularly to the Pope, was required. Once ordained, these men became known as Jesuit Priests and were expected to accept orders to go anywhere in the world.

Serving as a 'Soldier of God' they moved to extremely remote areas, often under harsh conditions. There, they lived humble lives while ministering and leading others to the faith. By establishing missions, or command posts, they were able to provide for themselves and those who lived with and supported them.

Samuel Fritz was born in Trautenau, Bohemia on April 9, 1654. He studied at the university in Prague before, in the year 1673, he entered the Society of Jesus as a novice. He was ordained as a Jesuit Priest in February 1683 and then sent to Quito, a city in what is now known as Ecuador, where he was assigned to the Omaguas Indians who lived along the Napo River.

After living amongst them for over a year, he made it a part of his mission to visit each of their villages. Spending about two months with each, he converted them to the Catholic faith then renamed each village using the names of patron saints. His influence amongst the natives did not go unnoticed by the Spanish government and so he was often called upon to settle land disputes or other such arguments as they arose.

When the pirates invaded Guayaquil and remained quite unreasonable regarding negotiations, once again Father Samuel was called upon. Summoned to Quito, he arrived only to be sent immediately on to Guayaquil with a large satchel of gold, should it be necessary to pay the demanded ransom.

When he arrived at Guayaquil and saw the skies darkened with smoke that was billowing up from the city, Father Samuel knew that the situation was much worse than expected. The chaos he observed as he approached the city saddened him deeply, however, the pirate ships were already disappearing into the horizon. Their departure assured him that order would be quickly restored.

Unwilling to risk the large amount of gold he was entrusted with, Father Samuel turned back towards Quito where he could be relieved of it and then get on with conducting the Lord's work.

He stopped to rest for the night in Helene, a small village by the sea. The next morning, he felt refreshed and ready to continue his journey. Before departing, he first walked to a small beachy area along the shore of the river to ensure that the pirates had actually departed. Sitting upon a large rock, he appreciated the gentle lapping of the waves and the cry of the seagulls overhead. Basking in the golden glow of the morning sun, he turned his face towards the warmth of a new day dawning.

Before long he was joined by a local dog. Obviously a mutt who had fallen upon hard times, it was dirty and not much of a mongrel, but it was friendly enough. When it shoved its muzzle into his hand, Father Samuel laughed, fondly brushing his hand across its head and down his back.

"I have nothing for you, my friend."

Accepting the offered affection but still unwilling to concede to his hunger, the dog began sniffing around the beach, skittering back when a wave threatened to soak his feet. With a friendly bark, it moved on down the shore.

"Good luck, my friend," Father Samuel called after him, chuckling as he pushed himself up from the rock.

Turning away, he noticed the dog sniffing excitedly around a bundle that had washed up from the sea. Then barking furiously, it skipped back only to leap towards it again with a growl and a bark. Curious, Father Samuel walked closer. His breath hitched as he realized that the dog had discovered a person who had obviously been washed ashore by the tide.

Father Samuel grasped the dog by his scruff to hold it, then poked at what he believed to be a lad, due to the size and the britches. Nothing. No movement. The legs, still in the water, rose and fell with each wave.

Well, now what to do, thought Father Samuel, considering his options with regards to his obligations to both God and man. First looking around to see if anyone would witness it if he should leave the body unattended, he glanced upwards.

"Why must you assign me such a task of randomness," he mumbled to the Lord, "when you know I am also entrusted with a great sum of money, which by the way, puts me in no small danger."

He reached down and grasped the body under the arms to pull it completely out of the water. Hesitating, he decided that it would be agreeable to God, as well as the locals who most assuredly did not know the individual, considering the fact that the body had been washed ashore, if he just said his prayers over the body, then notified the townspeople of the task of removing it.

Lowering himself to one knee, he rolled the body just enough to access the forehead. Placing his hands upon it, he prayed.

"Eternal rest grant unto them, O Lord, and let perpetual light shine upon them. May their soul, and the souls of all the faithful departed, through the mercy of God, rest in peace. Amen."

Feeling ashamed of his disgust over touching the water-logged body, he quickly swiped his hands across his knees and rose with a prayer.

"Forgive me Father, for I know it was a sin to feel such a way," he breathed out quietly "and I am most willing to pay penance in any way you design."

As if in response to his prayer, coughing and choking sounds came from the poor dead individual as it returned to life, ensuring Father Samuel's penance.

*****

Father Samuel wasn't just a little frustrated, he was angry. Yes, he had done the right and godly thing when he had discovered that the lad lying upon the beach was actually alive. With no one to assist him, he had mostly carried, but half dragged, him up to the house, fully intending to leave him with his hosts, who he would have generously compensated for their trouble. Having performed his duty to the satisfaction of both God and man, who could blame him for continuing on with his journey? He was uncomfortable being in possession of so many gold pieces and anxious to be rid of it. It simply wasn't safe to carry it over the countryside in nothing more than a satchel.

When the lady of the house emerged from the room in a state of great embarrassment, all were shocked when she explained that the lad was in fact a woman. Her husband and children all stood gawking in amazement as she explained how, when she opened the shirt to remove the wet clothing and it revealed feminine attributes, her hand was suddenly grasped then bent back quite painfully. Just as quickly, another hand clasped over her mouth to prevent her from calling out for help as she was pushed to the door and shoved through it.

Afraid and unsure what to do about the now unwelcome guest ensconced within the bedroom, the family prevailed upon Father Samuel to address the situation. However, when he entered the room, the creature had disappeared through an open window.

Relieved to be absolved of the blame and expense of leaving a stranger under their care, and happy that the situation had resolved itself, Father Samuel shared an abbreviated prayer with the family in preparation to leave. After first giving thanks for the shelter they offered, he asked God to watch over not only the family, but the poor missing creature as well, then quickly left.

*****

Walking along the abandoned road back to Quito, Father Samuel wasted no time. Listening to the chatter of the birds as he walked, he did not stop and enjoy them as he usually did. Satisfied that a day's good deed had been done and was well behind him, he enjoyed the moderate temperature and was relieved that neither heat nor rain would be slowing his progress. Only slightly concerned about the delay in starting his journey, he walked steadily until he heard a sound. Stopping, he looked around and saw nothing, so proceeded.

As he continued, an undeniable sense of being followed pricked him into heightened awareness. Not one to ignore his own internal warning signs, Father Samuel stopped and addressed the empty road.

"I know that you are there," he called out to the forest, "and so does God, as He watches over me."

Nothing.

"As we walk along, I will pray for you and your eternal soul should you chose to molest me, or to cause me any harm," he stated in a warm but firm voice.

Grasping the wooden cross hanging from his neck, he held it between his hands. Quietly but audibly, he recited a prayer and continued to walk in just that way.

Father Samuel was a simple priest, tall and thin with prematurely graying hair and a full curly beard. He wore a cassock made from palm fiber that reached only to his knees. His shoes, made of hemp, were plain but serviceable. He kept his hands folded in prayer around his cross and toted a heavy satchel upon his back. For several miles, nearly half of the day, they walked. Father Samuel and his omnipresent follower, known only by an occasional cracking of a twig and a prickling feeling across the back of his neck.

Stopping to rest under the canopy of a great tree, Father Samuel listened to the leaves rustling in the breeze and the chattering of birds above him.

"Well, well, well, what do we have here?" asked a sinister voice.

"So, you have decided to present yourself," stated Father Samuel, unperturbed by the sudden presence of two men. He was confident in the false assumption that if they meant him harm, they would have availed themselves of it hours earlier.

"Father, I heard you were on a special mission for the President."

Not surprised that word would have leaked out, as it always seemed to with efficiency within this particular culture, Father Samuel said nothing.

"I am going to have to relieve you of your burden, Father," stated one of the men as he walked towards him.

"But we promise to ask God's forgiveness afterwards," joked the man's companion in a gritty, throaty, chortle.

Just as they descended menacingly upon the frightened Father Samuel, a rumbling occurred within the trees behind them followed by the crackling whistle of the air being split. As if God himself protected his own, the side of one of the assailant's face split open, the source of assault yet unseen. With another snap and a whirling crack overhead, the second assailant's arm opened in a long slash. Frightened, the two men turned and ran in desperate fear, sure they had been truly struck by the hand of God for the deed they had been about to commit.

Father Samuel stood frozen in shocked silence. Nearly sputtering, he was unable to process what had happened, so quickly had it occurred. Suddenly, swinging from the trees as if an ape on a vine, the creature he had thought himself well rid of earlier that day dropped protectively before him.

Keeping one eye on the assailants, the girl seemed undisturbed as she released the end of her whip from an overhead branch with a mere flick of her wrist. Then, as she coiled it up to a circle, she yelled colorful epitaphs of dire warning to them in an odd combination of several different languages. Father Samuel, being fluent in multiple languages, recognized both English and French. He also identified a third language that he was yet unfamiliar with.

A few moments later, once his nerves had properly settled enough for cognitive thought and he was able to regain speech, Father Samuel spoke. He chose to speak in French, since that was one of the languages the girl had used.

"They do not understand you," he stated calmly, "but that would hardly matter since they are well and long gone."

Queen was fully aware that she would most likely be recognized as one of the pirates who had assaulted these lands. With nowhere to go after abandoning the house, she had sought momentary shelter within a barn located not far from it. Finding a worn but serviceable whip, she procured it and had been peeking out, unsure of where to go. That is when she saw Father Samuel leave the house, alone and strangely dressed. Curious, she decided to follow.

It didn't take long for her to realize that the strange man was traveling. He seemed to be a kind man, chatting and praying as he walked, and with no other plans, she decided to follow and watch over him. After all, a man wearing a woman's dress while walking along an open road with no weapons was very clearly someone of ignorance who had need of protection.

She was ready when the moment of assault arrived. She didn't even have to engage in battle, so easily were the men run off, which proved to be a bit of a disappointment. Determining that the strange man needed additional protection as he continued to his destination, she insisted upon staying with him. No amount of reassurances by him, nor begging, would detour her from her self-assigned mission.

Father Samuel saw the stubborn resolve in his unwelcome protector, despite his protests and many reassurances that he would be quite safe, and finally admitted defeat. At least they shared a common language and were able to communicate. Besides, this creature, above all others he had ever seen, certainly needed to be brought into the comfort of God.

"Father," he grumbled a prayer as they walked, "have I so displeased you that you would bring this creature for me to lead to you? I've no objection to flogging, should you so graciously allow it instead."

Chapter Twelve

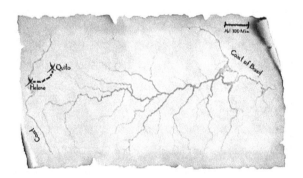

April 25, 1687, Outside the Capital City of Quito, Audiencia de Quito, Peru

Relieved to see the return of her unwilling companion, Queen stepped out of the forest as Father Samuel approached. Before he left, he had explained to her that he had to stop at the city for a meeting and to deliver the heavy satchel he carried. She was uncomfortable with the heavily populated city, so she chose to remain behind, waiting for him along the banks of a river where he told her she would be safe.

The moment Father Samuel left, Queen's imagination began playing tricks on her. What if he went to the Spanish officials and revealed to them where he had found her and what he knew about her? What if he chose to leave the city by a different route, stranding her there while waiting for his return? What if he returned with the authorities to have her arrested? It was maddening. Yet for some strange reason she trusted him. Forcing herself to remain calm, she waited.

Glad that his absence had been no longer than a day, she stood to greet him and noticed that he moved much easier minus the heavy burden across his back.

"You came back," Queen exclaimed with wonder.

"Did you have any doubts that I would," Father Samuel asked, "even after I gave you my word that I would?"

Queen shrugged.

"Oh, ye of so little faith," chuckled Father Samuel as he tossed a bundle he carried under his arm to her.

Queen caught the bundle. Looking at it, her gaze slid to him in question. With a nod, he indicated that she should open it. Queen unwound the bundle. A dress of light gray fabric with a long full skirt gathered at the waist and a full bodice, cut to form, rising to the neck and extending down the full length of the arms, unfolded. Confused, she looked up to see Father Samuel watching her expectantly, clearly pleased.

"What," she asked, looking at him as if he were daft while holding the garment out like the offending object it was, "am I supposed to do with this?"

"Wear it," he cried enthusiastically, clearly not grasping her distaste of it.

Queen rolled the dress up and pushed it back towards him, handing it back with a sad sigh.

"Only one of us can wear a dress," she stated with firm conviction, "and since it appears that it will be you, I thank you for relieving me of the nuisance and discomfort."

*****

July 1, 1689, tribal village of the Jurimaguas, Audiencia de Quito, Peru

When the rains started in February, no one had been concerned. After all, it was that time of year. In anticipation of the rainy season, Father Samuel, with Queen and their usual entourage of people from the Omaguas tribe, left a village located in a lower terrain where they had been staying. Traveling several days upriver, they had been welcomed in amongst the Jurimaguas with kind gestures and open hearts.

There, Father Samuel baptized and converted the indigenous people to the Christian faith, even building a church, though primitive in design and simple in structure, for their worship.

In early April, when the rains didn't cease and the water began to rise beyond the usual levels for the area, they became mildly concerned. In the spirit of an over-abundance of caution, they constructed a small but serviceable structure upon the roof of the church, should the need arise. Feeling the ridiculousness of a foolish but possibly necessary endeavor, they stocked it with food and other supplies.

That had been three months prior. Before the water rose to within a hand's width of the roof where they now resided. Before Father Samuel had developed a fever and grown weak with fatigue. Before the rats began openly fighting for what little food they had stored away. Before Queen was forced to stay awake nights listening to the grunting of alligators swimming around hoping for a morsel of food, dead or alive, to drop into the water.

Queen checked Father Samuel's temperature by laying her wrist across his temple.

No better, she thought wearily.

Instant fear of losing her friend rippled through her, causing her gut to clench and her breathing to become ragged. Perspiration dotted her forehead then ran down her temple to her chin and plopped to her chest. Leaning against one of the poles supporting their structure, she thought over the past couple years.

She had nearly drowned after being tossed overboard, and the knowledge of it still stung. On her own, she would have been lost in an unfamiliar world. At the time, following Father Samuel had seemed to be her only option. Fearing discovery as one of the pirates who raided these people if she appeared publicly, she knew that her options were few. In any event, never before in her life had she been exposed to any sort of society, so she had been unprepared to move amongst them.

From a harem to a pirate ship, she thought sorrowfully, then added with a small chuckle *to isolation in the jungle, with a priest, nonetheless.*

Attaching herself to Father Samuel was one of the best things that she had ever done. She knew at the time that he wasn't particularly happy with her presence, but someone who was desperate often did desperate things.

Resolved to never make him regret her presence or give him a cause to send her away, she endeavored to make herself invaluable to him. Overseeing his protection, she also ensured that his needs were met. Additionally, she challenged him to expand his reach far beyond what he would have ever imagined or could have been possible without her.

The rivers and outlets of the region were expansive and remote. In many places the jungle had closed in over them, blocking all passage. Most of the tribes of the region were remote and situated along them so they had never encountered any civilization other than neighboring tribes. Queen loved the constant challenge of navigating the fast-running waters, which were vast and unexplored. Traveling in canoes dug out from large tree trunks, she embraced the adventure and encouraged Father Samuel to allow her to navigate them, thus taking him to areas far beyond any scope imaginable had she not been with him.

In return, Father Samuel gave her peace. Yes, he had introduced her to his god. She accepted the fact of his beliefs and tried to understand them, but she had her own faith and beliefs, which he also allowed her. Through that mutual understanding, they mapped out a comfortable existence that was equally beneficial for both of them.

With Father Samuel, weighing needs was always principle. Life was simpler. Because they were always honest, extending help to the people instead of taking from them, they were always received kindly. They never experienced doubts about how their actions would be perceived. There were no unnecessary deaths, and hostages were nonexistent. If they had food, they shared it, trusting that more would come. When someone was ill, they did what they could until their options were exhausted, and then they prayed. They built churches and homes rather than destroying them. The fires they built were nurturing, meant to provide food and warmth, rather than destructive.

Once, she even helped Father Samuel wrap the wing of a bird they found and then nurture it back to health. Walking along a rugged path, they saw it pitifully flapping its wings against the ground. Stopping, they tried to catch it, but it evaded them. Father Samuel simply crouched close to the ground, insisting that everyone else also do the same, and waited. Finally, when the bird sat heaving with exhaustion, unable to fight any further, Father Samuel gently scooped it up.

A close examination revealed that the bird had a broken wing. They wrapped the wing in a splint and then spent the next several weeks nurturing the bird back to health. They spent hours each day looking for worms and bugs to feed it, carrying it along with them as they journeyed through the jungle. When the splint came off and the bird stretched its wings then flapped them wildly, Father Samuel tied a string to one of its legs to tether it to him. They traveled that way for several more weeks, keeping the bird close to protect it against predators until it was strong enough to take care of itself. After an initial struggle against the string, the bird seemed to accept its restriction of movement and happily perched on Father Samuel's head or shoulders. It accompanied him everywhere. Everyone was convinced that the two had bonded and that Father Samuel was going to keep the bird as a pet. On the day he announced that it was time to release it, all were surprised.

"How is it possible?" Queen exclaimed in awe and sadness when the little green bird happily flapped its wings and flew away from them.

"What do you mean?" asked Father Samuel, confused.

"You seemed to love that bird, yet you released it. It seemed quite fond of you, yet it flew away."

Father Samuel looked at her in his most peculiar way, a soft smile exaggerating his curly beard. Reaching for her, he brought his forehead to hers.

"It is the way of my god," he breathed out in a whisper, "that we provide and protect, while allowing all creatures the choice of their nature."

With reverence and faith, Queen tucked the moment away, preserving it within her memory for all time, too precious and tender ever to forget.

Now her friend was ill. Determined that he would not languish on an improbable rooftop island while waiting for the waters to recede, Queen began formulating a plan. Using sticks she collected as they floated past, she bound them together to fashion an odd but serviceable raft. At first her plan was to use the raft to go seek help and then return for him, so she built the raft small, allowing only for her weight. Upon hearing the grunts of an especially determined alligator swimming within the flooded church below them, she abandoned that plan and expanded the raft to allow enough room for both herself and Father Samuel.

When all was ready, she helped the weakly protesting Father to the raft. Though it was uneven and uncomfortable for him, it would float reliably. If Father Samuel remained very still, not disturbing the precarious balance of the craft, she was sure she could get him to help.

Two days later, on July 3, 1689, Queen pushed the raft away from the rooftop of the church where they had been stranded for almost three months. Fraught with danger and upsets, the journey took twenty-seven days.

Along the way, they encountered several very friendly natives floating upon rafts and in canoes. Although they were also in dire straits, they always shared with them what food they could spare. One comfortably situated family of five they encountered moving through the swampy terrain with two canoes secured together, even insisted upon packing themselves into a single canoe so that they could donate their other one to the cause of ensuring Father Samuel's comfort and ultimate safety.

When the canoe finally hit solid ground, Queen shakily climbed out of it. She did not even try to resist the overwhelming urge to fall to her knees and kiss the earth. Easily able to locate help from that vantage point, it took six men running at a steady pace while carrying Father Samuel for four days to reach the nearest Jesuit mission.

On July 30, 1689, Father Samuel was laid outside the gates of the Urubu mission in the Portuguese Colonial State of Maranhao. Satisfied that their undertaking was complete, expecting no reward or words of thanks, which would only have served to offend them, the men simply blended back into the landscape.

Chapter Thirteen

August 1689, Urubu Mission, Portuguese Colonial State of Maranhao

Unused to receiving unexpected guests, Father Theodosio Vegas was surprised to discover Father Samuel Fritz at his gate, desperately ill, and most shocking of all, accompanied by a woman.

Most of the tribal women of the region did not possess the usual global sensitivities regarding the fairer sex. Modesty amongst the tribes being nearly totally absent, he had become accustomed to the local attitudes and practices of frequent nudity, and the casualness of it between the sexes. Queen was not a tribal woman.

Wearing soiled pants and a blouse instead of the standard skirts of non-tribal women, Queen walked with the stride and easy confidence of a man. Still not lacking feminine grace or beauty, her presence was unsettling to Father Vegas. Unable to simply pretend she was a man, and yet also unable to keep himself from staring at her in open fascination, he mostly tried to avoid her. It was an endeavor that she did not make easy.

Father Samuel needed medicine that wasn't available in the remote mission. Furthermore, Queen was determined to protect him from the caring but misguided ministrations of their host.

When Father Vegas insisted upon trying therapeutic fumigation, knowing nothing about it, Queen had been willing to allow him to try. He closed the room, barring any fresh air from entering, then filled it with noxious smoke from a smudge of medicinal herbs. When poor Father Samuel's lungs protested in the form of violent coughing, she could allow it no more. In a rush, she threw open the windows, grabbed a bucket of water, and doused the offending object. She wasn't the least bit perturbed that she had also saturated and infuriated Father Vegas.

On a second occasion, Queen left Father Samuel's side for a few moments respite and fresh air. When she returned, she found Father Vegas sitting on the floor beside Father Samuel's bed. Father Samuel, burning with fever and having lost consciousness, lay with his arm extended over the edge of the bed. A thin stream of blood ran from a small cut on his forearm, dripping into a cup held by Father Vegas.

Outraged, Queen violently threw herself against Father Vegas, knocking him away from Father Samuel. When she did, the cup flew from Father Vegas's hands, splashing the blood that it held. The result was that the room looked as if a murder had been committed. Queen paid no attention to it as she immediately grasped Father Samuel's arm and pressed the tail of her shirt to the wound to stop the flow of blood. Covered in blood that had spilled from the cup, Father Vegas was furious and wildly protested her interference. She didn't care that he was angry, nor was she concerned over his soiled robes. Later, she refused to help clean the blood splattered room. As Father Vegas and his staff cleaned the mess, she stood guard over Father Samuel, stubborn and indignant and obviously satisfied with the justice of their toils.

Consequently, Queen no longer trusted Father Vegas. Afraid for her friend's life, she was determined to take Father Samuel to safety, so began preparing for another journey.

"This is absurd," objected Father Vegas, "and I must absolutely oppose you moving him!"

"You may oppose all you wish, Father," responded Queen defiantly, "but you will do so to my back and then alone, for you cannot stop me."

"The river between here and Para is unnavigable! Not even the natives would dare to try such a thing during this time of year!"

Queen narrowed her eyes at him in stubborn fury.

"They are not me," she stated sharply, "so they shouldn't."

Realizing he had no say in the situation, Father Vegas angrily threw up his arms in defeat, exasperated that he could be bested by a woman.

On September 11, 1689, Queen arrived at the Jesuit College in Gran Para, toting Father Samuel who was said to be *more dead than alive.*

*****

November 1689 Jesuit College in Gran Para, Portuguese Colonial State of Maranhao

Queen and Father Samuel, feeling much better, waited in his room for their host, Father Rector Juan Carlos Orlandini, to appear. After two months of the greatest care, Father Samuel had finally recovered from his illness and was ready to return to work in the missionary field. Aware that Queen was not comfortable around others, he did not want to delay their departure but felt he owed his friend a proper good-bye.

Not only had Father Orlandini seen to his well-being, but he had personally cared for Father Samuel through the darkest moments of his illness. From sitting through the night beside the bed to pray over him to dripping broth into his mouth for much needed nourishment, Father Orlandini had demonstrated a level of kindness and compassionate care only offered to those whom one considered a true friend.

When the door opened, Father Samuel stood as Father Orlandini entered somberly.

"I can never express my gratitude for all you have done for me," Father Samuel greeted him warmly.

"No, please, I did no more than you would have done for me," Father Orlandini humbly replied, "but there is something I must tell you."

Father Samuel noticed the grave demeanor of his friend and was concerned. The room filled with an awkward silence. Queen, instantly alert, stepped towards the men, prepared to act should it become necessary. Her hand fell absently to the whip she kept coiled at her waist.

"I am sorry that you cannot leave quite yet."

Obviously uncomfortable with the news that he was about to deliver, dots of perspiration broke out across Father Orlandini's brow.

"What's going on?" Father Samuel asked, sensing the gravity of the situation.

"I am afraid," Father Orlandini heaved a great breath in through his nose and blew it out through his teeth, "that you have been detained by Orders of the Governor, under accusations that you have been conducting yourself as a spy for the Spanish against the Portuguese. Accordingly, you are to remain here. As a prisoner."

Shocked, Father Samuel was speechless. Dropping his tall frame into a chair, he could not speak. Without saying a word, Queen stormed from the room.

Returning hours later, she silently stood before Father Samuel, each staring wordlessly into the other's eyes, until, placing her hand upon his shoulder, she lifted her chin defiantly.

"I will take care of this," she swore in a defiant whisper.

Father Samuel saw how determined she was and appreciated it. He had come to care deeply for Queen and was grateful for her fierce protectiveness. He did not want to hurt her, but there were some things she could not do. This wasn't a ruffian to be tamed or a river to conquer. This matter was outside of the scope of what she could do.

"Not this time, my friend," he said sadly, "you cannot help me this time."

"Trust that I will exonerate your name and be back to collect you."

Turning from him, she strode proudly from the room, determined that she would keep her word.

*****

Fascinated, Queen stood before the mirror unable to believe that she was seeing her own reflection. Pleased, Father Orlandini nearly clapped with delight, except for the odd expression across Queen's face. Clearly, she was completely unaware of her own striking beauty, but there was something more. Unsure of how to proceed in dealing with feminine emotions, he said a silent prayer before moving to stand in the mirror behind her.

"You are a very beautiful woman."

Queen looked more closely and tilted her head in a nod. Unused to the volume and height of her hair, she feared it would topple over. Reflexively, her hand went to it. Her beautiful long hair had been gathered and braided to half its length, which was twisted and coiled into a knot at the nape of her neck. The remaining length that fell from the top of the knot was tamed into a neat bundle of curls which rose to a height equal to the length of her hand. Perched on top was the most elaborate cap she had ever seen. A delicate crown of lace stood twice the height of her hair dangling multiple dainty ribbons. With the slightest movement of her head, the ribbons, falling to just below her jaw, gently fluttered and swayed, almost as if caressing the soft skin of her cheek. A gauzy veil of the same delicate lace cascaded from the back of her head to just below her shoulders, like a veil worn to shield her hair. Even more spectacular than the hair setting, was the gown.

Made from silk dyed the deep blue color of an angry sea, the tightly fit bodice, designed to accentuate the smallness of one's waist rather than curves, fell to her hips then flared out into a full skirt. It had a wired brocade inlay, ornately stitched with bright multi-colored and golden flowers that stretched from shoulder to shoulder then dipped to a point just below her pubis. A wide neckline scooped from the tip of each shoulder, stopping scantily just above her cleavage. To preserve her modesty, it was topped with gathered lace and a bow that nestled just over her cleavage. The sleeves, cut wide and large, were banded with the same flowered brocade fabric. Beginning at the shoulders, the wide bands joined the chest inlay then fell, circling her arm twice. It created an appearance that the flowers across her chest had grown in overabundance, so trailed their way to her hands, where they dissolved in a flowing ruffle of lace. The full skirt, worn over several petticoats, was simply cut and gathered in places with little bows, just enough to create a subtle flounce, before falling dreamily to whisper against the floor as she walked.

Queen had never before worn such an ensemble and was awed by her own appearance. However, she had some very serious concerns. She narrowed her eyes at her reflection and examined the dress from a more practical position. Equally important to appearance was her ability to protect herself should it become necessary. The gown was extremely heavy and tightly fitted so it radically constricted her movement. The tight corset underneath demanded that she remain fully upright, taking small rasping breaths, which would not be acceptable if she should need to fight.

Alterations were quickly made after she explained her concerns to Father Orlandini. Concealed within the skirt behind one of the bow-topped flounces was a large pocket. It was secured by the bow, which continued to appear as ornamental rather than functional. Within the pocket rested Queen's whip, ready for use should it become necessary, with the quick tug of the bow.

Father Orlandini was uncomfortable with the situation but there was no other option. The Spanish and Portuguese had been arguing over their territorial boundary lines for a long time. Priests, as representatives of

God, did not get involved in political disputes. They rarely paid attention to territorial lines and regularly traveled across them. That fact was well known by the officials of both countries and had always been respected. So, when Father Samuel Fritz appeared first at the Urubu Mission, then at the Jesuit College Mission in Gran Para, both located on the Portuguese territorial side, it wasn't unusual or extraordinary. His mission, located on the Spanish side, had been flooded out and he was ill to the point of being near dead. Urubu had not been equipped to help him, so Grand Para was the closest and most obvious place for him to have been taken.

With tensions rising between the two countries, the Portuguese, hearing of Father Samuel's arrival from the Spanish border, had obviously decided to make use of him in a political gesture. Unfortunately, Father Orlandini knew that if the Portuguese officials would go to such lengths as to arrest a highly respected Jesuit Priest such as Father Samuel, they were all at risk. The issue needed to be addressed with the Spanish officials, and quickly.

Of course, Father Orlandini had the connections to get an audience with the Spanish officials who ruled over the Quito Audiencia. But how could they contact them when they dared not risk sending a message, either verbally or in writing? Under the circumstances, they could not send a priest across the borders, it was too unsafe. Queen, being a woman and of little political interest, was Father Samuel's only hope. Sending her to do such a monumental task, however, was a concern.

She was unrefined. Her speech was passable, having been taught to speak Spanish by Father Samuel, and her wardrobe could be easily addressed. What concerned Father Orlandini was her lack of social etiquette and her masculine boldness. Hiring a seamstress to put together a limited but passable wardrobe had been an easy matter. Teaching her the refinements and social graces necessary to be taken seriously by the top Spanish official who could help them, was entirely up to him. From his perspective, it was a daunting task.

Dedicating two days to teach Queen proper dining and conversation skills as well as to coach her on how to address the political figures she was to encounter turned out to be ample time. She was a quick learner, and was not as devoid of feminine grace that Father Orlandini originally believed her to be.

"We need to discuss your name," Father Orlandini prompted what he knew could very well turn out to be a touchy subject with his protégé.

"What is there to discuss?" Queen asked, narrowing her eyes, "You don't even know my name."

Father Orlandini was surprised.

"But I thought it was Queen."

"I have never said it was my name," Queen countered, "only that it is what I am called."

"Well, that is wonderful," Father Orlandini exclaimed, well pleased that he would not have to offend her, "what is your name?"

Queen felt ill. She had been called Queen ever since Captain Townley had told her it was a role, or a title, and she had lived confidently up to it. A name was a part of you. It defined where you were from and who you truly were. She was not proud of Wajeeha, who had failed her Maharani so terribly, but her feelings ran much deeper than that.

Wajeeha was not only a royal princess and descendant of the Maharaja's of Koch Behar. She was a trained warrior who should have fought to return to her family. She had lived and worked upon two ships and had been in trusted positions with both captains. She should have made some efforts to return to her people, as she was bound to do. She hadn't. The shameful truth was that she did not want to return to the dull life of a harem, locked away from the world where the only things to occupy her were silks, jewels, and other female family members.

She had lived fully, seen the world, and experienced adventures beyond what she ever could have imagined. It hadn't always been easy and at times she had feared for her life, but she liked challenging herself and being challenged. That too was shameful according to her culture. She could never go home. The person she had been, Wajeeha, was dead. She had been swallowed by the role of Queen.

"I do not have a name that I remember," Queen lied.

Father Orlandini was aghast. Of course she had a name. Everyone had a name. Being wise, he knew there was more to the story, but chose to let it go.

"Then we must come up with a name for you. Presenting yourself as 'Queen' in a world of actual kings and queens may not be the best approach. There are people who might take offense, thinking that you design to elevate yourself. It could be dangerous."

"Then, just for this purpose, you must choose a more suitable name for me to use," replied Queen, amused.

Father Orlandini thought a moment.

"How about Maria?" he asked with a twinkle in his eye.

"Why are you amused?" asked Queen, "What does the name mean?"

"Maria means from the sea, or rebellious. Both of which quite adequately describe you, I believe."

He paused to ensure that he had not offended her. When he saw her smile, he was pleased.

"So, do you like it?"

As fast as a quick nod, Queen became Maria Queen, and she prepared to leave.

"Now do not forget to go slowly with President Mateo de la Mata Ponce de Leon. Let him seek you out. He can become a very difficult man. He is used to a certain amount of respect and reverence," Father Orlandini offered as parting words of advice.

"Since we have so much in common, we should get along well," laughed Queen, intentionally goading the poor Father.

"This is no laughing matter and is not funny," groaned Father Orlandini.

"And I am not joking," replied Queen with all sincerity.

Chapter Fourteen

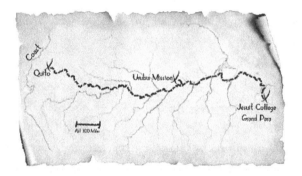

July 1690, Capital City of Quito, Audiencia de Quito

Queen could not sleep. It had been over six months. Six long months of waiting for a response from the King of Portugal, and still nothing. Rolling onto her side, she pulled the blanket with her. A hand reached out of the dark and stroked the side of her face, smoothing down her mussed hair.

"You cannot sleep, my darling?"

Mateo raised to his elbow and supported his head with his hand while gently rolling her towards him. Snuggling into the curve of his body, Queen slid her arm up and tousled his hair.

"I am worried about Father Samuel," she whispered, seeking reassurance.

"Though it feels like a long wait, it has only been a short time," Mateo wrapped his arm around her and softly stroked her back.

"That is what you say, but I don't understand why," Queen protested.

"Because I had to write to King Louis, of Spain, who then has to present the matter to his counsel for review. They then write to King Pedro, of Portugal, who also must go to his counsel. King Pedro must respond to King Louis, who will then pass the matter back to me. All of that takes time."

Queen tried to be patient but that was not one of her attributes. When she met Mateo, the President of Quito, she immediately set about enchanting him. Armed with the backing of the Jesuit missions, a political force unto themselves, along with a distinguished wardrobe and brains, all in a package of enchanting beauty, it hadn't been difficult for her to ingratiate herself into his social circle. After attending several social gatherings, she finally heard the gentlemen, one of whom being the President, talking of the border conflict between the two countries. Seizing the opportunity, Queen spoke of her concern regarding the audacity of the Portuguese to detain a Jesuit Priest under the concocted auspices of being a spy.

"If they are permitted to make an example of an important and exalted Jesuit Priest such as Father Samuel Fritz," Queen stated, "what does that say about the liberties afforded people having perhaps less affluence or influence?" then pointedly staring at the President, she continued, "Additionally, what does it say about our leaderships ability to protect us?"

Before she left the gathering, an aide to President Mateo de la Mata Ponce de Leon approached her to schedule a private interview with the President for the following morning.

In the time it took for her to fully explain Father Samuel's situation and to make an appeal for help, the President had become so thoroughly smitten by her that he would have done anything just for the company of her. He knew it was not just coincidence that Queen appeared when she did, needing his help. In his position it was more expected than unusual. Because of that, as usual, he had already made inquiries about her. He was aware that she was staying with, and being supported by, the Jesuit Missionary in Quito. He didn't care. He had no objection to helping them, and every intention of getting closer to Queen.

When he proposed to her that he would personally appeal to King Louis regarding the situation, he also suggested that she accept his offer of hospitality by residing in a home maintained solely for the comfort of visiting dignitaries. Accepting his invitation, she was moved that very day. Living there, Queen entertained him regularly. It wasn't long before he insisted upon the familiarity of a first name basis while in private, and she coyly welcomed him into her bed.

Not one to remain idle, Queen, then known as Maria Queen, learned what she could of the politics of Quito, as well as other parts of the world. Once informed with a working knowledge, she began advising Mateo in the form of suggestions, making herself an invaluable asset to him.

Because she had no political aspirations or connections other than the Jesuit Priests who had their own politics, Mateo felt safe in speaking openly with Queen about all matters of government. He appreciated how quickly she grasped all the fine nuances that were involved, as well as the many aspects of how the decisions he made reverberated through his people. Between them, there were no subject that was off limits.

It was through him that Queen learned that reparations of the damage she and her crew had done to Guayaquil had never been made. Having a bruised conscience regarding the situation, she made it her mission to ensure that the matter was addressed and that the city was restored.

And so it was that when he realized Queen's popularity and the positive effect that she had in promoting his own popularity amongst his people, Mateo cautiously highlighted her presence with him and allowed her to be intricately involved with the plans of rebuilding the city of Guayaquil. Satisfied, Queen indirectly oversaw what was a very personal matter to her, though why, President Mateo never either suspected or knew.

*****

June 1691

President Mateo de la Mata Ponce de Leon was engaged in a very important meeting with members of the Royal and Supreme Council of the Indies when Queen blasted through the door in a wave of steam.

"Why hasn't Father Samuel been told of the letter from Lisbon?" she angrily demanded, ignoring the instant fidgeting embarrassment of Mateo and the council members.

Mateo coughed into his hand in an awkward gesture, then quickly recovered his presidential decorum and forced a smile.

"Gentlemen, I don't suppose many of you have had the opportunity to meet the enchanting Maria Queen," to assuage any awkward personal suspicions the men might have regarding the nature of their relationship, Mateo emphasized the exalted endorsement of her presence by adding, "who has been a guest of Spain while waiting for correspondence from the kings of both Spain and Portugal."

Duly impressed, the men quickly stood and bowed in respect. As if they were not even there, Queen paid them no attention.

"That letter was received over a month ago and so far not even the local priests officially know of it," Queen declared sharply.

The President smiled awkwardly and turned to men of the council.

"And as with most women, she demands immediate attention to her concerns," he chuckled along with the men who rumbled in amusement.

With a broad sweep of his arm, he gestured towards the doors which were still open.

"Senorita Queen, will you please oblige me by accompanying me, so that we may discuss the matter in private?"

Without ever acknowledging his guests, Queen swept past the arm he proffered to escort her and marched out of the room in fast long strides.

To the amusement of his guests, Mateo tossed his hands helplessly into the air and rushed after her. In the hall, he caught up with her and firmly grasped her elbow to guide her to an office located on the opposite end of the building. Once the door closed behind them, he turned to face Queen, who did not wait for him to speak before pressing her point.

"How *dare* you withhold information which would not only free Father Samuel, but exonerate him as well!" she demanded.

A letter from King Louis of Spain, forwarding King Pedro of Portugal's response regarding the imprisonment and charges against Father Samuel Fritz, had arrived in May. In it, King Pedro censured Portuguese Governor Albuquerque for his actions in detaining Father Samuel. Not only did he proffer a formal apology, demanding that the Governor provide one as well, but he also ordered that Father Samuel be released immediately and then assisted back to his mission, with an accompaniment to ensure his safety, at the expense of the Royal Treasury.

Mateo knew he was wrong for the delay in forwarding the letters. He had agonized over it, but he simply was afraid that he would lose Queen when he did. She had become a welcome respite in his hectic life as well as a trusted advisor. He cared for her and wanted to believe that she cared for him also. He hoped that she would want to remain in Quito, staying on as his partner and mistress, but felt almost certain she would not. It stung his pride and wounded his feelings.

"Maria," Mateo the man, not the President, was before her. Lowering himself to his knees, he took her hands into his, "Por favor, forgive me, mi querida. I'm sorry. I know I should have forwarded the letters but... I delayed because...if you would only but assure me that you will remain with me..."

"How *dare* you presume to hold me hostage under such circumstances," Queen interrupted angrily, *"and how dare you think to force my affections!"*

Rising to his feet, Mateo protested.

"That was not my intent. Do you not see that I care for you? That I would keep you as..."

Queen had heard enough and angrily interrupted him.

"You would keep me as your whore for when you are tired of your wife!"

"You would say that after all I have done for you?" Mateo countered, further wounded, "I am the President! Think of all the good we can accomplish together!"

Queen drew herself up to her full height, resisting the urge to draw her whip out against him.

"Let me tell you something, President Mateo de la Mata Ponce de Leon, I was born in a palace with more prosperity and influence than you can ever even imagine. I have been challenged by men who were more intelligent and capable than you. I have even slept with men who are far more exalted than your King Louis or that imbecile, King Pedro. None have bested me and none could hold me. Why do you think you could *possibly* be the man to accomplish either feat? I am my own woman and go where I want, when I please, and with whomever I choose. I travel with Father Samuel because it pleases me and for no other reason."

Mateo was appalled.

"If you leave me, I could make you regret it," he dared to fire at her in desperation.

Unafraid, Queen rounded on him and stood directly in front of him, glaring straight into his eyes with a fiery warning.

"You could do your best, but I warn you that I *have* no regrets, and if you dare to even try, I will *destroy* you without a backward glance."

And so it was that Queen moved back to the Jesuit mission in Quito while arrangements were made for her journey to rejoin Father Samuel, who received the letters only a few days later.

*****

1705 Outside the City of Guayaquil, Audiencia de Quito

In 1704 Father Samuel Fritz received word that he had been promoted to the position of Jesuit Provincial Superior, overseeing the entire province. It had taken months for the Jesuits to find a proper replacement for him at his mission. Then, following an exhaustive training period to teach them the many cultural differences and necessary details about living and working with the Omaguas and other tribal people of his mission, they were finally ready to begin traveling to his new mission.

Beginning at Quito, they would make their way over land to Guayaquil. There, they were to gather provisions for the next leg of their journey, the remote village of Jaen. From there, they would enlist the help of tribal natives to travel by boat down the Maranon River, to where it met with the Huallaga River. Then finally, they would go on to Santiago de la Laguna, where Father Samuel would assume his new responsibilities.

Though neither Father Samuel nor Queen were sure how her presence would be accommodated under the constraints of his new position, each trusted that somehow it would all work out.

"Queen, how much distance do you suppose we have covered together?" wondered Father Samuel aloud as they traveled.

"I do not think of such things," Queen smiled, "but based upon the maps you have drawn, I suppose it is too great to determine."

Traveling the length of most every river in the region, Father Samuel had begun mapping them out in great detail. Not only had they been able to reach native tribes that had never before encountered outsiders, but they also created the first documented exploration of the rivers. As they traveled, Father Samuel grew excited and had become quite engrossed in his drawings. Queen simply enjoyed the challenge and freedom it afforded her. She loved being upon the water, even when it was difficult. Rough waters, places where the jungle growth blocked their way, hostile tribes. None of it daunted her. She loved it all, turning any difficulties into a personal challenge.

Following Father Samuel's release in 1691, they had returned to the Omaguas and resumed their travels. They soon discovered that the tribal people throughout the entire region had created quite a legend of Father Samuel. Apparently, during his absence a great earthquake had occurred and violently shook the earth. Because earthquakes were very rare, and certainly no one could remember ever experiencing one of that magnitude, the natives became convinced that God was angry about the treatment of Father Samuel. They heard he had been unjustly detained and were terrified that they would all perish if he was not released. Additional stories were glorified amongst the tribes, detailing his curing abilities, his strength and bravery in the face of adversity, and his ability to navigate waters, until they were convinced that Father Samuel was immortal.

In June 1693 a great number of gifts from one of the tribal leaders was brought to Father Samuel following an eclipse of the sun. The gifts were accompanied with a request asking him not to extinguish the sun. It took years to convince the people, though never fully, that Father Samuel was a mortal man.

The sky grew dark with swollen charcoal clouds hanging heavy and low as they approached the city of Guayaquil.

"It looks as if we are about to walk into a storm," noted Father Samuel.

They paused to assess whether they should seek shelter rather than continue, when they saw huge dark plumes billow up and blend with the clouds to linger over the city.

"It is a fire," exclaimed Queen with alarm, "a very large fire!"

They hastened along to render assistance and reached Guayaquil just before dusk. The smoke was so thick that the city was already fully dark. Flames provided the only light. The heat was so intense it felt as if their skin was melting from their bodies as they walked. Their lungs burned and refused to expand, as if even the air had been sucked out by the heat. The fire had grown so large and spread so quickly that there was nothing for the people to do other than seek shelter far back away from it, and pray.

Father Samuel and Queen worked tirelessly to help care for the wounded. Two days later, a storm blew in during the night and finally extinguished the fire. The next morning, in the growing light of day, the people of Guayaquil were finally able to assess the full extent of the devastation to their homes and their city. It was tragic.

Listless people with vacant faces wearing dirty scant clothing moved about in shock amongst piles of burnt timbers and ash. Children, many naked, wondered aimlessly, as cries for their parents went unanswered. Some people simply sat where they fell and covered their faces with their hands to avoid being confronted with what others, their eyes sweeping over the landscape of destruction, struggled to comprehend.

Queen remembered the last time she had walked the streets of Guayaquil, with her whip swinging and dancing overhead as she dragged Captain Grogniet through the burning city to safety. The fires were very similar in size. Confronted with a full understanding of the pain and destruction she and the sailors had inflicted upon these people, she was devastated. Though she never knew exactly how that fire had been started, of one thing she was certain, if they would have left Guayaquil unmolested, it wouldn't have burned.

Queen thought of the many other cities that they had plundered and burned and was ashamed. Always looking at what they took, she had never considered what they left. Now, forced to face it, she found the knowledge unbearable.

Father Samuel watched Queen move listlessly amongst the people. Driven by demons unknown to him, he could not understand her inability to sit and rest even long enough to eat and to restore her energy. As if possessed, she worked tirelessly hauling water, comforting children, and assisting others.

"You've got to rest," he implored her as she hurried past him with a cup of water intended for a child who stood nearby.

Queen took the water to the child, then turned weakly back to face Father Samuel.

"There is no time. There's simply too much to be done," she said wearily, with a wide sweeping gesture towards the city.

"Queen, we've got to be on our way," he gently reminded her, "these people have been through hard times before. They'll find their way, I promise. We've done what we could here. We'll continue to pray for them."

She knew Father Samuel was right and yet… She felt she owed these people. Years earlier she had left them in a fire, and now had returned to them in the same state. She felt that she was being presented with an opportunity to make things right and she couldn't ignore it. Turning from him, she swiped a tear from her cheek with the back of her dirty, soot-covered hand.

She had traveled with Father Samuel for seventeen years. She enjoyed their easy friendship, built upon a foundation of respect, and had loved every moment of their time together. She was happy to have facilitated him in filling his mission but felt that this was a calling for her to settle the balance of deeds in her life. *Her* mission. Turning away was not an option for her.

"I can't explain it to you, but I've got to stay. I need to help make things right," whispered Queen without turning to face him.

Father Samuel knew that Queen ran from her past. He never questioned her about it, but always believed she had played some part in the raid upon Guayaquil that had occurred just before he found her. Accepting her as she was, he had trusted her with his life multiple times and she had always proven herself worthy. Intelligent and fearless, she always did what she felt she must, and he knew there was nothing he could say to change her mind. He nodded in sad acceptance.

"When your task is complete," Father Samuel reminded her as he sadly laid a hand upon her shoulder, "you know where to find me."

Queen grasped his hand and pulled it to her cheek, where she held it.

"Do you remember that little green bird we found, and how we nursed it back to health then let it go?" Queen asked.

"Yes, I do," Father Samuel remembered fondly, "you were in awe that we did that, took care of it only to let it go."

"No, Father," explained Queen, turning to face him, "I was in awe with what you said about allowing all creatures the choice of their nature."

Remembering, Father Samuel nodded, and Queen continued.

"We have parted several times before. It pained me greatly each time, but I always knew that our journey wasn't yet over. Now, knowing that this time, Father, our journey has come to an end, I am suffering a pain so great within my heart that I know I could never again bear for it to be repeated."

Father Samuel was hurt, but he knew Queen well and so he understood.

"You are loved," he replied through tears he shed without shame as he pulled her towards him and placed his forehead against hers, "and you are always welcome back to me."

Queen nodded, drawing in the scent of him, imprinting it upon her memory.

"Do not look for me," Queen sobbed out through her tears, "but remember me fondly, my friend."

And so it was that Father Samuel continued on his journey while Queen remained in Guayaquil on her own mission to help the people there.

Chapter Fifteen

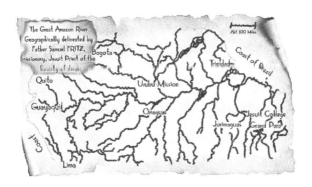

September 1708, Guayaquil, Audiencia de Quito

Queen sat on a hill overlooking the city and the bay, and leaned back, sinking into the tall thick grass. It was a beautiful day, and the birds were settled in the trees, all chattering happily. High pitched stuttering notes, warbled trills, clacking, grunting and honking filled the air. Parrots, kingbirds, toucans, oilbirds, all competed at a pitch that was deafening.

Red, pink, yellow, black, blue, white and green of every hue dotted the trees.

A gentle breeze swept in from the bay, cooling the intensity of the hot sun. Queen closed her eyes and let her mind wander, riding the sounds which surrounded her. In the distance, she could hear the hum of voices from the bustling port. And nearer, the laughter of children enjoying the long days before the rainy season set in.

Smelling rain, she opened her eyes and sat up, looking first towards the bay. Since returning to Guayaquil it had become a habit. The first place she looked when outdoors was always the bay. Scanning each ship, she searched for one familiar to her. Rarely did she ever see one. When she did, her breath hitched in response to the tingle that rippled down her spine. It caused the fine downy hairs on her arm and at the base of her neck to rise and her stomach to cramp, as if in fear or dread.

She didn't know why she responded in such a way. She certainly wasn't afraid, because she had nothing to fear. She did not dread meeting any of the pirates from her sailing days. In the unlikely event that any still lived, she doubted that they would either remember or recognize her.

The only ships she truly did not want to see were those that originated from India, which she never saw. Even if one were to arrive, the sailors from it would have no reason to ask for her. Besides, it had been too many years since she had been in India, and while there, she had lived too isolated within the harem for anyone to know her. Plus, she was sure that there was no one left alive who could recognize her.

She shook herself from that line of thinking and noticed that there were several ships coming and going from the bay. She sucked in her breath. It didn't bode well. Ships bearing strange flags that had no association with any known ports or countries were coming and going from the port of Guayaquil. Determined to learn more, she went to someone who would know the details about what was going on.

*****

When she entered the home of Señor Juan Perez de Villamar, Queen felt nostalgic. She always did when she entered the opulent homes of the wealthy, but that was where her feelings ended. With no desire to live according to the rules and restrictions demanded by wealthy society, she much preferred living a charitable life.

Helping the downtrodden citizens of Guayaquil, she was not scorned because of her preference of movement and comfort over fashion and style. However, she was not ignorant to the social prejudices of people such as Señor Villamar. Keeping the wardrobe provided to her by Father Orlandini, which Father Samuel sent to her after their parting, had been a wise and strategic decision.

Even if her gowns had become somewhat outdated, their original form had been so fine, surpassing the styles at the time in both construction and fashion, that she was still able to sport them without raising the celebrated eyebrows of wealthy citizens.

Queen walked onto the veranda where her host was entertaining a friend whom she recognized as being Señor Sebastian Alvarez de Aviles Obregon, and graciously greeted the gentlemen.

"Ah! Bienvenido, señorita, Queen," smiling broadly, Señor Villamar rose to his feet.

"Caballeros," Queen nodded in greeting and took the seat offered her.

"To what do we owe the pleasure of your company?" Señor Villamar reclaimed his seat and his drink.

"Have you seen the ships currently visiting our port?" Queen asked, wasting no time.

Both men nodded that they had.

"It is most concerning that so many fail to display a proper flag."

"Yes," agreed Señor Obregon, "we were just discussing that our new Corregidor has taken an interest in the illicit trade of cocoa, which may have something to do with that."

Queen narrowed her eyes at the men. When Señor Villamar gestured to offer her a drink, she held up her hand in silent refusal.

"What are your feelings regarding that?" she asked pointedly.

"Well," Señor Villamar shifted uncomfortably in his seat, "while we do not endorse the activities, we are aware of certain advantages should the situation progress favorably."

"I see," stated Queen sharply. She took a deep breath, "and do you also see certain disadvantages of that same favorable progress?"

The men froze under the icy gaze she pinned to them.

"Could you please expound upon that?" asked Señor Obregon awkwardly, breaking the silence, shifting his eyes nervously between Queen and Señor Villamar.

Queen smiled regally then spoke lightly, as if discussing the weather.

"The only way you can export the cocoa subversively is to do so through pirates. To use them, you must encourage them to our port and invite them into our city. They will not come unless they are courted with promises and proof of a substantial financial gain. While they are here negotiating the contracts, they will scout. They'll note the location of the promised exports, but also the wealth of not only the city as well as each and every individual within it, and any additional plunder to be had by them. Then, they will carefully assess your ability to protect it, knowing that first and foremost, just because you welcomed them in, you are too foolish to be anything but helpless in your own defense."

Embarrassed that they hadn't considered the very real potential for disaster, both men tugged nervously at their collars as she finished.

"Guayaquil has been devastated far too many times. We are now enjoying the fruits of decades of labor which was necessary only because of this very thing. Are we intentionally trying to hand our city back over to pirates, gentlemen? Or is it perhaps that we are simply allowing a fool and his misplaced greed to do it for us? I should think that any possible gains to be made under such an arrangement would be negated by the costs of recovering the losses from plunder, destruction and lives."

Having discovered the details of the unaffiliated ship's presence, her mission was completed, so Queen rose to her feet. With a cold hard smile, she nodded at her speechless host and his guest, then sashayed out the door.

*****

Office of Corregidor Jeronimo Boza de Lima, Guayaquil, Audiencia de Quito

Jeronimo Boza de Lima Solis y Pacheco was well pleased with himself. He stood in his office looking out the expansive windows that overlooked the bay of Guayaquil, when the door quietly opened and then closed. Annoyed, he turned to see who had intruded into his office without first knocking. Surprised to see the controversial Maria Queen, he jolted.

Clad in her customary britches and blouse, she sported her whip, the source of the controversy which surrounded her, which was secured to her side at the waist. Without speaking, she perused the shelves against the wall opposite his desk as if she were a familiar guest, or worse, shopping.

"What do you think you're doing," Jeronimo demanded in outrage.

Unconcerned, Queen simply glanced at him before turning back to the shelf. Then, lifting a priceless vase, she dropped it to the floor where it shattered with a crash.

"Just looking," stated Queen, as if her actions were of no consequence.

Apoplectic with rage, Jeronimo struggled to comprehend the audacity of anyone who would invade his office and so casually destroy a priceless treasure.

"How dare you!"

Unaffected by the shards of porcelain crunching under her feet, Queen went to the chair which faced his desk and casually slid into it. Then, with a gesture, she invited him to sit in his chair behind the desk.

"I will not! You will remove yourself from this office immediately or I will have you arrested!" exclaimed Jeronimo, sputtering with rage, "As a matter of fact, I will have you arrested anyway."

Queen chuckled and laid her hand upon her whip in a silent but clear threat.

"You *will* sit, or I will assist you," she demanded sharply.

Fearing her confident but deadly expression, Jeronimo obediently stumbled to his chair and plopped himself into it with an outraged huff.

Aware that should the Corregidor choose to try to have her arrested, the outcome would pose more than uncomfortable for him when she explained his efforts to defraud the king by engaging in illegal trade, Queen was unconcerned.

"Now," she began with an exaggerated sigh, "since we have established that you would like to keep what belongings of value that you possess, we will have a frank discussion about the people with whom you engage in business."

After a lengthy lecture wherein Queen enlightened the Corregidor of the probable outcome arising from his misguided efforts to court business dealings with pirates, Jeronimo sat in abashed silence.

"I had no idea," he stated numbly.

"Because you did not think," Queen stated as if he were a child before pushing him further, "and that is why I have decided to become your partner for a time. I will work without any pay, of course. That is, excepting a small donation which you will immediately make to aid the widows and orphans who still suffer from previous attacks upon our shores."

"My partner…" Jeronimo's anger refueled, "absolutely not!"

"You have no choice. Unless, of course, answering to the king, with whom I am a personal acquaintance, would be more preferable."

"You cannot work here! You're entirely unsuitable!"

Queen looked down at her britches with a laugh.

"I assure you that I will be dressed appropriately for the job, and am most capable of conducting myself with all the elitist feminine grace suitable for such a position."

"Why must you insist upon such outrageous terms?" Jeronimo demanded, "There is nothing suitable about a woman working, either here or anywhere!"

Unperturbed by his objections, Queen insisted.

"Because, quite frankly, I do not trust you. So, I will remain until I know you have fully extracted yourself from any illicit negotiations. Besides, you need me."

"How, pray tell, do you think you could be of any use to me?"

"Because I clearly know more about these things than you," stated Queen confidently, "adding to the fact that you have no choice."

*****

November 1708

"We've done it!" exclaimed Jeronimo happily as he burst through the door to his office.

At the window, Queen watched the last of the pirate ships sail from the bay. True to his word, Jeronimo Boza had allowed her complete access to all information pertaining to his dealings with the pirates. At first he begrudgingly resisted her advice, but quickly learned that she knew exactly how the pirates would react at each juncture, so he began to rely heavily upon her.

He realized the true danger he had risked to their city and was overjoyed that they, at long last, were rid of the danger. Queen wasn't so sure.

Spain was once again at war with not only the English and French, but also the Austrians, Dutch, and as usual, the Portuguese. Accordingly, all Spanish resources would quickly be targeted in an effort designed to economically cripple them. She had recently learned that many of the privateers had been recommissioned to focus solely upon Spanish assets.

When Jeronimo first engaged the pirates, he had enticed them to Guayaquil with demonstrations of great wealth and resources in not only cocoa, but also slaves, textiles, and ships. Further inducements were the wealthy merchants located within the city who could guarantee additional transactions. Understanding the logistics as well as the ilk of both privateers and pirates, it seemed unlikely to Queen that they would not return. When they did, it would not be to negotiate.

Feeling uneasy, she remained silent and continued to watch the ships fading from the bay until they disappeared completely. Because they had worked so hard, Jeronimo was disappointed that she didn't share in his excitement over their victory. Taking her hands, he smiled broadly at her.

"Why must you worry," he asked, "when you should be rejoicing? So, tonight you must join me for dinner to celebrate our victory together. After that, I promise to allow you to fixate upon the matter undisturbed."

Queen wanted to embrace his happiness. She wanted to believe, as he did, that Guayaquil had narrowly escaped danger. Accepting his offer, she allowed herself a brief respite from worry.

*****

Jeronimo Boza de Lima Solis y Pacheco gasped for breath as Maria Queen swept into the room. Wearing a gown bearing colors fashioned after the vibrant purple, white, and green of the Passion Flowers found deep in the local forests, she looked stunning.

Yards of soft green silk printed with delicate white flowers dancing around vibrant purple swirls embroidered with golden thread had been fashioned into a perfect vision of loveliness that accentuated her beauty. A lovely full skirt bloomed under a fitted low-slung bodice that dipped just enough on top to allow a peak of her cleavage. A neatly laid bow, dyed rich deep purple, matched the lace border that circled her wrists and hem.

"My God, you are beautiful!" Jeronimo breathed.

"You flatter me," replied Queen, suddenly shy and blushing.

"Never! Even angels are jealous in your presence this evening," insisted Jeronimo as he rushed to escort her to her chair.

They enjoyed the company of one another as dinner became an intimate and drawn-out affair that extended late into the night. When Queen indicated the time and prepared to leave, Jeronimo begged her to stay, raining kisses across her face and cheeks. When he reached her lips, he let his kisses linger, then deepen.

Drawn into the intimacy of companionship and desire, Queen returned Jeronimo's kisses with equal ardor.

*****

April 27, 1709

Queen waited nervously for Jeronimo to appear. She had news for him, but she wasn't sure how well it would be received. She was pregnant. They had been lovers for six months and though she knew he saw other women, she still hoped he would be happy and agree to settle down with her.

The pregnancy was a surprise, but still a blessing. She had given up the idea that she could conceive. Still young in heart and appearance, she had enjoyed the company of four lovers and yet it had never happened.

Jeronimo, just past the prime of his youth and half her age, also had no children, even though he had enjoyed countless lovers. They had discussed the possibility of pregnancy but dismissed it, thinking it unlikely. Queen was anxious to share the news with him.

She figured she was around four or five months along and was slightly embarrassed. Her monthly time had never been regular, so when several months passed by with no appearance of it, she hadn't been concerned. She attributed the fact that her waist was thickening to the richer diet she enjoyed while dining with Jeronimo. When she remembered the fluttering in her stomach that she had dismissed as gas, she felt even more foolish. When the baby finally gave her a distinct kick, she knew.

Though she knew how to remedy an early pregnancy, it was much too late to terminate this one and she didn't want to. She was excited to become a mother and was going to carry the baby to term. She hoped Jeronimo would be happy along with her.

"Maria!"

Beside himself, Jeronimo raced into the room hysterical with fear and threw himself on the floor at Queen's feet, where he buried his head in her skirts like a child.

Thoughts of the baby were pushed aside in the face of his panic. Queen dropped to the floor beside him and wrapped him in her embrace to calm him.

"What is wrong? What has happened?"

"They've come," wailed Jeronimo, quivering with fear, "just like you predicted!"

There was no need for explanation.

"Where are they? Do you know how many? On land or by sea? Have they shown themselves, or are they hiding?" Queen asked, fully grasping the situation and preparing to react.

"No. I mean…" Jeronimo took a deep breath to calm himself and collect his thoughts, "a fleet of ships have been spotted out at sea, not far from here. There are also a large number of men, I don't know how many but am told it is nearly an army, who are making their way up the coast by land, heading towards Guayaquil."

Queen knew exactly what the sailors were planning. Landing a distance away, they were depending upon the element of surprise to take the city at night. Marching in on land, they could take it quietly, then signal to their waiting ships to join them. Without resistance, they could take hostages and raid the city of its wealth while destroying much of it, then demand large ransoms. Sending out spies to track them, she developed a plan.

Based upon the sailor's reported location, it would take them several days to reach the city. With only a handful of citizens able to fight off an attack, she did not want to stir them into a panic by sounding an alarm. It would only result in them fleeing the city and into the very hands that they feared.

Queen understood that pirates rarely ever attacked without the element of surprise, so she devised a plan to fool them into thinking that Guayaquil was prepared for them and that they were in danger of being ambushed by citizens fully prepared and able to defend their city. It wouldn't totally prevent the situation, but it could minimize the destruction. She was sure they had already procured some hostages, so they could still demand ransom and goods in exchange for them to make a profit. If her plan worked, it would prevent unnecessary bloodshed as well as another total destruction of Guayaquil.

Coincidence played in the city's favor. It was time for the celebration of the Feast of the Cross. The timing couldn't have been more perfect. Several days later, on May 2, in honor of the celebration, a great bonfire was lit on the highest hill. In addition, large torches were liberally placed throughout the city, thrusting it from darkness to full light. Cannons and muskets were rapidly fired and the bells of every church in the parish pealed out in ringing celebration. To induce the citizens of Guayaquil to crowd the streets, for the first time ever the city sponsored the celebration in a rare and elaborate style.

When the sailors approached, they believed themselves to have lost the element of surprise, so they withdrew. The following day, instead of attacking the city, they sent an envoy demanding a meeting with Corregidor Jeronimo Boza de Lima Solis y Pacheco. Against Queen's advice, Jeronimo agreed. The following day he was taken to a privateer ship named *Duke* that was captained by an Englishman by the name of Woodes Rogers.

After a full day of discussion and negotiations, Captain Rogers found Jeronimo to be arrogant and lazy, as well as ignorant. Choosing an easier route towards victory, Captain Rogers generously plied the Corregidor with good food and drink and disarmed him with gracious manners. Outwitted and outsmarted by the captain, Jeronimo accidentally revealed to him that the people of the city of Guayaquil had been unaware of any imminent attack throughout their celebration. Having since learned of the presence of the sailors, they were not only unarmed and unprepared to defend their city, but they were also terrified and panicking. Incensed with the man's weakness to have put himself and his people into such a vulnerable position, the captain promptly shut down all discussions and had Jeronimo escorted off of the *Duke*.

No longer interested in friendly negotiations, Captain Rogers moved his fleet of ships directly into the bay and threatened to burn the city if the demanded ransom of fifty thousand pesos wasn't immediately paid. Panicking, Jeronimo sent word to all of the merchants and wealthy citizens of Guayaquil in a desperate effort to collect the required ransom. Queen was furious.

"You cannot do this," she pleaded, "if you come up with the money so easily, they will take it and assume there is much, much more! Don't you see, it will actually *cause* them to sack the city!"

"I don't know what else to do," explained Jeronimo, afraid to tell her what he had revealed to them, "they will not listen to reason!"

Not listen to reason, Queen silently screamed at him, *who the hell do you think you are dealing with? These aren't reasonable men! They are privateers, stealing from the Spanish under the protection of their own monarchs!*

Aware that Jeronimo was frightened beyond reason, she tried a different, more personal, tactic.

"My darling, you know I'm right. Please, listen to me if you want to save this city. I'm begging you... If you will not do it for me," she pleaded, "then do it for our child!"

She took his hand and placed it upon her belly.

"We are going to have a child?" Jeronimo exclaimed with wonder as tears flooded his eyes.

"Yes, my darling, a baby that is your son," crooned Queen, then to push her point further, she added, "whom you must protect with me."

Instead of inducing Jeronimo to listen to her about how to deal with the pirates, he immediately became protective of her and their unborn child. Promptly sending an elaborate gift of food and wine to Captain Rogers, he requested additional time to procure the required funds for the bribe. Using the time to send Queen to safety, he ordered her aboard a canoe in which she was to be rowed up the Guayas River to a village where she was to stay until he sent for her.

And so it was that Captain Rogers, forewarned by Jeronimo that the citizens of Guayaquil would attempt to flee, had sailors guarding the surrounding rivers. Quickly overtaking the canoe, Queen, along with two native women and four men, were taken aboard the *Duke.* On May 8, 1709, they departed the bay of Guayaquil heavily loaded with ransom as well as all matters of plunder that they had taken from the churches and wealthy citizens of the city.

Chapter Sixteen

October 1709, Open Sea Aboard the English Vessel, Duke

Queen worked quietly stitching the pants of one of the sailors. Since the birth of her son, she had withdrawn into herself. She just quietly moved about, blankly tending to his needs and performing her chores. She no longer engaged in idle chatter or conversation. Not even with Daphne, with whom she shared a small cabin.

In Guayaquil, Daphne had volunteered to travel up the river with Queen, to serve as her companion until they were able to safely return, and so was taken aboard the *Duke* with her. Frightened at first, Daphne had been comforted by Queen's firm grasp of the situation and was impressed when she spoke to the captain at the first opportunity, informing him that she had many useful skills which he could employ. Though he did not ask her about them, Captain Rogers noticed that Queen was pregnant and assigned her, along with Daphne to their great relief, a small cabin for their comfort and privacy.

That afternoon, the cabin, bare of furnishings or any other comforts, was supplied with two pallets and two blankets. Several large bundles of torn clothing that they were expected to repair were also delivered, along with the requisite needles and a supply of thread. Once Captain Rogers saw the skill of Queen's handiwork, she was immediately assigned the more difficult task of repairing the sails as it became necessary.

Daphne, with no previous experience as a seamstress, was a quick learner and eagerly applied her hands to the task, finding it far more preferable than caring for the cow, goats, chickens, or pigs aboard. She enjoyed conversing with Queen as they sewed and looked forward to the birth of Queen's baby.

In September, when Queen's pains started, Daphne helped with the labor, which lasted only hours, until she gave birth to a healthy baby boy. With tears in her eyes, Queen took the baby to her breast, stroking his little round cheeks as she suckled him. After that, she was never without him. She either carried him in her arms or in a sling fashioned after what she had seen while traveling amongst the natives.

It baffled Daphne that Queen had not named her son, referring to him only as *baby. Daphne, please hold baby while I fold the sail*, or *is baby hungry do you think?* She had not been around too many new mothers, and certainly never under such circumstances, so although Daphne felt Queen's behavior was odd, she wasn't overly concerned about it.

However, Queen's withdrawal was another matter. It had been over two weeks since they had engaged in any conversation. For some reason,

Queen seemed to have just stopped talking. Filling the silence, Daphne chatted on as usual with no response from Queen unless she was asked a direct question. Unsure what was happening with her friend, Daphne did not question her until she began to hear her crying at night.

"Queen, are you ill?" Daphne asked, "Is the baby ill?"

"No," sniffled Queen.

"Will you tell me what's wrong?"

"No."

With nothing else she could do, Daphne tried to help more with the chores and in caring for the baby. While Queen did allow Daphne to assist her with the chores, she never allowed her to help with the baby. If anything, she seemed to hover more intensely over him.

Unknown to Daphne, the truth was that Queen was fraught with terror over the future prospects for herself and her son. Having been on ships with prisoners many times before, she knew exactly what fate she and her son faced. Once they arrived at a port, their value as slaves far outweighed those of seamstresses, one with an infant no less, onboard a ship. They would be sold, perhaps together, maybe not. There was no way to know.

Queen was comfortable in the life of a sailor but could not perform the required duties with a baby who needed constant attention. Ultimately, she knew she had but two choices: the life of a slave or that of a sailor. If she could have had a guarantee that she and her son would remain together, the choice would have been easy for her. But even thinking of the agony she'd experience as slave who had not even the smallest assurance of her son's ongoing welfare, was beyond enduring. That her son would be subjected to a lifetime of slavery was also inconceivable to her.

Without the encumbrance of an infant, she knew she would be able to ingratiate herself with Captain Rogers and his crew, and so would be free. She had been watching them and knew that they suffered from inefficiency as well as a lack of skills and experience. She was more capable then ten men from his crew.

Queen had always done what she could to survive. Being *just* useful was a trait she could never afford. Circumstances had always required that she was always, always, *invaluable*. Not since she had been an innocent youth of fifteen had she considered the possibility of motherhood. Queen understood that her life was not conducive to motherhood. Taught how to prevent pregnancy in the harem, she had always ensured that it would not happen. Then, for whatever reason, with Jeronimo she did not take the necessary precautions.

Perhaps it was because she was unsure of her exact age. Maybe it was because she had spent so many years with Father Samuel, in the absence of female company, and simply did not think of preventing a pregnancy. One thing was certain, it wasn't because she wanted a baby or expected to get pregnant. Either way, when she finally realized she was expecting, she felt the strong pull of motherhood.

Holding her son for the first time, love for him washed over her, seeping through every cell and fiber of her being. It was larger and more consuming than she ever imagined possible. With it came the need to protect him. That she knew she couldn't was unbearable.

Weighing her options with those of her son, she saw only bleak, dark, misery. She knew what she must do. It was the most loving gesture she could offer him. While waiting until the time was right, she savored every moment that they had. In the end, she wanted him to know that he was absolutely wanted and loved beyond measure.

*****

Time was running out and she had to do what she must. She could not save both herself and her child. If she were allowed to choose, she would have gladly given her life for that of her son, but there was no choice. The simple fact was that while she could survive on her own, she would not survive while trying to care for a baby. Her son, only a newborn infant, would not likely survive without her. She would either have to go on living without him, or they would each die in their own separate misery.

Waiting for a time when Daphne would be gone, Queen showered her son with a lifetime of adoring affection, wrapping him in her eternal love.

One afternoon Queen and Daphne were working to mend another large batch of the sailor's clothing when someone pounded on their door. Disturbed, the baby scrunched his face and wailed in startled protest. As Queen reached for him, Daphne set her mending aside and pushed herself up to answer it. Grumbling, she opened the door and scolded the unashamed sailor for pounding on it so hard. After a brief conversation, she returned.

"Captain says there's a tear in one of the sails of the foremast that needs to be fixed right away," she explained with frustration, "and one of the shrouds needs repaired also."

"That's a big job, but the baby hasn't been feeling well and I'm concerned for him," explained Queen apologetically, "Do you think you can handle it?"

Although Daphne didn't want to do the task alone, uncomfortable with heights and not nearly as skilled as Queen, she didn't feel she could refuse. Gathering the necessary supplies, she paused before leaving the cabin and looked worriedly back at Queen.

"Are you going to be okay?" she asked, concern etched across her face.

"Yes," Queen replied distractedly, "I'm just worried about the baby."

"You worry too much," smiled Daphne before leaving.

Alone, Queen gathered her son to her chest and fed him, enjoying how he greedily drew sustenance from her body. When he was satisfied, she sang him a song as she rocked him. Before he was fully asleep, she ensured that he was dry and comfortable then settled him in her lap where she could look deep into his eyes and face to talk to him.

"You are a descendent of the most-proud and highly honored Koch Dynasty and the first Maharaja, Chandran. The son of Wajeeha Narayan who is now Maria Queen, and Jeronimo Boza de Lima Solis y Pacheco. Your father is the Corregidor of Guayaquil and will someday be a great leader. Your mother is a survivor, and she loves you more than anything in the entire world."

Queen placed a gentle kiss upon his lips and paused to hold her forehead to his, inhaling the scent of him. Without moving her face from his, she closed her eyes and slid her hand between them, firmly covering his face.

"I love you. I love you. I love you…," she repeated, over and over, to be assured it was the last thing he heard.

*****

Following the unexplainable and tragic death of her son, Queen carried him, accompanied by Daphne, out to the deck and across it, to the railing. Many of the sailors were husbands and fathers who had not seen their loved ones in years. They mostly tried to push their families from their minds, hoping they would live to return to them, and if they did, they would still be received affectionately.

Because they never knowingly took pregnant woman or infants aboard ship, it was a rare thing for them to be there. An infant aboard was almost unheard of and it touched the hearts of even some of the most seasoned sailors amongst them. Queen and her son evoked a bit of nostalgia amongst the sailors as they watched her with him in the first weeks of his life. His death scratched an ever deeper wound within their hearts. As she walked across the deck in small staggered steps carrying her little bundle, a couple of them jumped up to assist Daphne in supporting her.

The scene was so moving that the captain had the sails furled to slow the *Duke* down, giving the mourning group a gentler breeze with a moment of respite from the steady rolling pitch. In the short distance from the center cabin to the rail, more than fifty hardened sailors joined Queen in silent support.

Queen stood at the rail clutching the bundle that had been her son, feeling as if suspended between two worlds. One was overhead, where, as if screaming their own sorrow over the loss of her baby, the seagulls darted about like arrows, cutting through billowing white clouds that sped across a sapphire sky. The other was below, and the slate blue sea.

"I will be worthy of your sacrifice," Queen whispered with a promise, laying a final kiss upon her son's lips, "Now we can both be free. It is the only legacy I could give you."

After a silent prayer, Queen opened her arms. The bundle rolled from them and dropped out of sight; a life punctuated with a splash.

Unable to move, she remained standing with her arms open and extended, frozen with a grief that threatened to overwhelm her. Her one chance in life to love another being was wholly and completely gone. She felt robbed of the only child she was ever to have, and selfish to have made the decision that she did. She felt she would always be alone, just as she had always been, and it hurt.

Her feelings were raw and threatened to consume her. That was dangerous. Pushing them down, she tucked them deeply away, deeper than even the ocean. As she did, she hitched a sob, then swallowed her unshed tears and wiped the ones that had escaped from her face and nose. Then, pushing herself up with a deep breath, she thrust up her chin and slowly squared her shoulders. She did not move more than that, just stood looking out to sea until the sails had been hoisted and the breeze pushed against her once more.

Summonsing her strength, returned to her cabin and rummaged through the piles of clothing that were waiting to be mended. She found a suitable pair of britches and a blouse, then shed her skirts and prepared to once again become an invaluable asset to a ship's captain and its crew. She knew it would not be easy, but she had done it before, and never had she ever been more determined. Grabbing the whip she had previously lifted off a sailor as he slept off a rum induced stupor, she secured it to her waist then went in search of Captain Rogers.

*****

Queen went to Captain Rogers cabin and entered without knocking. Finding him there, she left the door open. Saying nothing, she waited.

"So, it *is* you," Captain Rogers stated, only mildly surprised at her appearance, "the queen of the high seas."

A defiant lift of her chin was Queen's only reply.

"I had suspected as much, hearing the rumors of you in Guayaquil," Captain Roger's chuckled, "though most think you are dead, swimming as an enchantress or a mermaid, luring sailors to their deaths or awarding them victories at your whim. There is even a song about you if you'd like to hear it."

"Your crew is sorely lacking and in need of training. Additionally, they are deficient in their number," Queen stated without preamble, ignoring his comments.

"I would agree with you on your first point, however, as to the second, we have suffered illness and losses. I've picked up every able-bodied men that I could in every port. So, in that there doesn't seem to be an abundance of sailors floating around seeking employment," Captain Rogers laughed humorlessly, "there is no immediate remedy."

Queen closed the distance between them. Standing before him, she scrutinized him, sliding her gaze over him from his toes to his head, where it stayed, piercing his eyes with her own.

"You've got a handful of strong able-bodied slaves you took from the Spanish. Use them. Train them."

"It would never work," Captain Rogers objected, "They'd run off at the first port. To keep them I'd have to hire even more men just to guard them."

"Many of them have always been slaves, working hard with no prospects for freedom. Make them free men, sailors, and you'll have a solid crew that will happily offer you their undying gratitude *and* loyalty."

"By God," breathed Captain Rogers in a moment of awe as he swept his palm across his brow, "that is brilliant!"

Wasting no time, he went to the men with his offer.

They needed no convincing. When he told them that they were no longer Spanish slaves, but British citizens, they whooped with joy. After being provided with clothing and proper English names, along with a draught of strong rum to seal the deal, they were taken ashore on an abandoned island where they were trained. Queen worked with a handful of seasoned sailors to supervise the training of not only the newly free sailors, but also the existing crew. Within a few months, Captain Rogers commanded one of the most able-bodied crews on the seas.

Chapter Seventeen

December 22, 1709, Open Sea on the Coast of Mexico

The *Duke* worked along with the ships *Duchess* and *Marquis*, sailing under a commission of the British crown, to take on the Spanish. With full crews that were ready and well prepared for battle, they began trolling for their enemy. It didn't take long for them to hear of a prize ship sailing towards them. The *Nuestra Señora de la Encarnación y Desengaño* was traveling from Manila to Acapulco. It carried one hundred ninety-three able-bodied crewmen and a plethora of treasures and supplies. Staying their course, they waited for it to appear.

On the morning of December 21, 1709, it was finally spotted. By noon, when attempts to engage it mostly resulted in simply chasing it across a watery landscape, the crews became frustrated. When it still wasn't defeated by the end of the day, Queen could stand it no more.

"Your tactics are all wrong," she stated angrily through clenched teeth, "the *Encarnacion* is much larger and swifter, which means you are going to have to be smarter."

Captain Rogers, open to intelligent reason, listened to Queen's plan and adopted it. Once night fell, the *Duchess* and *Marquis* were positioned so that the *Encarnación* was between them. Firing cannon rounds throughout the night not only allowed them to herd the ship where they wanted it, but also served to disorient its crew and allowed the *Duke* to slide in from behind, catching them unaware, until they were close enough to utilize small firearms. All that remained was to overpower the crew and board the ship.

With her whip cracking the air between the two ships then snapping down upon the frightened crew of the *Encarnación*, Queen was ready to join the men in boarding her when she heard a dull thud. Beside her, Captain Rogers fell to the deck.

Leaving the fray, Queen helped the captain to his cabin where she could inspect his wounds. There, she discovered that a musket ball had pierced his jaw and become implanted in the roof of his mouth. So though they had won the day and Queen finally had the opportunity to fully prove herself with the crew, acquiring another fine new vessel, their captain was wounded.

*****

September 20, 1710, Batavia, Dutch East Indies

"Oh, my dear, dear, Maria, I do so wish you would reconsider my offer and remain here," declared Elisabeth, wife of the Governor of Batavia, Abraham van Riebeeck.

Queen took Elisabeth's hand and held it fondly.

"I have so enjoyed my time with you, Elisabeth. I appreciate your warm hospitality," she sighed, "but as you must know by now, I do not easily stay in one place."

Bristling at the rejection, Elisabeth retracted her hand. Turning away from Queen, she watched the canals of the city slide by. The carriage gently swayed with the rhythm of the horse's hooves clopping along brick roads.

"It isn't fitting!" Elisabeth burst in a huff of indignant frustration, "that you, a lady of gentle breeding and composure, should ensconce yourself upon a ship of nearly heathens, sailing to God knows where! Not even if it *is* through a duty to the British crown, however vulgar it may be!"

Queen hated to disappoint her new friend but there was no other way. She could not succumb to the temptation of living a life filled with luxury and ease. She simply felt it would be too great of a disrespect to the memory of her son, whose life was sacrificed for hers.

After the battle to take the Spanish ship, *Encarnación*, renamed the *Batchelor* and an important part of their fleet, Captain Rogers had suffered mightily and was barely able to speak above a whisper. Queen, as well as several useless doctors aboard, had tried to help him but none possessed the skills to remove the musket ball from his mouth or to relieve his pain.

To make matters worse, one night when he was delirious with pain, he tried to walk and stumbled. As a result, he cut his ankle so badly it nearly severed his foot. In desperate need of medical care for him, the fleet stopped in Guam but found no physicians there who were qualified to care for him. They pushed onward until Queen remembered the tidy little city of Batavia in the East West Indies.

Though there were others aboard the *Duke* who had also been to Batavia, none could remember the way. Afraid to admit their lack of memory, they allowed the ship to wander for nearly a month until Queen realized that something was wrong and took the lead. Finally, on June 20, 1710, six months after Captain Rogers' original injury, the *Duke* slid into port of Batavia.

Easily locating capable physicians in the well-structured port town, Captain Rogers underwent several surgeries to remove not only the musket ball from the roof of his mouth, but also several bones from his lower jaw. More surgeries were then needed to remove all of the rear portion of the heel of his left foot, which had become badly infected.

While he healed, the crews of the ships did not sit idly by. Inspections of all three ships were performed and the necessary repairs were made. Discovering the *Marquis* riddled with worms, it was sold to their hosts for parts. In the meantime, the sailors trained hard and enjoyed the city.

Batavia was a lovely island city surrounded by well laid canals and channels that ran throughout it. Beautifully laid bridges and walkways joined wide streets paved in brick. Buildings and dwellings lined the roads and canals, all built with a solid construction that was designed to be aesthetically pleasing. Elaborate gardens, fountains, and statues dotted the city which also boasted a hospital, spin houses, rasp houses, and a large church. The people of Batavia, primarily Chinese, were kind and helpful to the ship's crews. They accommodated them without over-inflating prices and welcomed them into their shops and serving halls which provided ample amounts of good drink and food.

Queen realized that Captain Rogers would require a prolonged stay while he recovered. To ensure the good will of their host, when they arrived at Batavia, she immediately made an appearance on his behalf at the Governor's residence. Surrounded by canals, it was more accurately called a palace, or at the very least a castle. Rising in noble glory behind four large gates guarded by discreetly placed cannons, should protection become necessary, it was a large and beautiful fortress. Three long wings, equal size and length, nestled a courtyard framed with walkways that ended in stairs which provided access to them. Queen, possessing a limited but elaborate wardrobe, was well prepared to encroach upon such highly esteemed hosts and emerged nobly from her carriage before the center wing.

Escorted into a great hall, she was duly impressed. The walls sported brightly shining armor, elaborate tapestries, and flags from various countries. All trophies offering proof of successful plunder by the Dutch.

Queen stood before an elaborate golden lantern shaped clock that sat upon a pedestal. She was fascinated. It was covered entirely in gold that had been fully engraved and was topped with finials that concealed a little bell. When it struck the time with a rhythmic tinkling, like a child's laughter, she covered her mouth with her hand to stifle her squeal of delight.

"Quite lovely, isn't it?"

Queen turned towards the voice but remained distracted by the chiming of the clock.

"That was a gift from my parents."

Upon hearing that an uninvited guest, who was both female and lovely, had arrived, Elisabeth decided to personally investigate. Intent upon quickly dismissing the intruder, she was unprepared for the charming woman who had appeared to express her gratitude for the courtesies extended to the people aboard her vessel.

A friendship quickly developed between the women, both being lonely for female companionship. Had Elisabeth known the truth of Queen's position aboard the ship, she would have been appalled. However, it is also true that had she known the details of Queen's lineage, or of her acquaintance with the kings, though indirectly, of England, Spain and Portugal, she would have been duly impressed, even if a bit taken aback due to the recent conflict between the countries.

Queen, unimpressed by wealth or position, genuinely liked Elisabeth. What she lacked in intellect was compensated by a quick wit and a cheerful outlook that Queen found refreshing. Elisabeth's delight in showing her the beautiful countryside of Batavia with its beautifully laid farms lined with endless rows of neat hedges and narrow rock fences, thrilled Queen. Queen's exuberant enthusiasm charmed Elisabeth.

On October 4, 1710, when it was time for the *Duke* to sail, Elisabeth lovingly hugged her companion of four months.

"Please, dear, do hurry back without hesitation," she urged, "you are always welcome."

Queen knew she would never forget Elisabeth and would miss her, so tearfully returned her hugs. As the *Duke* sailed from the shores of Batavia, she vowed that even if they were to return, the pain of parting was so great that she would never again suffer it, even to see her friend, so she would never again visit her.

Chapter Eighteen

October 14, 1711, Upon the River Thames Near Erith, England

It was supposed to be a joyous and celebratory homecoming for Captain Woodes Rogers. He had circumnavigated the world, captured twenty Spanish ships, and plundered a countless number of Spanish cities. The holds of each of the ships were full of silver, gold, art, jewels, precious stones, as well as the largest collection of Spanish maps ever to be recovered. Most of his crew was safe, though many were discontent due to the manipulation of a certain James Hollidge.

When the *Duke* and *Duchess* with the *Batchelor* arrived in the port of Texel, Holland on July 23, 1711, before proceeding on to England, James Hollidge, an investor and part owner of the ships, met them. After speaking with several members of the crew and learning of the immeasurable wealth they had acquired, he manipulated the men into signing affidavits that voiced concern regarding Captain Rogers good intentions. Then, Mr. Hollidge also insisted upon performing a complete inventory of the holds before they sailed on. Not only did the situation cause them three months delay, but it was also an intolerable embarrassment and a blight to the name of Captain Rogers, as well as a foretelling of further problems.

"Why do you worry?" Queen asked, pressing her body to Captain Rogers' back.

Captain Rogers turned into her arms as she slid her hands up around his neck.

"Do I appear to be a monster, my dear, with my face disfigured and a limp to my step?"

"No, you look like a man who fought the devil and won."

To not have her by my side every day is the one thing that pains me about the end of the voyage, thought Captain Rogers as he kissed her deeply.

"What will happen to me," asked Queen, "and Daphne?"

Captain Rogers clasped her face between his hands.

"I have a home located in a discreet but accessible place rented for you," he whispered, looking sincerely into her eyes, "You will both be fine. I just need a little time for the holds to be emptied and the goods sold. Then, my dear, I will be flush once more and we will be off to our next adventure. In the meantime, it would be wise for you to change your name from one that is not most common amongst our enemies, the Spanish."

Queen pulled away from him, hurt.

"I have used the name Queen for most of my life," she challenged sharply, "it is who I have become, and I will not change it."

Captain Rogers laughed and pulled her back to him.

"I was merely suggesting," he cajoled as he laid soft kisses across her face, "that you change Maria to its English form of Mary."

Later that day, the *Duke* was secured in the harbor at Erith, England. While the crew went about their duties Mary Queen and Daphne were tucked into a carriage and taken to the quaint home that Captain Rogers had rented for them.

*****

April 1712, Queen's Home, Outside London, England

"Where have you been?" Queen demanded the moment Captain Rogers stepped through the door.

Captain Rogers took her into his arms and swung her around joyously.

"Have I not provided for you?" he asked sheepishly, "Have not all of your needs and wants been met? Have I not visited countless times?"

Initially, while at their first home, he had visited with regularity. Once Queen and Daphne relocated, his visits became infrequent. Queen knew a part of the problem was proximity, but that didn't do much to soothe her ill temper. The first house he had secured for them had been in Bristol, just a few blocks away from his own home on Queen's Square. It was large and supplied with a maid, but Queen found living there, and in the city, intolerable.

Filth littered the walks and streets in even the finest neighborhoods because as waste collected upon them, no one found the resolve to remove it. The air, filled with smoke and fog, suffocated her. Noise from the streets was as omnipresent as people who, like the mice and rats under their feet, scurried around in all matter of errands.

Then, Captain Rogers suggested that she and Daphne spend more time outdoors, walking through the park as members of the elite society they lived amongst. Queen found it equally distasteful due to the horses, bearing their pampered neighbors, which littered the walkways in all manner of filth. It was there where she was first confronted with the fact of Captain Rogers' fidelity issues.

She had known that he was married and had children. It was one thing when they were at sea where they shared a bed nightly for a period of over a year. To see him as he walked with his wife and children in tow, while sleeping alone, was quite another. After seeing them together, Queen knew she did not want to be confronted with the situation again, so new living arrangements were made.

Their new home was located just outside the city. Standing alone, it had no close neighbors and was set back from the road with a tall line of hedges to block the view from anyone passing by. Three upper rooms allowed Queen and Daphne each some privacy, as well as room for storing Queen's forever expanding wardrobe. The lower floor held a sitting room for leisure, a parlor for entertaining should they choose, and a dining room. A small separate kitchen was connected to the dining room by a covered walkway. Behind the kitchen, separated by a wall with a short door for access, was an open room for the chickens. All and all it was a comfortable arrangement which allowed privacy and leisure for both women. Queen was mostly content, but she missed the constant movement of being on a ship at sea and she grew restless with the long periods of leisure time.

Queen faced Captain Rogers and narrowed her eyes at him in anger.

"Maybe my needs surpass your money," she threw at him, tilting her chin up proudly, "and maybe my needs do not include an elaborate wardrobe that I don't even want."

Captain Rogers ignored her distress. Smiling broadly, he swept her into his arms and pressed big heavy kisses across her face until she laughed, then set her back upon her own two feet.

"I have wonderful news," he announced proudly, "I am taking you to meet Queen Anne."

Queen was speechless. It was a great honor.

"But how?" she stammered, "When?"

"In just a few days," Captain Rogers explained, "Sarah, my wife, is heavy with pregnancy and cannot go, so now I can easily take you, as a member of my crew, without unduly raising any brows."

Captain Rogers thought that she had missed his poorly veiled attempt to gloss over his wife's pregnancy and rushed on, but Queen was no longer listening. She knew it shouldn't have surprised her. Sarah was, after all, his wife. Wisely choosing to let the matter go, she began preparing to meet Anne, the Queen of England.

*****

May 1712, Kensington Palace, London

Having arrived promptly at the time they were instructed to appear, Captain Woodes Rogers and Mary Queen, in all their finery, waited for an audience with Queen Anne. Throughout the day, elaborately dressed people quickly rushed by, both coming and going, through a door located at the end of the long receiving chamber. At the end of the day they were frustrated to have been ignored and were preparing to leave, when a Courtier appeared and showed them each to quarters where they were told they would be housed for the night.

Queen was appalled with the conditions in the court of England's queen. Cats flourished, running freely to dissuade the many rats and mice which scurried along the walls of most every hall from making an overly obvious appearance. People were everywhere, scurrying about and tittering gossip. Though all of them were dressed in their finest apparel and sporting jewels that boasted of great wealth, without exception they itched and scratched, though discreetly, at the vermin and filth which infested them. Noxious odors pushed out all breathable air.

The stench of animal waste, though strong, was not nearly as noxious as the odor emanating from beneath the fine silks and velvets of the many esteemed guests. Rich and heavy perfumes replicating every sort of exotic spice and flower lingered in the air like a pernicious cloud, where it mingled with the stench of unwashed bodies.

That evening they ate their meal in another long, wide, chamber reserved for the lesser ranking guests of the queen. The food and drink were abundant and appeared tasty, but the presence of snarling dogs, with their teeth bared in angry aggression to compete for a morsel, was upsetting. Though the dining chamber was large, the air was heavy with an unpalatable bouquet of rich food, animal waste, heavy perfumes, unwashed bodies, and rotting teeth. It was so oppressive to Queen that she simply retreated to her room without eating even a bite.

The following day, holding a rose scented kerchief to her nose, Queen couldn't have been more relieved when she was finally called with Captain Rogers to the door at the end of the chamber. From there, they passed through a wide hall to an inner chamber which, though not as long and narrow as the outer one, was still very large. Heavy drapes were pulled across the many windows, barring any light from trespassing. At one end, a fire crackled and snapped in an oversized fireplace, casting shadows which danced in the flickering light. The pungent fetid smell of decaying flesh permeated through an overly sweet and heavy fog of incense.

Sitting across the room in an elaborately carved chair was the largest woman Queen had ever seen. Even the fullness of her skirt, obviously arranged, could not hide the huge mounds of flesh which spilled over the seat. Her hair looked as if it had been days since it had been pulled up and wound into its simple style. With her corpulent face drawn up into a squinting expression of pain, it was difficult to tell what Queen Anne's features were. Her bare feet were swollen and rested upon a velvet covered stool. One was carelessly bound in strips of white linen, evidence of puss dampened them.

"Your Majesty," stated Captain Rodgers as he performed a wide and sweeping formal bow.

At the sound of his voice, Queen startled from her shock and bowed in a delicate formal curtsy.

"Captain Rogers, we hear your adventures on our behalf were quite successful," declared Queen Anne, lisping through the rows of blackened nubs that were her rotted teeth.

"Yes, ma'am, though it also appears to have whetted the appetite of wolves," stated Captain Rogers in a voice tinged with bitterness.

"That is the way of men when profits are to be gained," agreed Queen Anne dismissively.

"My condolences, ma'am, upon the death of His Royal Highness. I was grieved when I heard of it, and was so very sorry that I was away at sea, so could not attend the funeral."

Queen Anne drew herself up rigidly in an obviously practiced pose of hurt and outrage, and looked at Captain Rogers with her eyes opened wide and her mouth pinched shut as if he had committed the most grievous offense.

"We shall never mention it again in our presence," grimaced the Queen in a strained whisper.

"Yes, your majesty," nodded Captain Rogers with an inward groan.

"Who do you have with you?" she demanded, as if she had just noticed Queen's presence.

Captain Rogers once again swept into a bow and introduced Queen to Anne, the Queen of England.

"Unto Her Royal Majesty, Queen Anne, I present the notable and noble, Mary Queen."

Queen Anne, obviously suffering with her vision, squinted towards Queen.

"Come here, Mary Queen," she demanded.

When Queen approached near enough, Queen Anne grasped her arm and pulled her closer.

"Are you an Indian from America?" she asked exuberantly.

"No, ma'am" replied Queen, using the opportunity to more closely study the woman's red blotchy face, "I am an Indian from India."

"Oh. Quite a disappointment. We were hoping for you to be from America. Not since Pocahontas was presented by King James have we seen a suitable Indian. She was quite the novelty. Very fashionable at the time," exclaimed Queen Anne absently, "We should have enjoyed it, were you to be an actual Indian."

"I am sorry to disappoint you, ma'am," apologized Queen.

A woman stepped into the room from a door concealed behind a curtain and signaled that their time with the queen was up.

"Abigail, do you see that Captain Rogers has presented to us an Indian, only not one as found in America, rather from India."

With barely a nod of acknowledgement, the woman addressed as Abigail gestured Queen and Captain Rogers towards the door. Backing from the room to prevent turning their backs towards the queen, when they reached the door, Queen hesitated.

"Madame, the queen is in great distress," she noted to Abigail, "I've skills in making poultices which could bring her some relief, if you will permit it."

Lady Abigail Masham, Queen Anne's dearest friend and senior Lady-in-Waiting and Mistress of the Bedchamber, nodded a doubtful assent.

"Though many have tried, so I am quite doubtful of your success, in that we have run out of options for remedies," she stated haughtily, "you may deliver your concoction to the guards at the back gate. Instruct them that it is to be delivered directly to me."

A month later, days after she had delivered the poultice, Queen was summoned back to Kensington Palace. This time she was not kept waiting, and was shown directly into the company of both Lady Masham and Queen Anne. After the requisite formal greetings and acknowledgement of the successful outcome of the poultice, Queen presented the monarch with a little cloth bag.

Squealing her delight to have received a gift, Queen Anne opened the bag and poured a gold locket into her hand. It was oval, half of the length of the Queen's smallest finger, and etched with a flower surrounded by a filigreed circle. Another flower, smaller in size, burst into bloom just above the circle. Excellent in craftmanship, Queen had received it as a gift from Mateo.

Perplexed, as if she had been insulted, Queen Anne's gaze slid to Queen and narrowed.

"Of what use, do you propose, would this adornment be to us, when we have the rarest jewels of every imaginable color and size available to us?" she asked haughtily, as if speaking to a child.

Prepared for the response, Queen wasn't the least unsettled.

"I am aware of the riches available to Her Majesty, having myself the favor of assisting several of her champions in obtaining them," Queen stated shyly before lowering her head, as if she was ashamed, embarrassed, and wished to snatch the locket back, "I thought, perhaps in error, that though Her Majesty is obliged to wear opulence in court, she would prefer a simpler piece in private. One that will not outshine her brilliance with its own."

"Then we shall wear it," stated Queen Anne, obviously well pleased.

With a satisfied nod, she directed Lady Masham to fasten it around her neck.

"Are you Catholic?" she asked quite suddenly before rambling on, "We do truly hope not, for we abhor Catholics. We find most of them having no principles at all."

"No ma'am, I am not Catholic, but I have found no particular distaste for them over any others," replied Queen soberly, "nor do they seem to me to be more devoid of principles than most others."

Queen Anne laughed.

"Do you wish to serve us?" she asked jovially.

"No, Your Majesty, I am not English, and my place is at sea."

"At sea! A woman amongst heathens! It would be outrageous except for the brownness of your skin. Do you think it is that which allows you to live as you do?"

"I am quite sure I do not know," replied Queen, unoffended.

"Then perhaps you have an affection for Captain Rogers which compels you to follow him?"

"No Ma'am, I took to the seas well before making Captain Rogers acquaintance."

"Good, for we shall never approve such a union," replied Queen Anne sharply.

Over the next two years Queen continued to make her poultices for the monarch. Being a person who enjoyed a quick wit and a slow temper, Queen Anne invited her to visit on several occasions and she did, until the queen's death on August 1, 1714.

*****

October 1714, Queen's Home Outside London, England

"Why can't I go with you?" Queen demanded.

Captain Rogers was frustrated. His life had been fraught with disaster and upset since returning to England. Sued by crew members and owners of the voyage, the matter wasn't settled until December 1712, when the courts ordered that the profits were to be divided into thirds. Two-thirds were to go to the owners, and the remaining one-third was to be divided amongst the ship's crews. His portion of the third went primarily to pay his legal fees.

The scandal of the situation had made his life unbearable. His wife, Sarah, had given birth to their son, but their joy dissolved into pain when the baby died shortly after his birth. At the same time, with the lawsuits hanging over them and his profits tied up in court, Captain Rogers was forced to sell his family's home in Bristol and acquire more modest accommodations. It was all too much for Sarah, so she left him, taking their three children with her.

To make some quick money by expounding upon his status as a national hero who had circumnavigated the globe, Captain Rogers published a book of his exploits titled *A Cruising Voyage Around the World*. Unfortunately, and to the ire of Captain Rogers, one of the officers from the *Duchess* also wrote a book. Though Captain Rogers' book proved far more successful, it was not enough to save him from financial ruin.

Desperate for additional funds, he even made a run to Madagascar for slaves. Queen disapproved of the voyage so refused to join him. It had been a long and miserable trip of an unpleasant nature that yielded only minimal profits. He vowed he would never repeat again repeat such a trip. He had been sure the death of Queen Anne, who championed him, would put the final nail into his financial coffin. So, he was relieved when England's new King George I advisors approached him.

The Bahamas had become a den of inequity without any form of government and was being ruled by pirates. Though it was a busy port dealing in commerce from around the world, because of the insidious people who ruled there, it produced no income for the crown. Unable to find anyone capable of ridding the islands of the pirates who would also govern with loyalty to King George, his advisors proposed that he offer the Governorship to Captain Rogers. Relieved to be presented with a solution to his financial ruin, Captain Rogers quickly accepted the appointment. When he told Queen about it, she immediately began making plans for a hasty departure, only to be disappointed.

"You can go, but not until I am able to restore some semblance of law and order there," stated Captain Rogers firmly.

"I have been on many vessels with the very same men and you damned well know it," retorted Queen hotly, "I am by far a more capable sailor than any other person you would have."

"Yes, you are a very capable sailor, but you are still a woman. Queen, you will stay here until I send for you and that's final."

Queen was unwilling to relent.

"I will not stay here saying good-bye to you each time you run off, hoping you will return, only to do it again! Especially when you go to sea, where I would like to be!"

And so it was that Queen and Captain Woodes Rogers chose to go separate ways. In the spring of 1715, Queen and Daphne sailed to America where they would be able to settle into a comfortable life in the clean air of the colonies. Captain Rogers went on to become the Governor of the Bahamas under King George I.

Chapter Nineteen

May 13, 1717, Anne Arundel County, Maryland, American Colonies

Prior to arriving in America, Queen realized that she did not have the sustainable funds to purchase land and immediately begin building a proper home. She appealed to the ship's Captain, Thomas Larkin, for help in arranging accommodations for herself and Daphne. He made several inquiries on their behalf. It was eventually decided that Daphne would indenture herself for the usual term of seven years. Once her time was up, she would be free. By then, she would know if she would rather remain in the colonies or leave to return to Guayaquil. Queen would be the temporary guest of James Carroll, where, in exchange for his hospitality and a small pay, she would assist him in creating an inventory of his belongings and help in managing his home.

Settling into his home, an estate named *Fingaul*, in September 1715, Queen soon learned that Mr. Carroll was an exacting and difficult individual. His specific methods of documentation could not be deviated from, so he anxiously insisted that Queen learn them. Though he was impatient for her to learn, he was not always thorough in instructing her. Accordingly, Queen struggled for months to learn his system before they were ready to begin the inventory.

Mr. Carroll's home was not extravagant, but he had many possessions and nothing could be omitted. Going through each room multiple times, they documented everything from furnishings to books, fine china to chamber pots, clothing to bed curtains, and looking glasses to candlesticks. So afraid was he that something would disappear, it was months before Queen was not looked in her room at night or searched before exiting his home.

Mr. Carroll's fortune was made by his own hands.

Though he was from a wealthy and influential family, the family money did not extend to him. When his uncle, Charles Carroll, arrived in the colonies from Ireland on October 1, 1688, having been dispossessed of the family holding, Ballymacadam Castle, by the English, he came through considerable Catholic connection. Through those connections, it wasn't long before he was appointed to the position of Attorney General to Maryland. There, Charles Carroll was able to amass a fortune. When his nephew, James Carroll, arrived, it was to work under the tutelage of his uncle, managing his lands and collecting rents. From that position, James saw the huge disparity between the gentry and the common man.

One day, a man with a family who was suffering from hard times and difficult circumstances pled with him for compassion. James, still living under the provisions of his uncle and working for minimal pay, took pity upon the man and loaned him the last little bit of money he had, giving him generous terms of a leisure pay back. The man, grateful for Mr. Carroll's generosity, not only paid the loan back with interest but also spread the word of his fairness.

Before long, Mr. Carroll made many such loans to anyone who owned lands, was invested in returning the money, and would tell others of his generosity. There, he discovered how a fortune could be made upon the masses of people who were neither wealthy nor impoverished.

While other nobility sought their fortunes chasing large investments with other men of their own similar circumstances, James Carroll built his wealth upon the less fortunate, a concept often misunderstood. Then, realizing and understanding the trappings of the wealthy yet displaced gentry, such as clothes, wigs, and carriages, all contrived to convey a level of wealth and position beyond their reality, Mr. James Carroll expanded his fortune by importing those goods.

He decided to travel to England with the goal of returning to the colonies hauling a bounty of illusion. By returning with trunks of brass, silver, and gold buttons, multiple wigs, hair powder and the finest fabrics, he could provide all the trappings designed to create the appearance of wealth and influence. Selling those items to individuals seeking to impress, while also extending lines of credit to persons in dire situations, Mr. Carroll created of himself a champion for both those people who were of moderate means as well as for the rich.

When Mr. Carroll announced he would be leaving for England in August 1716, Queen couldn't have been more pleased. That he arranged for her to reside with William Chapman and his new bride, Mary, was unsettling to her.

Mary was the over indulged daughter of a wealthy planter. She was also beautiful, so it was no surprise when she married William Chapman at the tender age of fifteen. However, marital bliss escaped the Chapman's when William discovered that his lovely young wife was completely inept at running his home. When he was approached by Mr. Carroll after making several discreet inquiries to members of the nobility who could help him with his situation, it was the answer to his prayers.

Under Queen the house ran efficiently. It was clean, tasty meals were prepared on time and within budget, the animals were tended to, and the slaves were well cared for and happy. It did not bother him that on occasion she was seen wearing britches and wielding a whip to the entertainment of the slaves. As long as she confined herself to the eyes of the slaves while dressed like a man and wielding her whip, causing him no undue embarrassment, he was well pleased with her.

When Mary disclosed to Queen that she was expecting her first child, Queen expressed all the normal congratulations and kept her doubts about it to herself. The pregnancy developed smoothly and that was a great relief to Queen, who was not inclined to suffer fits of whining, as Mary was known to do. That relief was only surpassed by a short and easy delivery.

"Queen," asked Mary as she reached for her baby, "do you think I will be a good mother to him?"

Settling the newborn into his mother's arms, Queen did not readily answer. Mary Chapman was a sweet young woman. She was capable of learning all the necessities of being a good wife and mother, but she was devoid of the interest in doing so. That is, she was lazy. With no patience for idleness, it was difficult for Queen to be patient with her.

"I think," replied Queen, weighing her answer carefully, "that you shall be a mother much like most mothers of wealthy planters."

Mary accepted it as a compliment and smiled adoringly at Queen, then snuggled into the blankets with her son.

The year that followed the birth of Richard Chapman was one of relative peace. Queen kept the home running smoothly while Mary continued much as she had. She entertained friends and family with parties and gatherings to ensure her social rank and status until she began to show with her second pregnancy.

Confined to her home in the last months of her pregnancy, the summer was miserable for Mary, who complained incessantly about the heat. When September ushered in milder temperatures, it was to the relief of everyone. However, by September's end that relief was swept away with grief.

On September 19, 1718, Mary's labor began as any other. When she had not yet delivered by the following day, the doctor was sent for. In the end, there was nothing he could do to save either the mother or the child.

Consumed with grief, William Chapman sat in his room and refused to see anyone. His parents, Thomas and Anna Chapman, grew concerned and took matters into their own hands. Finding a suitable young lady similar in age and appearance to William's beloved Mary, they introduced him to Rebecca Chambers. After a few properly chaperoned meetings, they were betrothed, and a wedding date was set for January 21, 1719.

Rebecca was anxious to establish herself as the new lady of the house while also distinguishing herself as being more capable than the late Mrs. Chapman. Finding Queen overly confident and much too lovely, she informed William that she did not require any assistance and insisted that Queen must be gone prior to the wedding day. In appreciation for her devotion to his late wife and son, William spoke to several of his friends on her behalf.

Sure she would not permanently remain in the colonies, Queen did not want to use what money she had saved to purchase a home or to dwindle it down in living expenses. When she was offered a position in the home of John Baldwin, it suited her needs perfectly.

John Baldwin had inherited not only a considerable amount of money with the death of his father, but also the responsibility of his three younger siblings. Their mother, Hester, was still in the home, but having buried her third and final husband, she had withdrawn to her rooms and left the burden of raising her children to their brother.

John Baldwin was an attractive man with aspirations of a career in the Legislature. He ran several plantations and worked to expand not only his wealth, but also his influence. He loved his siblings. Catharine was a very dignified fourteen-year-old, Mary, a precocious ten-year-old, and nine-year-old Thomas, was very inquisitive, but they were more than he could handle. It frustrated him that their mother was either unwilling or incapable of participating with them. Aware that they needed a woman's guidance, John happily welcomed Mary Queen.

"Miss Queen, we are all so happy to welcome you to our home," exclaimed John happily as he gestured to his solemn faced siblings who stood in a line according to their age.

"No Miss, and no Mary," said Queen with a quick wink to the children, "just Queen."

Thomas stepped from line and tugged upon Queen's sleeve.

"Do you know my name?" he asked.

"Let me think," replied Queen, studying him closely, "I believe that you look like you should be a Thomas."

Pleased, Thomas smiled with a nod.

"Are you a queen?"

"Well," laughed Queen, "I suppose that would depend upon who you were to ask."

"Really?" asked all three children simultaneously as their eyes flew open wide with excitement.

"I hate to disappoint you," apologized Queen with a chuckle, "but I am not an actual queen."

"Oh," breathed each of them in obvious disappointment.

"But I have known several queens, including Queen Anne," offered Queen in recompense for their disappointment.

Their esteem for their guest restored, the children circled around Queen and begged for stories of all the queens she had met.

*****

December 1719

"Was she truly so very awful, Queen?" asked Thomas about Queen Anne.

"She couldn't have been as dreadful as all of that," objected Catharine haughtily, "or she wouldn't have been the queen."

"She was exactly as I stated. The worst thing about it was that she was a very sad, very lonely woman who couldn't control her impulse for sweets or nastiness," insisted Queen, who then looked pointedly first at Thomas, who loved sweets, then at Catharine, who leaned towards a nasty disposition.

The children exchanged fearful glances and Queen chuckled.

"Off to bed, both of you," declared John, "your sister went long ago,"

With a nod and a bob Thomas and Catharine said goodnight and scrambled off to bed.

John laid the book he was reading aside.

"You're very good with them," he smiled softly at Queen, appreciating how the dim light of the fire softened her features. He slowly pushed himself up from his chair and moved to sit beside her.

Awkward with the situation, Queen pretended not to notice the warm affection of John's voice or the liquid way he moved towards her before sliding in next to her.

"Do you think the fire needs another log?" she asked, careful to keep the tremble from her voice.

"Queen, I..." began John.

Unable to find the words which would convince her of his true affection for her, John reached for her, then stopped. His hand hovered above her shoulder before sliding down the length of her arm in a slow languid movement, just grazing her sleeve.

"John, please don't," breathed Queen in just above a whisper, "you know I am much too old for you. The children, your mother, the staff, they would despise me and rightly so."

"They would never need to know. I love you, Queen."

"You cannot. You know nothing about me other than what you see, and I most assuredly am so much more."

"Don't say you haven't developed any affection for me, my darling, because we both know it would be a lie."

Queen knew she should stand up and walk away but she remained there, clasping her hands together in her lap, and felt lost. While she enjoyed the children and the busy life of caring for them, she wanted more. She had moved about for most of her life. It was adventurous and exciting, and she had come to the realization that she missed it.

She recognized that domestic life offered comforts and ease unavailable to her while on a ship, but she didn't relish either. She missed her whip, hated the burden of skirts, and absolutely loathed the catty social game. She even missed the sport of pirating, complete with the excitement of danger. She longed to be on a ship, swinging from ropes and sitting in the crow's nest where life was exciting and full, and she desperately wanted to be where it was warm. Unused to the harsh damp weather of Maryland, Queen often felt as if she would never be warm again. Never again would she complain of the heat if she could bask in the warmth of a tropical sun once more. She wanted to be at sea, back on a ship. Not playing house.

"Say something, Queen," pleaded John, "Don't you love me even a little?"

Why must men always ask that? The thought caused her to chuckle softly

"I can honestly say that I do not love you, John," she replied gently, "what I feel for you is more likened to attraction."

"Then we have a beginning. That's enough."

"Not only is it not enough, it's also entirely improper!"

"Who would know?" John reasoned, "it's just the two of us seeking comfort together. No one will find out. I promise."

*****

July 1720

"How could this happen?" John asked in horror.

"I do not know," replied Queen, equally alarmed, "I am not sure of my exact age, but I am not a young woman. I thought myself past the age to have a child."

"This cannot happen! What about the children? My mother? The neighbors and our friends? I will be a laughingstock. I'm ruined."

Queen didn't know how to respond. It was true. The situation was shameful. She, an unmarried woman of a mature age becoming pregnant by John Baldwin, a young aspiring gentleman. She, a woman of color. He, a white man. In British lands, nonetheless.

We will never approve such a union, Queen remembered what Queen Anne had said to her and applied it to this situation also. She knew that no one else would approve either.

There were many reasons to terminate the pregnancy. She was not content in the colonies. She needed more, so had decided to return to sea by the end of summer. If she had a child, then that could not happen. She was obviously not a young woman and that fact posed risks all by itself. People would scorn her for being unmarried and would think it was vulgar because of her age. She did not have sufficient money to properly raise a child and was without the means to obtain more. She had no great skills other than those she learned at sea or with Father Samuel, yet…

She still experienced grief over her son and could not bear to make that kind of choice again. She did not particularly care for the esteem of proper English society, so she did not mind their scorn, but she did have to rely upon those same people to make the money required to support herself. Most importantly, she wanted this child. Desperately. She wanted someone she could love and protect and who would love her back just because she was theirs.

She acutely remembered the feelings of emptiness and grief she had experienced after she had extinguished the life of her precious son and then dropped his lifeless little body into the sea. She had felt so empty and alone and had been positive that her punishment would be that she would never be allowed to foster another life, be a mother, again. It was the most devastated that she had ever been, either before or since. Yet, against all odds, she had another chance. A gift. An opportunity to leave something in the world that said she had been here, a child, a legacy. That was the only thing that mattered.

"It has happened," responded Queen firmly, "and so here we are."

Part Two

Chapter Twenty

"I will call you Phillis," whispered Queen, "Phillis Queen."

I've finally done it. I am a mother, and my daughter is perfect in every way, thought Queen as she nuzzled her cheek against her newly born daughter's face.

It did not sadden her that John Baldwin would not be a part of her daughter's life. Phillis was hers alone to love and care for. Though it was sad that she would not have a father to give her his name, Queen was happy to pass on a new legacy, one created by her alone. Her daughter was a Queen, Phillis Queen, and she would be raised to be strong, proud, and unashamed.

Aware that there could be no nuptials between herself and John and that she would be unable to remain within the Baldwin home under the circumstance, Queen returned to Mr. James Carroll for assistance. His uncle, Charles Carroll, had recently died and an inventory of his vast estate was required. So, he was happy to welcome her back because he knew she was able to make the detailed inventory in exactly the way he wanted it done and that he could trust her.

When the exhaustive inventory of his uncle's estate was done Queen would return to Fingaul to live. There, she would return to the duties of keeping his home running smoothly. All of her needs, as well as those of her child, would be provided for. In exchange, Mr. Carroll would assist Queen with avoiding the courts under a charge of having given birth to a bastard child, for which the penalties and punishment were severe. Queen happily agreed to the additional condition of work without any additional pay for a period that would be equal to that of an Indentured Servant. The only other stipulation was that when her child was born, it would not distract her from her responsibilities.

Queen enjoyed a short resting period of about two weeks after giving birth, and then returned to her normal duties. She did not mind working for Mr. Carroll and was relieved that he had no wife which she had to cater to. Mr. Carroll had never been married and did not seem at all interested in female companionship, so he rarely spoke to her. When he did speak, it was cordial and usually regarding the budget.

In addition to overseeing the cleaning, cooking, and laundry of Fingaul, Queen prepared the shopping lists. Mr. Carroll, a strict enforcer of budgeting, allotted a certain amount towards provisions, and maintained a two-part system to discourage theft. Queen worked with the staff to prepare the shopping lists. Several times a month another individual, usually the foreman or his wife, went and purchased the items. It was during those times, while the shopping was being done, that Queen had the time to visit Daphne.

Daphne was indentured until September 1721. She worked in the kitchen of Maureen Duval, who owned the estate neighboring Fingual, and was anxious for her time to pass so she could return home to Guayaquil. Each month she eagerly looked forward to seeing Queen so they could share in their excitement of returning home. Equally exciting, Daphne was overjoyed for Queen about Phillis and couldn't wait to meet her.

"Queen," exclaimed Daphne, "it is always so good to see you!"

When they greeted one another with their usual hug and Daphne desperately held onto Queen to extend it, Queen knew something was wrong.

"What's wrong?" Queen asked worriedly, gently pulling away to look into her friend's eyes.

Shifting Phillis, Queen dropped her arm over Daphne's shoulders and led her to a chair near the fireplace.

"This is so horrible," exclaimed Daphne, as she burst into tears, "I do not think I can survive it."

"What can be so terrible?"

She had never seen Daphne so upset and was genuinely concerned for her. Even when their canoe had been overrun by Captain Rogers' crew and they had been taken aboard the *Duke*, Daphne had been frightened but remained stoic.

"Queen," began Daphne sniffling through her tears, "I asked Mrs. Duval about my indenture because I wanted to know what was to happen when my time was up. I explained to her that I wanted to return to my country, so do not want the customary pay or clothing."

"Okay," Queen was even more confused.

"She said," bawled Daphne, "that I am a slave!"

"A *slave*?" cried Queen, "But you know that isn't true! The agreement was that you are to work for seven years and then are free. It was all in writing. In a contract."

"No," cried Daphne, "she said the law says that all negroes, regardless of how they got here, are slaves for their whole life and that no paper can say differently!"

Once again Queen shifted Phillis to wrap her arm around Daphne's shoulders. Then, she placed her cheek against Daphne's and gently rocked to comfort her.

"I'm sure there's a misunderstanding," Queen whispered softly, "we arrived as free women seeking a new climate with fresh air and cheap land. We've had a few setbacks, but we'll leave that way too. Free."

"Back to Guayaquil? Where it's warm?" sniffled Daphne, feeling much better.

"Yes," laughed Queen, relieved that her friend was feeling better, "back to Guayaquil!"

Daphne pulled out of Queen's embrace and looked at little Phillis, nestled sweetly asleep in her mother's arm.

"Oh, Queen," she breathed in awed wonder, "look what you went and did! She's beautiful!"

Queen beamed as Daphne scooped Phillis into her arms and crooned a soft song. Phillis opened her eyes and stared, as if studying Daphne, then gurgled.

"She's gonna be a serious one! She wants to have a conversation, not a song!" they laughed.

Enjoying the rest of the afternoon together, Queen helped Daphne with her work while they shared stories and gossiped, speaking in Spanish to keep their conversation private. Just as Queen was preparing to leave, Daphne shared with her the exciting news that she too was expecting a child.

"That's why I've got to know the truth about what Mrs. Duval said," she explained soberly, slowly shaking her head back and forth, "because this life…slavery…it just isn't right."

"I know," agreed Queen soberly as she thought of the horrible choice she had been forced to make regarding her son, "it's going to be okay."

When Queen returned, she did not have good news. In a rare moment of conversation with Mr. Carroll, she had taken the opportunity to speak with him regarding the matter. It was devastating.

"So, what does that mean for *me*?" she asked Mr. Carroll pointedly.

"Why, nothing," Mr. Carroll responded as he busily shuffled the papers across his desk, "One can clearly see that you are not a negro. You arrived with Captain Larkin possessing a certain measure of means. Though you work for me, it is with an understanding between us. There has been no agreement of indenture between us, just the promise and understanding that while you provide a service to me, I, in exchange, will protect and provide for you."

Relieved, Queen did not pursue the matter further.

"It's true," she somberly delivered the news, "I was able to speak to Mr. Carroll about it. All negroes and slaves brought into the province, as well as those already residing within it, regardless of why or how they got here, are sentenced to serve *Durante Vita,* for life, as a slave."

As Daphne grasped the gravity of her situation, she slowly crumbled to the floor. Drawing her legs to her chest, she wrapped her arms around herself and slowly began to rock, her pain too big for sound. Silent tears trailed down her cheeks as Queen went to her and sat behind her. Pulling her close, Queen wrapped herself around her friend in support.

"Surely there is something we can do, Daphne," Queen whispered through her own tears, struggling to encourage her, "I still have some money saved. It isn't much, but we can speak to a lawyer…"

They sat silently, each grasping for a solution, clinging as if together they could ward off the world which threatened them.

"No," Daphne spoke, breaking the silence as she shook her head, "I am doomed. No one listens to people like me. They don't want to hear anything I have to say. They can't even *hear* me through the color of my skin. *Because* of the color of my skin and for no other reason."

"We'll *make* them listen," begged Queen, "I've still got my whip and know well how to use it! We can run! There are ships out there that we can get to…"

Resigned, Daphne smiled weakly.

"Then what?" she asked bitterly, "I am not skilled like you. I'm not a fighter, so I would only be a burden to you. Then, with two babies too? We could never make it. Even if we did make it to a port or a ship, who would ever allow us aboard? This is Maryland in the great and mighty British colonies where we are *nothing*. We'd both be shot and our children would be raised as slaves, by slaves, if they even survived."

Queen knew her friend was right. Even though she did have some money left, it was certainly not enough to obtain the services of a lawyer.

Besides, what could a lawyer do in the face of such an ugly sweeping law that aimed specifically at the color of one's skin?

Running wasn't a real an option for them either. If it were just her, then yes, she could go and would make it. But it wasn't just her and she didn't have to run, she was a free woman and could just go if she wished. If she ran burdened by two babies and a woman who was unskilled in fighting, they would never make it. Never. As much as she cared for Daphne and hated what had happened to her, she had Phillis now. She had to look after her and protect her. She couldn't do anything to endanger her.

And so it was that the women, friends and sisters in spirit, made plans for Queen to raise Daphne's child as her own, ensuring its freedom.

Several months later, Queen was called to attend Daphne. Miserable with childbirth, Daphne, named Sarah by her owner, Mrs. Duval, labored so horribly that she was rendered unable to even remember English. She wailed piteously and constantly called for Queen. Finally, Mrs. Duval, took pity upon her and sent for Queen.

Taking charge of the birthing room, Queen ordered everyone out. Before the baby was born, she dosed Daphne with a bit of laudanum. When Daphne's daughter came into the world with a hale and hearty cry, Queen fed her a weakened mixture of laudanum, whiskey, and sugar before handing her to her mother.

"Are you absolutely certain this is what you want?" asked Queen, moving quickly to remove the thin soiled blanket from under Daphne.

"Yes," nodded Daphne as tears streamed down her cheeks, "it is the only way."

With a weak nod, Queen plunged a knife into the placenta she had removed from Daphne. Cradling it within the soiled blanket, she then massaged it to expel the blood it contained. Once the blanket had absorbed enough blood to give evidence of a traumatic birth, she laid it on the bed then gently wrapped the sleeping baby into a bundle, which she carefully tucked into her satchel.

"I've got to hurry," she apologized to Daphne, "before she stirs."

"I know."

Queen gave her friend a warm but hasty hug and a kiss over her cheek, then picked up the soiled bundle containing the bloody blanket in one hand and the satchel with Daphne's drugged daughter in the other, and turned to leave.

"Name her Nanny for me," Daphne whispered softly through her tears.

With a nod, Queen left and went to report the situation to Mrs. Duval. With grief in her eyes, she cradled the bloody bundle in one arm, carried her satchel in the other, and said nothing. Mrs. Duval's eyes slid over her as she approached. Queen shook her head sadly and pushed her gaze to the ground. Comprehension washed over Mrs. Duval.

"The poor, poor, dear," she exclaimed sadly.

"Yes," agreed Queen, "it is a tragedy for this to have happened."

And so it was that Queen raised two daughters, Phillis and Nanny. One the golden color of the sky just beyond the day's first light. The other, the rich brown color of a fresh cocoa nut found in the forest outside of Guayaquil. Rarely was she asked about them. When she was, she responded with a glare. Never would she have revealed the stories of their birth. They were both her daughters and she loved them equally, as mothers do.

Chapter Twenty One

Time passed quickly for Queen as she kept Mr. Carroll's home running smoothly and watched her daughters grow. They visited Daphne as often as time would allow but never felt it was nearly often enough.

Unsure of her exact age, Queen knew she was well past her forties, but she had aged gently. The years of living on ships, climbing and swinging their masts, and navigating the rivers and jungles with Father Samuel had kept her muscles supple and lean. Like fine wine, she only became more beautiful as she aged. It was as if the years had selected the prime season for each of her features and then preserved them there. She was never without men who pursued her and remained open to them only if the situation could benefit her little family.

In September 1721, she met Thomas Barnes, who quickly became besotted with her. On February 2, 1722, he bought a piece of land with one hundred fifty acres and a small house which she and her daughters moved into and enjoyed his frequent company. Though Queen knew he was married, it didn't bother her. She liked it that he had other commitments and elsewhere to go. It gave her time alone with her children when she wasn't working.

In 1724, Queen delivered a son she named Ralph. Because she continued to perform her duties and the children never disturbed either the house or him, Mr. Carroll did not object to their presence. Phillis and Nanny, uncomfortable around Mr. Carroll, ran away or hid whenever they saw him. He rarely, if ever, acknowledged their presence.

It was an unfortunate situation when Anne Barnes, through local gossip, discovered her husband's infidelity. In a rage, she demanded that the property where Queen and her children lived be sold. To guarantee it was done, she employed a friend and relative, Richard Barnes, to ensure that all of the inhabitants were properly tossed out and the documents were signed. On May 17, 1725, Queen moved back to Fingaul Estate with her three children.

Because of the children, Queen did not move into the manor, but into a small house just down the drive from the main house. It was comfortable and gave her easy access to work while keeping the children and their noise a safe distance from Mr. Carroll.

*****

While many people arrived in the colonies under contract, it wasn't long before the wealthy planters realized that it wasn't a practical arrangement. Developing a person into quality labor while providing for all their needs took a large investment of money and time. To have the limited use of those individuals, an average of seven years, only to see them walk away and apply their skills to developing their own lands, was frustrating. Far more practical was the use of slaves. They were an asset that was forever bound to their master and increased naturally through progeny. But all slaves were not the same.

By 1721, Mr. Carroll had expanded his business to include importing slaves. Ordering hand-picked specimens who naturally possessed the specific attributes required of his wealthy friends proved to be extremely profitable for him. By providing a specific list of qualities, he ensured that his shipments contained only prime cargo.

Accordingly, the slave population at Fingaul ebbed and flowed with business, and since Mr. Carroll owned other estates, it wasn't at all unusual for the slaves to be moved around according to the needs of each estate. It also helped in avoiding the tax collector from obtaining an accurate number. Although Queen was friendly with the slaves, because she was neither white nor of African descent, it made them awkward and uncomfortable with her, so she kept mainly to herself, preferring the company of her children instead.

Mr. Carroll was a greedy man who prided himself on outwitting others. He did not hesitate to take advantage of people where he could with impunity. It pleased him that Queen did not engage in gossip, never dipped into his funds or helped herself to his belongings, rarely spoke to him without having a purpose, and never asked him for anything which she did not earn.

On the evening of Christmas day, 1725, Queen was preparing to go home to her children. As she was banking the fire in the parlor, Mr. Carroll called for her to join him in his study.

"Yes, Mr. Carroll?"

"Marrrry Queeeeeen," he repeated, drawing out her name.

Mr. Carroll sat comfortably situated in a chair before the fire, swirling the drink in his hand. Unsure of what was required of her, Queen stood in the open doorway and watched the amber liquid sparkle through the cut glass.

"Come in," urged Mr. Carroll, "and have a seat."

Gathering her wrap closer despite the heat from the fire, Queen entered cautiously and slid into the chair beside Mr. Carroll's.

"Yes, Mr. Carroll?" Queen asked once again.

"Do you know what day it is?"

"No, sir," she replied, unsure exactly why, after all the years she had worked for him, he suddenly had the urge to have a conversation with her.

"It is Christmas, the day of the birth of our Lord," drawled Mr. Carroll, "and I have a gift for you."

Queen was shocked and instantly became cautious.

"While it is kind of you to think of me, it certainly isn't necessary."

"There is a price."

"A-a-a price?" stuttered Queen, narrowing her eyes.

"Yes. But a simple price."

Queen waited.

"I would have the simple price of your name."

"But, sir, you know my name."

"No," Mr. Carrol chuckled, "I know only the concoction of Mary Queen. I would have your *real* name."

Inexplicitly, Queen became frightened. Before she could respond, Mr. Carroll continued.

"Did you know that your name, along with your impeccable wardrobe, is why I consented to help you when Captain Larkin approached me regarding you?"

"No, sir," breathed Queen.

"I said to myself, *now James, here is a woman who understands.*"

"Understands, sir?"

Mr. Carroll lifted his glass to his lips. Finding it empty, he rose to refill it.

"Yes, Queen," he explained as he poured his drink then returned to his seat, "this land is filled with cast-outs of the worst sort. Sons not privy to inheritance or title, outlaws, and vagabonds. All stripped of significance and the privileges of their family titles. Oozing with the want to be important and respected, even if falsely. It doesn't matter. Just so others believe the picture of their lives that they so carefully manufacture."

Where is this headed? thought Queen in a panic she struggled to squash.

"When I came to this land I was young and nearly penniless. I was in servitude to my exceedingly wealthy uncle, Charles Carroll, and was assigned to manage his lands. Pitiful people who couldn't pay their rents or feed their children groveled before me. One day I took pity upon a man and loaned him my last shilling. It bought me the respect and well wishes of every home in the province. I realized then that perception is everything, Mary."

"That is very fortuitous for you, Mr. Carroll."

"Make them want what you have, Mary, and you are most powerful. Covet what they have, and you are reduced to a sniveling fool," laughed Mr. Carroll, caught up in his own understanding of people which was fueled by the drink he enjoyed.

He has become quite mad, thought Queen, saying nothing.

"We dress, walk, even talk, as people of means but yet... do we ever really know who is the cuckold," stated Mr. Carroll as he laughed at his own joke, "and who is the jester?"

"I'm not sure what you are trying to say, sir."

Mr. Carroll stared at Queen a moment, studying her.

"Because of my religion I have been stripped of political influence and am even unallowed to vote. But because I have what they want, I outshine them all. Money and influence, and the want of it, bridges everything."

"Yessir."

"They would shun me in public then beg at my back door, smiling, to get what I have, possessions or a loan. I've plenty of money to buy them all," laughed Mr. Carroll, drawing deeply from his glass once more.

Uncomfortable with her employer's obvious state of inebriation and unsure what exactly he was even trying to say to her, Queen shifted in her chair and looked pointedly at him.

"Is there anything else you require of me, Mr. Carroll?" she asked, "I have children who need tending to."

Mr. Carroll returned her gaze. Hard and fast, he looked at her.

"There is more about you that I suspect would provide a very good tale, Queen. You carry yourself as if you are, in fact, a Queen, yet you remain here shunning society as if in hiding. You came here from England but are most assuredly not from there. I know, based upon your coloring, that you are not negro. But I also know that your name is not Mary Queen," he stated soberly, "Therefore, I applaud your genius to have maintained your freedom from both man and the law."

He gestured to a small box sitting upon the table beside her and indicated that she should open it. Inside lay a small silver crucifix. Nodding her thanks, Queen rose and moved towards the door.

"Guard that which is yours, Mary Queen," Mr. Carroll ominously called after her, "or you will find yourself quite without it.

Chapter Twenty Two

Fingaul Estate, Anne Arundel County, Maryland, American Colonies

Life at Fingaul Estate remained quiet for Queen who worked and raised her three children in the peaceful countryside. In spring of 1729, Mr. Carroll became ill. No one was overly concerned when he went to stay with a nephew to recover. He died just a few months later, on June 13, 1729.

Through his strong faith and in support of the Jesuits, Mr. Carroll first secured his nephew's education, then left the remainder of his estates, including Fingaul and his slaves, to Jesuit Priest, George Thorold.

Other than the absence of Mr. Carroll, the transition of ownership of Fingaul to the Jesuits meant very little to Queen and her family. She continued to raise her children, living unmolested just down the road from the main house, and enjoyed the same comfort she had while he had been alive. That a variety of priests frequented the house regularly was no different, except that when they arrived, they stayed for several days at a time, using the house as a stop-over in their travels. Her children enjoyed a happy carefree existence and ran freely over the mission property. They played in the creek in the summertime and in the barns in the winter and helped out where they could as they became able. She continued to oversee the efficient management of the main house.

But there were other changes. Although the Jesuits were reluctant about slavery, they recognized the necessity of owning them for the productive economic health of their missions. They refrained from using the term 'slave' and instead referred to them as their 'negro servants' or their 'negro members of the family'. Although this baffled the slaves at the time, because of the other changes that came along with it, they embraced their new ownership with relief.

The priests also felt a moral obligation to care for the souls of their people and encouraged them to attend Sunday mass services where they were educated about God and were baptized. To facilitate them doing that, no one was required to work on Sundays or other religious holidays. They were also paid a small wage for any work they were required to do that was beyond their normal labor. Using the money to purchase small animals such as chickens, goats, and pigs, they were allowed full ownership of them, including any money they received from breeding or selling them. The same policy applied to the small gardens many of them kept behind their cabins.

The biggest changes, however, were regarding their families. The Jesuits felt morally obligated to keep families together, so they did not sell their slaves. Children remained with their parents who also remained together. Under the Jesuits, family units which were once loosely knit or nonexistent became strong and healthy. Skilled men and women could pass on their knowledge to their children. Because of it, a new sense of community and fellowship developed between the slaves who resided upon Fingaul that was unlike anywhere else, other than within other Jesuit holdings and missions.

Even though the slaves lives improved dramatically and they were considerably more content, they were still not free people and the Jesuits were firmly resolved that they never would be. Convinced that if the slaves were freed their mortal souls would be in jeopardy, the Jesuits solidly refused to give manumission to even the most loyal of them.

The Jesuits believed that they should serve as pseudo 'parents' to their slaves and that their role was to lead them as their errant 'children' to a loving and faithful life of servitude, guiding their heathen immortal souls to God. Freeing the slaves, even if they were able to purchase their independence, was not an option.

Issues of freedom did not concern Queen. The Jesuits had readily agreed that she would continue to work for them under the same agreement that she had with Mr. Carroll.

In January 1735, Queen's fifteen-year-old daughter, Nanny, fell in love and begged her mother to marry. Tom, a Cooper, was a nice young man who had been born and raised upon the Fingaul plantation. His father, Tomboy, and mother, Belle, had both been purchased by Mr. Carroll and had been together for many years. Tom had worked under his father from the time he was first able to walk and had developed into a highly skilled Cooper who was well liked and respected. He came from a loving home, so he had an example to provide the same to Nanny.

Although Queen wished her daughter would wait until she was older and then marry a man who was not enslaved, Nanny could not be persuaded to wait. When it was disclosed that she was carrying Tom's child, a wedding was quickly arranged, and the happy couple moved into a home in the slave quarters. On June 2, 1735, Nanny gave birth to her first child, Thomas. Two years later, on February 28, 1738, she delivered another daughter she named Mary.

The same year that Nanny was married, sixteen-year-old Phillis became smitten by their benefactor, Reverend George Thorold, who frequently visited the mission for extended stays. Queen was not overly concerned because she trusted him to discourage any untoward attentions he might receive from her young, impressionable daughter. However, when Phillis gave birth to a fair-skinned son, Johnny, just a short time later, Queen was incensed. Though she argued with Phillis about it, when Billy arrived on March 22, 1738, she resigned herself to the relationship.

With Susanna's arrival on February 14, 1740, Queen took matters into her own hands. After a brief but heated discussion with Father Thorold, the matter was resolved. He loved Phillis. Although he could not openly acknowledge their relationship or the children, he agreed to reside in the main house at Fingaul where he could more closely look after them. All were content for a time, however, on November 15, 1742, Reverend Thorold died, leaving the estate under the care of Father James Quin. Phillis gave birth to Father Thorold's fourth and final child, Betty, the following August.

*****

July 1745

One balmy summer evening, Queen stepped out of her house. It had been an unusually hot summer and that day was no exception. It was sweltering. Earlier, a light rain had moistened the baked ground and transformed the air into clouds of steamy fog that were muggy and close. Even the birds had been silenced under such an oppressive heat, but Queen didn't mind it. Wiping the sweat from her neck and brow, she went out into the yard to perch upon her favorite spot.

Not far from her cabin, a large old oak tree stood proudly boasting of its age in a thick, wide canopy of green. Underneath it was a log that had been turned up on end. It was so large that three grown people could sit upon it comfortably. She didn't know how long it had been there or who had placed it, though she had given it some thought over the years. She appreciated the sacrifice of what would have been a majestic tree. Several times she had tried counting the rings to determine the trees age but there were just too many. Instead, she offered her thanks to the log, recognizing the tree it had once been, and enjoyed it with gratitude. She slowly lowered herself to it then she drew her legs up to where she could wrap her arms around them and rocked back to prop her head against the trunk of the tree behind her.

"Mama says it ain't fittin' for you to sit like that."

Queen raised her head and slowly opened her eyes. Ten-year-old Thomas stood several feet away, staring at her intently.

"Well, since I'm her mama, she can't tell me what's fitting," replied Queen with a chuckle.

Thomas shrugged and climbed up to sit beside her. Sweat trickled down the sides of his face, clearing a path in the dirt layered there. His hair, normally kept neat and even by his mother, held strands of grass and bits of dirt. His dirty shirt was torn at the sleeve and caked in mud at the elbows, just like his knees. He wore no shoes, but that wasn't unusual for the summertime. Queen draped her arm across his shoulders, but it was too hot for such closeness, so she gave him a quick squeeze then drew her arm back.

They sat in companionable silence as she waited for him to talk. The eldest of her grandchildren, Nanny's son was a quiet boy with an active mind. His thoughts ran deep, with a wisdom beyond his years, and it often got him into trouble. He was not one to offer an opinion on matters that didn't involve him but was also unafraid to speak up if asked, and defend himself if objected to, even if it meant he had to fight. And he did fight. A lot.

Queen felt bad for him, so she defended him where she could and provided a safe haven for him when she couldn't. He lived within a house shared and surrounded by slaves and slave children. His father was a slave and his mother, though born a free woman, had a complicated status because she had married a slave. It made Thomas' situation difficult.

The slave children often shunned him, or worse, made fun of him. Of course, they also made fun of his sister, Mary, but she possessed a jolly disposition and rarely let it hurt her feelings or goad her into violence.

"What's on your mind, child?" Queen asked, looking up at the birds that dotted the branches, drying themselves after the rain.

"I *hate* Peter and I hate Sammy even *more!*" ground out Thomas.

"Is that a fact?" asked Queen, "and how much do you think that bothers them?"

"They say ma can't work as good as their ma's an' it ain't true! Ma just ain't as hard as their ma, but she work just as good!"

"And fighting them proves your point how?"

Thomas puffed out his chest contemptuously.

"Cause I told em that whatever be true or not 'bout my ma, I could take em both."

"And that has what to do with your ma?" frowned Queen.

"They ain't gonna talk 'bout my ma," insisted Thomas, "ain't no one gonna talk 'bout my ma."

"Or what," heaved Queen, "you're gonna fight them all?"

Thomas jerked his head in affirmation.

"You think you're that big? You gonna fight everyone? Well, child, you aren't, and you can't. What's more, your ma doesn't need or want you to fight for her. Let your ma take care of herself. The best way you can help her is by minding your business and taking care of yourself to stay out of trouble."

Thomas turned away. A moment later, several sniffles betrayed the fact that he was quietly weeping. Queen understood the internal battle that he suffered. She let him weep a moment before she addressed it.

"That's not why you were fighting, child. Now why don't you tell me what's *really* going on."

Thomas swiped angrily at the tears mingling with the sweat that rolled down his cheeks. Walking his fingers over the rings of the stump, he sucked in several long deep breaths to calm himself.

"Queen," asked Thomas cautiously, looking towards the road in a hard unseeing stare, "what's a priest slave?"

"Well," started Queen as she narrowed her eyes at her grandson, "it's a slave that is owned by a priest."

Thomas sucked in his breath with a scowl.

"What? That doesn't sit well with you?" asked Queen with a huff.

"I heard some men talkin' 'bout my pa, sayin' he was a priest slave and weren't no good 'cause of it," challenged Thomas angrily as he swiped at his nose with his torn sleeve.

"I see," replied Queen evenly, "and why does that upset you?"

Thomas turned his head to look at his grandmother squarely in the eye. Queen returned his gaze, raising her brow in question.

"Because my papa is better an' work harder den all of em!" declared Thomas fiercely, "an he make the best most watertight barrels of anyone!"

"Yes, he does," agreed Queen.

"So, they got no right treatin' him like he ain't 'bout nuthin'!"

Queen turned to face Thomas. Twirling her finger, she indicated to him that he should also turn to face her. Once he was situated, she gently cupped his chin and tilted it from side to side in close scrutiny.

"Look at you," observed Queen with a tsk, "fighting for a cause that is pointless!"

Confused and insulted, Thomas narrowed his lips into a hard line and knit his brows together but remained silent.

"Now, you listen and hear me very well, young man. Your pa is a priest slave and that is just a fact. You can fight it all you want but it doesn't change a thing. The priests own that man's body, child, and there isn't one thing we can do about it. But Thomas, there are some things we have that another person can't own. They are the things that keep us free, inside, where it counts. The only way you lose them is to *give* them away foolishly. Every time you use these hands to fight a worthless cause, you give away little pieces of the only part of yourself that is yours."

"Like what?" Thomas asked sadly, dropping his chin to his chest.

"Like what is inside here," Queen pressed her hand to his chest, then his temple, letting it linger a moment before grasping his hands. Turning them palm up, she held them there and continued. "Your thoughts and your actions are yours. The decision to be wise and just *let* people be stupid, or to *join* them in their stupid simple ways by fighting them, is also yours."

Thomas' eyes slid to his grandmother nervously.

"You 'shamed of me, Queen?" he asked timidly, fumbling with his fingers.

"Nope. I'm not ashamed of you. This is simply a lesson, Thomas," she replied softly, "and you need to learn it well. You cannot convince a fool against his will by beating him up. Child, one fight brings another and another and another. Each one gets bigger as people retaliate. It doesn't stop until either someone dies or is wise enough and strong enough to walk away. It takes a much stronger person to hold a punch than to throw one."

"But Queen," asked Thomas, "what if ya gotta fight? If ya just don't have no other choice?"

Queen sighed and thought before answering.

"If you are going to fight, make it for something that matters, when there are no other options. In those times, it should be for the life of yourself or those you love, *so you fight to win*," she finished in a voice that was hard and fierce.

Thomas shivered. He knew some about his grandmother's adventures at sea. He had heard stories about her all of his life. Many times over the years she had taken out her long whip. With a flick of her wrist, she sliced the air with whistle and a snap and could cut through tree branches or gently wrap the coil around a child's body. He loved the stories but enjoyed them best of all when she told them with her whip in hand, demonstrating.

"Will you get out your whip, Queen?"

"Not today," Queen chuckled, "it's too hot. Besides, I've got something to talk to you about too."

"You do?" asked Thomas, surprised and feeling very grown.

"Yes, I do. Thomas," Queen began reluctantly, "Father Poulton came to speak with me today about a new job."

"*A new job!*" cried Thomas, "Ain't you 'bout past workin' days?"

Queen huffed and fixed a glare on him.

"I'm sure not getting any younger but I still got a lot of life in me, Thomas Cooper, and don't you forget it!"

Thomas studied Queen's gray hair and fine wrinkles. He didn't know how old she was, but it didn't matter, she was his rock. She represented stability, intellect, steady support, and most of all, fun. She could climb a tree better than anyone, way up to the top where the branches swayed and the birds scattered. She could run faster than most kids, skip and hop too. She took time to play with him when most adults wouldn't. One time she even went puddle jumpin' with him. She had been there for him all of his life as a playmate and a wise friend.

"What that job gonna be, Queen?" asked Thomas, unconcerned.

"Child, it's like this," stated Queen as she fixed a narrowed gaze upon him, "Father Poulton is opening up a school for boys over at the Bohemia mission. He wants my help looking after them."

Thomas had been to the Bohemia mission several times with his father, delivering barrels he had made. It was a long way away, a day's travel to get there and back. He enjoyed the ride, bouncing along in the wagon, stopping to eat and to blindfold the horse before crossing the river each way. He liked the thrill of the river rising around the wagon as they crossed it, threatening to wash them away as it gushed and bubbled around in a rush. But he knew it wasn't a trip that could be made on a daily basis.

"*Bohemia!*" cried Thomas, "how ya gonna get that *far*?"

"Thomas, I'm going to go stay there awhile to help get things settled. I need to teach the servants there how to run the house properly as well as how to care for that number of boys. Uncle Ralph and his family are going with me to help oversee other things."

Thomas balled his hands into fists and punched the air.

"You're too old!" he protested, "why don't they just leave ya be? Ya already have a boy ta look after! *Me!*"

"Don't be that way, boy. Father Poulton *asked* me. He didn't tell me I've *gotta* go. I *want* to do it. Besides, you have a ma and a pa to look after you. These boys are being sent away to school all by their lonesome selves. They need someone to be there for them. To look after them."

"Lemme go wit ya," begged Thomas hopefully, "an go ta school with them boys."

Queen shook her head sadly.

"No, you can't. This is a school for rich white boys who are Catholic. Their parents want them educated with others like them. You aren't rich. You aren't white. You aren't Catholic."

"Queen, I can't be rich or white," reasoned Thomas hopefully, "but I could be Catholic."

Queen's breath hitched and she winced at the suggestion of embracing Catholicism. It wasn't that she objected to Catholics, the Jesuit priests had always been kind to her, especially Father Samuel whom she remembered fondly and continued to miss, but Catholicism wasn't her faith.

"I suppose you could, Thomas, but it still won't get you into that school," stated Queen firmly, "your name is Thomas Cooper. You're going to be a fine Cooper like your pa and that's no small thing."

Thomas felt proud. He squared his shoulders and sat a bit straighter beside Queen, listening to the chatter of the birds settling down for the night. Once the chatter ceased and the moon had pushed away the sun, Queen stood, ready to go in. After a few steps, she stretched her open hand back to Thomas.

"Come on, child," she encouraged, "you can wash up in the creek while I mend that shirt before your ma sees it. I'll send word to her that you're staying with me tonight."

Chapter Twenty Three

November 15, 1746, Bohemia Estate, Cecil County, Maryland, American Colonies

Father Thomas Poulton was concerned. Maryland had been settled as a haven for Catholics who wished to practice their faith but had been persecuted for doing so elsewhere. It was successful for a while and Catholics had enjoyed living amongst one another openly demonstrating their faith. That was no longer the case and hadn't been for decades.

As the Protestants migrated to the colonies, they brought with them their prejudices against the Catholics. When their numbers finally surpassed those of the Catholics, they rebelled against being governed by them. In 1689, after an armed conflict, the Catholics were forced to concede Maryland and turned over all authority of governance to the Protestants.

By 1702 any demonstration of Catholicism was illegal. Even saying the Holy Trinity was punishable. The law demanded that any offender caught saying it was to be bored through their tongue and fined. By 1718 Catholics were barred not only from serving in public offices or as public officials, but also from voting. Taxes for Papists, Catholics, were double than those of Jacobite's, non-Catholics.

Unwilling to abandon their faith, Catholics went underground. As for the Jesuit mission estates, the priests refrained from using the title of *Father* and used a much safer *Reverend* or *Mister* instead. Sometimes they used several different names to avoid drawing any suspicion from their Jacobite neighbors to acquire land and slaves or established private homes where they could gather in secret for mass. That was how they circulated with anonymity. However, when it came to educating their children, matters became more complicated.

Unwilling to relinquish their children to Jacobite instructors who would have seduced them into the belief that the Catholic faith was filled with mysticism, false idolatry, ritualistic practices, and was a bastion of evil, they sent their young boys to be educated overseas before attending the College of Saint Omar in France.

Leaving their homes and families at the age of nine, most of the boys were unable to return until their education was complete. Many did not see their families again for up to fifteen years and some never returned. Providing a solution to keep the boys nearer to their families, Father Poulton daringly opened a school at Bohemia.

Secrecy was imperative. Though many knew, or suspected, the true faith under which the boys were taught, none could prove it. The students who attended were hand-picked based upon their family's wealth and political influence or connections to the crown, and the numbers were kept discreet, never more than twenty. It was a huge risk. If it were ever proven that the school was driven by the Catholic faith, the law required that everyone involved would be subjected to severe consequences, including being sent back to England, banishment, imprisonment, confiscation of all property, and even death.

When the Bohemia school first opened, the Church of England's Reverend Hugh Jones, the rector of the parish, was angry. He outed it as a Papist school by printing a sermon in the Maryland Gazette titled *A Protest Against Popery*. Trying to inflame public protest against Catholics, and more specifically the school, he decried the faith as 'a tempest of the devil' and 'a bastion of evil' while demonstrating the piety of the Church of England.

Unwilling to let the slander go without redress, the priests constructed a response, an endeavor they undertook in united secrecy. However, unable to approach a newspaper to print it without disclosing the identity of at least one of the authors, they chose to privately print it as a pamphlet then distribute it widely.

When Reverend Jones heard about the pamphlet, he was incensed. Positive that it had been generated by the Jesuits, he angrily rode out to Bohemia several times and demanded a copy of it. There, he was greeted with open kindness, a denial of Catholic practices, and sorrowfully shaking heads that claimed ignorance to any pamphlet.

"This isn't over, Poulton," Reverend Jones threatened with an angry sneer at his last departure, "I know you're a Jesuit *Papist* trying to lure *my* flock away from me and from God."

In response, Father Poulton pulled himself up to his full height and stepped towards his nemesis. They engaged in a full eye-to-eye silent glaring battle for several moments before Father Poulton finally spoke.

"I think you are in a frenzied, boiling ball of panicked rage because your coffers are thinned. Perhaps you should look to God for guidance in constructing your sermons to inspire greater gifts, rather than harass those who have no influence over His will."

A few weeks later Reverend Jones once again utilized the newspaper. Because the Maryland Gazette was no longer willing to be involved in what was obviously developing into a feud of huge proportions, he approached Benjamin Franklin, who published the *Pennsylvania Gazette* and who agreed to help him. Reverend Jones' open letter addressed to *the Jesuits established in Maryland and Pennsylvania* was promptly published. In the letter, he denied being interested in the contents of the pamphlet but yet admitted to having asked 'the gentleman on whom it is fathered' for a copy so he could directly answer any 'sophistical fallacies or sarcastical falsehoods' that it claimed.

Concerned for the safety of his school, Father Poulton called a meeting with the Headmaster, William Waite.

"He is worried about our presence and isn't going to give up," explained Father Poulton with a weary sigh.

"We've done what we can. To produce another response will only serve to further provoke him," agreed Mr. Waite as he folded the November copy of the *Pennsylvania Gazette* with a rustle and set it upon the corner of Father Poulton's desk.

"Do you suppose it is even possible that he, in fact, really has not seen a copy?" asked Father Poulton doubtfully.

"No, Father," Mr. Waite chuckled, "he's seen it. He's just trying to ferret out proof of the author, which he believes is you, and agitate the people towards insisting that action be taken against you. It angers him that you are known to be a Papist and yet you sit upon a large plantation running a successful school and are being ignored by the authorities. Reverend Hughes feels that since you live in his parish, you must bow to him in body and money. You do neither."

"And I never will!" proclaimed Father Poulton angrily.

"Just be aware that it sparks his fury," agreed Mr. Waite.

"We need to immediately speak to the students as well as our negro families to ensure that they remain alert at all times. Especially when leaving Bohemia, they need to keep a vigilant eye out for possible trouble," stated Father Poulton as he rose from his chair to go and gather the students.

"It also wouldn't hurt to have only such staff that, if it should become necessary, could defend the property and protect the children."

After some deliberation, it was decided that several of the weaker or elderly staff members would be traded with other missions.

"What about Queen?" asked Mr. Waite.

"What about her?" asked Father Poulton as he fell back into his seat.

"She is old. If there's trouble, what could she possibly do?"

Father Poulton was shocked. Of course, he knew that Queen was advanced in age. Her hair, although still thick, evidenced by the heavy bundle of coiling braids, was white. The deep lines that extended from her eyes and crossed her forehead were accented by finer creases and slightly pleated lips. They all evidenced her age. However, she walked with a spring to her step, moving as spryly as the children, and was still quick witted and intelligent.

Several times he had stopped to watch her work with other servants who were far younger than she was or when she played a quick game with the children, and he marveled at how fluidly she moved. A few months earlier, she took pity upon a young lad who had no partner for a sack race and so joined the game. Concerned that she should be more careful with herself, Father Poulton later cautioned her against such vigorous activities. In response, Queen had bestowed upon him a scowl so fierce that if he did not know her better, he would have quaked with fear. So, when one of the boys overshot an arrow to where it landed upon the roof of the barn and Queen, using stilts rather than a ladder, worked to retrieve it for them, he kept his mouth shut and just watched her with awed fascination.

"My dear friend," laughed Father Poulton, "have you not truly seen the force who is Queen?"

"Yes, sir," responded Mr. Waite with a slightly offended hitch to his voice, "but you cannot deny that she is old."

"And you cannot deny," laughed Father Poulton, "that if you look at her more closely, past the gray hair and folds of her skin, she is spry. Quicker than either you or me. Besides, Queen rarely leaves Bohemia, only making an occasional visit to her daughters and their children at Fingaul. I doubt we need to be concerned for her. Plus, it is unlikely that Reverend Jones would bring the fight here, to Bohemia."

"But if he does, there are mostly just boys here. Young boys who are under your charge and whom *you* are responsible for," objected Mr. Waite, "and Queen sits as the final force of their protection."

"True enough," agreed Father Poulton, "but they are also the boys of very wealthy and very connected families. Even if he despises me, he would not dare to attract the wrath of them by harming one of their children."

*****

December 7, 1746

The day dawned bright and clear. After their lessons the boys hurried through their chores so they would have time for a few quick games of hide and seek before they were called to dinner. Queen stood in the yard and looked out towards the drive. A light breeze wafted and lifted a few escaped tendrils of her hair, chasing away any warmth she might have felt from the winter sun had she not been distracted. She lifted her face to catch its scent and smelled nothing unusual, but tiny barbs of warning needled across her flesh.

All day she had felt a sense of foreboding. It had been years since such a feeling had gripped her so firmly and she knew better than to ignore its warning. Many times in her experience, the fine line between life and death had been drawn by moments such as these and she never forgot it.

That night, sure that trouble was near, after the boys settled into their rooms Queen prepared to greet it. She removed her long full skirts and confining blouse and donned an old pair of britches with a loose-fitting blouse and a pair of men's boots. She knew if any of the boys or staff were to happen upon her and see her dressed in such a way, it would be shocking to them. She didn't care. There was evil business lurking in the night. Besides, she had no intention of being seen.

She quietly slipped down the stairs and went to the parlor. Without lighting a lamp or a candle, she moved a chair to the window and sat in the dark room peering through the curtains to the yard. There, she clutched her whip in her lap and waited, ready for whatever, or whomever, arrived.

When a faint flicker of light flashed through the winter bare trees, she slipped through the house and out the back door. By the time the soft rumble of horses approached and gathered in the front yard, she was in place.

Concealed by the shadows, she stood several feet behind the riders. Shadows cast by the torches they carried danced and shifted eerily. She could hear the rider's whispers over the nervous stomping and heavy huffing breaths of the horses.

"…and so, they shall burn by hell's own fire…" proclaimed one of the riders loudly as he raised his torch.

A loud hissing sound accompanied by a swish of air snatched the torch from his hand, drawing it back so quickly that it was instantly extinguished. Within a fraction of a second, another torch was snatched into the darkness. Then, like thunder, a whirring crack exploded over their heads followed by an immediate bellowing howl of pain from one of the riders and a gush of blood where his hand had inexplicably split open.

The horses, confused and afraid, squealed and froze, unsure of where to flee. Terrified yowls and wails of fear and pain rose to join the whistling of split air and crackling booms that filled the air around them in a ghoulish anthem. Sticks and branches from the trees began raining down upon them, further spooking the horses, who reared and bucked in fright, refusing to be controlled. Scarlet spread across the riders as their cheeks, backs, and arms were laid open with fine slashes.

One of the rider's lost his mount, falling with a hard thud, and was nearly stomped by his frightened horse as its hooves struck the ground. Freed from the restraining pulls of its rider, the horse bolted down the drive. The other horses raced after it, carrying their bleeding, vocally petrified riders away, who clung to them for dear life.

"Wait for me!" screeched the fallen rider, chasing after his friends in a staggered limp. Another whistle and crack rent the air and the seat of his pants opened with a bloody gash.

Satisfied and exhilarated, Queen stood in the shadows, listening to the hysterical screams of the men fade before silently slipping back into the house and up to her room. She did not see the curtains from the window of Father Poulton's bedroom drop.

The following morning, after the debris had been cleaned and while the boys were attending classes, Father Poulton waited for Queen to finish giving instructions to one of the female servants about the laundry. When she finished, she turned towards him.

"What can I do for you?" she asked, quizzically lifting a brow.

"Queen," started Father Poulton cautiously, "I was wondering if you could tell me anything about what happened last night."

"Looks like a storm blew through," Queen chuckled with a slight shrug.

"Mmm Hmm," sighed Father Poulton, "complete with horses hoof prints and large amounts of blood."

"You don't say. Incredible. How could that be?" wondered Queen aloud, knitting her brows together.

"Queen, I don't know how I could ever thank you," began Father Poulton, searching for the proper words.

Queen threw up her hands to stop him.

"The only thing I know about last night is that if there were folks here, they were intent upon wickedness. In that case, I'm sure that whoever they were, they have a new understanding of how your God protects you and those boys. I'm also pretty sure they will never dare to come back."

And so it was that the men who were intent upon burning down Bohemia with its residents sleeping inside, truly believed that they were struck down by God. Never seeing their assailant, they piously swore amongst themselves that Bohemia was indeed divinely protected and that God himself had wrought his fury against them for what they had planned. Relieved to escape with their lives, never again did any of them involve themselves in matters of politics revolving around the church, especially when it came to the inhabitants of Bohemia.

*****

For the next several years, Queen continued to quietly oversee the household at Bohemia. Boys from wealthy Catholic families arrived each year full of devout hope, filling the rooms with laughter and prayers before leaving to continue their education elsewhere. Father Poulton was happy with the success of the school and enjoyed a short time of peace and prosperity before his death on January 23, 1749.

By the end of the year 1751, prejudices and anger against the Papists grew so volatile that Catholics became afraid to send their children to be educated under the Jesuit priests, so the school at Bohemia was forced to close.

By then, time was catching up with Queen. Still sharp minded, she maintained watch over the activities of the house at Bohemia and regaled those who would listen with stories of her youth aboard privateer ships, her time with Father Samuel at Guayaquil, and the court of Queen Anne. It didn't bother her that most people simply enjoyed her stories, believing they were the product of the overactive imagination of an old woman. She knew they were true and had nothing to prove to anyone. She had lived her life exactly as she wanted and had been denied nothing. She had been afforded adventures beyond most people's ability to imagine, was an independent and proud free woman, had supported her children honorably, raising them to be honest adults who understood the value of hard work and good people. She helped the people she could and defended others where she was able. Though some might argue she took matters of the Lord into her own hands, she was proud of properly punishing those who she felt needed it.

When, at ninety-one years of age, Queen died on February 19, 1759, just a month after she helped her daughter Phillis bring little Johnny into the world, she went with the peace of knowing that she had lived wholly and left behind the greatest legacy a person could... her children.

Part Three

Chapter Twenty Four

March 2, 1765, White Marsh, Prince George's County, Maryland, American Colonies

Charcoal clouds raced in and crowded out what had been a beautiful spring day. As if in angry protest and the sun threw blazing arrows, lightning slashed the sky with a crack that was answered by a rumbling roar of thunder. Back and forth they argued in a spectacular display until the rain moved in to resolve the dispute and released a deluge of water. The rain quieted the lightning and thunder with its own beat that quickly faded, leaving behind a fog of steam. Then, as light pushed its way through in a soft glow, the fog dissolved to reveal a world that was greener and clean, with chattering birds that shook playfully, shedding water in droplets that scattered, before leaping into flight.

Phillis Queen stood in the doorway of their small home with her eleven-year-old son, Edward '*Ned*', and watched.

"A quick soaking is just what we needed to push out the flowers."

Ned, feeling very grown up, resisted the desire to roll his eyes at his mother. He didn't care about flowers. They were for women.

"Did you see that lightning?" Nanny called out in greeting as she picked her way around the puddles in the yard.

Holding her skirts high, she balanced one-year-old David on her hip and hopped over a particularly large puddle.

"Be careful jumping like that with my precious nephew in your arms," warned Phillis.

Nanny stopped directly in front of her sister and released an indignant huff.

"I've been carryin' children on my hip, in my arms, and 'cross my back most of my life, Phillis Queen, and don't ya forget it! After twelve children, it's more like I forgot how to walk without em."

"Well, you aren't getting any *younger* and don't *you* forget *that*," replied Phillis, placing her hands on her hips in a huff before she grabbed the baby from her sister's arms.

As the sister's banter dissolved into laughter, Ned saw an opening to slip away. Sliding across their little yard, he hoped his mother wouldn't notice. She did.

"Ned, where are you going?"

Phillis fixed a hard gaze upon her son, who raised his shoulders in a shrug. He shoved his hands deep into his pockets and grimaced.

"I dunno."

Phillis resisted the urge to tell him to stand up straight and take his hands out of his pockets as Nanny stood silently pleading for a few moments of privacy with her.

"Well, it's too wet to go off rompin' around and I need a few moments with my sister. Take David into the house to play with your sisters." It wasn't a request.

"Aw, Ma," Ned groaned, crumpling his face in disappointment.

"Don't you sass me, young man!" Phillis narrowed her eyes and pushed her index finger towards him, "Now do as you're told and come get the baby!"

"Yes ma'am," Ned muttered.

It was unfair. He was nearly a man, and here he had to go sit with a bunch of girls! As if watching his sisters wasn't bad enough, adding a baby was downright embarrassing. Mary was nearly eight years old. She could easily watch seven-year-old Sally, four-year-old Peggy, and two-year-old Winifred. Besides, girls loved watching babies and he most definitely did not. Feeling the weight of his mother's glare, Ned resignedly pushed himself towards the cabin. Before he took three steps, she called after him.

"Ned! You forgot David! Come grab him!"

Once he had closed the door to the cabin, Phillis turned to her sister.

"Talk."

Nanny checked both sides of the house to ensure they were alone. The wet hem of her skirt swirled around her ankles, trying to cling. Concern etched her face as she strode back to her sister and laid her palm on her shoulder.

"How ya feelin'?"

Phillis' breath stuck in her throat. A tear leaked out which she swiped away with the back of her hand.

"I'm fine. The bleeding has stopped, and the cramps have passed."

Nanny studied her through narrowed eyes.

"You are *not* fine, and you know it. You've got to talk to him, Phillis," she urged, "we gettin' too old to keep havin' children!"

"Well, what do you expect me to do about that?" Phillis pushed back.

"Tell him to stop sniffin' around," Nanny urged angrily, "Better yet, tell him if he wanna keep makin' babies, then find someone else. Ya've had thirteen children, nine of em his. Enough is enough."

Phillis was appalled at her sister's naivety. Father Lewis was a good man that worked hard and did a lot of good for their community, but he was not a man to be told what to do. While it was true that he had taken vows which prevented him from marrying, he was still a man. He had needs, physical needs that resulted in producing children.

"Nanny," Phillis warned sharply, "I know you mean the best but it's really none of your business."

"It is my business," Nanny retorted hotly, "You got all these children an' they need a mama. Who you think gonna have ta look after them if you can't?"

Phillis knew she was right but didn't know what to do about it. Some things were just too difficult to talk about and this was one of them. She had nearly died when she miscarried her last pregnancy and the pain was still too fresh. Father Lewis hadn't even known she was expecting again.

That there were so many of his children running around the mission was a difficult subject. It wasn't that he didn't have feelings for them, or at least Phillis wanted to believe that he did just as she wanted to believe that his feelings for her were sincere. The problem was that it created a certain amount of embarrassment for him when his colleagues visited. Though they never said anything about it, he knew they saw miniature variations of his face in Phillis' younger children. Just as if they looked closely, they would also have seen the same miniature variations of Father Thorold in her older children. It was even more pronounced with her children than other mulatto children because Phillis wasn't black, she was half East Indian and half white. Both of her children's fathers were white, so most of her children appeared nearly white. Their dark hair and eyes and olive complexions were the only hint of their heritage.

In any event, it wasn't unusual at most of the missions to have children born there who resembled the priests who oversaw them. It was simply something that wasn't flaunted or discussed. Still, there were times when Father Lewis was expecting a particularly pious or important visitor, so he would ask Phillis to occupy the children indoors. Stuffing so many children into their one room house for an entire day was never fun. Thankfully, it didn't happen often.

But none of that was the point. Phillis knew her life could be in danger if she were to conceive again. At forty-four years of age, she had given birth to thirteen children, including a set of twins. Added to that, there had been several miscarriages. Her body had had enough. Nanny was right to be concerned, she knew what she was talking about. With twelve children of her own, she had also been in the same position. It hadn't been easy for her to tell her husband that there could be no more children, but it had to be done and so she did it. In the end, Tom had taken the news well and supported his wife's decision, her health being the most important thing.

"You're right," Phillis sighed, "I will talk to him tonight."
Nanny eyed her sister suspiciously.

"Promise?"

Phillis nodded. Nanny knew what Phillis was afraid of and felt bad for her but persisted.

"Sister," she said softly, using the endearment they had always used since they were children, "it ain't that he want more babies. He likes you, so don't worry, he'll still come sniffin' around."

Phillis chuckled a bit but did not want to be pushed further, so the matter was dropped.

******

March 17, 1765

In his bedroom, Father Lewis moved a chair to where he could sit by the window, warm and comfortable, and look out at the brisk spring morning. From that vantage point, he could see people moving about in all directions. Several men stood outside the mill at the bottom of the hill and talked using animated gestures, obviously in a heated discussion. Just beyond the mill were the quarters.

Several neat and efficient little houses made from rough-hewn logs that had been notched and fit together then chinked with mud on the outside and plastered on the inside, sat in a tight group. Smoke streamed from each of the chimneys in ribbons that opened to form what looked like a dark cloud that had been misplaced, slung over the houses on a bright day. Behind each house were various coops for chickens and ducks, animal pens for goats, sheep, and pigs, as well as patches of brown earth waiting for spring to be planted. Only one house, belonging to old Tom and Susanna, Phillis' daughter, had no garden because Tom preferred making brooms and kitchen wares.

Father Lewis was proud of his people's industry and encouraged it. When it was possible, the slaves were paid for work that was excessive or not within the scope of their normal chores. They used that money to buy small animals to raise or tools to make what they wanted, which they could then sell. The money was theirs to keep. Most often it was reinvested. Several of the people did very well in their trade which was evidenced in better clothing, heads held higher, and the admiration of their peers.

But that wasn't why Father Lewis sat watching them. It was because of Phillis. She had been acting strangely for over two weeks. They had maintained a standing arrangement for years, and now something was different. On the evenings when he desired her company, he lit a candle and set it in his bedroom window where she could see it and come, letting herself quietly in. They mostly met in the bedroom but there were times when they sat in the parlor before the fire and talked. A couple of times they even sat in the dining room and shared a meal or a glass of wine. Never had she failed to appear until recently.

While Father Lewis knew that Phillis had been with other men before him, he didn't think she had ever been with anyone from the quarters. Her children were certainly fathered by white men. Although she was friendly with her male peers, she never seemed flirtatious or showed them any affectionate interest. Never before had Father Lewis been concerned that Phillis would entertain anyone other than himself, but that was because she had never given him a reason. However, something had changed.

Four times Phillis had ignored him. Four times he had lit the candle and sat, waiting for hours on end, and she never showed up. Four times he had gone looking for her to illicit some explanation for her absence and yet had heard nothing but vague platitudes about how she was tired, or one of the children were sick. It was as if she was no longer interested in him and it stung.

To even think about the possibility that Phillis would step out on him infuriated him. She was *his* and by god he didn't share. If he found out that she had shared herself with another man, he would kick her and her whole squalling brood off of his mission. He didn't care that many of the children were his. She should have been more careful in preventing it.

Phillis, Ralph, and Nanny, and all their children, had lived off the charity of the missions all of their lives. They were fed, housed, and clothed and should be grateful for it. As free people of color, it was expected that they would be able to provide for their families themselves. However, their mother had an arrangement with the late James Carroll and when he died, she and her children came along with the estate.

Mary Queen had been a valuable employee until the day she died. Her children were too and so there was never any reason not to continue to extend to them the same arrangement. But that didn't change the fact that they owed a debt of gratitude of which they seemed ignorant.

Father Lewis pushed his fingers into his temple. The situation with Phillis was driving him to distraction. He closed his eyes as he moved his fingers in a circular motion and said a silent prayer for relief.

As if his prayer was answered, when he opened his eyes he saw Phillis and Nanny, arm in arm, talking as they walked through the quarters. It gave him an idea.

Chapter Twenty Five

"You want to know *what*?" asked Nanny in outraged shock.

"Simply if your sister might be seeing someone..." Father Lewis' voice shook nervously, "a...a...another man."

"How dare you!"

How dare I? She dares to speak to me this way, Father Lewis thought bitterly, *when I am simply trying to have a civil conversation of a rather delicate nature?*

"How do I dare?" he asked snidely, "I dare because of the obvious nature of our relationship and also because she has given me reason to suspect that perhaps there is someone else."

Nanny could not believe what she was hearing. That it was about her sister infuriated her. That it was coming from a Jesuit priest who shared her sister's affection made her even madder. Rage shivered through her as she released her breath, blowing it out slowly, and straightened her spine. It was what her children called her 'hot mad' look. When it appeared, they all ran because it was always accompanied with a steely calm and a slashing tongue.

"Father Lewis," Nanny began in a low, hard voice, "my sister been nothing but good to you all these years while you misused her, body and soul. She birthed your children, buried little Johnny, and even miscarried several babies without complaint. All while you stand and piously preach 'bout what the Lord want and don't want, pretendin' that you's it, when we all know what's what and who is really who."

Father Lewis was too shocked to find the words to silence her.

"Phillis never took no vows to nobody about nothin'! She got a *right* to entertain whoever she want. For you, a so-called man of God, to question her integrity while ya violate your vows is straight from the devil hisself and ya should be ashamed! The reason she ain't come runnin' when ya put your little candle in that window," she pointed towards it, noted his surprise that she knew that particular detail, and let her breath out in a *humph* before continuing, "is 'cause she *can't* get pregnant again or it may kill her. She been afraid to tell ya 'cause she don't trust ya!"

"Stop!" Father Lewis found his voice, "You will stop your blasphemy this minute! It is vile to God, and I will not tolerate this abuse!"

"I ain't blaspheming no one but you," Nanny retorted hotly, "and ya do a mighty fine job of bein' vile to him without my help!"

"Nanny Cooper, *you* are the one that put those ideas into Phillis' head," Father Lewis, red faced and pushing his finger into her angry face, accused, "you have strayed and are playing God, deciding who can conceive and predicting if they live or die!"

Nanny didn't budge or back down from him. Instead, she pulled herself even taller and pushed her own finger into his face in retaliation.

"And where were you when she was bleeding her life away, passin' the baby she just done lost? Where were you when those children, *your* children, needed watchin' 'cause their momma be too sick ta do it? I'll tell ya where *I* was... wipin' up blood and feedin' children, *that's* where!"

"Get out! *Get out of my home immediately!*" roared Father Lewis.

Nanny laughed, then aimed her parting words.

"This ain't even your house," she fired, her voice calm and cold, "this is a Jesuit mission and belongs to the church. Ain't that what you always say?" she tsked, "If my momma was alive, she'd take out her whip an make ya dance!"

Father Lewis grabbed Nanny by the arm. His fingers bit through her sleeve as he marched her to the front door. Using his other hand, he threw the door open with such force that it bounced against the wall and bounced back, hitting him so hard it nearly knocked him down even as he tossed her out.

The following day, Nanny received word that she was to pack her belongings because she was being transferred to a different location. Father Joseph Moseley was establishing a new mission in Talbot County and Nanny was to join him along with her eldest son, Tom, and his wife, Francis, known as *Frank*, and their children; Lucy, twelve, Davy, nine, Nancy, six, Paul, four, and two-year-old Henny.

With the new mission being located three day's travel by wagon from White Marsh, Nanny knew she was being sent there in retaliation for the previous day. Storming to confront Father Lewis, she marched to his door and pounded upon it with her fists. Father Lewis was expecting her.

He opened the door with a cordial smile and invited her in with a quick wave and a nod of his head. Without moving to enter, Nanny began the speech she had rehearsed.

"You knows I got six children at home under age ten an a husband that work all day."

"Please, come in," smiled Father Lewis.

"I'm fine right here," retorted Nanny, "besides, weren't it just yesterday you threw me out?"

"Yes," replied Father Lewis airily, "however, today I must *insist* that you come in."

His eyes, hard and cold, evidenced the truth of the mood under his light tone and cordial manners. He stepped back. With a wide sweeping gesture, he motioned for her to enter. With a cautious step, Nanny moved to just inside the door, which promptly shut behind her.

"I ain't goin'."

"Yes, you are," responded Father Lewis firmly.

"Ya can't *make* me," Nanny retorted hotly, "I'm a free woman! Free as you or any other white person be."

Father Lewis laughed.

"Yes," he agreed, "you can refuse. However, if you do, you are to remove yourself and your children from White Marsh. As soon as you do that, I promise you I will sell your husband so far south that you will never, ever, hear from him again."

Nanny froze. The air in her lungs solidified and she could not breathe as fear washed over her, punching its way through her gut to clutch her heart in its angry grasp.

"You would not dare," she breathed out in a choked whisper.

Father Lewis knew he had won. He moved to stand in front of her, so close that she felt the heat from his body. When he lowered his mouth to her ear, she felt his hot, stinking breath.

"You will go as penance for playing God," Father Lewis whispered, "or your family will starve and your husband will die."

And so it was that Nanny, with only her eldest son, Tom, and his wife and five children, left her family to help establish the new mission, named St Joseph's, in Talbot County, Maryland. Her youngest child, David, was less than one year old.

*****

March 20, 1765, St Joseph's Mission, Talbot County, Maryland, American Colonies

Nanny's eyes were dark and shadowed from unshed tears as she bounced along in the bed of the wagon. She wrapped her arms around two-year-old Henny and absently stroked her head. Pulling her fingers through the little coiled ringlets that framed Henny's sweet brown face, relaxed and innocent in slumber, she watched them pull straight, then spring back into place.

Paul had grown restless, sandwiched between his baby sister and their momma. He held a small twig that he had picked up along the way. Using it, he concentrated upon drawing shapes in the dirt on the wagon floor where they sat. Little balls of dirt and debris popped and slid with the jouncing and sway of the wagon, disturbing his efforts to create a recognizable picture. Annoyed with her brother's futile efforts, six-year-old Nancy reached for the twig to take it from him. When Paul quickly snatched it back from her, her fingernails raked his arm.

"Ma," howled Paul, bursting into tears, "Nancy done scratch me!"

"Did not!" objected Nancy, "he done it all by hisself tryna keep me from gettin' the stick!"

The adults, burdened with larger worries, ignored the children. Their mother hung her head over the side of the wagon and vomited once more.

"Can't you two see dat momma ain't right?" scolded their older sister, Lucy, from the rear of the wagon, "Stop dat fussin!"

"But she done scratched me," cried Paul, "an I didn't do nothin'!"

"Enough," ordered David, who sat scrunched in the center, "We ain't carryin' on over a little scratch or a small stick."

Grabbing the twig from Paul, he broke it in two and shoved one half towards Paul and the other towards Nancy. When neither child reached to receive them, he shrugged and tossed the pieces over the side of the wagon.

"Won't be much longer now," announced their father, who drove the wagon beside Father Moseley.

The distance from White Marsh to the new mission site was over seventy miles. They traveled in a wagon pulled by a large ox and the journey took them three long days. While at first the children were excited with their new adventure, they quickly grew weary, cold, hungry, and uncomfortable. Initially, the older two had tried to entertain their three younger siblings but they quickly ran out of ideas for play in such a confined space. The adults were no help at all.

Nanny, miserable with grief over leaving her husband and young children, had simply bounced along in silence. Frank, suspicious she was expecting another child, had grown ill by the end of the first day due to the constant movement. She walked most of the second day, letting the kids take turns in joining her, but when they wandered off or dragged behind, she made them all get back into the wagon and stay there. By the end of the day, poor Frank's feet hurt so badly that she was forced to stay in the wagon for the remainder of the trip. Their father drove, listening to Father Moseley's excitement over the new mission, complete with animated descriptions of how they were going to create 'a hub to spread God's word.'

At the end of the third day, the oxen left the road in a lumbering gate and traveled a short way through a forested area to a clearing. Their journey was finally over.

"Whoa!" Tom called to the oxen and the wagon jolted to a stop.

In the clearing were three ancient structures, all covered with vines and in poor repair, groaning to hold themselves up past knee-high grass. The small center building was in the best shape. It was built with thick rough-cut boards held into place by rusty nails. It had not been chinked, allowing the weather to flow freely through its one room, and there was no fireplace or chimney. In the center of the dirt floor a shallow fire pit had been dug and was circled with fist sized rocks. Above it, there was an opening in the roof to allow smoke to escape. To the left of that structure, about a hundred paces, a lopsided tobacco barn struggled to stand. A little further out, on the right, was the dwelling intended for slaves.

Though the slave cabin was a similarly structured as the main cabin, it was smaller and had no door. The roof, once branches woven with sticks and twigs from the surrounding trees, had fallen in. Debris covered the floor.

No one spoke as they despondently wove their way through the long grass, checking out each pitiful structure, to see their new home. Insects hummed loudly around them, a forewarning of the night and days to come, when, soft as a whisper, Nanny exhaled and turned to Father Moseley, her eyes filled with mirth.

"Father, I *know* why I be out in this wilderness, I angered Father Lewis," she breathed in a voice that grew stronger and louder as it mingled with laughter, "but I think you might've made somebody *far bigger* than him a whole lot madder, bein' a *white* man ta end up out here!"

Chapter Twenty Six

November 16, 1767, White Marsh, Prince George's County, Maryland, American Colonies

The earth glistened under a blanket of frost. Cobwebs shimmered and sparkled like lace draped across and woven through the grass and the leaves of every tree. Shadows slowly stretched across the yard as the last bit of night struggled to stay. Roosters crowed out their greeting to the day and were answered by the bleating of sheep and a cow calling out to be milked. From the quarters, the sound of voices mingled with the fragrant smell of woodsmoke and rode a gentle breeze to the small guest cabin located across the yard from Father Lewis' home.

Inside, Father Ashton sat rigidly on the floor beside the bed under a crucifix, the room's only adornment. The thick curtains hanging over the single window were drawn tight. No fire had been lit to knock out the winter chill that was raising goosebumps over his naked back as he prepared for his morning prayer ritual.

On the floor before him was his Instrument of Penance, a scourge he felt befitted a Jesuit priest, which he had created. It was the most important part of his daily rituals. Seven cords of different lengths, varying from the span of his hand to the length of his arm, extended from a rope handle.

Each cord possessed three flagellation objects, two knots and a cross, spaced unevenly.

Born in Tipperary, Ireland, twenty-five-year-old Father John Ashton grew up in a country in conflict with England. In 1752, when England began confiscating Irish lands and awarding them to English soldiers, his family lost their estate. His father had been angry and bitter, often taking his frustration out on his son, until his death on August 8, 1758. Young, landless, and penniless, John Ashton entered the Society of Jesus in Watten, Belgium on September 7, 1759. Though he struggled, he was eventually ordained, then remained there until being assigned to assist Father Lewis in Maryland. The internal demons he struggled with followed him there. Tormented, he fought them every day through prayer and ritual.

"Hear me, Lord, for I have sinned and have fallen short in your eyes. I will not spare myself your righteous judgement so that I may be returned to your heavenly grace even though I know I am not worthy."

Grasping the scourge by the handle, he sucked in his breath and held it. A violent yank of his arm towards his chest sent the cords whizzing over his shoulder to land across his back with a soft thud. Wincing, he blew out his breath as he flicked his wrist to dislodge one of the crosses that had partially embedded itself into his back.

*****

February 21, 1768

"Mama, why do you keep opening and shutting the door?"

Phillis turned from the door to the fireplace and grabbed a rag she had left lying there. Using it, she lifted the lid of a pot hanging over the fire and leaned into it, inhaling deeply, then smiled. The rich savory scent of cornbread, made special with pork fat, wafted up and tickled her nose. Satisfied, she replaced the lid.

"You know Uncle Ralph is coming for Sunday dinner and I'm excited," she replied to ten-year-old Mary.

"But Momma," sang out five-year-old Winifred as she twisted the hem of her dress in her hands, "Uncle Ralph comes a lot. Why this be different?"

"Because today is special," Phillis replied as she swatted at Winifred's hands, "and he may have a surprise!"

"We love surprises," shouted Winifred happily as she joined hands with seven-year-old Peggy and nine-year-old Sally. Laughing and shouting gleefully, the three sisters skipped in a circle until, tripping over their thirteen-year-old brother, Ned, they fell across him in a heap.

"Get off me!" shouted Ned angrily as he shoved them aside and scooted down the wall.

Just as Phillis was about to scold her energetic daughters, someone knocked on the door. Her children's troubles were instantly dismissed as her eyes widened with excitement, pulling her brows up, and she quickly swept off her apron.

"Good Lord! They're here!" she cried, patting her hair, "Mary, get the girls up and smooth their dresses."

She threw open the door, swinging it wide with a burst of excitement. It was a devastating blow when she saw her brother standing alone. She tried to hide her disappointment, but her hopes had been dashed as quickly as if they had been doused with icy water on a hot summer day.

Ralph saw his sister's exuberance dissolve into disappointment and felt horribly about it. He had tried, but there was nothing that he could do. Holding his hat in his hand, his shoulders slumped as he tried to explain, reaching for words that wouldn't come.

"She couldn't come yet," he faltered, "she wanted to, begged to, but Father Mosley said he needs her til spring."

With her chin on her chest and tears stinging her eyes, Phillis toppled towards her brother and leaned into him.

"It ain't your fault," he tried to comfort her, "Nanny shoulda known better than ta go struttin' up to Father Lewis the way she done. He's mostly a good man, but he's proud and got the white man's streak in him."

"It was because of me," Phillis swept at the tears streaming down her cheeks, "she was trying to protect me."

"Where she didn't have any business. It was a matter between you and your man, a proud white man, and she should have let you take care of it in your own time," objected Ralph, "besides, you know she ain't exactly like us."

Phillis drew back from him in shock.

"What do you *mean* she isn't like us?"

Ralph tilted his head and narrowed his eyes at his sister.

"Woman," he warned, "now don't go getting your feathers all in a ruffle…"

"She is *exactly* like us," Phillis interrupted him furiously, "raised by the same mama, on the same mission, feeding her children the same way we do! The only difference is that she made someone mad and now her babies are growing up without her. Her husband died alone, heartbroken…."

"Phillis, *stop*," Ralph injected, "you know that isn't what I meant. She's darker than us, a *lot* darker, and she married a slave. Tom was a good man. He was good to Nanny, but he wasn't a free man. For that matter, if anyone knew the truth about Nanny and her real mama, she'd be in a far worse mess."

Phillis could not believe that her brother dared to say the words. Throughout their entire lives, they each understood Nanny's circumstances at birth was never to be spoken aloud. They had all visited Daphne, Nanny's biological mother, until she died, but it had always been as friends. Daphne had hugged and loved on all of Queen's children equally. She never showed any partial feelings to the child that was of her body. Queen had also loved them all equally fierce and had claimed each one of them through blood and love. Remaining silent about those truths was the only way to keep Nanny safe and free. *They can't repeat what they never heard,* Queen had always said. Yet Ralph stood at her door and said the unsayable! However, he did have a valid point.

With her short, round, pert, nose, tight coiled curls, dark complexion, narrower shoulders, and shorter stature, Nanny didn't look like any of them. She looked more like the African slaves, though she was from Guayaquil. When Queen had been asked about it, and she frequently was, she had simply responded with a glare, and no one ever pushed the issue with her. Then, further complicating matters, Nanny had married a slave.

"I just hate it, is all," Phillis didn't want to argue, "and I was so very excited to see her. I'm disappointed."

"She's doing well," Ralph assured her, "and looking forward to coming back home in the spring. She misses you too, but being away from her children has been especially hard on her."

Later that evening, after a hearty dinner of pulled pork, cornbread, and boiled beets, the kids settled down on their pallets lined against the wall while their mother and uncle sat at the table talking.

"Phillis, is somethin' going on around here that ain't right?"

"What do you mean?"

"I just been noticin' that there seem to be a lot of people at the Marsh that are injured," Ralph broached a subject that had been on his mind for several months, "and it seems that it's always the left hand or an elbow."

Phillis paled. She knew Ralph was protective and she didn't want to make him angry. If the things she heard about Father Ashton were true, she knew it would infuriate him. She had already nearly lost a sister to her temper. Ralph's temper was far worse than Nanny's.

"Well, you haven't seen anything like that in *our* family, have you?"

"Not that I reckon. But still, seems kinda odd to me," pushed Ralph.

Pursing her lips, Phillis nervously scrolled her finger across the table in circles.

"What aren't you tellin' me?"

Phillis took a deep breath and began.

"Father Ashton seems like a nice enough young man, but I hear he has odd ways. Odd, *evil* ways," she whispered so the children wouldn't hear.

"They say he whips himself every morning! I didn't believe it, but several times I've seen a bit of blood, just a speck here and there, seep through his shirt, over his back."

"*Whips himself,*" Ralph could hardly believe it, "no nigger wants ta be whipped and you say there's a white man whipping *himself?*"

"Yes, it's true," nodded Phillis, "and he's quick to viciously punish the slaves too. He grabs their fingers and twist them out and back so bad that they need to be popped back into place. Just after he got here, in the fall, a man named Abraham was working here on loan, helping out at the smith shop, and Father Ashton stopped by. A spark hit Father Ashton's arm and burned a little hole in his sleeve. Father Ashton made everyone but Abraham leave the shop. People said they could hear Father Ashton praying and Abraham hollering all the way down the road. That night Abraham self-freed himself."

"He ran away?" Ralph was shocked.

Rarely did the slaves run away. The odds of succeeding weren't good and besides, where could they go? No slave would risk their lives sheltering them, they couldn't blend out in the free world with their darker skin, they had no means to provide for themselves. Plus, there was always a reward for their return, making it profitable for someone to turn them in. Additionally, these were priest slaves. Their lives were generally much easier than other slaves and they knew it.

"Yes. After looking for him all night, Father Ashton sent word to Father Matthews, at St. Inigos mission where Abraham was loaned out from, to let him know in case Abraham ran home. Father Matthews was so mad he rode his horse to a lather getting here to talk to Father Lewis. He said Abraham was a good man who worked hard and wouldn't have run off unless something dastardly had happened, but no one has heard from him again."

Ralph blew the air he was holding out slowly.

"Whhoooeeeee! Somethin' real bad musta been done to that poor man," he exclaimed, "for him to have run off like that."

"Yes," agreed Phillis, nodding, "and ever since then, I've been hearing whispers about Father Ashton. When he gets mad, he starts spouting bible verses about how God agrees with the awful things he's getting ready to do. Then he hurts folks, mostly on their hands. Word amongst the slaves is that when Father Ashton gets to preachin', people start hidin'."

"He can't be doin' people like that," Ralph drug his hands across his forehead.

"Now, Ralph, we both know it's wrong but we also both know that you can't fix it. So, whatever you're thinking, just stop it right here, this very minute," Phillis scolded, "I've already lost my sister because she thought she could right a wrong that wasn't any of her business. I don't want to lose my brother too!"

"What can he do, Phillis? I wouldn't talk to Father Ashton directly. I could just let someone know."

"Like Father Lewis? You saw how that worked out! The priests will protect each other. They'll circle around him and then kick you out! Where would you go? You've worked for room and board at these missions your whole entire life! Think of your wife, who is still a slave, and your kids! How would they manage without you? Please," begged Phillis, laying her hand across his, "leave it alone. The priests are in and out of here all the time. It won't take long for them to discover it for themselves."

It didn't sit well with him, but Ralph knew Phillis was right. Nodding, he looked out the window.

"It's late and I need to get home, but promise me one thing…" Ralph took his sister's hand and stood, drawing her up with him, "…if that man puts his hands on any of you, your children, Nanny's children, any of our family, you'll get word to me."

Phillis agreed with a nod.

"I ain't jokin' around 'bout this, Phillis," Ralph pushed sternly, "maybe some people can't do anything to help themselves, but we're free people and we can. It might not be easy, but we're made of strength. We are Queen's children, so we'll fight back, and we'll survive just fine."

Chapter Twenty Seven

June 6, 1775

With a pleased smile, Tom carefully stretched a piece of thick leather over the last, a tool carved from wood into the shape of a foot, and tacked it down to form the upper part of a shoe. He grabbed another thick piece of leather that he had cut into the proper shape the previous evening and then softened overnight in a bucket of water, and he sat down on his shoe bench. Before he began, his eyes slid over the room, and he paused. He couldn't have been more pleased.

After thirteen years spent living with Thomas Barnes, a cordwainer, to learn the art of shoemaking, at twenty-one years of age he was finally able to work on his own, in his own shop. Returning to the White Marsh mission and his family had been an obvious decision. Working there, making shoes for the slaves in exchange for room, board, and provisions, was a comfortable life. His entire family had done it ever since his great grandmother, Queen, had arrived in the colonies. Though they never had much money, they also didn't have all the concerns and difficulties that other free people of color did. They were all comfortable and happy.

When he arrived at White Marsh, he spent an entire week reacquainting himself with his mother, Susanna, his grandmother, Phillis, and the rest of his family, before presenting himself to Father Lewis, who greeted him warmly. Although he was a single man and so would have normally shared a cabin with several others, because he needed space to perform his craft, he was assigned a cabin to himself. It wasn't much but it was all his and he was proud of it.

There was nothing unique about the cabin. It was the standard single room with a dirt floor, an adequate fireplace, and no windows, with just a small table and chair standing alone in the middle. What made it special was the shoemaker's bench he had placed just inside the open door.

He had made the bench himself under the guidance of Mr. Barnes and it was his prized possession. When closed, it appeared to be a wooden box with a bottom hinged opening. A set of swinging legs seemed oddly placed on the door until it was pulled down, revealing four drawers, and the legs were secured. What unfolded was a bench under a toolbox. It was all proportioned to him so he could do his work efficiently.

The toolbox held everything he needed within arm's reach. In it was a sharp awl for poking holes through thick leather, an excellent ax and fine carving knives to make lasts and soles, a variety of hammers, lengths of waxed hemp, leather, glue, and his lapstone for molding the soles. He had worked very long and hard to earn everything he needed to be a great cordwainer, making good and comfortable shoes that were also serviceable.

Humming a jaunty tune, he sat on the bench cradling the lapstone and placed a leather piece in the center of it, where he pounded it with a hammer to form it. He had been taught that slaves didn't need much shaping of the sole, but he disagreed. If anyone needed comfortable shoes it was the slaves, and he wanted to make sure they got good ones that would last.

"You seem mighty pleased with yourself."

Startled, Tom nearly smashed his thumb.

"Hello," without getting up, Tom greeted the stranger, obviously one of the priests, who stood in the open doorway, "I'm sorry. I guess I was pretty much into my work and so didn't see you."

"I see that," agreed the stranger with a pinched frown and a jerk of his brows, "perhaps you should refrain from making so much noise, humming, as you perform your tasks."

Tom laughed jovially.

"Well, Father...?" He looked at him questioningly, seeking a name.

"Ashton," the stranger provided, "Father John Ashton."

"Okay," Tom forced a smile across his face even though he instantly disliked Father Ashton, "Father Ashton, it's a pleasure meeting you. My name is Tom Queen. I'm the new Cordwainer. And since I'm making so much noise pounding out this leather, I doubt a little bit of humming is going to overly disturb anyone."

"Are you one of *the* Queens?" asked Father Ashton dubiously, giving Tom no time to respond before he continued, "The bible says that what comes out of a man defiles him."

Tom felt the icy bite of Father Ashton's cold voice and matched his tone with equal conviction.

"It also says to sing in grateful praise, addressing one another in song."

Impudence! snarled Father Ashton silently before dueling back.

"There is no condemnation for those who are in Christ!"

Tom was born on the mission but had spent most of his life living as an apprentice with the Barnes family. They were the kindest most God-fearing people he had ever known. They raised their children with scripture, citing them for every circumstance that arose, and required everyone under their care, children and apprentices alike, to also learn them. Accordingly, Tom was well prepared to duel with Father Ashton in scripture, but unfortunately, he did not yet know the depth of his opponent's pride, and so he did not understand the gravity of his mistake in doing so.

"Love one another with brotherly affection," Tom's voice increased in speed and volume as he cited the scripture, "Romans."

Father Ashton held his breath in indignation with his cheeks puffed out until his face turned beet red and he looked nearly ready to burst. Then, he blew the air from his lungs in an angry huff and erupted.

"Render to all what is due to them!" he shouted as he kicked the legs of the bench, causing them to fold and dump Tom to the floor. Heavy tools fell from the drawers that spilled open and smashed into Tom before they crashed to the floor. The heavy lapstone Tom held fell from his lap and struck the floor with a loud clunk.

Still clutching his hammer, Tom sprang to his feet. Raising it to strike, suddenly he stopped. Bracing for the blow, Father Ashton hunkered down and wrapped his arms over his head when suddenly, the realization of what he was about to do washed over Tom, dampening his rage. Slowly, he forced himself to lower the hammer to his side

"When you discipline a man with rebukes for sin…" he choked out in a restrained fury that was quickly being replaced with shame, "…you consume what is dear to him. Psalms."

Father Ashton rose cautiously and stretched to his full height to where he stood face-to-face with Tom. Each of them felt the breath of the other across their face. Obstinately, neither man moved as beads of sweat dotted their brows.

"I must turn my eyes from looking at worthless things," whispered Father Ashton, snidely breaking the spell.

He turned away, stepped through the door and out of the cabin, then slowly walked away.

"Psalms," he hollered over his shoulder without turning back.

Needing to have the last word, Tom called back out to him.

"Do not cause your brother to stumble. Romans."

*****

June 15, 1775

Day after day, Father Ashton returned to Tom's cabin. He never approached it. He just stood several paces away and stared. Ignoring him, Tom continued to work. Though he found it unnerving, he resisted the urge to shut the door. With no windows for light or air, it was simply too hot to work in a closed-in space. Finally, frustrated and hot, he realized that Father Ashton clearly wanted another confrontation, so ignoring him was of no use. Seeing no other options, Tom was willing to oblige him.

"The wrongdoer will be paid back for the wrong he has done. There is no partiality. Colossians," he called through the doorway.

With his hands held together before him, as if in prayer or deep contemplation, Father Ashton stepped closer to the cabin.

"You are one uppity nigger," he drawled.

Unaffected, Tom did not move. It wasn't new to him to hear such an insult; he had been a part of several confrontations that had turned in that direction. With fair skin and proper speech, he could easily pass for a white person and that fact seemed to upset white people. Even his beard, long and full when combed, seemed to irritate white men who envied it.

"The Barnes family did you no favors treating you soft, making you think you're better than you actually are," taunted Father Ralph, "which is just a nigger. Bastard born man of a nigger whore who will be invited into hell upon her death."

Aware that Father Ashton was baiting him, Tom struggled to swallow the rage that instantly boiled within him. He turned from the door and stepped to the table in the center of the room. Breathing slow and deep, he leaned against it with his full weight, supporting himself with both hands.

Father Ashton was encouraged. He knew his words had struck their mark. He wanted Tom to strike him, welcomed it even. Suffering was the condition of man that brought him closer to God. Besides, if Tom would dare to strike him, he would go to jail. Then Father Ashton would finally have the over-inflated Queen family right where he wanted them, at his mercy.

"The Lord knows the thoughts of man," he goaded, slowly stepping into Tom's cabin to make an easier target of himself, "Psalms. He knows the violence that you are thinking as if you had already done it. You are already damned!"

"If anyone thinks he is religious and does not bridle his tongue," Tom responded without moving, "this person's religion is *worthless*. James."

"How *dare* you question me and blasphemy my religion," blasted Father Ashton.

Father Ashton grabbed an awl Tom had left lying on his bench and charged forward. With an angry roar he slammed the sharp tip through Tom's left hand, just below his third and fourth fingers. Tom roared in a bellowing howl of pain. The awl stuck clear through his hand to the table, its handle wobbled from the impact.

Tom used his right hand to pull the awl. Embedded in the table, it resisted at first, then sprang out. Holding it up, Tom spun around, wielding it as a weapon, ready to thrust it into Father Ashton. He was not there. Tom leapt to the door only to see him racing down the path.

"All who take the sword, will perish by the sword! Matthew," Tom angrily hollered to the retreating figure, "Damn you to hell, Ashton!"

*****

"Tom, *please*," begged Susanna, "there's gotta be something we can do. You just got home! I missed you so bad for too many years! Besides, you're so happy with your new shop!"

Tom gently pulled his mother into his embrace, careful not to disturb his bandaged hand, and held her there a moment. Her arms slid around him, wrapping him closer.

"Mama, I can't stay," he whispered, begging her to understand, "I'll kill him. I swear I will."

Susanna gently pushed her son back and placed her hands on either side of his face to look into his eyes. They were hard and sure.

"All right," she conceded with a tear, "but what are you gonna do and where are you gonna go?"

"I don't know yet, but it seems just my luck that we're at war. If I'm going to fight for my life, it might as well be a fair fight, with a gun in my hands."

Susanna's breath hitched and Thomas regretted worrying her.

"I'll be back," he assured her though he was uncertain, "I promise."

*****

Susanna sucked in her breath and held it until her lungs screamed for air. She could not believe it. It was outrageous and unconscionable, utterly unbelievable, yet there it was, right in the paper for everyone to see!

SIX POUNDS REWARD.

RAN away from the subscriber, living near Bellair, on Patuxent, in Prince George's county, Maryland, a mulatto fellow called Tom, a shoemaker by trade: he is about one and twenty years old, 5 feet 9 or so inches high, stoops naturally, he is fair, but has a remarkable beard when he lets it grow; he has the look of a rogue when sharply spoken to and discovers a great deal of assurance and impudence in his conversation. As he has always lived in the neighborhood of Queen Anne's, the Governor's Bridge, and Bellair, and been acquainted with the priests of this province, his conversation may easily discover him: It is likely he may call himself free, and have a forged pass under another name, or he may probably be concealed and kept at his trade in Annapolis, or in the neighborhood of Bellair, on Paxtuxent, where he lived, by some white people, who make too familiar with my slaves to my great prejudice, and whom I hereby forewarn from having any dealings with them, either in the shoemaking business, or in any other way, without my express consent. Whoever secures the above fellow in jail, or brings him home to me, will be entitled to the above reward, from

JOHN ASHTON

Furious, she snatched the paper from the table and stormed out the door.

*****

Father Ashton pulled the door to his cabin shut. His knuckles turned white against the knob as he used it to steady himself. Holding his breath, he winced against the raw burning that radiated from his neck to his waist. The thin linen shirt he wore, soft and light, offered no relief from the morning sun, shining hot and bright across his back.

Lord, strengthen me to do your will, for I am but a weak and lowly man, he silently prayed, *I have repented and been punished. Today we will begin anew.*

He embraced the pain and relaxed into the lesson of remorse and the humility it offered, then began walking. After a few steps, he stopped.

Marching towards him was the lovely Susanna Queen. His throat constricted. Everything about her was beautiful and alive. The skirt of her floral dress danced around her legs, teasing him with a quick silhouette of shapely legs before her knees punched it forward. Her neat bun, tucked beneath a hastily placed bonnet, bobbed gently to the beat of her stride. Escaped tendrils of long black hair, in sharp contrast to soft buttercream of her skin, pirouetted delightfully with the loose strings of her bonnet, stroking her face and neck. Round full breasts strained slightly against her bodice as she huffed from exertion and anger. Father Ashton stood and watched her approach, drinking in the vision of her with the thirsty lust of a lonely man.

"What is the meaning of this?" Susanna demanded, thrusting the crinkled paper she held against his chest.

Unprepared for such an onslaught, Father Ashton stumbled backwards, stammering through a quick transition from fanciful lust to defensive outrage. The paper drifted to the ground like an over-sized leaf.

A breeze swept it up and tumbled it several times before gently depositing it several feet away.

"How *dare* you post a reward for my Tom," Susanna pushed against his chest, "when you know he's as free as you!"

"You *pushed* me," Father Ashton cried in outrage, "you actually put your hands on me and pushed me!"

Susanna placed her hands on her hips, tapping her toe furiously, and stepped closer. In spite of the breeze, she smelled the stench of him and resisted the urge to back away.

"You deserve a horse whippin' for calling out my Tom as a slave," she hissed.

Anger, lust, and something else he could not define, shivered through Father Ashton. He curled his lips into a snarl as his lids narrowed over hard glazed eyes. His face transformed as if possessed.

Warning tingled in Susanna's throat then slid down her spine where it landed and knotted in her belly.

"You are gonna leave my Tom be," she growled, stepping back away from him, "You messed up his hand, deviled him into leaving so he wouldn't kill you, and now you're gonna leave him be."

She turned toward the house where Father Lewis lived and went there to speak with him in an effort to protect her son.

*****

Father Lewis was concerned about Father Ashton. Although it wasn't unusual for priests, particularly younger ones, to self-discipline through wearing coarse clothing, fasting, and whipping, Father Ashton's zeal was a bit alarming. Many times he had observed spots of blood seeping through his assistant's shirt and seen grimaces of pain when he thought no one was looking.

Father Lewis had also noticed that discipline was being rendered against the slaves and other workers with increasing frequency and harshness. Although he didn't like it, feeling that workers were more productive when they were happy and provided for by people who genuinely cared for their well-being, he also felt that Father Ashton was still young and learning. Eventually, he thought, Father Ashton's proclivity towards such harshness would surely fade and he would settle into maturity.

And so it was that Father Lewis assured Susanna that Tom was free to leave White Marsh but would be sorely missed. He then ordered Father Ashton to discontinue his post in the paper.

A few months later, Father Lewis noticed Father Ashton's unusual preoccupation with Susanna, though he tried to hide it, as well as the increased severity of his infliction of self-punishment. So, Father Lewis transferred Susanna to another Jesuit mission site, known as St. Thomas, to keep her safe and to remove the temptation of her which so obviously tormented poor Father Ashton.

Chapter Twenty Eight

October 11, 1784, White Marsh, Prince George's County, Maryland, United States

Father John Lewis couldn't have been more excited. What started out as a normal day filled with tedious chores and endless correspondence, had turned into a wonderful day filled with possibility. Shortly after the noon hour, the assistant to Father John Carroll had arrived and informed him that Father Carroll would be calling upon White Marsh that evening for a formal meeting. The assistant also cryptically advised Father Lewis that Father Carroll would be making *a most special announcement.*

For thirty years Father Lewis had worked on the Jesuit missions. After spending eleven years at Bohemia, he transferred to White Marsh in 1765, where he remained. For all of those years, he had lovingly devoted every bit of his energy to the work of God and the Roman Catholic Church. From traveling long distances under miserable conditions to gather his flock, to toiling in the fields, creating them even, to keep the missions profitable and fed, he had been as a true disciple of God. There had been no sacrifice too great.

Appointed Superior, Vicar General, over the British colonies, he had maintained the mission's profits and good standing for decades. Back in

1772 the Holy See in Rome had approved the suppression of Jesuits, resulting in their expulsion from countries all over the world. Father Lewis had successfully navigated the political landmine, ultimately negotiating an agreement where all Jesuits under his appointment signed a document offering submission to Rome. As a result, he had saved the colonial missions, retaining them in good standing under the Roman Catholic Church.

When the American Revolution started in 1775, Father Lewis had provided what sustenance they could to support any soldiers who asked, regardless of what side they fought on. Because of that, they had successfully maintained a very difficult politically neutral position. Once again, he had kept the missions afloat under dubious conditions.

When the war finally ended in September 1783 and the British colonies became the independent country of the United States, his position needed to be redefined as Superior, or Vicar-General, to the United States. Calling upon his top four men, they gathered on November 6, 1783, and drafted a petition to the Holy See, under Pope Pius VI, asking for formal recognition of him in that position.

There were no other candidates under consideration because there was no one else who was as qualified as him. He had already served in the position for decades, so his appointment was strictly a matter of title, a mere formality, and should have been approved immediately. That was over a year ago. After several months passed by with no response from Rome, Father Lewis finally asked Father John Carroll to look into the matter for him.

Father Carroll was from one of the wealthiest, most well-connected families in the colonies. Born in Maryland, he had attended the school established by Father Poulton at Bohemia before being shipped off to Europe. There, he attended the finest schools, further expanding his connections and influence amongst elite society, before becoming a Jesuit. When he returned to Maryland in 1773, he was still young enough that his many contacts who could obtain information concerning just about anything, as well as have influence in political matters regarding either the government or church, were still vibrant and viable. Father Carroll was the perfect person to discover what was going on in Rome to cause the delay. Certain that Rome was simply taking its time in order to plan and prepare a special event for him, Father Lewis trembled with excitement. He could hardly stand the wait for Father Carroll's visit. He just knew he was finally going to be rewarded by the church for his loyal and spiritual dedication over so many years, decades. It was beyond exciting. After all, how often did one become the first Superior of a newly formed country?

He planned to celebrate with Phillis later that night, so he set the candle in the window, ready to be lit, and went to wait for Father Carroll's arrival.

*****

Welcoming his guests into the study, Father Lewis was perplexed. He had not been expecting Father Ashton to accompany Father Carroll. Of course, he knew the men were friends, a fact that baffled him given Father Ashton's concerning moral qualities, but this was a business matter of the highest order. Not only that, but it was also a special and meaningful moment for him, one he didn't particularly wish to share with Father Ashton.

The relationship between Father's Lewis and Ashton had become strained. Father Ashton had become secretive and irascible, taking his frustration out on everyone, including Father Lewis, but especially the black workers. It had become so tense between the two men that Father Lewis had finally resolved to dismiss Father Ashton. However, aware that Father Ashton was very well connected with people of influence and money and could be relied upon to retaliate against him, he wanted to wait until after his official appointment as Superior. That way, he could squash any troubling mischief before it even began.

"Welcome, gentlemen," Father Lewis beamed as they sat, "shall I have refreshments brought in?"

After a few moments of idle talk, he could bear the suspense no longer.

227

"So tell me, what have you heard from Rome?" he asked expectantly.

Father Carroll breathed a heavy sigh through his nose and pinched his lips together. Father Ashton leaned forward like an expectant school-boy.

"Well," began Father Carroll hesitantly, "I have received a mixed bag of news. Frankly, I'm not sure where to begin."

"Mixed news?"

Perplexed, Father Lewis's brows darted up. Father Ashton leaned even further forward, looking as if he was going to topple from the chair.

"Actually," Father Carroll cleared his throat in discomfort, "although this is quite awkward, there is no other way to go about it, so I'll just say it. The Holy See, in their infinite wisdom, has decided to appoint *me* as the Vicar-General, Superior, to the United States."

Father Lewis began to tremble. His face turned pink, then crimson.

"*You?* But you weren't a candidate! You weren't even up for consideration! There was no one up for consideration other than me, the *only* qualified person, by the way, who has already been in the position for decades!"

"I'm sure this comes as quite a shock. It certainly was a shock for me also," began Father Carroll.

"Lies!" burst Father Lewis, feeling as if he had been robbed, "Don't patronize me! I've been around for too many years not to know how things work, either here or in Rome. You know *exactly* how this came about and I want to know!"

"At this point, I don't think that is important. It has been done. I will be receiving the formal notice any day," replied Father Carroll, forcing his voice to remain calm and even.

"What do they expect of me," sneered Father Lewis, "to just accept being usurped, then walk casually back into the fields to work like a slave?"

Uncomfortable with the situation, Father Carroll fixed his gaze upon the ceiling and stuttered.

"Actually, no," supplied Father Ashton cheerfully, "I believe they stated that your labors have already imposed such an obviously heavy burden upon you that you now require repose rather than arduous labor."

Pleased that his jab met its mark, Father Ashton's eyes gleamed merrily when Father Lewis looked ready to explode with rage as he leaped from his chair and stomped to the window. There, he looked out into the starless night and said a silent prayer to steady his breath and calm himself. After a few moments, the low rumble of laughter began rolling from him as events of the previous year were arranged in his mind, creating a picture of clarity. Turning back to his guests, he walked back to his chair. Sniggering, he plopped heavily into it.

"So," Father Lewis began, swiping his hand across his forehead, "Father Ashton, where do you fit in all of this?"

Father Ashton gaily slid his gaze from Father Lewis to Father Carroll and then back.

"I'm sure I don't know what you're suggesting," he drawled lazily.

"Oh, come now," cajoled Father Lewis, "we both know you're involved. But we also know that you'd never perform a task without recompense. Suddenly, it all makes sense to me. Your complete lack of decorum or respect towards me, the cruel way you punish and abuse the workers, your absolute sense of entitlement over all things, and the way you beat your back bloody. Every. Single. Night. From the guilt of it."

Father Ashton's eyes went hard, glazing over in fury, but he refused to allow Father Lewis, a man dispossessed of status and position, to goad him into a hasty response.

"Now that you mention it," rushed Father Carroll, anxious to end the entire ugly scene and unwilling to sit between two nemesis who circled for a fight with their swords already drawn, "to allow you a much needed rest, I have appointed Father Ashton Procurator General."

"Why, of course you have, you disgusting bastard."

"As the new Procurator General," injected Father Ashton smugly, "I will help hasten you into a very much needed retirement by inviting you to begin two days hence."

229

Father Lewis turned to Father Carroll in shock. It was unheard of to transition into retirement in so little amount of time. When Father Carroll refused to meet his gaze, or respond, he knew he had been completely outplayed. His position, the mission, his livelihood, had all been neatly swept out from under him and there was nothing he could do.

"And what if I should refuse your generous offer, choosing instead to stay on here at White Marsh, continuing to do the Lord's work, though relieved of the additional responsibilities of the position of Superior?"

Father Carroll sucked in a deep breath and held it while Father Ashton smiled cold and dark.

"That, my dear friend," Father Ashton stated in a voice to match his icy gaze, "is not possible. You will remove yourself from White Marsh. To where, I do not care."

Releasing his breath, slowly blowing it out, Father Carroll lifted his hand to silence the men. He knew that for either of them to leave the evening feeling overly abused would only serve to undermine his new position. Additionally, both men were well established, possessing many connections that, should they lash out against him, could very potentially damage him. He needed to at least try and make the situation more palatable for Father Lewis.

"I think, Father Lewis, it would be best for you to seek repose at Bohemia, away from Father Ashton whom you are in discord with at this time. There, you may enjoy your leisure time and are free to engage in whatever duties you choose."

And so it was that two days later Father Lewis left White Marsh after a warm and heartfelt parting with Phillis and her children as well as the rest of the workers who resided there. Father Ashton did not appear to say good-bye to him. Instead, he was already busy making plans of his own, the first of which was the return of Susanna. Moving to Bohemia, Father Lewis stayed there until his death on March 24, 1788.

Chapter Twenty Nine

October 24, 1784

Susanna had been gone from White Marsh for nine long years. When she finally returned, she went first to her mother. Crying, Phillis wrapped her arms around her daughter and pulled her in close, holding her there in a long heartfelt embrace. Although they had visited some over the years, it had always been just for stolen moments on the rare occasions when Phillis could take time to ride to the St. Thomas mission with Ralph. Having her daughter in her arms, knowing she was back home, felt good and right. Both women were excited to have the opportunity to sit down together and really talk.

There was so much to catch one another up on, not the least of which was getting acquainted with three-year-old little Kelly, Susanna's youngest child, who shyly tucked her face into her mother's shoulder.

"She's as beautiful as ever," exclaimed Phillis, stroking Kelly's cheek with her hand then sweeping it back to smooth her curly hair, "and look at that head of hair!"

"Don't I know," exclaimed Susanna with a laugh, "I can't keep it neat to save my life!"

She plunked Kelly down to play with Betsy, a doll made out of corn husks. Easy to make, corn husk dolls were the only dolls any of them had ever enjoyed. Most children had many of them, but remaining loyal to Betsy, Kelly wanted no others.

To make them, several corn husks were stacked then folded in half. A string tied an inch down from the fold created the head. Some people drew faces on their dolls, Susanna never did, so Betsy was faceless. Separating the husks into three strands on both sides then braiding them, gave Betsy her arms. Another string tied half-way down created a waist. The ends of the husks that hung below the waist were spread to make a full skirt. If they wanted a boy, the ends were simply divided into two parts, then tied at the end to make legs and feet. Once formed, the doll was placed in the sun to dry. Almost every child could make at least a fair looking doll by the time they were four or five years old. To the relief of their parents, the children spent many hours happily content while playing with them.

Once Kelly was settled with Betsy, Susanna joined her mother at the table to catch up. The news was worrisome.

"Father Lewis was sent off just like that?" asked Susanna, shocked that he was treated so cruelly from the priests whom he had supported for years.

Phillis, emotional at the telling of the events, used her sleeve to swipe at the tears that spilled from her eyes.

"Yes," she nodded, "with barely a chance to say good-bye."

Susannah reached across the table and placed her hands over her mother's, gently squeezing them in an affectionate hand-hug.

"Ma, I'm so sorry."

"There was nothing he could do, being cheated so cruelly by someone he trusted," sighed Phillis.

"He trusted *Father Ashton?*" burst Susannah in shock.

"*No,*" Phillis defended Father Lewis, "of course not! You know he would never have trusted that man with an ear of corn, even if he needed it to feed the pigs! But he did trust Father Carroll. Of course, he never understood why those two were friendly, being so different and all, but he trusted Father Carroll to help him. It was all such a shock."

The two women sat a few moments in reflective silence.

"I'll always be grateful to Father Lewis for helping me to escape Father Ashton, who was always watching me with that weird look in his eyes… It mostly nerved me but scared me some too. Something wasn't right about him."

Phillis turned her hand over and grasped Susanna's. Pulling her slightly towards her, she leaned into the table. Her worried mother's eyes fixed upon her daughter. Susanna remained silent, returning her mother's gaze with a tired sigh.

"Be careful of that man, child. There's a wickedness about him that's just dangerous," whispered Phillis, gasping through a sob, "sometimes he seems okay, but at the slightest little upset he gets a look in his eyes that's just devilish. Pure evil. Always, the next day some poor soul walks with his fingers twisted or burned, or worse. Much worse."

Susanna felt a lurch deep in her gut. She recalled tending to the wounds on Tom's hand before sending him off into the big unknown world. Every day she watched for him, clinging on to the promise he made before he left, *I'll be back. I promise.* And he would. One day. She had to believe it, but it had been nearly ten years and still there was no word.

During the war, Uncle Ralph had ridden out to the St. Thomas mission to let her know he'd gotten word that Tom had enlisted with a North Carolina regiment, where he fought to create a new nation. She was proud of him, fighting on the winning side for a cause that had meaning. But meaning for who?

White people had cried out against the restraints put upon them by the British crown. Seeking 'independence and liberty for all', they sparked a place in the hearts of blacks that none had ever dared to entertain. A place where black people existed as a part of the 'all' in the human race, so they cheered on whichever side seemed the most likely prospect to freedom.

Both sides needed the black people so they made many promises of what life would be like for them once they had helped to win the war. Promises of liberty and freedom were strewn about like a whore with her favors. So, with high expectations, black people bravely took up arms, some as slaves with the promise of freedom in exchange for their service, others as free men.

Some slaves self-freed themselves, running away from harsh masters or unable to resist the bellowing call of liberty rolling throughout the land, shedding the threads of bondage for the role of soldiers. Others were offered up to serve in the place of their white masters who were either too busy or afraid to answer the call when they or their sons were drafted.

Free men were recruited to volunteer. Many did, seeking an opportunity denied them because of the darker shades of their skin; the promise of land, respect, and the independence of equal choices and opportunities available only to white men.

In the end, 'independence and liberty for all' only meant all white men. Though some slaves gained their freedom, most were already back in bondage either with their former masters or new ones. Free blacks simply returned to their communities and farms, both sorely neglected while they were gone, and began again to eke out a living.

But the conditions and culture had changed in the hearts of blacks. The spark had been lit with dreams and hope of freedom and it would not be extinguished. Trust was broken between blacks and whites when promises weren't kept. To complicate matters, both blacks and whites had seen the essential contributions and impact that the black soldiers had made to the cause. The black man, both slave and free, had seen himself as significant and capable. It scared the white man, finally understanding his integral need of the black people beyond just beasts of labor.

Susanna hoped that Tom had been smart about volunteering. She hoped that he had been one of the lucky ones and had gotten some land or money. Then, shedding his beard, his only obvious link to 'tainted' skin, she prayed he had gone on to live as a white man, unafraid to stand up to people such as Father Ashton. Clinging onto that hope, she discussed it with no one lest they try to take it from her. Slowly, it became her truth. It was why he did not return to her and explained why she had not heard from him. It was that belief which kept her heart from breaking and her soul from weeping over the loss of him. It was also the only thing which kept her from wanting to kill Father Ashton for taking him from her.

Her eyes red from unshed tears, Susanna turned her attention back to her mother.

"I've seen Father Ashton's rage," she assured her mother, "and you can be sure that you won't ever catch me near him."

*****

The sun slid below the trees taking its warmth with it. Moving by the light of the moon, Susanna shifted her sleeping daughter's weight to her hip and tucked the corners of the blanket around her. Nuzzling her head against her mother's breasts, Kelly clutched onto Betsy, made a few soft murmuring sounds, and drifted contentedly back to sleep. Susanna smiled. God knew she loved both of her children with all her heart, but for some reason it seemed she loved Kelly harder than she had Tom at the same age.

At forty-four years old, she had two children by two different husbands, both slaves. Many years her senior, her first husband, Tom, had been quiet and serious, preferring to keep to himself making brooms and kitchen wares. Spare with words and affection, he had shown her he loved her by always seeing to her comfort. When she became pregnant, everyone living in the quarters had been surprised, believing old Tom was beyond the age of producing children. Susanna had loved him and his quiet ways. After he died, when little Tom was still young, it took her years before she could consider seeing anyone else.

Meeting Kelly's father had been an entirely different experience. Simon, a mulatto, was a loud and exuberant young man filled with passion and energy. Never afraid to demonstrate his affection, he swept Susanna up in a storm of emotions. Life with him had been fun, filled with laughter, angry fights followed by full nights of making up, and excitement. It was that very thing that took him away from her.

Simon wanted to do something important and significant. In September 1781, when a large contingent of French and American armies marched through Maryland on their way to Virginia, he saw his opportunity. Self-freeing himself, he left his pregnant wife and unborn child to join in the cause. Susanna never heard from him again.

Having lost two husbands and her son, Tom, she had become very aware of how fragile relationships could be. Perhaps her feelings were simply a result of the natural aging process coupled with the maturity of realizing that nothing lasts forever. So, in remembering to embrace each moment as they are given, it only *seemed* that she loved little Kelly harder.

Pushing the matter aside for another day's contemplation, Susanna opened the door to her cabin and slid inside. Laying Kelly down upon the bed, she gently kissed her cheek, pausing a moment to breathe in the sweet scent of fresh air and sunshine that lingered on her. Susanna tucked the blanket around her and let out a contented sigh. When she stood, a hand clasped firmly over her mouth.

"Even from birth the wicked will go astray," a sinister voice whispered into her ear. The hand pressed harder, pulling her head back until she could feel the moist heat of fetid breath across her face, "for those who live according to the flesh set their minds to things of the flesh."

Fear shivered through Susanna as she felt whiskers scrubbing her cheek. Her chest constricted and her mind froze. Her heart raced in desperate need of oxygen. A few moments seemed like an eternity as thoughts of her daughter's safety fleeted through her mind. The need to survive washed over her like a fever, slowing her heart to a dull thud.

Father Ashton felt Susanna's surprised panic. The power of it exhilarated him. Still clasping his hand over her mouth, he held her full length against himself. His free hand wandered feverishly over her body, desperately exploring her curves.

"A whore is a deep ditch. She lieth in wait, as for a prey, and increases the transgressors amongst men," he whispered once more into her ear, thrusting his loins against her.

Consumed with lust, Father Ashton's hand fell from Susanna's mouth to her breast and squeezed.

"Please don't do this," Susanna pled in a desperate whisper, "not with my daughter right there."

"What she sees, my lovely Delilah, will be up to you," Father Ashton replied as he buried his hand in the folds of Susanna's skirt, seeking the moist heat hidden beneath it, "for you have tempted and taunted me beyond my ability to refrain from you."

His voice was filled with resolve, and Susanna knew there was nothing she could do to stop him. *This horrible thing is going to happen, no matter what,* she thought with despair.

If you can't beat them, rule them, the voice of her grandmother, Queen, sounded from a distant memory.

Twisting under Father Ashton's roving hands, Susanna turned to face him. She did not want to be raped in front of her daughter. If she fought him, Kelly would surely waken and be scarred for the rest of her life. Though she reviled Father Ashton, she knew the only course to protect her daughter was to either stop him from ravishing her, or to just allow it. Testing his mettle, she pushed against him. Roughly, he grasped her closer.

"You're a priest," she reminded him in an angry whisper, "a man committed to God!"

"Yes, but I am still just a man, and I will finally see done what you have promised for all of these years," Father Ashton replied, his voice low, not a whisper, but still cold and hard, "For our own sakes, He made him who knew no sin to sin, so that we might know the righteousness of God, who will extend to us mercy and forgiveness in all things."

Susanna's fear dissolved into heavy anguish as she convinced Father Ashton to remain silent enough not to disturb her daughter in exchange for her complicity. Numbly, she lay on the hard earthen floor as he pounded his thrusts into her, using her like a rutting animal. Bracing against the pain, her nails dug into his already scarred back, hurling him into ecstasy.

And so it was that an understanding developed between Father Ashton and Susanna. She would cooperate, unresisting to his physical demands, keeping her mouth shut about them, and he would not harm, or alarm, her daughter.

*****

July 15, 1785

Father Ashton stiffly looked down at the squirming bundle Susanna held out for him to see. What did she expect? That he'd take one look at it and dissolve into a sniveling heap of sentiment, dropping to his knees in professions of undying gratitude? She should know better. It unnerved him that she stood silently before him with her cold, blank, stony expression, staring at him expectantly.

He knew Susanna wasn't exactly afraid of him, but she didn't really like him either. She merely tolerated him. It was particularly annoying because she made no efforts to hide that fact. Always polite, she lacked even the pretense of warmth that came from kindness, never giving any more than was required. She allowed him the use of her body but showed no interest in him and seemed devoid of any pleasure herself. That fact alone made him feel weak, less of a man, and was infuriating.

As a rule, Father Ashton loathed the unnecessary chatter that most women indulged in. However, there had been moments when he wished Susanna would speak with him. Just a simple conversation. Twice he had tried. It was useless, and yet it was probably for the best. Most women, lacking in proper intellect and experience, only served to frustrate men when they opened their mouths. Everyone was better off if they kept their empty-headed frivolous chatter amongst themselves.

That she stood before him with a wad of fabric, waiting for him to inspect the sniveling little being she produced that was wrapped inside, was annoying. He wanted to flee.

She is devoid of all intellect! Father Ashton thought, then added with a sigh of relief, *at least she produced a male.*

Because she stood blocking his passage to exit the small room, and out of the tiniest bit of curiosity, his eyes slid towards the bundle she held. The child was completely concealed behind a flap of blanket that was grasped in little flailing hands.

Can she not do anything right? he grumbled to himself.

Unable to resist the urge, he awkwardly raised his hand to move the blanket. Susanna flinched protectively, stilling his hand. He ground out a growl of irritation and gently pushed the baby's fist, still grasping the corner of the blanket in his perfect little fingers, down to his side. The blanket slid down with it.

Two large, beautiful brown eyes looked sleepily up at him as little pink lips puckered, blowing tiny spit bubbles. Father Ashton's chest constricted.

This was the most perfect child he had ever seen! Oh yes, he had seen many newborns, being a priest, and had always believed them to look quite ghastly. They were all little creatures with pointed heads sporting swollen slit eyes over smashed noses and nonexistent lips. They didn't even have enough flesh to fill out their oversized, wrinkled, loose skin, and were usually dappled with hair where it shouldn't be. This child, his son, was different. He was absolutely perfect.

"What is his name?" he breathed, unable to look away.

"Charles," Susanna replied flatly, "Charles Queen."

"Charles is an acceptable name," Father Ashton replied, "he may keep it."

Little Charles had a perfectly round head, plump rosy cheeks, and pink flesh filled skin. His big brown eyes were open wide and studied his father as if he knew that he was the one responsible for his very existence and he was grateful.

This is how God must surely feel, thought Father Ashton, swallowing the tug of emotions that threatened to overwhelm him.

Never in his life had he felt so well satisfied with himself.

Behold, children are a heritage from the Lord... A reward, he silently recited to himself, *Psalms.*

It had been a long and tormented year for him. Days and nights were spent in barely controlled lust and followed by agonizing punishments. Never had he been so miserable. He was plagued by constant thoughts and dreams of Susanna and the need to possess her. Every cell of his being cried out to be near her, see her, and yes, God help him, touch her. The more he tried to resist, the more she occupied his every thought, even haunting his dreams.

He struggled to regain some semblance of control and spent many hours studying the bible, reciting what he believed God wanted and expected of him. *It is good for a man not to touch a woman. He that knows no woman, cares only for the things that belong to the Lord and of how he may please the Lord. But he that has a woman, cares only for the things that are of the world.* To remind himself, he repeated the words, a loose interpretation of several verses found in 1 Corinthians 7, over and over. However, no matter how many times he recited them, he always reverted back to his own wicked thoughts.

Since arriving in the colonies, Father Ashton often fantasized that he was like Abraham of the bible who was called by God to leave his own country, journeying to unknown lands, where he was to become the founder of a new nation. Then, even though Abraham was nearly one hundred years old, God began giving him children, progeny to build a new nation.

Like Abraham, he had also followed God's call to new lands and had tried to live a life of obedience, but after all, he was just a man. Now, though it was unlikely that he should ever have children, here was a male child made from his own loins. It was proof that, like Abraham, God saw him and was pleased and had chosen him to build a legacy. It made perfect sense. It even explained why he was obsessed with Susanna, of all people.

Though Susanna was beautiful, she was not a young woman. She rarely spoke to him, so it wasn't her great intellect that drew his attraction. Obviously, she had no positive social significance. He hadn't understood what it was about her that spellbound him so, but his perfect son suddenly made everything clear. Susanna was his Hagar, the handmaid to

Abraham's wife, Sarah, who gave Abraham his first child, the beginning of his legacy. Beyond that, she was insignificant.

"He's white," Father Ashton proclaimed, withdrawing from his thoughts but still staring at Charles in awe.

"He'll darken up," replied Susanna flatly, then intentionally baiting his temper she continued, using the slave talk that he hated, "it always take time fer dem t' color up, 'specially when they's more white dan not."

Instantly agitated, Father Ashton's face turned hard.

Why must you always open your stupid mouth? he asked silently, stiffly withdrawing his hand from his son. He knew she used slave-talk to annoy him, and he refused to allow her to goad him with it.

"*More white* is a nonsensical term," he arrogantly pushed back at Susanna, who shrugged indifferently.

"My grandmother Queen was from India, not Africa. My momma is a mulatto. My daddy was white, a priest. Charles' daddy, you, are also white and a priest," tilting her head to one side, Susanna locked her gaze into his, then threw the verbal barb she knew would rattle the composure he struggled to maintain, "so then, I guess you could say he's more priest than anything else."

Without another word, Father Ashton spun on his heels and left the cabin in long angry strides.

Chapter Thirty

September 1785

Tired and irritable, Susanna firmly grasped her daughter's hand and tugged her along the steep path which would take them home. Rarely did they venture up the hill, but help was needed in the kitchen, and she was obliged. Besides, she liked helping in the kitchen because it always meant extra supplies. It wasn't unusual that at the end of a day she could take enough supplies home to generously share with her family as well as others. Such was the case that day, so in addition to herding Kelly and carrying baby Charles, she had a large sack slung over her back. It was burdensome and heavy.

"It's bad enough that I'm hauling this load like an old mule, Kelly," she griped, "but you draggin' your feet is gonna trip me up."

"Sorry, Ma," little Kelly responded, even though she wasn't, "but do ya see how pretty the water is shinin'?"

When her mother released her hand to shift the baby, Kelly ran forward with her arms spread, embracing the glory of the river. Susanna looked down the hill past the overseer's house, next to rows of little cabins where the slaves and indentured workers lived, just beyond the fields of yellow tobacco which seemed to pour into the river as the mature plants next to it grew smaller in size. The sun danced over the river in a dazzling display, sparkling across the bright blue trail of slow-moving water. Mineral deposits colored its banks and shallow spots white, as if snow had settled and refused to budge even under the hot summer sun. It was a spectacular contrast of white against the vivid green of the trees and grass growing along the banks. It looked magical.

Having walked up and down the hill all her life, Susanna rarely took time to notice or appreciate its beauty. She smiled at her daughter.

Kelly was at that wonderful age where she was just beginning to discover and explore the world she was in, noticing its beauty with innocence and awe. This was her first experience of looking out from a higher vantage point and she was enchanted. Embracing the joy of watching her, Susanna waited until she was startled by a greeting on the path behind her.

Once a good-looking boy with kind eyes and a jolly spirit, life had not been kind to Joseph Edward Kelach. Growing up in Ireland, he knew that his parents had once deeply loved one another, evidenced by their six children in as many years of marriage. Through the years, love alone did not prove enough to keep them happy as they struggled to provide for their brood. His mother, with so many children to care for and a bent towards complaining, began nagging at her poor husband. Overworked and underpaid and getting no appreciation at home, he escaped to the local pub to fortify himself before going home to his surly wife. Years of failure accompanied with his wife's misery had produced a guilt so great that his spirit simply died. When one day he came home, fully intoxicated, bearing the news that he had lost his job, his wife responded with a storm of insults so berating and unending that the burden simply became too heavy. The very next night he took his own life.

Being the eldest child and a son, the responsibility of providing for the family fell upon Joseph. There was no job too big or too small that he wouldn't do as long as it paid. Most days he was able to honestly put food on the table. When he couldn't do it honestly, his family still had to eat. Stealing a chicken here or there, some vegetables from a garden, and once even a pie resting in an open window, seemed harmless enough. But he grew careless and so was caught. Charged with theft, after a quick appearance in front of a country judge he was placed on the next ship headed for the colonies and straight into the Revolutionary War.

He felt bad about leaving because he never got to say good-bye to his mother or siblings, and he worried about who would provide for them. But then again, it wasn't exactly a choice. With nothing else he could do about it, he simply boarded the ship and watched his home fade off into the horizon. What surprised him was the relief he felt. Suddenly, he was responsible for just one person, himself. It was liberating.

He served just one year with the British Army, seeing no action. When the British troops finally withdrew from the colonies, renamed the United States, in November 1783, he saw his true chance for freedom. Instead of boarding the ship to leave with them, he walked away. However, remaining in the new country proved more than difficult.

Broke, unable to support himself, and with the promise of food and clothing in exchange for honest work, he quickly indentured himself to a plantation that seemed to be the most affluent one around. There, he quickly learned that wealth was not always as it seemed, promises were not always kept, and some abuses were more painful than hunger. He ran away.

Reinventing himself as Edward Kelly hadn't been hard. Indenturing himself with the Jesuit missionaries was the best choice he had ever made. Sure, the days were long, still planting tobacco, but he did not fear being beaten and every night his belly was full. Any extra money he made was his to keep. He worked alongside the slaves and though they didn't embrace him as one of their own, there was a mutual respect between them.

It was the most comfortable period of his life. His skeletal body filled out with muscle and flesh, he had no worries, worked hard, slept hard, and counted off the months until he would be free to leave. By then, he was sure, with proper planning and saving, he would be able to purchase some property where he could settle in, meet a good woman, and raise a happy family.

He had seen Susanna around White Marsh and knew she was a part of the very large Queen family, who were seen as a sort of royalty amongst the slaves. They were mostly hard workers, so had earned the privilege of being fluid, choosing where they worked and how, as long as the job got done, which it always did.

The men were protective of their women and the women quietly ruled them. There were many jokes flying around about the Queen women being queens with no room for a king, but no one was quite sure how they did it. Very few of them were openly tied to a man. No marriages. No cohabitating. No apparent dalliances. Lots of rumors. Never had anyone seen any of the Queen women nag or abuse anyone unless they were crossed. Then, it was said, hell rained down on the poor soul who dared. Instead, they were seen helping in the fields when needed, organizing the children to carry water and support the workers, sharing food, clothing, or whatever else was needed with someone new or down on their luck, and bearing children.

The Queen women had lots of children. From Edward's estimation, the Queen family, spread across five Jesuit missions, represented over half of the entire workforce. He had heard stories of how old Phillis and Nanny's mother arrived at the mission when the man she worked for left his estate to the Jesuits. She continued with them under the same arrangement, then passed that legacy to her children. It was interesting enough but didn't concern him.

Walking up behind Susanna, Edward knew he startled her and was mildly surprised about that fact. It wasn't as if the path wasn't well traveled throughout the day.

"I didn't mean ta scare ya none, lass."

Flustered, Susanna shifted Charles' weight, causing the bundle over her back to shift. The sudden jerk of it nearly toppled her. Edward quickly grabbed the sliding bundle, easing the weight of it so she could balance herself until she was stable.

"Thank you. Sorry. Kelly was just so excited… she's never been up here. I got excited for her. I wasn't paying attention," Susanna rushed on in a flurry of frustration and nerves.

"It seems like you've got quite a load for such a little thing," Edward smiled to put her at ease, "why don't you let me help you?"

"Oh… I don't have much further to go," objected Susanna, relieved that he was already helping her to remove the load from her back.

Edward set the heavy bag, filled with sweet potatoes, corn meal, a sparse slab of bacon and other items, on the ground and winked at little Kelly, who stood staring at him.

"Who you be, mister?" asked Kelly, her fascination with the view replaced with curiosity about him.

Edward looked at her with an exaggerated expression of feigned surprise and hopped to attention.

"Edward Kelly at your service," he drawled, removing his hat in a large sweeping gesture, "and you, lass, are the prettiest thing these eyes have ever seen."

Kelly smiled with a giggle.

"Mr. Kelly…" began Susanna.

"Just Edward, I beg of ya," Edward interrupted, retrieving the bag, "why don't you allow me the honor of escorting you fair maidens to your destination?"

With a nod and a smile and without waiting for Susanna to agree, Edward replaced his hat and began walking. Kelly, basking under the glow of his compliment, happily skipped along beside him. Susanna smiled and trailed along, quickly catching up with them.

"Okay, Edward, I'm Susanna Queen. I live just there," she smiled, relieved not to have to carry the bag any further, and pointed out her cabin to him.

"Another lass?" Edward asked with a nod towards the baby.

"No," she slid the blanket from the baby's face, "this is Charles. Say hello to Edward, Charles."

Swinging the bag at his side, Edward glanced at the baby as he walked and stumbled, hoping Susanna hadn't noticed his misstep. He had expected the baby to have his sister's coloring. The Queen family ranged in color from very dark to nearly white. Susanna could have easily passed as a white woman. Kelly was the color of brown cotton. Charles was even lighter than his mother.

Curious, he thought, recalling other rumors he'd heard about the Queen women. A few of them had married slaves held either on one of the missions or on surrounding plantations, but most remained single. Though almost all of them had children, none claimed the fathers. Even the two sisters, Phillis and Nanny, differed dramatically in coloring. It was widely speculated that Phillis was the child of the man who left the property to the Jesuits, while Nanny must have been fathered by a slave. However, no one had any proof other than their obvious skin color. It was also said that Phillis' children were by one of the priests. Again, it didn't concern him, so he never bothered to ask anyone about it. Besides, he had learned that a person learned more just by listening. Questions shut mouths and the slave population at the missions were very protective of the Queen family

"Ya got yourself a good strong lad, Miss Susanna."

Susanna's cabin stood in a huddle of others. They were mostly occupied by Queen family members, who stopped to stare at them as they passed. Susanna knew word that she had walked home with the white indentured man would quickly get back to her mother who would, within the hour, be at her door, wanting details.

"Simon," she called out to her brother who gawked as they passed, "ya need help catching your eyes when they pop?"

Stifling a chuckle, Edward grinned broadly.

When they arrived at Susanna's door, she turned to him.

"Well, you might as well come on in," she grinned, her eyes sliding over the quarters, "they're gonna talk, so we might as well give em something good to talk about."

Game to be included in causing a slight stir, Edward nodded with a mischievous grin, grasped Kelly's hand, and followed Susanna through the door.

The cabin was small but very clean. A table, oversized for the space, stood in the middle surrounded by several straight-back chairs. Additional chairs were scattered haphazardly, as if Kelly had moved them around while playing. The fireplace on the wall opposite the door was neatly banked with just enough soot to keep it burning evenly. Two rope beds, small but serviceable with straw ticking that had been recently fluffed, were neatly made and rested along opposite walls. Each had a little trunk at the foot. A rope had been strung the length of the cabin and held a blanket dangling at one end. When pulled down the rope, the blanket would just clear the table in the middle. There were no windows. The only opening was the door, which was left open for light and decency.

Susanna handed Edward a tin cup of water, fresh and cool from the river, which he enjoyed while they sat and talked. Before long, Phillis arrived in a flurry of curious energy. Taking it as his cue to leave, Edward playfully tousled Kelly's hair and left with a promise to return.

The Queen family quickly grew used to seeing Edward sitting with Susanna, either inside or in front of her cabin, or happily playing with little Kelly. As a warm friendship grew, they shared confidences. He shared with her the circumstances of his life and the secret to his identity, and she shared details of her life with him, gradually feeding him tidbits of her relationship with Father Ashton.

Edward didn't want to press Susanna about her relationship with Father Ashton, fearing she'd think his interest was other than brotherly affection and concern, but he sensed something was wrong and felt uneasy about it. He had noticed the strained look across her face when she spoke about it. He could tell by the hard set of her shoulders after Father Ashton had visited her that something did not sit well, and she was not happy. When he saw bruises circling her wrists, he could no longer let the matter go.

"Does he hurt you?"

Susanna stiffened, sucked in her breath and held it.

"Not exactly," her voice cracked through the breath she released.

"What does that mean, Susanna?" Edward pushed.

Through tears gone too long unshed, Susanna revealed the whole ugly truth of her arrangement with Father Ashton. Edward was appalled.

"We can make this right," he promised, "so he will *have* to leave you alone."

"I've tried," Susanna protested, "but he'll hurt Kelly and maybe Charles too, or one of my other family members. Besides, I'm pregnant again."

Edward breathed a sorrowful sigh. Susanna had become like one of his sisters. He wasn't able to be with them, but he hoped if any of them found themselves in such a predicament, there would be somebody to stand up for them and help them in his place. With that resolve, he vowed to help Susanna.

And so it was that Edward sought the advice of Father Diderick, a priest whom he fully trusted, and the two came up with a plan.

Chapter Thirty One

February 1786

Outraged, Father Ashton sat in his finely appointed parlor opposite his old friend and Superior, Father John Carroll. The dainty cup, comically delicate in his large hands, shook and clanked in the saucer as he tried unsuccessfully to set it down. Liquid sloshed over the rim as he steadied it with both hands.

"Is this a joke?" he asked in outrage, as if unable to believe the accusation brought to him.

The set of Father Carroll's jaw said that he was serious.

"That is preposterous!" exclaimed Father Ashton angrily, pushing himself up from the chair. He stood with his thoughts in a scattered panic, then plopped back down.

"It would seem that the indentured man, Edward Kelly, filed a formal Petition of Paternity with the magistrate just today," Father Carroll spoke in a slow, steady tone, secretly enjoying Father Ashton's distress, "I offered to bring the document out to you," Father Carroll lied, "but the magistrate claims he must do it himself. For legal reasons."

"*Kelly* filed the paternity papers?" Father Ashton fired, "I saved that scoundrel! Gave him a job, a place to live, food in his belly!"

"In *this*," Father Carroll folded his hands together, placing his index fingers against his lips, "his allegiance is most *definitely* to Susanna, and he does not mind the scandal or particularly care about your outrage."

Father Ashton pulled a thin flask from under the chair cushion, uncorked it, and filled his teacup. He took a long deep draw, emptying the cup, refilled it, then replaced the flask back under the cushion without offering any to Father Carroll.

"Well, it isn't as if this sort of thing is new or unheard of," he chuckled, "half of the Queen family are the whelps of former priests."

Father Carroll wasn't amused.

"But none have been declared as such," he responded coldly, pointing out the obvious, "and none have become an embarrassment to the church."

"Can Kelly even do that," asked Father Ashton doubtfully, feeling the calming effects of the liquor, "even if it were true? It is none of his business."

"Is it true?"

Father Carroll leaned forward to press the matter when Father Ashton didn't respond. After a moment of silence, Father Ashton laughed.

"Your silence tells me that it is true. To be honest, I wasn't completely surprised. People talk. But I must ask, what are your feelings for this woman?"

Father Ashton looked at Father Carroll incredulously.

"She is no more than a broomstick to me."

Father Carroll nodded.

"Very well. Then we will defend the matter for you."

He picked up his cup and pushed it towards Father Ashton, indicating the subject was closed, business was over, and they were back on friendlier terms. Father Ashton filled it from his flask.

"I had a similar situation once," Father Carroll mused, "lovely little house wench in England. Tossed her a few coins and she scampered away."

The following evening, after a visit from the magistrate, Father Ashton repented, punishing himself with savage blows across his back. Then, with a belly full of liquor to dull the pain and numb his conscience, he went to Susanna's cabin.

*****

Susanna was waiting. She knew Father Ashton had been served with the petition that day and was going to be angry. Edward had offered to stay in her cabin to protect her, but she couldn't let him. She didn't want to be responsible for anyone getting hurt, most especially Edward. He had proven himself to be a good friend and ally. Although he was young and strong, she wasn't sure he would be able to overpower Father Ashton, who was used to pain, if the situation became violent, which it was surely to do. Besides, she wanted no witnesses because she wasn't sure that she wouldn't kill Father Ashton herself if she were forced to defend herself.

When she had first seen Father Ashton's back, with thick layers of scars over skin that was mottled with long, angry, red and purple streaks that were splotched with green and blue bruises, she was horrified. She asked him about it several times, but her questions were met with cold silence and an icy warning to never mention it again. To anybody. She didn't, but she watched and listened.

She eventually learned that his wounds were self-inflicted. While at first it confounded her that anyone would intentionally injure themselves *repeatedly*, before long she began to understand why he did it and it gave her power.

Father Ashton was a sanctimonious, self-righteous, and arrogant man. He held the delusional belief that he was an extension of God's hand sent to live in the human world amongst lowly creatures, other people. That his divine self had to suffer the embodiment of human form was his cross to bear while fulfilling his higher purpose. That he also suffered human impulses, desires, wants, and needs, was a foul and exasperating element of his existence. Believing pain was not only the by-product of survival but also the means to get closer to God, he mercilessly punished himself with savage creativity.

She knew she was the cause of most of his angst. It was her only weapon against him. Her power and revenge. When she felt him looking at her, she moved more fluidly, breathed from her chest, tilted her head in just such a way, and silently spoke her revenge, *this is gonna be painful and I'm not one bit sorry* – all to make his blood boil with desire for her, which must be punished.

For her, it had become a calculated game. When he hurt her, she always spoke a silent warning to him, *you'll be paying for that*. Then, she waited for the opportunity to absently thrust her chest forward and push out her bottom to raise his lust. Just enough to result in the guilt and shame that must be punished, but not usually enough to spark his lust into action. When he did take her, not only did he brutally beat himself because of it, but she also got to see the results of her actions across his back. That gave her some small comfort in bearing it.

It was a complicated and twisted relationship that Susanna did not know how to escape, but desperately wanted to protect her children from.

When Edward came up with the plan to have Father Ashton removed from White Marsh, she felt as if her life had been saved. By getting a public, legal, declaration of paternity against Father Ashton, the church would be forced to also find that he took advantage of his position there by having a sexual relationship with her. Because he violated his vows and it had become a matter of public knowledge, the church would have no other choice but to dismiss him. They hoped that the church would remove him immediately to avoid the scandal. If not, it was going to be a dangerous time for Susanna. Either way, she knew she was going to have to do something drastic to save her skin. That is why she developed a plan.

Earlier in the day, after settling the children at her mother's house, she asked for Queen's old whip. Following a multitude of questions and reassurances from Susanna that everything would be okay, Phillis sadly went to the trunk where it was stored, neatly coiled and wrapped in burlap, and retrieved it. Handing it to her daughter, she kept hold, pulling it back a bit when Susanna reached for it.

"The most important thing you've got to do is take care of yourself, child. For the children, if for no other reason."

Unshed tears stung the back of Susanna's eyes as she nodded.

Waiting in the dark cabin, she was ready for him. She had moved the table from the center of the room, pushing it with the chairs against the wall and into the corner. She stood tall and proud, whip in hand, opposite the door and in front of the fireplace.

Riding a storm pushed by rage, Father Ashton burst through the door in a drunken fury. Susanna's heart raced but she was in control and did not move. She saw a glimmer of sudden confusion in Father Ashton's eyes when he entered, but it vanished instantly when they landed upon her.

"I'll kill you!" he roared leaping towards her, his claw-like hands grasping for her neck.

Growing up, Susanna loved it when Queen pulled out her whip. She didn't do it often, but when she did, she always made it interesting and fun, showing the children how she could slice through tree branches or gently coil it around their arms. *It's all in the arms and the flick of the wrist,* she'd said. Then, she helped whoever wanted to try, letting each of them have a turn. Raining compliments down upon each of them, she assured them that, with practice, one day they could be as good as her. They knew it wasn't true, but that wasn't the point. It was fun and they felt special.

Susanna wasn't as good as some of her family members, but she could crack the whip and reign it back into a coil with the flick of her wrist. It looked impressive enough to fool an untrained eye into believing that she knew what she was doing. No one needed to know that she didn't have either precision or control. After all, there never really was a reason for her to have such a skill. However, threatened with the rage of a man who liked to whip himself, she was ready to turn the tables on him. It was risky, but she was desperate.

When Father Ashton lunged for her, she leapt aside.

Glad he's good and drunk, thought Susanna when she saw him stumble.

It all happened exactly as she planned. When Father Ashton stumbled, Susanna used her foot to shove him down. Then, stepping back, she flicked the whip, keeping half of its length coiled around her hand due to the size of the room. It cracked over his back, causing him to buckle and freeze with a shock of pain. Susanna spoke in that instant, using the same icy cold tone he used to frighten her, and for the first time she addressed him by his given name.

"You've been a bad man, John, very bad, and God doesn't like it."

Father Ashton spun around to face her, heaving with shock and fear. But there was something else that Susanna didn't expect to see. Respect? Pleasure? She sucked in her breath and held it until her lungs hurt, in desperate need of oxygen. Then, taking a long calming breath, she pushed forward.

"Turn back around, John. Now! So I can do God's work."

With another flick of her wrist, a soft whirring sound ended with a crack in the air. Father Ashton startled and twitched. Then, to her surprise, he slowly pushed himself up and turned to the wall where he placed his hands and leaned into it.

"Forgive me, Father," he cried to the ceiling, "for I am not worthy."

Susanna knew there was no room for mercy. Father Ashton did not respect mercy. He loved no one, not even the God in whose name he prayed.

"You are mean," Susanna cried out with a flick of her wrist. Over and over, she hurled back at him all the insults he had dealt her, punctuating them with a bite of the lash across his back.

And so it was that Susanna and Father Ashton developed an even more twisted relationship built upon his desperate need to be punished and her need for revenge against him. Through it, they became intertwined in a contorted distortion of need.

Susanna remained silent to the court regarding the petition for paternity and the charges that Father Ashton had fathered Charles, so it was dismissed. Edward Kelly was removed from White Marsh, finishing his term of indenture under Father Bernard Diderick, who had sworn out an affidavit with the court supporting Edward Kelly's claim of paternity and charging Father Ashton and Susanna Queen with fornication.

In 1787, Father Diderick made a formal complaint to the church Superior, Father John Carroll, pushing the matter. To avoid any potential scandal, Father Carroll opened an internal investigation. In January 1788, he informed Father Diderick that there was no evidence to support any claim that Father Ashton had had a sexual relationship with Susanna Queen.

Chapter Thirty Two

July 23, 1788

The only sounds were the steady drumming beat of rain as it pounded the already water-logged ground, the crack of lightening, and the booming call of thunder. No one spoke because after sitting together in the small single room for two days they had run out of things to say. Even the children ceased their play. Curling up in a heap against and across one another like a litter of puppies, they napped or simply lay watching the adults study their hands in boredom.

Because of the rain, the firewood which provided the only light or heat to the cabins was soaked through. The people of the quarters moved several of the piles into the barn so it could dry out. Then, they agreed to move into larger groups, doubling, even tripling, the occupants of each cabin in an effort to preserve what fuel they could.

Phillis, with her children all grown and having the rare privilege of living alone, opened her home to Proteus, Gervais, and Ned, along with their wives and children. It was crowded to say the least, but they were family and that's what families did. No one thought they would be together for more than a day or so. Just until the rain stopped.

At first it seemed like a reunion more than a shelter. Though they all lived on the mission just houses away from one another, they were normally too busy with their own chores and families to get many opportunities to gather for casual time together. The women enjoyed exchanging recipes and tidbits of gossip they dared not repeat amongst others. The brothers joked and poked at one another. By the end of two days, there was no more gossip, the recipes were forgotten, jokes were no longer funny, and boredom settled in.

Finally, able to stand it no more, Phillis stood and went to the door, cracking it open just enough to peek out.

"Wind is picking up," she announced the obvious.

The wind pressed against the door, assaulting her with rain. She pushed her weight against it to force it shut. Swiping her sleeve across her wet face, she turned back to the room and her family. She was irritated.

"Are we just gonna sit in the dark and sigh all day?" she asked, hands on her hips.

"Mama got a wet stripe from head to toe," laughed Proteus, her third son born just minutes before his twin, Gervais, who he chucked on the head, "Look! Just a strip of wet where she cracked open the door."

Gervais was not amused to be woken with a smack to his head.

"What ya go an do that for?" he grumbled, shoving his brother back with his shoulder, "I ain't botherin' you."

"Just think it's funny is all."

"Well, I don't, an' I was tryin' ta sleep."

"How much sleepin' can a man do?"

"However much the good Lord can give him if his dumb brother'll leave 'im alone."

"Two full grown men bickering like children," Phillis scolded, "you being fathers too," she added, sucking through her teeth.

"This ain't good," sighed Ned, "not a bit. The crops are ruined for sure."

"I ain't sorry 'bout that. Not a bit," Gervais stated with a hard voice, absently covering his good hand over his other, splinted, one.

The room fell into awkward silence. Father Ashton was angry at Gervais over, well, everything. It wasn't unusual for Father Ashton to become focused upon a victim then follow behind them for days until he became focused upon someone new. It was unusual for Gervais, who was a hard worker, to draw such unwanted attention. Confident in his work, he did the worst thing possible, he talked back to Father Ashton.

A punch to the gut accompanied by a gruff warning never to do it again hadn't set well with Gervais. Instead of cowering in fear as he was expected to do, he pulled himself up tall, spreading his shoulders wide, and glared back into the eyes of Father Ashton in silent but direct defiance. Moments later, four men crossed the field and grabbed Gervais then held him while Father Ashton twisted his middle finger until it snapped out of place. As if that wasn't bad enough, from that day forward Father Ashton hounded him, shadowing his every move, while spouting a steady stream of criticism and insults laced with bible verses. All designed to goad a response from Gervais which would give Father Ashton an excuse to do worse. Far worse.

But Gervais, proud and stubborn, wasn't foolish. He knew the kind of damage Father Ashton regularly inflicted upon the slaves. He had seen how many of them had been beaten and tortured. Never so bad that they were rendered unable to work and never on their dominate side. Over time, their hands became disfigured and misshapen, and they were never able to use them normally. Gervais bit his tongue, bided his time, and prayed that Father Ashton would quickly become preoccupied with someone else. It took over two long weeks, far longer than usual. Gervais felt bad to be so relieved when Father Ashton pounced upon a new victim, but at least it was no longer him.

A sudden pounding on the door broke through the silence.

"De river risin'!" a male voice called through the door before Phillis could open it, "gots ta move de livestock!"

In an instant, the room filled with activity as the men grabbed their hats and raced out the door to do what needed to be done. It was a welcome respite from boredom. That evening when they returned water-logged and weary with exhaustion, they were greeted with a warm bowl of stew and a thick slice of cornbread drizzled with honey.

"This ain't good," sighed Gervais, clawing at his closely cropped wet curls, "if it don't stop raining…"

A loud splintering followed by a hard thud shook the cabin. Ned jumped to the door, opening it just as a series of claps followed by a resounding boom exploded above them. A rumble resonated through the cabin and bounced off the trembling walls. As if orchestrated for effect, multiple bolts of lightning ripped through the sky. Light flashed across the yard giving him blinking peeks of a large tree laying just a few paces from the door.

That night, the cabin shook and trembled under the fury of the storm. Wind howled and screamed like a demon circling it in search of entry. No one slept and no one spoke; there was no use in competing with the haunt of the storm.

Long before sun-up, one of the children screamed out in panicked terror. By the time the adults were fully alert to assess the problem, a drove of mice invaded the room. Possessing no fear, they scampered in from under the door and squeezed their way in through the chinking of the walls, then scurried up to the rafters in droves, all seeking higher ground.

Fear and panic dominated the cabin. Shadows of flailing arms, swinging blankets, and people swatting with anything they could lay their hands upon danced across the room to the cacophony of screams, squeals, thunder, wailing, and gushing water.

The first rush of water gushed under the door then pushed it open with a bang, flooding the cabin in a wave. Hysteria ensued with the sudden shock of finding themselves ankle-deep in cold water.

"Stop!" Phillis called out, pressing her fingers to her temple in a quick gesture to gather her wits.

Like statues, they froze, eyes wide as saucers, sliding between one another.

"The river is flooding!"

Hysteria shifted to purpose.

"We gotta move up the hill," Proteus exclaimed, plucking up his youngest child, standing nearly knee-deep in the rising water, and placing her upon his wife's hip before grabbing the next child.

Babies and toddlers were quickly tied to their mothers and older siblings, leaving the men unencumbered to assist everyone. Trembling with fear and trepidation, they sloughed through the rapidly rising water and fled the cabin into a world eerily transformed.

*****

Cabins groaned in distress as they struggled to stand against the violent onslaught of rising water, wind, waves, and debris. Water fell in swirling torrents and pelted against them only to twist back and slam them again. They were nearly swimming more than walking as they pushed through waist high water. Lightening flashed and booming thunder threatened violence against them. There was no choice but to push forward.

The Queen family joined others making their way to higher ground. Babies, insulted by wet and cold, cried. Small children, afraid, clung closely to the bigger ones who set their jaws and continued. A mother screamed as her child was swept away, grabbed by the roots of a tree speeding by. Her shrill cries, muted by thunder and carried by the wind, were unintelligible and desperate, as if a fiend had swept in and snatched them out of the air before they could be heard.

Climbing the hill to where the main house stood, none looked back to see through the flashes of lightening what had become of their homes. There was nothing they could do and no point in rushing towards heartache. Gathering in the barn, the people of the mission huddled together in shocked silence, comforting their children as they listened to the storm rage on.

The following day the children became restless. Grouping together by age as children naturally do, they played. The younger children imitated their parents in normal life. The older children played a game of dropping stones and picking up sticks. All were quiet in deference to the grim worry of their parents.

Phillis organized the women into chores, dividing the responsibility of cooking, tending to wounds sustained in their flight, and removing the waste of so many people. The men took turns keeping watch over the livestock, moved the previous day to the back side of the hill and then higher. They also constantly assessed the damage to the barn, main house, and kitchen, to ensure everyone's safety. All prayed.

By noon the following day, there was a lull in the storm. All rejoiced that it had finally blown itself out. Then the wind shifted and they were hit equally hard from the other direction for the remainder of the afternoon and into the evening. That night, the storm finally blew over and the people were able to sleep.

The next morning, Phillis stood on the side of the hill and waited to see what the light would reveal. The sun dawned bright and hot, slowly unveiling the destruction. Unable to take it in all at once, she pressed her fingers to her eyes and struggled to meld, bit by bit, what she saw to reality.

The river had pronounced its superiority. Rising to an incredible level, it had claimed all of the land around them. The hill, their refuge, had been transformed to an island surrounded by violently rushing water. Acres and acres of crops carefully planted in the spring were swallowed and gone. Of the cabins that still stood, and there were few, only the peaks of their rooves could be seen. Trees, their thick round trunks that once stretched endlessly towards the sky as if they reached for heaven, lay scattered across high grounds like broken soldiers on a battlefield. Full branches had been twisted free from mature trees and tossed in amongst twigs and leaves, making mangled heaps that stretched across every inch of what little land there was. Limbs and trees with their roots still attached bobbed and spun in the racing current. Hundreds of years of growth wasted in the time span of one horrible storm. Chairs, articles of clothing, and portions of what was once a cabin sped by in the rushing water. Fish slid by where they shouldn't be.

Shaking, Phillis sank to her knees, then down, where she stayed until horror turned to numb escape. She realized this wasn't their first hurricane. In that moment they were all safe. Later, the water would recede, and they would rebuild. They always rebuilt, slowly putting their lives back together until the devastation became just a distant memory, a salute to the struggle of survival. Though this time was worse by far, that made it no different. Once again, they would make it through together. They would replant, rebuild, and reclaim their lives. They would thrive.

Chapter Thirty Three

May 11-18, 1789

Assembling in the chapel of White Marsh on May 11, 1789, were Fathers James Pellentz, Robert Molyneux, John Ashton, Charles Sewall, James Walton, and Henry Pile. There, they met to discuss the concerning issues they each had with regards to their respective missions. On the agenda were finances, including their wages and pensions, fundraising and financing, the new academy at Georgetown, the overabundance of slaves being supported by the missions, and most importantly, the selection of the first Bishop to the United States.

The first day was reserved for travel and greeting one another. The second and third days they discussed finances, securing their wages and pensions, and the distribution of the profits from tobacco. The fourth day they established a chain of command regarding the new academy at Georgetown and the necessity of appointing a clergyman as Principle there. The fifth day they discussed slaves.

Historically, the Jesuits tried not to separate slave families. But due to the expenses of having to rebuild because of the damage wrought from two hurricanes in as many years, as well as declining crops, the expanding slave count was too expensive to maintain. Additionally, with so many people engaging in commerce, buying, selling, and trading from their gardens, they had created a situation where the Jesuits were in competition with the slaves in selling their produce. It drove up prices for those items which had to be purchased.

Something had to be done to save the missions. As a solution, the priests agreed that the managers of each mission would determine exactly how many slaves were necessary to maintain their mission. The rest must be sold. Once a number was established, all superfluous slaves were to be sold every three years, including anyone over the age of forty-five years and any children too young to be productive. Additionally, slaves were no longer permitted to buy or sell any items from other missions or plantations, or engage in commerce in any way without specific and express permission of their mission manager.

The sixth day, a Sunday, was reserved for worship and prayer. On the seventh day, they voted to elect John Carroll as the first Bishop to the United States.

*****

July 13, 1789

Rain turned to steam under the golden summer sun. Leaves from a giant oak tree gently rustled in the breeze as it shrugged off the last remnants of a summer shower, releasing a cascade of shimmering droplets that looked like magic raining over the Queen family, who crowded under it. No one there noticed the beauty of it as they huddled together under the leafy canopy, making room for everyone until they stretched outwards, shoulder to shoulder, baking in the moist heat. No one minded the additional moisture or the heat, all were focused upon the matter at hand. It was of the utmost of importance and the family's sole focus.

Although nothing had been announced by the priests, everyone upon the missions knew of the Jesuits intention to reduce the number of workers. Families would be divided, couples would be ripped apart, contact between parents and children severed. With nothing to be done about it, the slaves waited in excruciating anticipation.

Father Ashton knew that word of an impending reduction in the number of slaves had spread and wielded it about as a weapon. Added to the constant fear of personal injury was the ultimate threat of being sold. No one felt safe. The strain of that threat collided into reality if Father Ashton's attention was drawn to you, it was terrifying. No one dared to call attention upon themselves. Several of the slaves began plotting an escape, planning to self-free themselves and their families.

The Queen family was in a different position. With only a few exceptions, they were all free and always had been. Every one of them had been born at one of the missions where they grew up watching their parents and older family members work, passively learning how things were done. When they became of age, they slid easily into a job, generally the same as their parents. They were all leaders who lead by the example of hard work and good sense, so they were respected and trusted, but there were a lot of them.

It started with one woman, Queen, who had three children, Phillis, Ralph and Nanny. They had twenty-eight children between them, twenty-six still living, that ranged in age from fifty-four to twenty-three. Those children also had children and grandchildren. In all, the Queen family numbered over two-hundred people. That didn't include the slaves who were married to a family member, or those who were born by a woman outside of the family network. Though the family provided a solid workforce in the middle, it also held many elderly people and youths who were unable to work but still had to be provided for.

If what they had heard was true, that anyone over the age of forty-five or too young to work was to be sold, what did it mean for their family? Were they to be sent away? Would some of them be allowed to stay and others forced to go? What about the husbands or wives that were slaves? What did they need to do to purchase their freedom? Where would they go when they left? How soon was all of this to take place?

So many questions without answers were quickly churning into panic. "Listen up," hollered Ned through cupped hands, "we can't boil the water before the chicken's plucked. Somebody's gotta go and find out what's what."

Silence blanketed the yard as all eyes shot to him in silent agreement. Without any formal discussion, it was unanimously decided that he should be the one to approach Father Ashton.

*****

December 1789

Sucking in his breath through clinched teeth, Ned anxiously swiped his palms across his shirt. Grateful for the cold, he paced nervously before Father Ashton's door. Several times he had spoken to the irascible man only to be put off and rudely dismissed with no answers. Because several of the slaves whom they had known their entire lives had been recently sold with no notice, the Queen family was rapidly growing anxious.

The laws regarding slaves and their children stated that any child born of a slave man was to be a slave *as their fathers were.* So, most of the Queen women did not openly identify the fathers of their children. Without a place to point a finger, proving they were the progeny of a slave, the children were then presumed to be free. However, there were exceptions within the family.

Nanny had married a slave, Tom, who fathered all of her twelve children. But neither she nor any of her children were ever considered to be slaves. Nanny's daughter, Mima, had married Allen, a slave. They had two children and were expecting another. By virtue of their dark skin, Mima was considered a slave until Allen's death, and their children were all slaves. Monica, another of Nanny's daughters, had married a slave named Will and they had three children who were considered slaves, but Monica wasn't. Ralph and his wife Nel, also a slave, had three children and although the children were considered free, they still needed to secure Nel's freedom. Of course, there was Susanna, who had two children by slaves and one who was mulatto. Neither she nor any of her children were considered slaves. But all these assumptions about statuses were from before.

Before life changed. Before they needed to worry about individual family member's birth status. Before Father Ashton. They needed to know exactly what position Father Ashton was going to take regarding the family so they would also know exactly how many people it was going to be necessary to buy.

Gathering his courage, Ned used his fist to pound on Father Ashton's door. When no one answered, he pounded again, only harder. Ned knew Father Ashton was home but what could he do if the man refused to answer his door? Frustrated, he lifted his fist to deliver another series of blows when the door flew open.

With one hand on his hip and the other on the door frame to block entry, Father Ashton stood with his face contorted into an irritated scowl.

"Ned," he grumbled, raking his hand through his hair to his beard, "what do you want?"

Careful not to further agitate him, Ned diverted his gaze, keeping it on the ground rather than look at him directly in the eyes.

"We need ta talk."

Father Ashton moved aside and invited him in with a jerk of his head.

Working under the assumption that any Queens born into the family were free, Ned chose to address only those family members who had married into the family as slaves. Scraping his hat off his head, he said a silent prayer then began talking.

"There's been talk that you'll be gettin' rid of some people. The Queen family is the biggest family here, so we figure some of us is gonna have ta go too," began Ned, ignoring Father Ashton's piercing glare. "We're grateful for our time here, an we wanna keep things right with the church, but we gotta stay together."

"You're grateful…" stated Father Ashton icily, "*grateful!*"

"Yessir."

Father Ashton stepped to the window. Turning from Ned, he looked out towards the hill that sloped down to the fields and quarters. There, he noticed that people were working industriously. His gaze slid across the landscape to the river. Its banks were full and the currant was swift. Unable to resist the urge, he searched for Susanna, who he did not see. For a long moment he remained silent. The air was heavy with his rage and pregnant with thought.

"Generations upon generations, born, cared and provided for, fed, sheltered. And all you have to say is that you're *grateful*?"

He turned to Ned and gestured for him to move closer. Keenly aware of Father Ashton's tendency towards sudden violence coupled with an intense dislike for him, Ned didn't want to be any nearer to him than was necessary. When Ned didn't move, Father Ashton flicked his fingers at him once again. Ned had no choice. Hesitantly, cautiously, he moved closer. Father Aston laid his hand upon Ned's back and slid it up to his neck, where he applied a slight pressure.

Ned stiffened at the touch.

"Do you see all those houses?" Father Ashton asked, increasing the pressure to a faint squeeze.

Ned gulped and nodded.

"Mine. All mine. The land and everything on it, is mine," Father Ashton squeezed steadily harder, "and that includes *everyone* who lives on it."

Ned was angry but frightened. His neck felt as if it were being held in a vise, but he knew he could easily end that. He was much larger and stronger than Father Ashton. What frightened him was that he so badly wanted to retaliate with lethal force. Many nights he had lain awake fantasizing about how he could exact just retribution for all the injuries and pain the man had inflicted upon various members of his family. He had prayed for a reason, any reason, to do just that. He had even prayed that when the time came, they would be alone, with no witnesses.

Finally his prayers were being answered, but it was too late. It pained him. His family needed Father Ashton in order to purchase their loved ones and preserve their families. If he were to disappear, it could very well delay things beyond the time to save them. Besides, who knew who would replace him to run the mission. A new caretaker would take his time before negotiating with his family and they needed a fair price quickly. They simply couldn't afford to pay premium rates for healthy adults.

Ned pushed down the urge to overpower Father Ashton, swallowing the bile that rose because of it. A sharp tang burned his throat as it slid back down to boil in his gut. He pushed his head up, elongating his neck for some relief. Father Ashton's grip tightened.

"I understand. That's why we want to pay," Ned grounded out, "we want to be fair."

"Is it fair that your family drops brat after brat knowing that they can't provide for them, and without a care that you will require me to do so?"

Father Ashton pushed Ned's face into the window with a thud. Anticipating the glass splintering under the pressure, Ned's eyes squeezed shut. The window held. Father Ashton shoved Ned's head against the windowsill, releasing him. His head struck, cutting his temple, and bounced off. Ned saw stars as he stumbled. He shook his head to clear it and blood trickled down his face. Father Ashton drew his fist back and thrust it into Ned's belly. Falling to his knees, Ned rasped for air. Father Ashton stood over him with his hands cupped. Exhilarated, he laughed his pleasure at seeing Ned on his knees and gasping for air.

"Under the circumstances, I would expect you to pray," Father Ashton chided, "and the bible is very clear on how. Do you hear me, Ned?"

When Ned didn't respond, Father Ashton grasped his hair and pulled his face up.

"Look at me when I speak to you!"

Ned obediently opened his eyes. Father Ashton smiled.

"That's much better. Now," he exclaimed in a voice filled with false bravado, "all is not lost for your family. Nothing will immediately happen, so there is time for you and your family to gain a proper understanding of your positions here. Psalms 30 makes it very clear. Learn it, then go and return to me with the respect that God requires. Now repeat after me.

"Oh Lord, this man hast brought up my soul from the grave and kept me alive that I should not go down to the pit of hell. Of this saint, I give thanks at the remembrance of his holiness. Though his anger is but for a moment, in his favor is life. Though our weeping may endure, in the end there is joy in knowing that in my prosperity, because of his gifts, I shall never be moved."

As Ned repeated Father Ashton's twisted interpretation of the bible, rage coursed through him, sizzling his veins. When Father Ashton threw him from the house, it was a welcome relief. Ned collected his hat, which landed several feet away, and angrily slapped it across his knee several times before placing it upon his head. Then, he went to speak with his mother.

*****

Fueled by the unsated need for violence, Father Ashton kicked the door to Susanna's cabin open only to find that she was not there. Yanking a chair from the table, he turned it towards the door and sat to wait.

When Susanna approached her cabin, she immediately noticed that the door was not only open, but it was askew, hanging lopsided from just the upper hinge. That could mean only one thing, John was there and in a fit of temper.

With a quick squeeze to Charles' hand, she told him to go join his sister at her mother's cabin. When he hesitated, she nudged him along and stood watching him go.

"And Charles," she called after him before he rounded the corner of a cabin and out of sight, "don't come back until I come to get you!"

Slowly walking on, Susanna cautiously approached her cabin door. With the sun in her eyes she could not see in, but heard Father Ashton's heavy breathing even before he spoke. Unwilling to enter, she lingered outside.

"You are plotting against me!"

Unsure how to respond, Susanna remained silent. She knew Ned was determined to get some answers and had tried several times to talk to him.

She had not known that Ned was going to push the matter again on that day.

But what else could they do? The Queens were a family and were determined to stay together. In order to do that they needed information. Specifically, who they would be required to purchase and for how much.

Further agitated by Susanna's silence, Father Ashton leapt to his feet and closed the distance between them in two long strides. When she jumped back away from him, he slapped his hands onto her shoulders, turned her around, and marched her like an errant child through the door.

"What in God's name are you planning?" he asked as he pushed her into the chair he had just occupied, "exactly."

Susanna took a long slow breath, drawing it deep into her lungs, she blew it out slowly.

"Nothing," she shrugged, "we're not planning anything in God's name. Just ours."

Father Ashton slapped her.

"Try again."

Susanna's face stung and her eyes filled with tears that spilled down her cheeks.

"We know we gotta go. Our family has gotten too big. We see how the mission is selling off people and have heard about how people who can't work have to leave. More than half us Queens are too old or too young to work. All we want is to go together. That means we gotta buy some of us, and we will, fair and square, but we need to know for how much, so we can plan."

Father Ashton laughed dark and mirthlessly.

"Revelations. The unbelieving and the abominable, the whores and all liars, shall have their part in the lake which burneth with fire and brimstone," rage smoldered in his voice as he spoke, misquoting the bible, twisting it to suit his purpose, "for those who give themselves over to fornications, going after strange flesh, are set forth as an example to suffer the vengeance of the Lord."

Susanna knew he was prepared to make her suffer and there was nothing she could do to stop him. Her eyes pleaded for mercy, and it sickened him. Holding her by the hair, he punched her squarely in the face. Pain exploded in her head behind the crunching sound of cartilage breaking. Intoxicated by the blood spurting from her nose, Father Ashton placed his cheek against hers, breathing in the coppery scent of her blood as it mingled with his own sweat.

"Your family can rot in hell," he breathed, "but until then, they are mine and will go nowhere until and unless I allow it. You will never leave with my son. You Queens think you are so smart, playing coy by not naming the fathers of your bastard children. I am not ignorant. I know every one of those children were fathered by slaves. Just look at Kelly! Spawn of Satan. Child of a whore and a slave. She is the child that bonds you to me as my slave. Think of that every time you lay your eyes upon her."

Unable to believe what he was saying, Susanna closed her eyes and slid from the chair to her knees. When she opened her eyes again, she met his cruel hard gaze with raw anguish. A scream built in her chest then rose up her throat, exploding in a siren of rage and bitter torment. The punches that followed did not silence her, but the chair crashing over her head did.

Father Ashton did not mind that Susanna could not respond or that her head lolled from side to side when he took her.

When she finally did open her eyes, he pulled her to her feet. With the command that she dare not fall, he placed the whip in her hand. In hiccupping sobs, Susanna begged him to leave. When he refused, she viciously applied the whip against him with all the rage she had before sinking down into a corner where she stayed.

Later, lying bloodied and in pain with her cheek pressed to the cool floor, all she could hear was the wind from an incoming storm scraping the branches of a tree against the roof, the birds chattering outside her window, the creaking of her door swinging loosely on one hinge, and the distant crunching of heels across the gravel as Father Ashton stumbled home.

*****

Overhead, the sky was clear, the clouds blown away with the storm. After a while, the sun disappeared as night fell and the earth was still. Not even the birds exchanged their normal evening chatter as the people of the quarters settled down to bed without their normal rustling. It was as if the world held its breath in dreadful anticipation.

The next morning dawned with low hanging clouds that blanketed the earth in fog, a final shield to dim from clarity the beginning of a new era upon White Marsh marking a period of fear and misery.

In their separate cabins, the Queen family rose and sleepily began their morning rituals. Phillis threw fresh coals into her fireplace and placed a pot of stew left over from the previous evening meal over it. Mothers gingerly drizzled precious golden honey over cornbread. Children scrubbed the sleep from their eyes with their fists. The men slid into their pants before standing, then slipped out to relieve themselves before stiffly making their way to work. The horses stomped a demand to be fed as harnesses were prepared.

Ned stood in the open doorway of his cabin, waiting. He wouldn't spend much time thinking about the previous evening. He didn't have the luxury of time and needed to stay mentally alert, prepared for anything.

He had gone to his mother's home and let her clean the wound on his head, fussing over him as she did, and wrap his bruised, possibly broken, ribs. As she fussed, he told her what Father Ashton had said. Though she didn't respond, he knew she would think about it, mulling it over, around and around in her head, until she developed a plan.

Then Susanna showed up.

Beautiful, bright-skinned Susanna with the angular jaw and perky slender nose. Always clean and neatly put together with fresh skirts and blouses in good repair. Her hair, always neatly wound into a large knot nearly the size of her head and secured just above her neck. Susanna, who was proud of her appearance and carried herself that way. Never with her head down or slouching, she always squared her broad shoulders and walked with purpose.

That was not the Susanna who showed up at their mother's house. She had been unrecognizable. Ned cringed remembering. Falling through the door, she laid on the floor naked and bloody. Her hair was a tangled and bloody mass, splintered with bits of wood and debris. Her face was smeared and splattered with blood over deep purple bruises that were already forming. Bite marks were on her shoulders and arms. Her nose, swollen several times its normal size, was crooked and obviously broken.

When Ned picked her up and moved her to their mother's bed, she held onto him, desperately clinging as if for her dear life. When their mother joined them there, Susanna grabbed onto her too. Frantically, she threw her arms around their necks and pulled on them as if to shield herself from whomever would do this to her.

Ned didn't need to ask. He knew.

Back at Father Ashton's for the second time in a day, he didn't knock. He stormed through the door to find Father Ashton laying naked across his bed. Ned found no satisfaction in the angry red welts, puckered and bleeding, that spread from Father Ashton's neck to his buttocks. They belonged there. He deserved worse and Ned was the perfect one to give worse to him.

Grabbing him by his foot, Ned yanked a surprised and frightened Father Ashton off of the bed. Crashing to the floor, he rolled into a twisted heap just as Ned's fist slammed into his jaw.

"If you hurt my sister again," Ned, his voice hard and cold, growled into Father Ashton's ear, "Ever. Again. I will kill you. I swear."

Without another word, he left the way he had entered, storming out the door.

Now, contemplating the foreshadow of Father Ashton's fury and his capacity for revenge, Ned was still not sorry for what he'd done. He'd do it again if he had to. He knew his sister had been involved with Father

Ashton for a long time. He never liked it or understood why, but it made no difference. Father Ashton had no right to harm her so grievously. As her brother, Ned felt compelled to protect her and he would do just that, even if he had to suffer because of it. Anyway, one way or another, they'd be leaving soon. How bad could it get?

Chapter Thirty Four

June 11, 1790

Gingerly choosing her steps, Phillis followed the narrow winding path that ran next to the river. She needed time. Time to think and contemplate. Once she had gone as far as she dared, she carefully lowered herself onto a large rock. Silently, she chuckled. She had traveled this path her whole life. At one time, many years ago, the distance hadn't seemed very long. When her children were young the rock had served as the marker for them to turn back and head home. *When you get to a rock that stands as tall as you, turn back*, she'd told them, *you've gone far enough*. Now, it seemed that every year the rock moved downriver, making the path longer and more uphill.

Drawing the hem of her skirt up between her legs, she fanned herself with it, then tucked it into the waist and sighed with a heavy heart. She was worried about Ned. She was worried about all of her children, but particularly Ned.

Don't worry, Mama, he'd said, *we'll soon be gone from here and rid of that man. I can take anything for a time.*

That had been months ago. Six long months. Six months of twisted and dislocated fingers, broken ribs, cuts, and torment. Ned was strong, but everyone had their limits.

At almost seventy years of age, Phillis had never seen anything like Father John Ashton. He had been bad enough when Father Lewis, bless his poor, tormented, departed soul, was in charge of the mission. But at least then there had been some fear of reprisal.

Looking back, she clearly saw that she and Nanny should have picked up their children and left the mission at the same time that Father Lewis left, with his blessing. But life doesn't always make sense when you're in the middle of a bad situation. So, we flounder, bouncing along, just hoping to hang on and wade our way through, until there is no end in sight. And nothing to hang hope onto.

Phillis didn't know what to do to resolve the situation or how to go about it. She wasn't a young woman anymore. It would be hard enough for the younger generation to leave. How could she possibly manage? Where would they go? And how had things changed so dramatically from the happy, carefree days of her youth?

On second thought, had she ever been truly happy? Had her family? Had Queen been happy when she began living under the arrangement with Mr. Carroll or had it simply been convenience? It was hard to see through the shards of what their life had become.

Remembering, Phillis picked through the details of her life and her family's lives. There were tears but there were also happy smiles. They had struggled but they had also thrived, worked hard, played hard, had children, even buried a few. Queen had lived to a ripe old age; older than any other person any of them had ever heard of outside of the bible. She and her siblings were old too, very old. *Yes,* she decided with a silent nod, *they had been happy.* Where did it go? What had happened?

Father John Ashton happened, she scowled.

Starting with his arrival, fear penetrated their lives. Not just the fear of something going wrong at work or having an isolated bad day. Real fear. Fear of being in the wrong place, which was wherever he was. Fear of drawing his unyielding attention. Fear of injury or worse, death, under his wrath. Dreading each day because of the knowledge that his proximity at the mission made the likelihood of contact with him and his unstable moods so much greater.

How could we let him steal our happiness? Question the value of who we are until we changed ourselves into a reflection of what he saw? Phillis thought of Queen. Rarely did anyone call her by any other name. Even her children had rarely ever called her mama, or ma, and the grandchildren followed suit. She had always been Queen. Confident and strong in who she was, she dared anyone to defy or challenge her. She was a refined lady who dressed and spoke better than most white people and expected her children to also.

When did that change? Phillis wondered, recalling the varied degrees of slave talk within her own children and family.

Queen had been entertained by pirates and royalty alike. Comfortable in the presence of either, she slid through their worlds with ease and confidence. When questioned about it, she would explain; *there is one world, and we all live in it together. No one is better or worse than anyone else. There are just different circumstances, choices, skin colors. You have to make the best of what you've got and where you are. You determine who you are going to be, on the inside, where it matters. That is where your kingdom lies,* she said as she placed her hand over her children's hearts, *how you rule is up to you. Make noble decisions, stand up to challenges with courage, always welcome good thoughts. Those things can never be taken from you without your permission. Always be your own Queen.*

Remembering, Phillis tilted her head and narrowed her eyes. Suddenly, slowly, the pleats over her lips stretched and disappeared. Her eyes rounded, made larger by the pull of her brows, as a smile swept across her face. Her slim shoulders rose and fell excitedly with every breath as she pushed herself away from the rock. Pulling herself up tall and straight, she walked with renewed vigor back the way she had come.

*****

Silence enveloped the barn as members of the Queen family gathered. Waiting for each of their children to appear, Phillis and Nanny stood towards the back, holding hands in solidarity. They wore grave expressions as they watched each one of their children enter, evaluating their strengths and weaknesses.

Feeling the weight of scrutiny upon entering, each of their children slid nervously to the side to make room for the others. First Mary, Henny and Winifred. Then Pricilla and Fanny with Charity, followed by Thomas, Simon, David, Monica, Betty, Proteus, Gervais, Billy, and Peggy. Johnny, Mima, and Ned assisted Susanna, who trailed after Ralph, Henry, John and Mary. Once all were present, they stood silently, weighing the gravity of the situation, and waited for their mothers to speak.

"We are all the children of Queen," began Phillis, her voice piercing through the silence, "her children and their children. Free born, without the restraints of slavery. Free to choose whether we will stay or leave this place. Though we have had happy times here for many years, now someone is hurting us. Hurting our children. Raping and beating our women. Threatening our freedom.

"Father Ashton is attempting to steal everything that we are! He wants to strip us of everything that Queen stood for and taught us by trying to rip away our basic freedom. He is using the sands of time with the hope that we have forgotten!"

Phillis' voice hitched back a sob. She closed her eyes, drew strength from a supportive squeeze to her hand from Nanny, then, opening them, she faced her family. With eyes red from tears she refused to shed, her gaze skipped to each face present, stopping to drill the gravity of the situation into their eyes, where the soul, needing no words, speaks deeper than anything she could say.

"We have *not* forgotten! We *will not* forget! We will not let *others* forget," she paused once more to slide her gaze over her family before continuing, "and we will not be bullied or beaten any longer. I have appealed to the church to save us from this monster, and they have refused. It would seem that there is no beating him. That we have been abandoned by the church in seeking protection from him. That is unfortunate, but they don't know us. They are wrong. They do *not* own us. We have forfeited nothing to them. They have forgotten that we are the children of Mary Queen and what she taught us. We will remind them. If we can't beat them down now, get them to concede, we will *rule* them tomorrow!"

*****

July 12, 1790, Home of Gabriel Duval, Prince George's County, Maryland, United States

Four sets of eyes stayed fixed upon Gabriel Duvall's long angular face as he explained the details of the Mary Butler case. Phillis and Ned, along with Nanny and her son, Tom, all leaned forward in tall straight-backed chairs, hanging on to every detail.

Mary Butler was the great-great-grandchild of Eleanor *Irish Nell* Butler, an Irish indentured servant, and Charles, a slave. The law specifically stated that any white woman who married a slave should serve his master for the lifetime of her husband. However, after several unsuccessful attempts to win their freedom, the Butler family, through Mary, successfully proved that while there was cohabitating between Nell Butler and Charles, wherein children were indeed produced, there existed no proof that they had in fact married. In November 1787, the court ruled that because no conviction of marriage existed between the two, Nell was not a slave and her children were born to a free white woman, as free individuals. Accordingly, Mary Butler and her children were determined by the court to be free.

Additional Butler cases were quickly filed. With the implication of their free status evident, if they were able to prove they had descended through Nell or Mary Butler, the parties most often were awarded their freedom by their owners without the bother and expense of going to court.

"So you see, there have been several cases within the past three years where certain individuals have proven their claims for freedom," Mr. Duvall concluded.

"But Mr. Duvall," exclaimed Tom, "we're already free. Everybody knows it. We just wanna go an live in peace."

Phillis, Ned, and Nanny nodded in agreement.

"I understand," agreed Mr. Duvall, "however, in light of Father Ashton's recent claims of ownership of you and your family members, plus the added fact that you have lived under the care of the Jesuits for generations, this could be a very treacherous situation."

Once again, everyone nodded in agreement.

Mr. Duvall, a local attorney, was not without compassion for the Queens. White Marsh neighbored his own estate. He had met the current proprietor there many times and had found him to be arrogant, outspoken, and packing a temper full of steam. John Ashton, he had decided, was best left alone. A fence between their properties, where each stayed on their own side, kept them on good terms.

"Have you ever tried to leave?" he asked.

"No, sir," answered Phillis, "we've never had a reason to want to go anywhere else."

His fingertips together, Mr. Duvall rested them under his chin in contemplation while the Queens waited expectedly. They had a compelling claim, and he was intrigued. It was the kind of case that provided an opportunity to make a real name for himself, but he really didn't want to get involved. If they resided anywhere other than upon his irascible neighbor's estate, owned by the Jesuits no less, he would have jumped at the opportunity.

"Mr. Duvall," Phillis broke the silence, "I meant to congratulate you and Mrs. Duvall on the birth of your son. January, wasn't it?"

"Yes," Mr. Duvall beamed, "January twenty-fifth. We named him Edmund Bryce, in honor of Mrs. Duvall's family name."

"How lovely. A big strapping son, I'm sure."

"Absolutely. A healthy young lad, for sure."

"Well, Mr. Duvall, how would you feel if someone hurt him? Broke his bones. Tormented every day of his existence into a living hell."

Mr. Duvall paled. His fingers fluttered nervously to his lap then quickly grasped the pen laying on the desk. Dropping it, he nearly raked his fingers through his hair before stopping, as if reminding himself not to disturb his carefully arranged locks, and reclaimed his pen.

"That is what Father Ashton is doing to my son, Ned," Phillis pushed, her voice calm but hard, "every... single... day. My poor daughter is also tormented and disturbed, barely able to care for her children, who are also Father Ashton's children, because of how he tortures her. We need your help, Mr. Duvall."

They soon came up with a plan. All blood members of the Queen family who were not implicated in slavery in any way would pack their belongings and attempt to leave White Marsh. If they succeeded, they could then begin negotiating to purchase the remaining family members. If they were prevented from leaving, Mr. Duvall would file a petition for Ned's freedom first.

Because the family was so large and many of them had married or had children with slaves, the risk of filing all the petitions together was too great. Failure would mean the enslavement of all. When he suggested filing first for Phillis, a direct descendant of Mary Queen and their best shot of success, she rejected the idea.

"I'm old," she stated firmly, "and he's going to kill my poor Ned if this goes on much longer. Ned goes first. Save my son."

Mr. Duvall reminded them that if they failed, Ned would be legally declared a slave for life, which would automatically implicate her into the same status.

"If that would happen, then we're right back to where we are now," declared Phillis, pushing her chin up in stubborn pride, "and we'll start over. But we're Queens, we won't fail."

Mr. Duvall nodded in agreement. That night he prayed a special prayer for the Queen family, asking that they be allowed to leave White Marsh in peace. He knew it was futile.

And so it was that when the Queen family attempted to leave White Marsh, they were prevented from doing so. Father Ashton, having heard of their plan, had men armed and ready to defend his right of ownership over them. Haughty and proud, he did not question their easy retreat as they returned to their cabins.

On October 17, 1791, the Sheriff of Prince George's County Maryland, arrived and delivered a Petition for Freedom in the name of Edward 'Ned' Queen. Father Ashton was incensed.

Chapter Thirty Five

October 22, 1791

Peeking around the corner of the barn, Ned shifted his weight, poised to pop back if he should see any signs of Father Ashton. There were none. He walked across the yard, not too fast, not too slow, and slid into the tree line. It was safest. Safer than the path that everyone used

He had successfully avoided Father Ashton for five days. Five days of carefully plotting his movements, keeping his head down, his voice low, and maintaining a low profile. Five days afraid to sleep in his own cabin, waiting until after dark to quietly slip into a random cabin, taking care not to stay with family. Family cabins were the first place Father Ashton would begin looking if he wanted to find him.

Mr. Duvall had assured the Queens that Father Ashton would be afraid to torment him too badly in response to the Petition. *Included in the Petition are the orders that Father Ashton not remove you from the state or obstruct you in any way from attending court. He must continue to feed and clothe you and use you well, which means not to abuse you,* he had said, *It would be foolish for him to do anything now. It should buy you some relief until we can get to court.*

Mr. Duvall obviously didn't know his neighbor very well. He didn't understand how cruel the man could be. How he was always careful not to injure his people in a way that would be openly obvious to any visiting priests or prevent them from performing their chores. How his diabolical goal was simply to extract a painful and hellish experience, and how much he enjoyed it.

Father Ashton's punishments were designed to hurt the body, but mostly to destroy the spirit and soul of his victims. Always in the name of God.

No, Ned knew that Mr. Duvall was wrong and that he was not safe. Far from it. Father Ashton would have received the petition as a personal affront and a challenge to his authority. He would probably be more careful about hurting him, maybe even killing him, ensuring there were no witnesses, but retribution was assured. It was only a matter of time. A cat and mouse game.

They share the barn and they both know it, thought Ned, *but even a mouse survives if it hides good enough and runs fast enough.*

Mr. Duvall told them it would take about six months to get all the evidence together and present his case.

That will allow us to attend the next court session, which will be in May, he'd said.

May! Six months away! At least it was winter and they weren't planting or in the fields. Hopefully it would be a hard cold winter, driving them all indoors.

I gotta be one smart mouse, breathed Ned.

Hidden by a jumble of brush, he waited until several men passed by, walking together in a loose group. He rustled the leaves and they slowed, tightening the space amongst themselves to allow him to join them undetected by a casual observer.

Everyone working at White Marsh knew that the Queen family was free, had always been free. Until Father Ashton's arrival, they had always been acknowledged by the mission proprietors as free. So, when word spread that Father Ashton had claimed Ned's freedom, outrage was fueled. At the news that Ned had managed to hire a lawyer and was fighting back, they all hoped and prayed for his success, but none coveted the position he was in. Discussions and arguments abounded throughout the quarters.

To further complicate matters, when he returned to White Marsh after the first meeting with Mr. Duvall, Ned shared what he had learned with his best friend, Patrick Mahoney. The Mahoney family was the second largest single family at the Jesuit missions.

It was said that Patrick's great-grandmother, Ann Joice, had been born in the tropical islands to a black native woman and a white sailor who took her to England with him when she was just a child. Desperate and alone after the death of her father, Ann entered into a contract of indenture with Lord Baltimore. He brought her to the colonies where, in exchange for passage, she would work for him. When Lord Baltimore left to return to England, he passed his assets, including Ann's contract, to his brother-in-law, Henry Darnall.

Henry Darnall was a wicked and greedy man who refused to give Ann her freedom once she had completed the term of her contract. Instead, he burned the papers in front of her then threw her into a basement cellar to prevent her from running away. Months later, weak and abused, she was finally released from the cellar, but only after submitting to her enslavement.

Ann had several children, all born into slavery, who knew and passed on her story. When three of her sons, horribly mistreated and in a desperate situation, were found guilty of killing their abusive overseer, they were hanged. Their bodies were then quartered and placed on stakes throughout the county as a warning to other slaves.

The Darnall's, said to be cursed because of their evil ways, eventually fell into financial ruin, so sold their assets to many of the local leading families, including the Jesuits.

When Patrick heard about Ned's visit to Mr. Duvall, he too went and asked Mr. Duvall to represent him and his family in pursuing their freedom. It did not help Ned's situation when three days after Father Ashton received Ned's petition, he also received ones for Patrick and his brothers, Daniel and Charles.

Sure Ned was instigating a legal mutiny, Father Ashton questioned, and had questioned, any and everyone. His half-hazard investigation only served to fan the flames of curiosity and speculation throughout the quarters.

Both Queen and Mahoney family members were barraged with questions and advice from the slaves. Some, afraid and untrusting of the legal system, suggested that they self-free themselves, just run. Others encouraged them to persist, opening the way for future generations. All watched and waited in nervous anticipation of Father Ashton's response.

Passing the tool shed with the group of men, Ned dipped behind a barrel. In a squat, he scanned his surroundings before pushing up to his height. He started to walk back to the shed where his brother, Gervais, worked, when something struck him on the back of his head.

Specks of light flashed through the darkness that threatened to engulf him. Voices spun in his head, fading and indistinguishable. Ned felt himself falling, spinning, being pulled into a deep void of nothingness.

*****

Laying with his cheek pressed against the cool earth, Ned struggled towards consciousness. His head felt as if it was made of lead and his neck was too insubstantial to bear its weight. Pain buzzed through his body like a swarm of bees. He sank gratefully back into the void.

Hoo. Hoo. Hooooooo.

Hoo. Hoo. Hooooooo.

Ned's eyes twitched as stars danced in his vision behind his closed eyes.

Hoo. Hoo. Hooooooo.

Hoo. Hoo. Hooooooo.

Leave me alone, Ned wished the owl would stop its noise and leave him alone in his misery.

Hoo. Hoo. Hooooooo.

Hoo. Hoo. Hooooooo.

Then, suddenly alert, his eyes shot open. Ribbons of light broken by dark strangely shaped shadows surrounded him. His head felt as if it were exploding. Moving it only aggravated the excruciating pounding within. Careful to remain stock-still, he slid his eyes around to explore his surroundings. Slowly, some of the shadows took form. Several rakes, shovels in varied sizes, and barrels stacked three high.

He tested each muscle with a twitch. There were heavy cuffs joined by a thick length of chain around his ankles. He stretched out his hand and flattened it against the packed soil floor underneath him. A sigh of relief flooded through him as he recognized where he was.

He was in the old supply shed out beyond the far fields. It wasn't much, but knowing where he was gave him an anchor. A place to orient around. A mental focal point. It was enough.

Over the following week, Ned slowly gained strength. When he woke each morning there was a tray of food. Watery stew, hard corn pone, and water. He never saw it delivered. Sure that Father Ashton would never stoop to delivering the trays himself, Ned wondered who brought them. Who else knew where he was and what had happened to him?

By the end of the week, he was finally able to stand against the weight of the chains when a sack was thrown over his head before he woke. The brutal beating that ensued returned him to the miserable state of the previous week.

For months, the process continued. Each time his recovery took a little longer, but just as he was able to stand, he was once again beaten without mercy or compassion.

*****

April 1792

Time had long ceased to exist in any recognizable form. Days and weeks melted into one another separated only by periods of suffering, the agonizing process of healing, and the torment of knowing it was all only to be repeated.

When conscious, Ned tried to stay grounded. He filled his mind with thoughts of his mother, memories of happier times, and of the rich smell of simmering stew and hot corn bread on a chilly fall day. Finding places of comfort in a cage of misery was his link to the world. It tethered him to life and promised his return.

When he healed beyond standing, then was able to walk the length of the chain, a good four paces, he became guarded, afraid of what was in store for him. When more time passed, he became anxious that his meals were slightly more robust and wondered what was going on.

Did he have a friend, someone secretly looking after him, afraid to openly help but willing to risk the few extra pieces of meat buried in a richer broth? Regardless of why, one thing was clear, somehow he was going to have to get himself out of this mess. He needed to be ready. He had to do what he could to prepare himself for any opportunity, no matter how small, to escape. He began stretching and moving his muscles. He took inventory of everything in the small shed and sat for hours devising ways to create weapons from them.

One morning he woke to the steady rhythmic patter of rain from a spring storm followed by the hard tapping of drops that fell through the leaky roof and splashed into the puddle that had become the floor of the shed. Beyond the stench of shed, he could smell the change in the air outside. Spring was arriving. That meant he had been locked away for about six months.

Rolling to his side, he eased himself up and mentally checked himself over, feeling each muscle in turn, as he did every time he woke. Though he was still stiff, particularly in his back, the worst of the pain had resolved.

He stepped towards the tray resting where it did each morning, just outside of his reach, and stopped just as usual, a few feet from it. From there, he planted one foot and pushed the other out as far as the chains would allow, then stretched his body to reach for it. All while praying against a fall, which would result in bruising pain from the tug of the chains around his ankles. Using his fingertips, he nudged the tray closer until he could grasp the side and pull it towards him.

Settling the tray on his lap, Ned froze. Something was different. He looked around before he realized that the chains had been removed. He had just performed his entire morning routine out of habit rather than necessity. How had they been removed without his knowledge? How had he slept through the removal of heavy clunking chains? Who had done it? Why?

The tray toppled as he jumped to his feet. Its contents, his only meal of the day, spilled and became a part of the expanding puddle in the center. Ned's heart raced as he jumped towards the wall and pressed himself against it to peek outside for any sign of movement.

How long ago was someone here, he wondered, frantically moving, inch by inch, around the shed to see his surroundings from every vantage point, *and when would they return?*

Satisfied that no one was lurking outside, he plopped himself down to think.

I've got to do it. Now. What if it's a trap? Doesn't matter. It's a chance. I might be killed. That's better than living as an animal. What if they're waiting, expecting me to run? Then fight, Ned argued with himself.

He quickly grabbed a length of chain and cautiously opened the door then slipped out. The air, crisp and cool, was clean and filled with the green scent of new growth, sunshine, and wet earth. The trees and grass glistened in shades of blue, green, white, and yellows that were so bright in contrast to the dim browns of the shed, he had to pause to shield his eyes. Drawing in a long deep breath, he oriented himself back into a world of color and clean air.

When his senses stopped reeling, he checked his surroundings once again, though through squinted eyes. His legs felt wobbly but there was no time to wait. Taking off at a slow and careful but awkward jog, he headed towards the wood line. He was going to find Mr. Duvall.

*****

Tree limbs raked across Ned's cheek as he tore through the brush in a race against time. He wasn't foolish enough to believe that he had been left untethered without the consideration that he would try to escape. But what if someone had tried to help him by giving him the opportunity to run towards freedom? He couldn't afford to weigh the options.

Losing his footing at the opening of a ravine, he slid. Down he went, tumbling head over heels, until he landed with a thud at the bottom. Gathering his bearings, he jumped to his feet. The incline was too steep to make it easily back up. He scanned the area for another route but didn't see any. So, scrambling on his hands and knees, he slowly made his way. When he finally reached the top, he threw himself up to level ground. There, he lay panting to catch his breath.

Thank you, God, he prayed silently.

Just as he rose to his feet, he was struck on his head from behind. Hurling himself forward to avoid falling back into the ravine, he fell and slammed his head against a rock just before his vision exploded in a burst of stars.

Pain buzzed through his head and body like swarming flies. He struggled to maintain consciousness. The ground underneath him felt soft and squishy from spring rains as he fell back onto it. He felt his back sinking into it as Father Ashton straddled him and grasped his hair. Darkness swaddled him as a fist pounded into his cheek. He never felt the bite of the little crosses tied onto the scourge as it rained its fury upon him,

When Ned woke, he could hear the trees scraping the roof and knew he was back in the shed. Someone moved to stand near him, or over him, so he knew he wasn't alone. He didn't open his eyes and tried to regulate his breathing to give the appearance that he was still asleep. He was in such pain that he couldn't do it. Adding to his misery, raw hunger gnawed at his belly. He bared his bloody teeth in a grimace of pain. Something landed against his face with a thud. A fist? A boot? He couldn't tell. Over and over, it rained down on him, first on his chest, then his back, and then over the length of his body.

Later, he didn't know how long it was or even if it were night or day because his eyes were swollen shut, he willed his heart to stop beating. He focused upon the soft thump, thump, thump in his chest, commanding that it stop, until finally he swore that he felt it slow down and knew he approached success. Calm washed over him with the certainty of death. He whispered a soft goodbye to his mother.

*****

Before she even saw him, Phillis was aghast at the condition under which Ned was being kept. The air, drenched with the stench of blood, sweat, and waste, was heavy, as if even the oxygen had fled the oppression. The boards that made the walls supporting the tiny structure were not designed to provide shelter or security for a living being. It was just a place to store field implements, so it was damp and chilly inside.

Her son was heaped in the center of the room and Phillis fled to him. Falling beside him, she resisted the impulse to gather him into the shelter of her arms. Her hands, shaking with worry and fear, moved over the length of his body, hovering in search of a place where she could touch him without causing him further injury.

After she carefully removed Ned's clothing, Phillis grabbed a bucket and ran to the creek to get water to wash him. As layers of dirt and blood slowly melted away, the revelation of hundreds of small cuts over the length of him horrified her. She examined each of them closely. Only half of the tip of her finger slid into them. They were not deep. Relief swept through her.

She wanted to go and get help in moving him away from the center of the room where water and body waste pooled, but she had been warned that if she left, or if anyone else arrived, Ned would be moved and his whereabouts would never be shared again. Her aging body fought against her will as she struggled to gently push him clear of the puddle. Her stiffened joints rebelled. It was no use. There was no way to move him without causing him further pain, but it had to be done. Finally, pulling his hands over his head, she grasped his wrists and murmured a brief but sincere apology, then tugged.

Once he was settled, clean and dry and covered with a light blanket, she sat beside him and talked. She spoke of the weather and crops, shared stories, gossip, and rambled about anything she could think of. As if only the sound of her voice could keep him alive, she kept talking.

Ned slowly became aware of a dim voice reaching out to him through the fog. Wrapping itself around him, it eased and caressed the worst of his pain and comforted him. He did not want comfort. He wanted the pain, needed it even. It was the answer to end the misery his existence had become.

Go, he silently pled to the voice, *let me go.*

As he pushed it away, a fresh wave of pain washed over him like a tide sweeping across his body. Giving himself over to its murky waters, he welcomed it. The voice disappeared as he sank back into a silent void.

*****

Once again, Ned heard the voice. It had become familiar and persistent, dancing its way around him, enticing him, drawing him to it. There was something more about it that he could not place. It nagged at him, and he pushed it away until, slowly, realization grew as if it were whispered into his consciousness. His mother was there. Wrapping himself in the safety of her voice, he allowed it to carry and comfort him.

"My mother, Queen, do you remember her? Of course you do. Who could forget her," it was a statement, not a question, "and her wonderful stories... all true.

"She once lived a pampered life in a big palace. She wore beautiful jewels that were as big as eggs and in every color of the rainbow. In the palace were strange men with high feminine voices who carried long curved knives. They protected the women who were both warriors and pampered flowers.

"When the palace was attacked, she was taken captive and put aboard a ship where she was to be taken to be sold as slaves. Instead, she made the best of the situation and learned to become a sailor. She loved sitting way up high in what they called the crow's nest. It was higher up than even the very tips of the tallest trees and she could see for miles. She loved seeing the water sparkle and large fish, both dolphins and sharks, swimming around below as she rode way up where the birds flew around her.

"One day she was tossed overboard. She washed ashore where she lived in the jungle and traveled on long flowing rivers in canoes that were dug out of trees. Birds of every color filled the air. Many of their calls were so strange she said we wouldn't even recognize them as birds. The bright green of the jungle dotted with colorful flowers and birds was so vibrant and beautiful that she said it stole her breath.

"The way she described it I felt I could almost see it, so I loved to hear about it.

"But then, always, she told me about the trials of living on that ship and in the jungle. Being the only woman amongst rough hard sailors was difficult. To support themselves they attacked other ships and innocent villages, often burning them down to steal their food and riches. They even raided the churches and were often forced to kill anyone who resisted or fought them.

"In the jungle, traveling through all of that beauty, they were riddled with insects so big they were nearly the size of a grown man's hand. In the water were alligators and fish that could eat a human in minutes. There were strange tribes that flattened the heads of babies with boards and used sharp knives or sticks to put strange marks over their faces and bodies.

"I hated for her to tell me about those things. It scared me and made me have bad dreams.

"When she told me about the beautiful things in her life, I always leaned in real close, never wanting to miss a single word. When she stopped, I begged her to continue, even if it were retelling the same story again and again. But when she told me about the ugliness, I buried my face under my blanket. If I didn't have one, I threw my skirt over my head and begged her to stop.

"One day, she pulled my hands down and ordered me to keep them in my lap. Of course I did, nobody defied Queen even for such a simple thing. Then, she pulled my skirt off of my head and tilted my chin up, keeping her hand under it, just like this," Phillis gently cupped Ned's chin. Her fingers spread across his cheek like butterfly wings as she brought her face close to his. Her expression was hard and her eyes were misted with love. Her gaze bored into him as if she could press it through his closed lids.

"She looked at me just like this and said, *Phillis, I always wanted to be a mother but believed it would never happen. I had a child once, a son who would've been your brother. I wasn't a young woman and believed he was to be my only child. And yet his life would have taken the lives of not only both of us, but also the lives of others who trusted me with theirs. So, my son's life was sacrificed.*

"*It was a cruel bargain and I paid dearly for it, but I always lived in such a way to honor his sacrifice. In the end, I was blessed with not just one, but three beautiful children and a life longer and richer than anyone has a right to.*

"*Through that experience I learned one of the most important lessons that life has to offer; suffering and happiness are woven together like fabric. Each strand is dependent upon the other to make something that is useful, good, and even beautiful. Any attempt to leave out even a single thread spoils the whole thing, making all our efforts useless, resulting in waste.*

"*I will always tell you of both beauty and suffering. One, to show you the possibilities of life. The other, to remind you that there is always a cost. There cannot be one without the other in equal exchange. It is a part of life that deals with the laws of nature and the rules of balance.*

"*Phillis,* she said, *if you hide from suffering, as you do under that blanket, you will also never get to know happiness. Yes, you will suffer at times, but if you bury yourself in it, wrap it around yourself, which we all do from time to time, happiness will pass you by, unseen. Opportunities will be lost, unknown.*

"Always remember that life is for living. Most days you just get through. They pass unremembered as just a notch in the strand of your existence. Sometimes you get to sit in happiness. Then, stay present in every detail. Burn them into your memory to call upon later, in the times when you suffer.

"When you are suffering, remember that you can choose to either embrace it, walking through it in strength and wisdom, clinging to those stored up memories for comfort, or let it sweep you away.

"Always remember that pain and sadness promise better times. One will accompany and balance out the other. Great pain promises great happiness. Both eventually pass but they are the threads where the fabric of life is created and where my stories lie, she said. It is what we pass on, share, and are remembered for. It is also the place that allows joy."

Sure he could hear her, Phillis squeezed Ned's hand and choked back a sob before continuing.

"So, my son, whatever you must do to find that place in yourself that wants to live, do it. It may not seem like it right now, but this suffering that you are experiencing promises a great happiness. It will be a joy to be passed down through the ages. It will be your legacy. To pass it on, you must survive."

When Ned woke, surprise and disappointment to be alive surpassed his agony. He had thought he would die, welcomed it even, but it wasn't to be. His face contorted with pain and renewed fear, he opened his eyes.

Chapter Thirty Six

May 31, 1792

Susanna gripped the table to remain upright. It was bad enough that she was so ill, but to be attended to by the haughty and arrogant Dr. Charles Worthington only made the situation worse.

"I should think," he sniffed, looking her over with derision, "that a woman of your particular age would know better than to fall into such a condition."

Susanna narrowed her eyes and took a deep breath. Pulling it in through her nose, she counted to five, then blew it out.

"Of *course* you are ill," the doctor continued as if he were speaking to a small child who went out into the rain then came in surprised to find themself wet, "what else would you expect at your age?"

Susanna wanted to stomp upon his shiny silver shoe buckles, kick his knees right where his pristine silk stockings met his breeches, and punch him in his overly powdered nose, before strangling him with the ribbon which restrained his long, also powdered, locks. Taking another deep breath, she resisted the urge.

"Thank you, Dr. Worthington," she walked to the open door, "for tending me. I'm sorry to be such a bother."

Pulling the door from where it was propped open and against the wall, she held it.

"Don't worry," he huffed, "the bother was not for you. It was for the good Father Ashton."

"Hmmm," breathed Susanna, nudging the door.

Dr. Worthington exited with a flounce. In three long strides he stood beside his carriage where, with a huff, he waved his hands impatiently to urge his driver to hurry to assist him. Susanna watched with disgust as the poor driver, decked out in an ostentatious uniform that seemed ill suited for the weather and his position, tripped over himself to accommodate his master, who struck him.

"Yes," Susanna muttered under her breath, "John will definitely have to be punished for this."

Closing the door, she leaned against it. Her hand moved over her unborn child.

That evening, after washing the memory of the doctor's touch from her body, Susanna waited for John, sure he would come. Later, when she woke in the wee hours of the morning and he had not appeared, she climbed into her bed where she slept restlessly.

Weeks later, when John still did not come to her, she became desperate and went in search of him. When she arrived at the barn, he was expecting her. He had gotten the report from Dr. Worthington, along with a whole rambling diatribe regarding the voracious libido and prolific reproductive ability of negros. Susanna, he'd said, was a grotesque example of their unique ability to become enceinte so late in life; further proof that *they* were animals and so were less than white people.

Father Ashton's problem wasn't that Susanna was pregnant. It was that she was pregnant with his child at a time when he had finally put to rest the gossip and charges pertaining to her with the church. Even after Father Carroll closed the investigation, finding no evidence of a relationship between himself and Susanna, the matter had continued. On and on were questions, letters, comments, and snide innuendos whispered behind his back. It was simply annoying.

When Susanna appeared at the barn trying to trap him into a public admission that the child she carried was his, he refused to let her speak. Even if the only others present were slaves who had no bearing under the law or in the church, they still talked. Word would spread across the missions and eventually, quickly, it would fall into the ears of a sanctimonious do-gooder like Diderick, who would start everything all over again.

Sending Susanna to her cabin, he ordered her to stay there until he came. If he wasn't too tired, he would go that night. Might as well address the matter before she mucked everything up. He had worked far too hard and was far too powerful to let someone like her mess things up.

*****

Susanna pulled the corners of her blanket more tightly around herself as memories flooded through her in an overwhelming gush. Her pregnancy with Charles had been awful. Her only friend had been Edward Kelly, and he, trying to save her, had messed things up, made everything much worse. Father Ashton had been so angry that she had believed he was going to kill her. That fateful night was when they both surprised themselves in forging a new kind of relationship. Gone was Father Ashton, except in public. John took his place.

Susanna shuddered and drew her legs up, wrapping her arms around them to save herself from drowning in the memory. She laid her head on her knees and let out a strangled groan.

John was a very naughty boy who loved sex and beauty, both sins, and had to be punished because of it. Afterwards, he slunk out of her cabin wearing his shame across his back in long angry stripes that oozed with blood and puss.

At first it had been exhilarating. A way to get even for all the wrong he had done to her and her family. To punish him for his hurtful, insulting ways. To mark him as only she could do. It was a permanent reminder to him that she *did* have his baby. All the nay saying and denial in the world couldn't change that fact.

Then, there was that one time when everything changed and she could no longer stomach the perpetual abuse of it. She had just finished an especially brutal whipping when John slid down the wall, sobbing, and crawled into the corner. Surprised, but still feeling no compassion for him, she simply pulled a chair over, a few paces from him, and sat watching him with detached interest.

Drawing himself into the smallest ball possible, he pushed himself further into the corner as if it were a great mouth and could swallow him whole if he could only push himself into it hard enough. There, he cried the angry frightened tears of a child, wincing and ducking his head defensively against an assailant seen only by him. All while begging his father for mercy and love.

When he finally noticed Susanna sitting there, watching, he slid towards her, hesitant and slow, then pulled on her skirts as if he were a toddler asking for permission before laying his head in her lap. There, he begged her to love him, pleaded with her to make his father stop, and sobbed out his grief.

It was then that Susanna realized that John wasn't mentally balanced because of the horrible abuse his father had dealt him. Never having come to terms with the shame inflicted upon him by the one man who was supposed to have protected him, he punished any misdeeds that kept him from perfection, the price of his father's love. Without it, he could not be whole. But his father was long gone. Dead. Buried with him was the only chance of his son becoming whole.

When John turned to the church he found a new father. One who also made demands of perfection coupled with the threat of withholding the ultimate prize, entrance into the kingdom of heaven, if he failed. Of course he would fail. Everyone failed.

Even though the bible says that we are all sinners and destined to fail in our pursuit to live in the image of Jesus, John could not accept it. For him, love and acceptance were always a prize that was dangled over conditions that could never be met and so could never be obtained.

Susannah never mentioned that night to him. She knew he had been too lost to even remember it and he would never forgive her if she did.

For her, that night changed everything, and she began to see John differently. In public he was Father Ashton, a cruel and heartless man who was just like his father. In private he was just poor John and she served as an extension of his father's cruel hand, hurting and whipping him. In those moments, a child. She hated it all. Hated him for making her beat him and hated herself for doing it. She hated all it represented.

Because she could not talk to him about it, they persisted. Him, seeking illusive perfection that he could never achieve. Her, because if she didn't, the whip would be turned upon her. Neither had a choice.

That night, when he went to her cabin, he laid down the rules as to how the matter of her pregnancy would be addressed. She would tell no one anything, admit nothing, and stay out of sight as much as possible. She was not to even look at him outside of her cabin and was never, ever, to approach him or speak to him unless he spoke to her. Then, and only then, could she speak to him, saying nothing beyond what was specifically required.

To make sure she fully understood the rules, he made her repeat each one until she had committed them to memory, exactly word for word. That way, if she broke them, she could not fool herself into thinking that she did not know why it was necessary for her to be punished.

When he left, as he pulled the door shut behind himself, it seemed to boom in her ears with finality. She did not know whether to be relieved over the loss of the man, or sad for the grief of the little boy within him. Not wanting to contemplate it, she melted into her blanket and slept.

And so it was that in January 1793, Susanna delivered a healthy baby girl. John named her Elizabeth, after the wife of a priest named Zechariah from the bible. Both Zechariah and his wife were righteous and lived according to God, who favored them.

The church, upon hearing of the birth of Elizabeth, once again pursued the matter of Father Ashton having a sexual relationship with Susanna Queen, which he denied. When he was formally pushed to answer questions about it by the Bishop, Father John Carroll, he became annoyed and responded by telling him, *you will finally know of the matter only upon my death.*

Chapter Thirty Seven

March 1794

Phillis watched Ned as he wandered aimlessly through the yard. She was worried about him but didn't know what could be done to help him. He had been through so much over the past year. Too much.

The previous fall, after the world had shifted into a colorful display of reds, orange, and yellows and the mornings glistened with frost, she finally left the small shed to confront Father Ashton. Convincing him to allow her to have Ned carried to her cabin had been surprisingly easy. She had simply pointed out that she had stayed in that shed nursing him for nearly six months. It was bad enough baking in the heat of the summer, but her old bones would be damned before they would freeze through the winter. Without any argument, he agreed. It was a relief to have Ned where she could keep him both warm and properly fed. She was sure it would help in speeding up the process of restoring his health.

What she didn't know was that her visit had provided a quick solution for Father Ashton as to the matter of Ned repeatedly not appearing for court. The court terms where they heard petitions for freedom were scheduled every May and November. So far, Ned had missed four court dates. It had been an easy matter for Father Ashton's attorneys to get the continuances, citing scheduling conflicts and other such things, but they had warned him that he was eventually going to have to produce Ned to have the matter heard. After two years of delays, getting another continuance was going to be difficult.

Because of the unfortunate circumstances of Ned's health, if he were to appear in court it did not bode well for Father Ashton. Allowing Phillis to take over his care under better conditions was the only reasonable solution. Besides, it had become tedious ensuring that food was taken to them every day. Keeping the other workers and staff away from the far shed had also proven more difficult than he had originally believed it would be. Phillis's insistence upon moving Ned had relieved him from having to make the decision himself.

Once in his mother's home, Ned began to noticeably improve. First, his hollowed cheeks filled out with a layer of flesh that softened the angles of his skeletal frame. Then, he began acknowledging the presence of others, silently watching them as they moved around the cabin. It was months before he was able to stand, then months more before he could take a few steps. It wasn't until the following fall that he was able to walk out of the door, and then only under a tremendous straining effort and with considerable pain. But even though his health slowly improved, he rarely spoke, never smiled, and slept often.

Maybe he will never come back to me, thought Phillis with a heavy heart and a sad sigh.

Ned wasn't the only one of her children causing her concern. She was also worried about Susanna. Even though Susanna had never admitted it, Phillis knew that Father Ashton often visited her and that both Charles and Elizabeth were the product of those visits.

Having had a long-term relationship with Father Lewis, Phillis understood how those types of things worked. Even though they lived in relative isolation at the missions, a relationship with a priest always called for discretion. Especially with the church trying to make an example of Father Ashton to other mission managers.

Why won't she speak to me about it, thought Phillis with frustration, *when she knows that I, of all people, would understand?*

Many nights Phillis laid awake mulling it over in her head. Susanna wasn't happy. She had not been happy ever since she lost her son, Tom, but it was only when she began seeing Father Ashton that she had really changed, sinking into a sad and distracted place.

She could only compare watching Susanna to the experience of watching a puppet being manipulated. She moved through her days without experiencing them. Her smiles never reached her eyes, tears never flowed, and she no longer engaged in any meaningful conversation. She never asked about others or volunteered anything of herself.

That means whatever is going on, it is eating her from the inside out, sighed Phillis, remembering a poem Queen taught her when she was a young girl.

It had been summertime and very hot. Due to heavy rains, the creek was full and flowing fast. It looked cool and refreshing with the water bubbling over rocks instead of rushing around them. The kids wanted to go for a swim but their parents had told them no. Instead, they were only allowed to sit on the bank where they could dip their hands into the cool water and splash it up on their faces, necks, and arms.

A group of them excitedly ran down the path to where the bank was smooth and covered in white sand. Breaking the rules, they all waded in, just to their ankles, and began splashing one another. They had so much fun they didn't even notice that before long they were all in up to their knees where the water pushed against them, making it harder to stay afoot.

Suddenly, one of the smaller girls took that extra step back to where there was a drop-off. She lost her footing and was immediately swept away with the currant. Ralph went after her and dragged her to safety. When she emerged, she was frightened but otherwise okay, except that she had a big knot on her temple where she had hit her head on a rock.

They were afraid to tell their parents that they had broken the rules and gone into the creek. Instead, they constructed a story saying the girl had lost her balance and fell into the river and that Ralph had saved her life. It seemed plausible enough.

The girl's parents didn't believe the story. Their daughter was a very smart and agile girl. She would never have stood as the children claimed, leaning over the creek where she could have fallen in. Even if she did lean in such a way, she wouldn't have fallen. Instead, they decided that Ralph must have pushed her in and the others were lying to protect him. Afraid, the poor injured girl simply refused to speak of it or answer any further questions. That only served to further stir her parents concern, causing them to widely disparage Ralph's good name and character throughout the quarters. No amount of talking could persuade them that their version of events wasn't what actually happened. The more anyone said, the more convinced they were that the children's stories were lies to cover up Ralph's misdeed.

Afraid that people would become convinced that Ralph was a wicked child, Nanny and Phillis couldn't eat and had horrible dreams.

Within days, Queen heard the stories about the events at the creek. After speaking to several of the children who were there, she knew they weren't being honest. Settling her daughter's side-by-side into chairs, she asked them about it just once. Then, waiting for them to respond, she sat across from them and stared into their eyes, long and hard, without saying another word. Afraid to admit the truth of their lies, neither Nanny nor Phillis would answer past the silent tears pooling in their eyes.

Finally, Queen took a deep breath and said, *A secret kept is a tear wept. A secret held is joy swelled. Release the fear, dry the tear. Share the joy, we all rejoice.*

It was enough. With those few words from their mother, they understood that keeping ugly secrets ate you up inside, just as they were experiencing. The only way to make it better was to tell the truth. The only secrets that were good were the ones that could eventually be shared. Relieving themselves of the stress, they told their mother the truth.

Happy to be released from the burden of their secret and vindicate Ralph's good name, they didn't even mind the whipping that followed. They each, including Ralph, got one good smack for breaking the rules and entering the creek, and an additional harder wallop for the lie. Though they all did go on to break rules from time to time, earning plenty more spankings, none of them ever forgot the lesson about keeping secrets.

Susanna was an adult with kids of her own. Phillis didn't need to know her secrets, but understood that sometimes people need permission to forgive themselves.

Back when Mr. Duvall was first hired, he made a few inquiries to several of the neighbors who had been in the area since the time when Queen had first arrived. He found that Queen had been very well respected and trusted throughout the community. She was best known for always having a good story about exotic faraway places and was especially liked because of them.

Her stories were often passed around as topics of interest or just good gossip, often returning with added tidbits and additional details. When that happened, Queen never minded. She just laughed, exclaimed that people will be people and as long as she knows the truth, the heck with them. She just kept retelling her stories, always the same, and let people do with them what they would.

So, when word spread that her children were being claimed as slaves and that inquiries were being made about the situation, many people clamored to tell what they knew. In fact, there were so many people that Mr. Duvall needed help in talking to them and sorting out truth from fiction. He needed to bring on another attorney.

Phillip Barton Key, a fellow Marylander, was an attorney who came from a very wealthy and connected family. After the conclusion of the Revolutionary War, where he served on the side of the British Loyalists, he left the colonies and went to England. There, he attended a prestigious law school and returned to Maryland in 1785 to practice law. Willing to work pro-bono, or free, he was the perfect addition to help with the Queen case.

Working together, Mr. Duvall and Mr. Key spoke to many people, conducting interviews about what each person knew about Queen and her family. Then, sorting fact from fiction, they settled upon several key witnesses.

First, Mr. Richard Disney, a wealthy planter who was a neighbor to Mr. James Carroll, the owner of Fingaul before he bequeathed it to the Jesuit missions. Mr. Disney claimed he knew Phillis and Nanny his entire life. He said that his mother claimed to have delivered Nanny and that she remembered it clearly because it was her first delivery as a midwife. Although that fact caused no small discomfort to Phillis and Nanny, they reasoned that they were in no position to refute the good Mrs. Disney's word by correcting her after she was dead and gone by stating that she actually delivered Phillis, not Nanny.

Mr. Disney also testified to the fact that Captain Larkin brought Queen, a fine lady, into the country from England, and that when she arrived, she possessed such an elaborate wardrobe that no one wanted her to work for them. That he also stated that Mr. Carroll had finally relented and bought Queen was of no account. Worst case scenario was that it could be inferred that perhaps Queen had indentured herself for a term. In any event, she would have been a free woman.

The next witness they chose was a gentleman by the name of Thomas Warfield, a former laborer and overseer who did business with individuals associated with the Jesuit missions. He also had knowledge that Queen was brought into the country by Captain Larkin. He further testified that she stayed for a time in the Chapman home, verified that he had known Phillis, a bright yellow mulatto woman, his entire life, and knew that she was the mother of Ned.

Mr. George Davis, another planter, corroborated both of the other gentlemen's testimony.

All three testimonies were from people who personally knew both Ned and Phillis and that they were the descendants of Mary Queen, who had arrived in the country from England with Captain Larkin.

Of course, the attorneys representing Father Ashton would say that Mary Queen was purchased as a slave, but their ability to come up with any such testimony was vague for two reasons: One, not only was it untrue, but people had also genuinely liked Queen, frequently referring to her as Queen Mary, and they did not want to cause damage to her family. Also, most of the people who had personal knowledge of Queen, her arrival in the colonies, or her arrangement with James Carroll, were dead.

At one point, Father Ashton's attorneys even produced a transcript of Mr. James Carroll's will. In it, Mr. Carroll bequeathed to his nephew, Anthony, a slave by the name of Mary. Since Mary Queen was the only person named Mary working at Fingaul at the time, they reasoned he was referring to her. According to that, they said, Mary Queen was clearly considered a slave by Mr. Carroll. However, upon inspection of the original will produced by Mr. Carroll, it was discovered that in the transcription of it, the name Meg was mistakenly written as Mary. The transcriber apologized for his error and the issue of Mr. Carroll's will was dropped.

In the end, they could only produce two witnesses. Both relied heavily upon hearsay and gossip.

Caleb Clark stated he knew both Ned and Phillis, but he did not even know that they were mother and son. Although he had heard of Mary Queen, it was only through the gossip of his mother, Mary Clark, and his grandfather, Mareen Duvall, both dead, who had lived within eyesight of James Carroll's home at Fingaul. He collaborated, through stories he had heard over his lifetime, the details of Captain Larkin arriving from England with Mary Queen, but stated, according to his mother and dead aunts, James Carroll and Mary Queen were often heard quarrelling about the subject of her freedom and that James Carroll was heard promising her that it would happen *by and by*.

Deborah Lusby claimed that her father, Edward Lee, her uncle, and a close friend, all lived in the same neighborhood where Fingaul was located. Because of that, she had known of Phillis for over thirty years and had never heard anything mentioned about her or her family being entitled to their freedom. If any of them were entitled to freedom, she was sure she would have heard someone mention it. She also confirmed that Nanny Cooper and Phillis Queen were sisters, and that Phillis was the mother of Ned as well as multiple other children including Susanna, Mary, Gervais, Proteus and Winifred.

Everyone agreed. Ned had a solid case and was very likely to win the freedom of the Queen family. However, getting their day in court was frustrated by the repeated delays asked for by Father Ashton and his attorneys.

Finally, in February 1794 Mr. Duvall and Mr. Key came up with the idea to push the matter. They knew that Father Ashton and his attorneys delayed the case to put off the inevitable loss of the Queen family. They represented over half of the mission's workforce, so a large portion of their tradeable assets, who by virtue of the same provable descendancy, would also be free. Filing multiple claims, keeping them limited to only those who fell directly under Queen's children, would demonstrate to the court, without outright stating it, that the delays were being produced to prolong and preserve Father Ashton's assets. That was against the rules of law and justice and was a crime. If they dared to cause further delays, it would be seen as the blatant flouting of the judge's authority.

In late February 1794, Mr. Duvall sent word to Phillis and Nanny asking her for all of the names of their children being specifically held by Father Ashton at the White Marsh mission. There was no need for more. After all, they were from the same family and so all directly descended from the same woman. Obviously, the remaining family would also be free.

Phillis and Nanny spoke with each of their children and warned them not to breathe a word to anyone. The only one which gave them any cause for concern was Susanna. While listening to the plan she had become even more withdrawn, absently playing with her fingers in her lap while chewing her lower lip. Both Phillis and Nanny had noticed it, but neither mentioned it to the other. Susanna was Phillis' daughter, so Phillis would talk with her.

The following day, Phillis wasn't surprised when Susanna casually told her that she would be over for dinner, without her children, so they could talk.

When Susanna arrived, she was relieved to see Ned outside, moving slowly around. She needed to speak with her mother privately. It was a conversation that Ned, of all people, would not understand and didn't need to hear.

Speaking to her mother, Susanna tearfully described her relationship with Father Ashton and her confusion about it. She conceded that while he could be a vicious and unpredictable man, he was also a poor soul, broken by his father, that just needed to be loved. Being the father of two of her children, she also didn't want to do anything that would disrespect him in her children's eyes.

Phillis listened and let Susanna talk even though she didn't agree with her. After a few strategically placed questions, the truth of Susanna's greatest fear was finally produced. For years Father Ashton had abused his power, the people he was entrusted to care for, his religion, and his colleagues. Often times he had schemed up elaborate plans against them in Susanna's presence. Then, when he reported back to her on how successful he had been, he demanded that she punish him for the wrong that he had done. She was afraid. If they succeeded, the reach of his power outside of the mission allowed him to harm them even if they were no longer under his authority.

Frustrated, Phillis listened to her daughter's concerns then sat holding her hands as she cried. When Susanna's tears were spent and only red eyes, a tear-streaked face, and a sniffly nose remained, Phillis handed her a glass of water and a kerchief.

"Now take a deep breath with me and listen very carefully to what I've gotta say."

Taking Susanna's hands into hers once more, they both pulled in a long soothing breath and blew it out together.

"Daughter," she continued, "you are no longer a young woman and you've suffered in ways that you shouldn't have had to. Inflicting pain on other's, even when you're forced, hurts your heart differently than when you're the one being hurt. It's still suffering, nonetheless.

"Queen used to tell me that there is nothing in this world, good or bad, holy or evil, that people are not capable of doing under the right circumstances. What you must ask yourself is not why you did those things, because we already know that, but what actually created the situation. Then, if possible, avoid being in that situation again. We both know that until now you've had no choice of the situation.

"Now, when a person *willingly* repeats what they know and feel is wrong, it eats their soul. It's their shame to carry. But when a person is *forced* to do something, it eats the person that forces them. It's *their* shame.

"You now have a chance, maybe the only one you will ever get, to walk away from it all. To stop doing what you know is wrong and avoid being in the situation ever again. If you don't take it, then it becomes yours by choice. Take it. Leave the shame with him, where it belongs. You won't walk alone. We'll go as a family and help each other through it together."

"But, mama," sniffled Susanna, "what if we lose?"

"Then we will hold our heads high because we tried and do what we must to protect ourselves. Remember, no one can take from you that which is truly yours," Phillis' hand fluttered to her daughter's chest, "what is in here," then her forehead, "and here," then laid them on her shoulders, "are all that we truly possess. No one can take them from you without your permission."

Feeling stronger but still afraid, Susanna nodded.

"Besides," Phillis laughed, pulling her daughter closer as she leaned in for a hug, "we are Queens, daughters of Mary Queen. We don't fight to lose. We always, *but always,* fight to win when we're right and we never, *ever*, give up until we do."

And so it was that in April 1794, just one month prior to Ned's case being heard, Attorneys Duvall and Key filed twenty-one petitions for the freedom of the descendants of Mary Queen and their children.

*****

May 23, 1794

Ned stood in the yard of his mother's cabin and watched the fog crawl across the fields until it surrounded him so thickly that the world was

313

reduced to vague shapes buried in a haze of grey mist. It gave him solace. It was fitting that the world faded into mist on such a morning. He remained there, standing very still, and waited for the sun to rise.

It was court day and his lawyers insisted that the matter was going to be heard. He wasn't so sure. So many days, years, had passed. Each time they had been hopeful. Each time they had been disappointed.

This time he was actually going to go. He would appear and watch his attorneys fight for his liberation from Father Ashton. Though he knew they would be in a court of law and surrounded by lots of other people, that knowledge gave him no peace. He didn't trust the man anywhere, or under any circumstances.

He wasn't sorry that his family couldn't go to court with him. Lately, it seemed that in their presence he felt lonelier than ever. They all had such great expectations of him and hailed him as their hero. He was the one that was to wager the battle and win the war for them. The unspeakable fear of possibly losing his case lingered in the back of his mind, but he wouldn't let it take form. He couldn't. He just pushed it away as often as it came. He would not lose. He could not lose. He must win.

If he won, when he won, he knew he wouldn't be allowed to return to say good-bye to his family. Father Ashton would never allow it. It didn't matter because his win would settle everything for them too. After all, his freedom ensured theirs since the path was the same.

Standing in the courtroom, fear bloomed in his belly and grew until sweat beaded across his brow and nose despite the mild May temperature. When he saw Father Ashton enter, smiling and greeting people as if he were hosting a party instead of attending court, Ned was gripped with terror. He struggled to remain on his feet as violence roared through him, demanding that he react. He didn't dare. Court was about to begin.

And so it was that a jury was called and the case of Edward "Ned" Queen versus John Ashton was heard. Though neither party could testify against the other, depositions were read, testimony was given, attorneys from both sides argued their cases, and the matter was turned over to the jury to decide. In the end, the jury found that Mary Queen, the grandmother of Edward, "Ned" Queen, was not a slave and that he had descended from her as he alleged.

"Therefore," the judge, the Honorable Michael Stone, announced, "it is adjudged by the court that Edward Queen, the Petitioner, be freed and discharged of and from the service of Reverend John Ashton. It is also considered by the court that the said Edward Queen recover against the Reverend John Ashton the quantity of 1,997 pounds of tobacco, as well as receive pay for the costs and charges incurred by him to bring about the pursuit of his Petition."

With the sweep of his pen, the judge, by the dint of his authority, put an end to the charade that the Queen family were not free and made Ned a wealthy man.

Chapter Thirty Eight

March 1795

Nothing was going as it should. It had been five months since Ned had won his case and for the Queen family it seemed as if their world had been turned upside down. Father Ashton was supposed to have let them all go. Instead, he stubbornly hung on to his claim of ownership of them all.

In August, three months after Ned won his case, the Jesuit's paid Philip Barton Key to stop representing the slaves against them. He agreed and took the money under the assumption that they would be releasing the Queen family for the obvious reason that their claims had already been proven. When that didn't happen, he had no other option but to continue in his representation of those twenty-one cases he had already filed, regardless of the agreement he had made or the money that was paid. It was preposterous that none, not one, of the Queens had been offered their freedom.

Not only were they not free, but the privileges they had previously enjoyed over the whole of their lives had been revoked. They were no longer allowed to leave the respective missions where they lived, additional overseers had been added, and they were not to receive visitors or communicate with anyone outside of the missions. It had become nearly impossible to speak with any of them.

To make matters even worse, the Jesuits were selling members of the Queen family not actively engaged in petitions against them. At the time they had filed the additional twenty-one cases, they had chosen to file only for Phillis, Nanny, and their children. Once it was established that Ned, by virtue of his mother, was free, then so would her other children be free, as well as their children and so forth, making the other claims redundant.

Because Ralph, Queen's son, lived at Bohemia rather than White Marsh where most of the Queen family lived and so was under a different manager, they had not filed for him or his children. Once it was established that Queen had been a free woman, all of her children, including Ralph, would presumably fall under the same status.

Learning that Ralph's son, along with his wife and child, were sold just the previous month, had been a blow to Phillip Key. To then find out that Nanny's granddaughter, Phillis, along with her three-week-old daughter, had been sold in January, leaving behind her four-year old daughter, Clara, only to be sold one month later to a different buyer, was horrifying. Once they had been sold away from their family, bestowing the rights of ownership upon a new individual, they would have to pursue their claims with that individual. But first they would have to have access to someone who could represent them. Under the circumstances, it was unlikely.

Unable to talk sense into the Jesuits, Mr. Key wracked his brain for a way to stop them from disseminating the Queen family before they could have their cases heard. He could think of nothing. As long as an individual did not have a claim for freedom already made and they were being held under the status of slaves, they fell under the direct jurisdiction of their owner, who had the right to sell and trade them at will.

He had spoken to Ned several times since his court date and knew that he struggled. At first, Mr. Key had been certain that once the dust settled around the blow of the verdict, the Jesuits would see reason in the obvious conclusion that they would have no choice but to allow the Queens their freedom. He had been wrong, and Ned's distress increased as the delays mounted.

So, after assuring Ned that everything would be fine, Mr. Key suggested to him that he should go and establish a home in a place where he would be ready to receive his family enmasse once their cases were won.

Taking his advice, Ned went to Baltimore where he was well removed from the missions and people who knew of the situation and yet he wasn't so far that they couldn't get word to him. It was difficult for him to leave his family behind and begin building a life without them. It had been a huge adjustment learning to navigate the world as a free man, making decisions about where to live, seeing to his own needs and having to finance them himself. Especially when he wasn't fully recovered from the abuse inflicted upon him by Father Ashton. But he learned quickly.

The only visible remains that he had suffered such torment were multiple scars, mostly small, and a rocking limp. But some scars, the worst ones, weren't always so easily discerned. He rarely smiled and carried his shoulders sloped and low, making them appear as if they were sliding off his body. His fists were almost always stuffed deep into his pockets. He always wore a grimace, as if in pain, which he was most of the time, and was easily winded, huffing and puffing at the slightest exertion.

As he thought of the abuse suffered by Ned, Mr. Key's brows pulled up, his eyes sparked, and his face lit with inspiration. He had an idea. Perhaps he could not go to the court with complaints about how the Jesuits treated their slaves or interfere with how they traded and sold them, but he could make the judge aware that the twenty-one members of the Queen family whom he represented were in grave danger.

Hopefully, he thought, *we'll prevent years of delays, saving those people that we can.*

And so it was that on March 20, 1795, Phillip Key filed a case in the court of Prince George's County Maryland on behalf of Edward Queen, seeking damages against John Ashton for false imprisonment and assault. In support of his claim, he stated that John Ashton, *with force of arms, using swords, staves and knives, did beat, wound, imprison and ill-treat him without any reasonable cause and against the laws of the State of*

Maryland, from October 15, 1791 until May 18, 1794, the space of three years, and that Edward *was obliged and compelled to expend and lay out several large sums of money for his release and the deliverance from the service of John Ashton, who caused great damage to him.*

*****

May 1795

It seemed as if the earth trembled in anticipation. Leaves, crisp and new and not yet their full size, fluttered against one another in excitement. Crickets melodically rubbed their hind legs together in song, calling for their mates. Birds chattered all around as if sharing with one another the events of their day before ruffling their feathers and settling in to be lulled to sleep by the gentle sway of the trees. On the ground, brittle remains from the fall sheltered a host of insects in a thick, moist carpet. The moon hung low and full, a golden glowing ball of light that illuminated the clouds as they traveled across it in shades of muted orange. Behind them, the twilight sky was a palette of sweeping strokes of blacks, blues, and grays. The evening spring air, crisp and cool, was invigorating. All was as if even God endorsed the plan laid out by the Queen family members, gifting them with perfect conditions. They were going to self-free themselves.

Gathered by the old shed at the end of the farthest field were Simon, Billy, Matthew, Isaac, Lewis, Tom, Jack, and Paul. All grandchildren of Nanny. No one spoke. Everything that needed to be said had already been shared. Weeks of planning, considering every conceivable outcome, had wrung from them all equal doses of fear and excitement. Some of their siblings and cousins, too afraid to take the risk of running, had backed out. With each of their departures, plans were changed, sparing them the knowledge of any details which could place them in danger.

The arrival of Tom, Nick, Fanny, and Billy, Phillis's grandchildren, completed the group. All who were expected were present and accounted for. It was time to begin.

Fanny disappeared into the shed and emerged with a bundle of clothing she had previously stored there in a barrel. Piece by piece, she had removed small items from the laundry that she took in, careful to only take one of a small item, and only if there were multiples. It was frustrating and worrisome, and she had fretted with how she was to get all of the necessary clothing for everyone. Then, one day she was walking back from a delivery, having received special permission to leave the mission unattended for that express purpose, and she was gifted with such a rare opportunity that she simply knew it was put there by God himself.

Hanging on a line to be aired were three full men's suits and several fine lady's dresses. Even the shoes dyed to match the dresses were there, hanging by their strings, though they were much to dainty for the calloused feet of a field hand.

Normally she didn't travel so close to the house when she crossed through that particular property, but that day something told her to. Maybe it was because she had stopped by the Duvall property to deliver a message for her mother, so needed to make up the lost time, but she preferred to believe it was divine intervention.

She knew the people who lived at the house, a family of five who had fallen on hard times. They ran a small store in town and kept only one slave, an older woman who had been with them a very long time. A quick scan of the yard assured Fanny that no one was around.

Wasting no time, she assessed the dresses as she ran towards them, choosing one most suited for her purpose, then yanked it off the line. In a single fluid movement, swinging the dress over her shoulder, she ran down the line pulling the items she needed. Shift, stay, petticoat, a hanky for her, and two coats, shirts, and breeches for the men. Stockings and ribbons for all. As she pulled the ribbons, her last items, in a single swipe, the door to the house opened and slammed with a bang. Fanny froze in time that suddenly seemed to stand still, knowing that she had been caught. The ribbons streaming from her raised hand to the line, fell and dangled. Their long loose ends danced as if laughing at her.

With nothing left to do but turn and face her captor, Fanny closed her eyes and slowly shuffled her feet, turning around with her arms wide and wrapped around the stolen bounty. The old slave stood, her hand still on the knob of the door, and watched. Her eyes were not mean and accusing as Fanny expected, but neither were they friendly. She did not yell curses or rain insults and accusations at her. She just stared, hard and sure. Fanny waited, feeling as if the old woman could see through to her very soul, and stared silently back. Her chin jutted up in a slight but proud movement, even as the air refused to move through her lungs. Then with a nearly imperceptible nod, the old woman, having made her decision, turned the knob and inched the door back open. Without turning from Fanny, she eased backed into the house and shut the door. Relief flooded through Fanny. She gasped for air, squeezed the bundle to her chest, and ran.

Everything they had planned and done was all for this moment. The choice to self-free oneself, to run, was never easy, but they felt they were left with no other options. While their parents waited for their day in court, one by one family members disappeared, sold away from their mates, siblings, friends, and family. Young children were being taken from their mothers and placed in a world where they would become as strangers, unable to recognize the person possessing their same nose, mouth, or eyes, even if they should ever see one another again.

They each knew it was simply a matter of days or weeks before they would also be sold. Even if their parents won their cases, it was too late for all of them. Father Ashton had made it very clear that he was going to make each one of the Queen family members file individually. They would be under his rule for years while waiting for their cases to be heard. During that time, he would keep twisting and breaking their hands until they grew with gross deformities, burn and scar them to disfigure a pretty face or to mar too perfect skin, and make them suffer for the audacity of their parents to have claimed their freedom. All while he sold off their loved ones as further punishment, claiming his right to do so as the vindication of God.

Slipping into the shed to change her clothes in privacy while Tom and Billy changed into theirs outside, Fanny emerged transformed. The sloping curves of her slender body filled the dress where it would have otherwise been slightly too large. The moonlight brightened her skin to a milky glow. Having earlier powdered her face and tamed her curls, smoothing them into the graceful style worn by white women, she was the perfect picture of a young white lady.

Enchanted, Phillis' Tom dipped into a sweeping bow. He too was transformed. The soft waves of his toffee-colored hair were pulled back and secured by a black ribbon under a fine hat which fell lopsided as he pulled himself back straight. Fanny and the others looked at him with pride, but he quickly dismissed it. He couldn't afford to think of anything but what they had ahead of them.

Because there was so many of them, they had decided that the best course of action was to divide into groups. They had a carriage that was seldom used and had been carefully transformed to be unrecognizable as one belonging to Father Ashton, and two of the finer horses from the stables to pull it. Tom and Fanny would ride in it, playing the part of a white planter and his wife rushing to the side of her dear nearly departed mother. If asked, they would say they brought two drivers, Simon and Isaac, so they could continue their journey without the need to stop for rest. Nick, having cinnamon colored skin and thus too dark to pass as white, was the perfect one to pose as Tom's grooming assistant. Phillis' Billy, who could also pass as white, wore the other suit, only without the coat. He would pose as an irascible planter who had stubbornly and successfully tracked down his discontent slaves and was escorting them back home. He would travel with Jack, Paul, and Nanny's Tom, who posed as his slaves. Brothers Lewis and Matthew were more comfortable traveling together, keeping out of plain sight. Nanny's Billy preferred to travel alone. All were going to Philadelphia, Pennsylvania where they would meet in one week's time. With everything ready, they bid one another safe journey and left, fading into the landscape of a beautiful spring night.

And so it was that on May 1, 1795, Father John Ashton published an ad asking for the return of the Queen family members.

Twelve Pounds Reward.
Prince-George's County, May 1, 1795

ABSENTED themselves from my service since the Late Prince-George's and Anne-Arundel county courts, the following twelve NEGROES, calling themselves QUEENS; *Simon, Billy, Jack, Lewis, Isaac, Paul, Matthew,* and *Tom,* very black negroes, and *Tom, Billy, Nick,* and *Fanny,* of a brown complexion; they are all young, hearty, and well made negroes, and quitted me for no other reason but because they were not set free at the last court. As I have recognized for the said negroes I conceive that I do not forfeit their services, nor lose any share of my authority over them, before trial; I do therefore promise the above reward to any person who will inform me where the aforesaid negroes may be found, and be witness against such persons as harbor or employ them, or TWENTY SHILLINGS for each one. I likewise forewarn all persons from harboring or employing the said negroes at their peril, as I am determined to prosecute every such person agreeably to law.

JOHN ASHTON

Months later, Fanny became very ill and needed medical attention. A physician was called and came to attend her. Deliriously talking through fever, she revealed enough facts that the physician who treated her grew suspicious and began making inquiries. Offering to transfer her to where she could receive more skilled care and better medicine, instead, he returned Fanny to White Marsh and Father Ashton.

On April 21, 1796, less than two weeks after her return and just six days before her family's case was heard in court, Fanny was sold south.

Chapter Thirty Nine

April 27, 1796

It was a bittersweet day for the Queen family. The air was heavy with the weight of what it held for them. If they won their cases, as they were sure to do, the family would be divided. Having learned from their experience following Ned's victory, they were under no illusion that their victory would compel Father Ashton to concede any of the remaining Queens their freedom.

Over the months leading up to their day in court, they embraced their time together, spending every moment they could, sharing their love and possessively tucking it into their hearts and minds where memories were indelibly etched. On the week when their case was to be heard, they counted the days as well as the hours and minutes.

Rising before the sun had even dawned on the day of court, they all gathered together to share a sober meal before an emotional parting. As she was climbing into the wagon, Phillis paused for one last time to take in her surroundings.

Looking back at her cabin, she was once again overwhelmed with the memories which raced through her mind. They left her bewildered as she pondered them and how they had all culminated to such a circumstance.

Pushing them away, she shook her head, squared her shoulders with a tsk, and allowed her son to assist her into her seat.

The sky was beautiful with large cottony white clouds that drifted lazily across a deep sapphire blue. The air, crisp and fresh, carried a hint of Wood Hyacinth, one of her favorite flowers. It's sweet woodsy scent gently tickled her nose. She closed her eyes and turned her head toward it, drawing it deeply into her lungs where she held it. It was a gentle reminder that even with all of the recent ugly events, this too was a part of life, and it was beautiful.

The trees raced down the drive in a line as they passed, their branches waved softly in the breeze as if they were saying good-bye. It was a sign. A good sign.

Waiting for their case to be called, Susanna stood rigidly beside her mother. Her arms strained under the weight of her daughter as she gently rocked her to sleep. The rich scent of a meat pie drifted by and teased her stomach into a hungry growl. Turning to look for the source, she saw Father Ashton pass by, casually chatting with his attorneys as they walked. Only a subtle stiffening of his back and a quick shift of his gaze indicated that he had seen her. Pity for him tugged at her.

He needs to possess me, and he can't, she thought, pulling herself straighter, *not even if he wins and then owns me. He can use me to punish himself for everything that he cannot be, but that is all. It is all I will ever give him and all that he can take from me. The rest is mine which I refuse to allow him to have.*

When their cases were called, Susanna grasped her mother's hand and walked with her family, all with worry lines etched across their faces, through the courtroom doors. It was where, though they could not speak on their own behalf, their fates awaited them.

They entered a long corridor where they were instructed to stand. At the end of the corridor, the attorneys stood at a bar before the judges, who were seated on a curved bench. There were openings on both sides. Each were packed with people who had crowded in to watch.

Susanna nervously pulled at her earlobes as she glanced around at the people gathered there. Never before had there been such a case, a large family claiming their freedom in mass. It had become a spectacle. It seemed that their lives had been opened for all to see and had become the fodder for gossip and speculation. It felt as if the very memory of Queen was being challenged and it hurt. Once again Phillis took Susanna's hand and gently pulled it down where she held it by her side, a silent offer of comfort.

Susanna looked down at their joined hands. Both were pleated and aged through lives of toil and child rearing, but they were united in blood and experience. Giving her mother's hand a gentle squeeze, they stood clinging together in silent hope.

Their lawyers had tried to describe for them what was going to happen in court, but the experience was so far removed from any other that they had ever experienced, they were unprepared and overwhelmed. As the day wore on, they grew anxious and filled with nervous energy.

Finally, and quite suddenly, it was over as the judges found once again that Mary Queen had not been a slave. Announcing each of their cases by name, they were relieved of the scourge of slavery and Father John Ashton. They had been unburdened of him by their mother and grandmother, Mary Queen, and her legacy of freedom.

Afterwards

On May 10, 1796, Edward "Ned" Queen's claim of false imprisonment and assault against Father John Ashton was brought before court. It ruled that *he take nothing, but be in mercy for his false clamor* and that he pay John Ashton *four hundred and thirty-three pounds of tobacco* for his costs to defend himself in the case. An appeal was filed but was never heard. Ned died February 23, 1798, just three years and nine months after the verdict that declared him free. He was buried at St. Peters Pro-Cathedral in Baltimore Maryland, a church where Father John Ashton had performed its very first mass.

Even after winning her freedom, Susanna continued in a tumultuous relationship with Father Ashton, returning to White Marsh in June 1800. There, he allowed her to build a cabin where she lived. In May 1801, after years of struggling with lawsuits and a drinking problem, Father Ashton removed himself from the directorship of Georgetown College and as the manager of White Marsh. In the years that followed, Susanna moved back and forth between White Marsh and Father Ashton's private residences until his death on February 18, 1815. In his will, he left his estate to Susanna's children, Charles and Elizabeth, finally answering the question of their paternity.

Several of the Queen family members who were freed in 1796 remained around White Marsh where they could continue to see their children and spouses who were still being held as slaves. Many of them were sold to other plantations throughout the slave-holding regions of the United States. Petitions for freedom continued to be filed by them against their various owners for decades.

In 1830, Georgetown College authorized the construction the Gervase building which was completed in 1838 and held the first hospital located there. To recover the costs of building it, two hundred seventy-two slaves were sold to a plantation in Louisiana, ending Jesuit slaveholding in the United States. Amongst the men and women sold, there remained several people who were listed with the surname of Queen.

In April 2019, the students of Georgetown University voted in favor of establishing a reparations fund for the descendants of that sale and created a list of the names of individuals who had been sold. On it were the names of seventeen Queen family members.

Sneak Peak of my
exciting upcoming title!

A BETRAYAL
OF
FREEDOM

Chapter One

December 1655

If it is true that our lives are fated towards a predetermined destiny, then I say that God must be cruel as he moves us along our paths amongst others of greater or lesser favor than we possess. Feeling betrayed, we walk through a life that rarely turns out as one hopes, with expectations only sometimes met and disappointments frequent. Such has been the story of my life.

Born to Richard and Mary Davies of limited means, I was welcomed into my family on Christmas and baptized on December 30, 1655. My brother, John, was then 5 years old. Many believe that a Christmas birth suggests a certain gift of favor with God. My life is testamentary to the fact that this is not so.

I do not recall any particular hardships in my early years. My family lived in a modest home on Mark Lane in London, England, just beyond the Tower. I suppose, looking back, that my parent's marriage was not favored by mum's family. Because though I recall some small contact with them, the memories are vague and usually end with my mum silently wiping her tears as we were transported home in a fine conveyance unequal to what we enjoyed in any other time, which would most often be our own two feet.

In spring of my tenth year, my life was forever changed. John and I were confined within the boundaries of our home due to an infestation of the city by rats, fleas, lice, and other such pests. Though we were prohibited to leave our home or to open any windows, we peeked from behind the curtains to watch the streets. They were lined with conveyances of all manner, the occupants constantly pestered by people recently beggared as they attempted to flee in order to rid themselves of the discomforts of our city.

Strangely, it was then that mum began going out more frequently. I suppose, by necessity she rose early and often times left the house with my father, before the full light of day, as he headed to work and she to locate some scarce food for our meals.

One day early in the fall, my mum did not appear in the morning. Even as the noon hour approached, she remained in bed. Within that very same day my father returned home early. Finding her ill, he left to summon medical attention for her.

Upon his return, having been unable to locate help, my father fled through the house straight to mum's bed where he quickly gathered her to himself. At once there occurred a great pounding and commotion upon our front door as two men crashed through. When they had learned of mum's illness, they followed my father home. Determined to take her, they wrestled mum from father's arms.

Those men carried mum out of our home wearing nothing more than a nightdress, wrapped in a blanket, and with only a few words of solace to us. It was the only time I ever saw my father weep and it alarmed me so acutely that the pitiful site will always remain with me. Not knowing what to do and desperate to reclaim my mum, I followed those men for many blocks until they entered a small house lying at the edge of the city.

It was not the state of disrepair or the filth that surrounded the place which frightened me, but the large red cross painted upon the door with the words, *LORD HAVE MERCY UPON US* inscribed above. I stood frightened, staring at the door for only the briefest of time before it opened and expelled the two ruffians who had taken my mum. Immediately, they pointed to the cross and demanded that I leave "under orders of the king himself" until such time that the painted cross was changed to white.

Almost daily I returned and willed that mark to transform itself from the color of blood to one of hope. Months later, it finally did. Again I stared at that door for long moments before I approached, fearing a trickery of my eyes, until a woman opened it. She looked worn, haggard, and much aged beyond her years. Upon seeing me, she stopped and stood staring at me without expression. She did not speak.

Love driving my courage, I asked the woman of my mum. The pitiful being spoke flatly as she told me that she did not know which of the many corpses who had exited her home had been my mum, but that none, save a very few, had left outside of a wagon. That is how I learned of my poor mum's passing.

Only months later, my life was once again thrown into chaos. It was unequal to any other event experienced during not only my lifetime, but also the lifetimes of all who resided within our city. London was burning.

Some say it was God's retribution for the masses of people leading unholy lives, though most did not spend time contemplating a meaning and set about to preserve what possessions they could.

The fire spread, fanned by a wind that was surely touched by the very heat of hell. We gasped for breathable air and were cast into perpetual darkness as smoke blocked out the light. Burning embers rained down, surrounding everything with a hellish threat, claiming all space where they landed with bursts of flame. There soon became nowhere to go nor paths to exit, excepting one, the River Thames.

Forced to flee from our home when it too was swallowed by flames, I was separated from my father and brother, ushered along within a frenzied throng of panicked people. The rodents, also fleeing, ran in great masses amongst the people, often hitching a ride upon their backs, causing even more hysteria.

For several blocks I was swept along until suddenly I was scooped off of my feet. I heard a woman's voice shout *save yourself*, before being plunged into the watery depths of the river. Gasping, I surfaced, then was immediately grasped by my arm and pulled over the curved top of a small floating trunk. I clutched onto it with all my might, bobbing in the great wake and splashes of others who joined me there. All around me, every manner of possessions floated or sank as people fought to gain access to them.

The rats swam amongst the people, also seeking solid footing, often upon the head of a hapless individual who immediately unraveled from panic to hysteria, sinking into the water as they violently slapped away their unbidden passenger.

I do not know how long I remained in the water, time distorting itself in such moments. I was finally pulled out and into the arms of a woman who was perched upon an overly crowded but unknown surface. There, I remained in her arms. I focused upon her soft voice as she crooned to me a child's lullaby to block out the sounds of horror around us.

I cannot recall how we finally escaped the river. But afterwards, having nowhere to go with my father and brother's whereabouts unknown to me and the streets of our beloved London unrecognizable in the aftermath of the fire, I remained with the woman, Isillet, and her husband, who cared for me as if I were their own.

We resided in a shack surrounded by many others which were all put together with the cruelest of means. They created a shanty town just outside of London. It housed those downtrodden souls who, because of the plague, had already suffered the loss of family and friends upon whom they could rely for assistance. Creaking with the wind and leaking in rain, our shack was cold but at least it held.

There, I quickly became accustomed to the lack of food and water. I learned that clothing, even in poor repair, could surpass the preciousness of jewels. I did not despair over my wet bedding when it rained, it being only a blanket, and felt relief at the simple gift of it remaining dry through the night.

My dear father finally found me almost a year later and tearfully took me into his arms. It was then that I resolved with a ferocity only those who have known the cruelest of suffering can accomplish, that never again would I allow myself to get into a situation where I would suffer so greatly. So began the path to my complete and utter destruction.

I returned to Marks Lane and began devising a plan. Gaining the permission of my father after months of pleading, I dressed in the finest clothing I could accomplish and visited my mum's sister, whom I scarcely knew. After several hours of conversation to gain her favor, my aunt consented to assist me with securing a position amongst her acquaintances as a companion to one of the daughters of the gentry within her social circle.

Before long, in the year 1669, at fourteen years of age, I was ensconced in a brilliant home which afforded the luxuries only great wealth could provide. Dressed only slightly beneath the quality of my companion, I attended her lessons with her to ensure that she learned them. Music, comportment, reading, language, penmanship, and the proper folding of linens were all bestowed upon me, as well as access to her social environs, though peripherally, which I normally would not have aspired to achieve.

By the time I became eighteen years of age, I found ways to gain the notice of my companion's friends with the hope that my accomplishments, coupled with a pleasing face, would outweigh my lack of social standing and find me worthy of an offer of marriage. Sadly, before my well executed plan met its fruition, my companion was arranged to be married.

Upon her departure I would return to my father's home.

Nearing the end of our time together, and subsequently our lessons, I was quite despondent with grief. When our tutor questioned me about it, I availed him of my fears; that I would be required to suffer a marriage to a shopkeeper, or to a man of other equal standing. Having grown accustomed to a more commodious lifestyle, I was ill prepared to withstand such a marriage, nor dispositioned to embrace such an arrangement.

My well-meaning tutor listened sympathetically and encouraged me in the understanding that I had no choice but to take my future boldly into my own hands. I was bereft of how to accomplish doing so, until one day he proposed a plan so simply obvious that I could not deny its brilliance.

The colonies were gaining popularity amongst the nobility as the king sought to fortify his hold there. With so many wealthy and titled individuals, and their families, going there, they had the additional need of commoners with skills. Likewise, a need was created for young gentle ladies, such as myself, to be employed in the same manner that I was accustomed, as a companion to their gentle daughters.

The esteemed Lord Baltimore was seeking just such a person for a position. What good fortune I felt when it was agreed upon that I would travel by ship to the colonies to reside within his household. I would be ensconced within one of the finest and most well-connected homes of the land. After four years, I would then be well acquainted with the gentry people there and in a perfect situation to conduct myself into an advantageous marriage. While I was no great beauty, I did possess a loveliness that was often complimented upon. It would serve as an additional advantage. It was also a further security that such a union could be easily managed.

Excited, I wrote to my father of the good fortune which had befallen me. His response was angry and outraged as he forbade me to go. Nonetheless, I signed the contracts of Indenture without my father's blessing and remained silent to him about them as preparations were made.

I had no wish to depart London without bidding my father and brother farewell, though I feared they would bodily restrain me to prevent my going. So, with men-at-arms to guard against such a happening, I went to them on the eve of my departure. They were not pleased but there was nothing they could do other than angrily demand that I stay, and then tearfully bid me farewell.

On July 9, 1674, I boarded the ship, *Constant Friendship,* and sailed with forty-three other passengers from my beloved England, towards the colonies and a hell of my own creation.

If you are interested in researching for additional information or wish to research your family history, here are some websites that are a valuable resource:

Life and Labor under Slavery: the Jesuit Plantation Project
https://jesuitplantationproject.org

The National Archives US
https://www.archives.gov/

The National Archives UK
https://www.nationalarchives.gov.uk/

O Say Can You See Early Washington DC Law & Family
https://earlywashingtondc.org/

The Georgetown Slavery Archive
http://slaveryarchive.georgetown.edu/

Maryland State Archives
https://msa.maryland.gov/

Early Colonial Settlers of Southern Maryland and Virginia's Northern Neck Counties
https://www.colonial-settlers-md-va.us

Race & Slavery Petitions Project
http://library.uncg.edu/slavery/petitions/

Free African Americans
http://www.freeafricanamericans.com

Indentured Servants of Colonial America

https://www.landofthebrave.info/indentured-servants.htm

Family Search
https://www.familysearch.org

Ancestry
https://www.ancestry.com/

The Queen Family Heritage Foundation
https://queenfamily.org/

Georgetown Reflects on Slavery, Memory, and Reconciliation
https://www.georgetown.edu/slavery/

About the Author

Cynthia Marlowe is a genealogist and the author of the nationally acclaimed novel *SOLD!* She lives in eastern North Carolina and is frequently called upon for research, public appearances, and life coaching. She is a veteran of the US Army and has a passionate love affair with the written word. She enjoys spending time with her family, carpentry, spending time at the beach, and traveling off the beaten path. She loves engaging her readers and looks forward to hearing from them. If you would like to contact her, please visit her website at: https://www.cynthiamarlowe.com/

CPSIA information can be obtained
at www.ICGtesting.com
Printed in the USA
BVHW071218181121
621925BV00007B/337